THE FOREST BRIDE

Highland Secrets, Book 2

Susan King

ARE YOU SIGNED UP FOR DRAGONBLADE'S BLOG?

You'll get the latest news and information on exclusive giveaways, exclusive excerpts, coming releases, sales, free books, cover reveals and more.

Check out our complete list of authors, too!

No spam, no junk. That's a promise!

Sign Up Here

www.dragonbladepublishing.com

Dearest Reader;

Thank you for your support of a small press. At Dragonblade Publishing, we strive to bring you the highest quality Historical Romance from some of the best authors in the business. Without your support, there is no 'us', so we sincerely hope you adore these stories and find some new favorite authors along the way.

Happy Reading!

CEO, Dragonblade Publishing

Additional Dragonblade books by Author Susan King

Highland Secrets Series
The Scottish Bride (Book 1)
The Forest Bride (Book 2)

Celtic Hearts Series
The Hawk Laird (Book 1)
The Falcon Laird (Book 2)
The Swan Laird (Book 3)

Three lasses, three ladies, three brides all
Born and flowering in Kincraig's hall
One shall loose an arrow in the heart of greenside
One shall heal a king and woe betide
And one shall be the harper's bride . . .
                    —Prophecy of the Keiths of Kincraig

Love and thanks to all my readers

PROLOGUE

Merry Margaret

As midsummer flower

Gentle as falcon

Or hawk of the tower

—John Skelton, *Garland of Laurel*, 16th c.

Scotland, The Highlands
April 1297

"A FEY CREATURE. Scarce more than a child." Standing at the window of his mother's solar, Duncan Campbell gazed down at a slip of a girl who waited in the bailey yard of Innis Connell Castle, his father's island stronghold in Loch Awe. The visitors, Sir Robert Keith and his daughter Margaret, had arrived by boat to discuss the betrothal affixed between Duncan and the girl ten years earlier.

He drew a sharp breath, recalling the tense discussion about the matter with his father, Sir Colin Campbell, chief of that clan. Seeing his son's insistence on dissolving the agreement, his father had reluctantly promised to broach it with Robert Keith.

Though Duncan had not seen his would-be bride for years, he saw now she was neither child nor yet a woman. In her moss-green gown and plaid cloak, with hair like bright copper spilling in loose curls over her shoulders, she was a faery-like creature.

"She is lovely." Lady Janet Sinclair came to stand beside her son.

"True, but good saints, Mother. The lass is only Isabel's age."

"Thirteen. Your sister is fourteen and will marry later this year."

"Too young. Even I am not ready to marry, at just twenty and newly knighted. I told Father we should void the betrothal, since I must leave to fulfill my knight service. The lass should not have to wait even more years for this marriage to be made."

"This alliance has considerable advantages. You know that."

"Aye, but I gave my pledge to King Edward and must report in the south. I do not know when I might return. Or if."

"You will return. I know it, I." She smiled. Whenever his mother used that phrase, Duncan knew it came from more than logic. His mother had the Sight that ran in her family; he respected it, if he did not quite understand it.

"I hope so. As for marriage, I have no fortune or castle, and as a younger son with five brothers and a sister, my portion one day will be modest."

"Caelin Mòr Campbell of Lochawe will not let a son of his be a landless knight. You will have Brechlinn Castle upon your marriage—or later, when he is gone."

"I appreciate it. I do." Somehow he could not look away from the girl, that innocent wee beauty—and he the demon about to destroy her hopes. "Brechlinn is all but a ruin. It will take coin and work to improve it." In truth, he loathed the idea of riding for the English king, and would rather put time and muscle into that dear old castle. "Someday I will return to the Highlands and marry. But not now."

Someday. The sticking point. The betrothal had been made long before he or the Keith girl understood it. Both families were pleased by the alliance, but King Edward's expectations took precedence over those plans. Indeed, the king's intentions in Scotland could alter the future for everyone. Nothing felt secure.

In the yard, his father emerged from the keep to welcome the guests. Colin Campbell had a thundering presence, tall and beefy in a plaid cloak over a long tunic of ochre wool; Sir Robert Keith of Kincraig was lean and dark in a blue surcoat. As they grasped hands and spoke, young Margaret turned in a dreamy circle, arms out, cloak swirling. She was coltish, sweet, her hair a sunset glow as she turned.

He recalled the tiny spitfire he'd first met when she was but three and he ten years old. She had been a wee thing with red-gold curls who clapped with delight when the betrothal pledge was read, then followed him about the hall. To his great embarrassment at age ten, she had climbed into his lap and cooed the proper Gaelic form of his name spoken in the ceremony—*Donnchadh Dubh*, Black Duncan, for his nearly black hair. Finally the nurse came to fetch the child.

"This one is fiery," she said as picked her up to carry her away.

"My Donnchadh! My Donnchadh Dubh!" Margaret had shrieked. *Dona-kha-dhu*, her plea heartbreaking, his discomfort keen.

"Duncan Dhu," his mother said then, dipping into his thoughts as she so often did, "let the wedding proceed while the marriage waits. That lass will be good for you, and you for her."

He sighed. "I know you and Father are disappointed, but I feel it is the honorable thing to dissolve it and not ask her or her kin to wait longer."

She patted his shoulder, though he towered over her. "Your father is pleased you stood up to him. Few dare argue with Caelin Mòr. He will talk to Kincraig."

Duncan nodded. He had trembled to present his opinion. Cailean Mòr—Big Colin—was great in size, heart, courage, reputation, and stubbornness. But the man loved family above all, and so he had listened.

"I know. But this is my responsibility."

"And this is a good match. Her father is an influential lord, her kinsman is Marischal of Scotland, and her great-grandfather is

Thomas the Rhymer, respected for his counsel and prophecies. Her family has power and position. And I have a good feeling about this girl." She gave a wise smile.

"Aye. But my future is uncertain. I know the tocher must be repaid if no marriage takes place, and I will pay it. It is my debt."

"You are a good soul and a good man. So like your father." She ruffled his dark hair. "The black hair, those dark blue eyes, the cheeks that stain pink with your thoughts. Like him in your heart and your stubbornness, too. But—"

"Thank you. But?"

"But you have such reserve. You hold back. You are thinking of honor, I know. But that lass has a wild spirit." She indicated the girl spinning about below. "She can teach you something."

He huffed. "She deserves better than a younger son of a clan chief."

"Your father is a powerful Highland earl and cousin to the mighty Bruces. That bonny lass will not find a finer match than Duncan Campbell, who completed his studies in law and natural philosophy at Saint Andrews. We are proud of you."

"I may never use those studies if Edward has his way."

"Your father's position as justiciar in the north is heritable, but your brothers are not interested in that work. You studied law, so he wants his judiciary role to go to you."

"And I am honored." His brusque, decisive father was stern and fair, and his role would be hard to fill; nor could he think of his father gone. "They say King Edward will not allow Scots to hold heritable positions. Those may go to English lords instead."

She sighed. "He would erase our character even as he takes our land and goods."

"Some of us are determined that will never happen."

"This marriage alliance could help that effort one day. Think of that."

"Mama," he said gently, "leave it be."

She patted his arm. "I must welcome our guests. Your sister will entertain the girl this afternoon. I am thinking you should keep your distance from her until later."

"I will take a hawk out to fly." He needed to get outside to think.

When his mother left the room, Duncan glanced out the window again, still feeling regret and guilt, though his decision was necessary. Below, Margaret Keith whirled again; she had a wildness that reminded him of the hawks in his father's mews, untamed and spirited regardless of jesses and expectations.

He did not want to hurt the girl. He wanted marriage someday, but felt compelled to focus on knighthood and a need for freedom, justice, and honor. Too much was unknown. A decade earlier, Scotland had lost a good king down a cliffside on a rainy night, and later, the little princess who inherited his throne had died too. Edward of England stepped in like a vulture, appointing Sir John Balliol to the throne—Edward's Scottish puppet, many said—ignoring eligible warriors in the royal line, chiefly Sir Robert Bruce and Sir John Comyn.

If the younger Robert Bruce claimed the kingship, Duncan felt sure fates and fortunes in Scotland would improve. So far Bruce had made no move. Until he did, Duncan would ride for Edward as he must. But he would rather join what some called hotheads—a growing faction of young Scottish lords determined to fight for Scottish freedom. That felt more like honor to him.

He took the stairs to the yard to head for the thatched-roof mews. Among those stubborn, magnificent birds, he could find peace and purpose, and perhaps sort out his conflicted heart.

CARRYING A GOSHAWK on his gloved fist, Duncan crossed a broad meadow, his plaid cloak of green, blue, and black fluttering about his knees over a long tunic of brown linen and woolen trews. As he walked, the bird cheeped, blinded by a leather hood topped with a jaunty feather.

"Restless and ready to fly? I feel that way too, lad," he murmured.

One never knew what to expect from a hawk, a wild thing

that likely complied with humans only because they proved a regular source of food and shelter. Birds of prey were pragmatic, somewhat lazy creatures, accepting captivity only so long as it pleased them. Never fully tamed, they might decide to fly free at any time.

His father's mews was known throughout the Highlands for its excellent birds and a skilled falconer who had infinite patience for the hawks, falcons, and owls Sir Colin kept. Duncan had learned much in that tutelage. Leaving home and ending the betrothal to fulfill his knight service troubled him, but his sense of honor and his need to build a future for himself gave him little choice.

Ahead, the long isle was a stretch of flowered meadow, woodland, and shore, where the gleaming blue loch rippled on a pebbled beach. He headed toward a cluster of pines and birches thinking to release the hawk there.

At the mews, he had learned that his sister had taken a kestrel and their young guest had asked for a bow and quiver to practice archery. Walking over the meadow, Duncan glanced around for Isabel and Margaret, determined to take a different direction if he saw them.

But soon he saw his sister running toward him, cloak flying out, dark braids bouncing. Behind her came a groom carrying a bird on his glove. Seeing Duncan, she ran faster, waving. Something was wrong, he realized.

"Isabel!" he called.

"Duncan!" She stopped, breathless. "We need help."

"What is it?"

She pointed. "Lady Margaret is back there. We must fetch Papa's falconer. She is up in a tree with a bird."

He stared, incredulous. "A tree?"

"One of the tall pines there. She sent us to get help—she found a wounded bird. Could you help her—oh, perhaps not," she said, aware of his change of heart.

"I will help. Take the gos, Isabel." Duncan handed the bird

over, its wings fluttering in the transfer to her glove. Then he crossed the meadow in long strides.

Near a cluster of tall pines, he saw a slight figure in a green dress seated on the grass. Duncan had the odd thought that she looked like a woodland sprite, delicate as the new green on the trees. Despite what he promised his mother, he wanted to help.

"Lady Margaret?"

She shaded her eyes with a slim hand as he stopped with his back to the sun. In that moment, he was lost for words.

Seeing her earlier, remembering a truculent toddler, he had not expected beauty in the girl. But she was stunning, a faery princess just on the verge of womanhood, with creamy skin, rosy cheeks, and eyes of hazel green under dark brows; her hair, a rich and ruddy bronze, wafted over her shoulders in long loose curls.

She stood with awkward, leggy grace, willow-thin, tall for a young woman. Wobbling a bit as she favored one foot, she smiled. "You are Duncan Campbell!"

He took a step back. Though he was a man now, a knight, the incandescence of such uncommon beauty tossed him back to bumbling, uncertain adolescence. "Uh, I—"

"I am Margaret Keith." Her soft, husky voice was enchanting.

"Lady Margaret. My sister said you went up a tree."

"I was, but fell out just now. I am fine. Bruised my ankle, see." She drew up the embroidered hem of her gown to turn her foot in its narrow boot.

Dumbfounded, he looked at the pines. "You went up there?"

"Aye. So, you will soon be my husband?" Her smile was impish and bright, with pretty teeth and tiny side dimples. Duncan faltered. This gorgeous creature should be cherished, protected, not cast aside. He felt a new wash of guilt.

"About our, uh, betrothal—" He did not know how to say it.

"I remember our promise outside a church, and now we will plan a wedding. Are you nineteen now? I am thirteen."

"Twenty. A knight. You are very young."

"Fourteen this summer. Thank you for waiting for me to

grow, Duncan Dhu."

That she remembered the name touched him. His heart sank. His hands went clammy. "Er, my sister said you had trouble."

"Look there. Do you see the bird?" She pointed toward the pines.

He saw a flash of white and silver: a falcon perched halfway up the tallest pine. Now he felt on solid ground. He knew birds better than he knew girls.

"A falcon! Not one of ours."

"It was in the tree. I am afraid I shot it by accident. I feel terrible."

"I doubt you could shoot a falcon." He noticed the bow made of good ash, lying in the grass beside a quiver of arrows. It would take strength to pull it. She looked too fragile for that. "They are the fastest creatures in all the world, so fast you would barely see her before she was gone. You did not shoot her."

"I hope not. But I was practicing—and then I saw her not moving." Tears welled in her green eyes.

He was ill-prepared for tears. "If she is injured, I might be able to catch her." He walked toward the trees.

"How do you know it is a she?" The girl followed him.

"All falcons are 'she' until we know otherwise. And that one is big enough to be female now that I see her better. They are larger than the tiercels, the males, you see."

"If you were smaller than me, I would be a giantess!" She laughed.

He huffed, feeling enormous beside her. Stopping, he looked up at the bird. "Odd. It is sitting halfway up, though falcons normally seek the highest perch."

"I may have wounded her. I tried to climb up to help, but I fell. Can you go up?"

"I think so." The bird had not moved even with humans nearby. It was wounded for sure. Wondering how to capture it, he tested a couple of branches.

"Pardon me. I need to remove my shirt." He waggled his

fingers and she understood, turning her back. Quickly he removed his falconer's glove, undid his wide leather belt and sporran, tugged at the plaid draped over his shoulder, and stripped off the long tunic until he stood in shirt, woolen trews, and boots. He shrugged off the shirt and slung it over his bare shoulder, then drew on the heavy glove. He would need it.

The bird fixed large dark eyes on him, its white brow angled sharp and wary. It was a female—a gyrfalcon, he realized, for her chest and wings were nearly white, liberally speckled with gray. Her wicked talons flexed on the branch, but her legs were still blue-gray, indicating her youth. When she lifted one wing, the other stayed close, as if she could not fly. As he moved closer, she shifted a little, and a tiny bell on her anklet chimed above the leather jesses looped around her leg.

"She is a trained bird," he said. "A young one. See the gray specks on her wings? She will turn mostly white in a few months."

"Pretty thing. Her jesses look tangled on the branch."

"I will go up and see." Climbing the pine next to the central one, he ascended until he crouched just above the bird. She twisted her head to watch, dark eyes piercing. Duncan froze in that devilish stare and judged his next move.

Slowly he grabbed another branch and eased his way across to the tree where the falcon perched, pausing above her. Now he could see the bird was weak, her body quivering, likely with hunger as well as injury. With luck, she would let him capture her; a trained raptor would have learned that a human could provide food and safety.

Lifting the shirt, he dropped the linen like a cloud over the bird, reached down, and scooped her up swiftly. Startled, tangled in linen, she fought, but Duncan trapped her, nudging his heavy glove beneath the lethal talons. She caught hold of the leather while he worked to free the jesses, the little bell chiming.

Cooing soft reassurance, he cautiously descended and dropped to the ground. Margaret Keith followed as he carried the falcon out to the sunny meadow.

"There, bird, safe you are." The creature cocooned in his shirt trembled. "Margaret, in my sporran there is a falconer's hood."

She fetched the pouch and found the small leather hood. When he popped it over the bird's head to shut out the world, the falcon went still. He handed Margaret his shirt and balanced the bird on his glove.

"She seems well trained," the girl said.

"The glove and hood mean security to her. Otherwise she would fight me fiercely." He looped the jesses around his fingers as he spoke.

Margaret held his shirt to her chest. "You know birds."

"Some." The hooded bird was still as Duncan probed her chest, her wings. Finding crusted blood beneath one wing, he saw an ugly dark puncture, half-healed. "She was hurt a while ago. Likely the arrow dropped away. Not yours," he added.

"Oh, thank the saints!" He heard her little sob of relief.

"Her crop is thin. She has not eaten for a while. There is a bit of raw meat wrapped in the sporran. I brought it for my goshawk but sent him back with my sister."

She handed him the wrapped meat. "I have sisters too. Tamsin and Rowena. And a brother, Henry."

"Do you? Here, dear, take this." He offered the bloody chunk to the bird, snatching his fingers away as the sharp beak tore down.

"Here, dear," Margaret repeated, handing another dripping bit to him. She was not squeamish, Duncan noticed with approval, as he fed the bird again.

"Safe now, my lass," he told the falcon.

"Safe with us," Margaret echoed. "Is she badly hurt?"

"I do not know yet, but she cannot fly." He indicated the puncture beneath the wing. The girl did not flinch as she peered at the wound. Duncan admired that.

With the bird on his glove, he could not easily dress again. "Lass, hand me my plaid if you will." He stood as she draped it over one shoulder and then helped fix his belt. She fetched his other things and grabbed her bow and arrow, moving quickly and without complaint, though she limped.

"It is a good walk to the castle. Your ankle—can you walk?"

"I am fine." She limped beside him and he walked slowly for girl and bird both. Margaret clutched his things to her chest, smiling.

"Thank you for saving the bird. When do you think was she hurt?"

"A while ago. She must have escaped her falconer and headed north. They like to fly north, these birds."

"What sort of falcon is she?"

"A gyrfalcon. The largest of the falcons." He was proud of his knowledge of birds, and glad to talk of falconry rather than marriage just now. "Her tail is long and straight, and she has the large dark eyes and arrow-shaped brow of a falcon. When she is an adult, she will be larger and mostly white. The snowy white sort are rare. She is a valuable bird," he added.

"Jer-falcons? I have heard they are special birds, especially the white ones."

"Well done to spot her. You saved her life."

"You saved her! I only saw her."

"She let you see her, and let me capture her. She knew we could help."

"Oh, look!" The girl paused short, so that Duncan bumped into her, touching her slim shoulder for a moment. "See?"

Glancing up, Duncan saw an elegant bird, pale and swift, arrow across the sky and slip between tall trees. "Another falcon! Curious."

"I saw it earlier when I was waiting here. Is it a gyrfalcon too?"

"Could be. Silvery gray, and a bit smaller than the female. A tiercel. A male." Then he saw the gray falcon perched at the highest point in a tree. The gyrfalcon on his glove made a chupping sound. "He must be a wild bird. But she noticed him."

"Papa says only kings can own gyrfalcons. Could they belong to King Edward?"

"I wonder." The same thought troubled him. He peered at the gyrfalcon's anklet and jesses. "There is some tooling on the leather." With his free hand, he examined the faded markings on the tattered strips. "It looks like—aye. Three lions rampant." He frowned.

"King Edward! Could she have flown here from England?"

"The king may have brought hunting birds to Carlisle, where he is staying. She could have flown here easily from there."

"And the other bird? Is he her mate?" She pointed upward just as the pale gray tiercel left its perch to disappear among the trees. "Perhaps they escaped together. Escaping the evil king!"

She looked delighted with her fantasy. Margaret Keith was a romantic soul, Duncan realized. He shook his head. "Falcons mate for life, but this gyrfalcon is young, and the tiercel looks wild. Falcons do fly wild in northern Scotland."

"She could have a wild mate." She smiled at the romantic idea. "But if she belongs to King Edward, she must be returned."

"First she must heal. Then we will decide." He meant his father. She smiled as if he meant the two of them.

"Will she fly again, our gyrfalcon?" Her lovely smile was distracting.

Our gyrfalcon. "With luck. She needs time."

"Only a king can fly a white gyrfalcon. Could we even keep her?"

"A man could lose a hand, even his head, if he owns one or flies one for sport."

"What if no one knows? You said they fly wild in Scotland."

"Some do. The white sort come mostly from Norway. But wait." An idea occurred. He took one of the jesses. "Take hold of the other piece, lass."

She closed her palm over it. "Now what?"

"Margaret Keith, swear to me now on this bird's jesses, that you will never tell that we found royal insignia on this bird."

"I swear it." The trust in her voice, her eyes, made him falter. "It is our secret. And our bird." Her bright smile cut him like a knife. "A promise as solemn as marriage."

He gulped. "Margaret. There is something you should know."

"I want to tell you something, too."

His news would ruin anything else. "Say it, then."

"We pledged one secret, so here is another for our trust. Listen. I saw you in a vision. We were married." She smiled so sweetly that his heart broke, then and there.

"Did you." Vision? What a dreamer she was. He must tell her now.

"My great-grandfather has a seeing stone. He calls it *clach na firinn*, a truth stone. The Queen of Faery gave it to him, you see. He is True Thomas. Thomas the Rhymer. You may know his name." She beamed when he nodded. "The stone has a hole through it, a magical opening that shows the truth and the future if you can see it."

He huffed. "Such things do not happen."

"They do! I looked through his seeing stone. And I saw something. Instead of the room where I stood, I saw a knight and a lady. It was you—and me."

"But we only met as children. And then again today."

"But I knew it was you and me, older than we are now. We each carried a hawk on a glove. We were married. And so happy."

He frowned. "That is a fancy. You saw what you wanted to see."

"I saw the truth through that stone. I know it, I."

That phrase gave him pause. His mother used those words when she had a strong premonition. Then he shook his head. "A pretty dream."

"Not a dream. My Grandda called me a forest bride. He said one day I might have sadness and strife, but happiness would come. I reminded him that I was already betrothed and would be married soon."

Duncan gazed far down the meadow. "What did he say to that?"

"He said, 'bonny wee forest bride, wait and see.' But we will not be married in the forest. We will be married in a chapel. So that part is silly. Though I do love the forest best of all."

"Silly." Far off, he saw a people coming from the castle across the long meadow toward them. He had only minutes left alone with her.

"I shall visit you often to help train our gyrfalcon. And her mate. Oh, he is gone!" She looked up.

"You are a wee dreamer, Margaret Keith." He felt sad to say it.

"Papa says I am a dreamer like my sister Tamsin. Our sister Rowena is a practical sort. You will meet them soon. It is good to have dreams."

She was so young. He felt old suddenly. "Dreamers get their hearts broken."

"—and one day my husband, a brave and worthy knight, will be rewarded by the king for rescuing a precious falcon. That is, if we tell the king." She wrinkled her nose.

In the meadow, he saw them running—his father, his mother, his sister, the falconer, and Sir Robert Keith. There were only moments left. This mess was his doing, and as a courteous knight, he was obliged to tell the lady the truth.

"Lady Margaret."

"My family calls me Meg. And your family calls you Donnchadh or Duncan Dhu."

"Aye." He could not use her affectionate name. Not now. "Our betrothal—must be dissolved."

"What?" She tipped her head like a hawk, green eyes wide, fixed on him.

The others were approaching. The bird shifted, clenched on the glove. "The agreement must be undone." His heart thumped. "I am sorry."

"But we are supposed to marry!"

"I must go away for a long while. Royal orders. I cannot marry now."

"I would wait!"

"I do not want you to wait so long for me."

"You do not want to marry me." Her brow puckered, her lip wobbled.

"Not true," he said hastily. The others were nearer, calling out. "I must fulfill my knight service and cannot take a wife yet. Listen, please—"

"Stop!" Tears pooled in her eyes. "Stop! I hate King Edward. I hate you! I want to be your wife but you do not want me!" She stepped back. "Take care of our bird—" On a sob, she threw his things to the ground and spun away.

She ran, limping and stumbling, curls fanning out like flames. Her father reached her first, taking her in his arms as she cried. Then he scooped her up to carry her to the castle.

Duncan stood, gyrfalcon on his fist. Intent on knighthood, he had meant to give Margaret her freedom. Instead, he had hurt her, and felt stabbed through the heart as well.

His father ran toward him. "God's bones, Donnchadh, why is the lass so upset? Where is your shirt? And what the devil are you doing with a white gyrfalcon? *Ach*, now we are in for it!"

CHAPTER ONE

Scotland, Stirlingshire
April, 1307

"I T IS NOT far now, I hope, Lady Margaret," the young girl said, riding beside Margaret as their small escort traveled north on a road leading into the Highlands. They had ridden for hours since leaving Kincraig Castle that morning.

"Not far now, dear," she told the girl. "Sir Hugh says we will reach the Firth of Clyde soon to meet the boat your father is sending for you."

"Ireland is lovely, I hear. Will we reach there tonight?"

Margaret smiled. "Lady Lilias, you are in a hurry! It was arranged for us to sail to a Hebridean isle to spend a few days there until another boat arrives takes us over to Ireland. Your father is not free to meet us, though."

"I know Papa will not be there, but one of my uncles lives in Ireland. We will see him soon. I do like to hurry," Lilias added, giggling. "I talk too fast and move fast too, but Papa says those are traits of a someone with a quick wit. I promised him to try harder to be patient. But I am anxious to see my uncle and cousins in Ireland. My half-brother Rob Bruce is there too," she went on. "Will you stay with us for a while before returning home? Everyone at Kincraig has been so kind to me while I have been there. I appreciate it. I know my father does too."

"I feel as if you are like one of my sisters now, and not just

Bruce's daughter sheltered at Kincraig. We have been happy to help you and help King Robert, too. Scotland needs him now."

"I am glad you are with me on this journey," Lilias said. "I am a bit nervous, I confess, with so many troubles now. Papa fears some harm may come to me, but I am just his daughter outside of marriage. Not very important. But he is concerned about me and my half-siblings now that his queen and his daughter Marjorie, and a few of my aunts and cousins were captured by English and are so cruelly treated in England."

"It truly is distressing. He wants to ensure your safety because he loves you very much," Margaret said. "And we are safe in the company of Sir Hugh, Sir Quentin, the men from Kincraig, and those sent by Bruce." She glanced around at the escort party of eight men; she would not tell Lilias that no more men could be spared to accompany them due to the war effort. She smiled. "And soon we will sail away on an adventure."

"You like adventure, Meg," Lilias said. "You are so strong and brave. I wish I were more like you and your sisters."

She laughed. "You are all that and more, I think. You have not had the chance to find out. When I was your age, I was dreamy and impulsive. But I learned quickly that life is not always good to dreamers. I had to learn to be bolder."

"Then I will learn too. Can we continue to practice archery in Ireland? I have enjoyed lessons with you so much."

"I am sure we can find time for it there." Margaret reached back to pat the yew bow strapped across her saddle, then smoothed a hand over the leather quiver hooked over the pommel. Having a weapon to hand made her feel a little more secure. Truth be told, she was not entirely certain of their safety that day.

Before they left Kincraig, she had overheard her brother, Sir Henry Keith, discussing the journey with their brother-in-law, Sir William Seton. Both had seemed concerned, wanting more men for the escort and regretting that they were not free to go along, having assignments elsewhere. Henry was a deputy sheriff in

Selkirk, and Liam, Tamsin's husband, had a task to take care of for Robert Bruce. She sensed their concern, for the English were a perpetual threat in Scotland—and Lady Lilias was precious goods.

"I would prefer to travel with you," Henry had told Margaret. "But I must obey King Edward in gesture if not in spirit."

"I will see to her wellbeing," Margaret said.

"You are so protective of her—and you have a good hand with a bow, come to that." He said it lightly, but Margaret took his praise to heart.

With Henry often away, and their sister Tamsin married and living at Dalrinnie Castle, and their sister Rowena away too, lending a hand in local infirmaries, Margaret had taken on the role of chatelaine at Kincraig. She had learned to take charge of the castle household, and the castle's garrison filled with Scots knights loyal to the Keiths as well as Bruce.

She hoped that young Lilias did not fully know the threats that might affect her. As the oldest daughter of Bruce's so-called bastard children—whom he loved equally—Elisabeth Bruce deserved protection. As her friend and foster sister of a sort, Margaret felt a sincere responsibility toward her.

Ten years ago at Lilias's age, Margaret had been happy, whimsical, and trusting, dreaming of her future—until her heart was broken by an annulled betrothal. Tragedy and illness had followed. Yet trouble had forged a strength in her that she might not have acquired otherwise.

She had abandoned dreams of a happy marriage, accepting that she might never marry. Her father had made other attempts to find her a match, but he had died sooner than anyone expected. Instead of marrying, she became resolute, stubborn, and more determined than ever to watch over her home and family. That included Lilias Bruce.

Lady Elisabeth de Bruce was just thirteen, but her father might soon look for an advantageous marriage for her. He had been secretly crowned King of Scots a year ago, and even with much on his mind, the safety of his family was paramount to him.

Feeling a surge of affection, Margaret glanced at the girl. Lilias was lovely, with dark, wavy hair, a fine-boned face with her father's high-set cheeks, and blue eyes so dark, they turned twilight purple at times. One day she would be a beauty. Today, she was perhaps the most valuable lass in Scotland, and did not even know it.

Her mother, the daughter of a Scottish lord, had died when Lilias was born, having dallied with young Robert Bruce before they could marry. His sister, Lady Christina Bruce, had raised the child with her own brood; yet months ago, Lady Christina had been captured with Bruce's queen and the other women. King Edward had refused to negotiate, confining a few of the women to iron cages and shutting the rest in convents. Determined to rescue them, Bruce was also taking measures to protect Lilias and his other illegitimate offspring. He knew Edward would hunt for anyone close to him.

"Here is Andrew!" Lilias said. Margaret looked up. The son of the late hero Sir Andrew Murray was another young person Bruce valued. "Perhaps he has news."

Margaret smiled as Andrew Murray drew up his horse beside them. Thirteen also, he was tall and lanky, still sweet-faced as a girl, with wide brown eyes and a tangle of golden curls. Andrew had come to Kincraig at age nine, sent by his widowed mother to foster under Sir Robert Keith. Sir Andrew Murray had perished of battle wounds when his son was small. A close friend and advisor of Sir William Wallace, Murray was revered in memory. And his son felt like another sibling to Margaret.

"Riders ahead," Andrew reported. "Sir Hugh Stewart sent men to see if they are the ones we are to meet."

"Soon we will sail!" Lilias beamed bright enough to banish any dark cloud. Margaret felt a nagging sense of worry lift for a moment.

"I expect King Robert will send a fine ship for us," Andrew said. "They do say the king has a fleet of eighteen birlinns of forty oars each. What a sight that would be!"

"He will not make a show of fetching his daughter," Margaret said. "Likely he will send a smaller ship, old and plain, and we will hope for fog to veil our escape."

"We have sun and blue skies and we are off for Ireland. I can hardly wait!" Lilias smiled again. "Look at that beautiful hawk! That is surely a good omen for our journey."

Margaret looked up to see a hawk, wings spread wide, feathers fingered at the end, tilting and sailing overhead. She thought of Duncan Campbell then—a habit she could not seem to break. Every hawk and falcon reminded her of Duncan and the beautiful white gyrfalcon they had rescued together.

But Duncan Campbell was gone, deceased in captivity, so her father had said. The gyrfalcon would be gone by now too, either returned to King Edward or lived out its years. Still, every bird of prey in flight looping overhead reminded her of Duncan Dhu and dreams that would never come to be.

Now she felt once again a twinge of that broken heart. But her life had changed. She had changed, becoming strong and independent. But if she let the memories slip in, she felt the old hurt like a blow. She had forgiven him long ago, especially knowing that he dwelled in heaven with the saints, where she could think of him kindly.

At first she had been angry, then sad; soon after, she and her mother had fallen so ill that her father had taken them to Lincluden Priory to recover. There, word had come of Duncan Campbell's death. Mourning him in those bittersweet days, her love for him had grown. Sir Duncan Dhu Campbell transformed into the ideal love she would never have, the man she would never marry, the knight who could never be equaled.

And so over ten years she had refused, adamantly at times, four offers of marriage. At twenty-four, she was not wed and might never be. She had accepted that future. None could compare in her mind—in her heart—to Duncan Campbell.

Her father had not agreed. Had he lived, he would not have given up looking for the best match for her. Henry, busy after he inherited, meant to continue the search, but so far, he had had no time for it. Margaret told herself she was content, she was strong, and her siblings needed her.

"What does a hawk signify?" Andrew asked.

"It reminds us to be determined and purposeful," Margaret said. "Or it can be a sign that we are protected and watched over, as if we have an angel on high."

"I like that," Lilias said. "White falcons look like angels. Have you ever seen one?"

Startled, Margaret said nothing. The hawk vanished into the trees.

"Something is happening up there. Look." Andrew pointed toward the head of the escort. Suddenly Margaret heard shouts, and saw Sir Hugh and other knights take off at a gallop toward a group of men riding out of the trees that lined the road.

"Is that our escort to the firth?" Lilias asked.

"I do not think so." Margaret felt a cold chill of fear. "Lilias. Andrew. Get behind me." She reached for her bow. Even riding sidesaddle, she could try to shoot if she could keep her balance. Heart thumping, she prayed she would not have to try.

"Dear God," Andrew said. "Who are they?"

Riders were barreling toward them now, swords out. They were not Keith men, and certainly not Bruce's men, Margaret was sure. They carried shields and wore badges on their arms and surcoats that she did not recognize. The seven or eight descending on them wore chain mail and surcoats and were heavily armed.

"Quick!" she cried. "Get off the road into the trees!" Turning her horse, she led the way down a grassy slope toward a fringe of oaks and beech trees. But the horsemen pursued them, hooves pounding. Before she reached the trees, Margaret heard Andrew cry out and Lilias scream. Snatching an arrow from her quiver, wrapping the reins around one arm, she turned, lifted the bow as best she could, nocking an arrow, and shot. The bolt hit the ground. She nocked another, aiming as her horse cantered, with

Lilias and Andrew riding alongside. She shot again. Hearing a cry, she thought she hit an attacker.

A glance in the distance showed a skirmish underway. The men of their escort struggled to hold off the attackers, while two Kincraig men and one of Bruce's men rode after Margaret and the younger ones to try to protect them.

But it was too late. She heard Lilias scream again as a man grabbed her; saw Kincraig men knocked from their horses; heard Andrew shout in protest. She groped for another arrow but she lost her grip on the bow when an ambushing knight rode up, grabbed her in a beefy arm, and dragged her over his saddle.

When he knocked her hard across the head, she slumped.

CHAPTER TWO

COMING OUT OF a gray fog, she looked around. The ambush had happened so fast, she hardly understood what had occurred. The enemy knights had taken some of them away. She rode across her captor's lap, reluctantly leaning on him to avoid falling. Looking ahead, she saw Lilias, still on her horse, her hands tied, the horse's reins in the keeping of one of the attackers. The girl was struggling, kicking, trying to get free. The knight reached over and took hold of her cloak in case she managed to squirm away.

Margaret squeezed her eyes shut, struggling for alertness. She recalled the flash of swords, a flurry of arrows, the *thunk* of long poles that jousted men from their horses. Remembered her horse neighing in alarm, remembered shooting—where was her bow? Gone.

Lilias had been taken first, dragged screaming as she was tossed over a thug's lap and carried away. Then Andrew, flung to the ground, was quickly subdued and tethered with a rope to stumble with the good knights of their escort who had been captured and were still on their feet. Other good men lay on the ground.

Glancing behind her now, she saw Andrew, Hugh Stewart, Quentin Douglas and a few other men walking, hands bound, bleeding from wounds, some limping.

To her left was a vast loch through a screen of trees. Guessing that was Loch Lomond, she knew they were traveling north. Yet soon they veered to the right through forestland, heading northeast. A few moments later, they stopped briefly, the knights conferring, pointing. She and Lilias and the men were kept under close guard. When her captor remounted, he pushed her behind him, so that she had to cling to him or fall.

He should have kept her in front of him. Her head was clearer now. If she had a chance to grab his dagger—or even to just slip away—she would have to take it.

The knights rode single file along a rough forest path. One side was a steep slope carpeted with ferns and studded with saplings. It made Margaret think of games she had played with her brother and others in the forest around Kincraig. She had loved climbing trees, leaping branch to branch, rolling down hills to jump up and run. She could do that now.

Taking the risk before she could think further and let fear hold her back, she let go of the man's belt and slid down and away. He grabbed for her cloak as she fell, snatching hold, tearing the wool. Her cloak pin popped open and the cloak spread as she tumbled to the ground. She grabbed the cloth but missed the pin.

Rolling down the ferny incline, feeling sticks poking into her sides, she slid to the bottom and scrambled to her feet, launching into a run. Men shouted, and one or two slid down the hill in pursuit. But she slipped away into the forest, cutting behind trees, farther and farther away each time she paused to look, to breathe.

"Eh, let her go!" someone shouted. "We will come back. We have what we want for now. Come on!" Horses began to advance along the path at the top of the slope.

She turned and fled.

Running until her breath went ragged, she fell to her knees, then rose and ran on. Branches smacked, leaves slapped her face and hands, roots tripped her, bracken snagged at her skirts. She plunged onward through the greenwood, heart slamming.

Finally she stopped where the forest was thick with tall pines. Her breath heaving, she ducked under the drooping boughs of an ancient pine and leaned against the trunk, hidden. Piney fragrance filled her nostrils, the scent and the quiet forest calming. After a while she peered out. No one seemed to have followed her.

She listened, hearing wind and rustling leaves, chirping birds, the burble of a nearby stream. Beams of sunlight threaded green and soft through leaves and boughs, undisturbed by human movement. Her wild path had taken her well off the beaten path. Safe for now, she sat back with a sob, burying her face in her hands.

Lilias was gone. Andrew was gone. The knights of the escort were taken, a few left killed or wounded. And she was lost in an unknown forest.

Touching her forehead, she felt a tender bump there, then flexed her right knee, which felt twisted and bruised. She pushed the pine branches aside to look out again at a forest redolent with green and earthy scents and spring growth. She had plunged so deep into the woods that she heard only the sounds of nature. There was no trace of men, no voices, chinking armor, horse hooves.

Sliding to sit, she tucked her arms around her legs and lowered her head and waited for the urge to cry to lessen. She would not cry. She never cried. Not any longer.

Leaning her head back, her coppery hair loose of its braiding, forehead and knee throbbing, she felt on the edge of panic. She made herself breathe, calm, reminding herself that she was safe and free. And somehow she must help the others.

First she had to understand what had happened. She thought back.

Her bow was gone, as well as their baggage and her horse.

She counted. Three good knights, two from Kincraig and one sent by King Robert, laid sprawled on the earth. Six others, including Andrew, taken prisoner, wounded and tied with rope. Three others, also left on the ground, had been enemy men. Sir Hugh Stewart and the captured men had been bloodied and limping. Thinking back, she guessed a dozen attackers had descended upon them, armed and ready.

A chilling thought occurred. Had they been waiting for the escort, aware that Bruce's daughter was with them? But how had they known?

The area they rode through, along the eastern shore of Loch Lomond, with the loch to her left, was in the region called the Lennox. She knew it belonged rightfully to the Earl of Lennox, a Bruce ally. But Lennox had been outlawed by the English, and his lands had been confiscated. King Edward had awarded them to Sir John Menteith, a Scottish lord who catered to Edward and would therefore benefit. She had heard Henry and other men discussing it at Kincraig. Was Menteith involved, since they rode through the Lennox, or was the attack just a coincidence arranged by brigands and thugs?

Perhaps she was in the Lennox, but she did not know more than that. She was far from home, certainly; Kincraig Castle was two days south at least. No one would know that something had happened until their escort failed to arrive as expected.

What she knew for certain was that she had not protected Lilias and Andrew. She had tried to defend them, but the odds had been against her. Her bow and arrows, a gift from Thomas the Rhymer, were gone now—along with the beautiful cloak pin Thomas had given her.

She felt struck to the heart. Not only Lilias and Andrew, but the precious things Thomas had entrusted to her. Tears rose in her eyes. She dashed them away.

Searching for the silver chain and pendant she wore around her neck, tucked inside her bodice, she was relieved to find it still there. Grandda had given her the little charm stone that he said a queen had given him. It reminded Margaret of him—and the trust he had placed in her.

But the lost cloak pin held the large blue stone he had called his truth stone. She pulled her green cloak close to find the rip in the wool where the silver-framed pin had been torn away. The pin and the pendant had been gifts to Thomas from the Queen of

Faery, so he had said, and thus both pieces were enchanted. Someday she would know how to use them, he had told her. But he had died before she could ask more.

In his will, he had entrusted to her the pretty pendant and his *clach na firinn*, his truth stone. The greater power lay in the brooch, and it was lost now.

She wrapped her fingers around the pendant, finding it a comfort after the shock of the day. The silver filigree frame held a translucent crystal pink as dawn, carved in the shape of an arrowhead. Grandda had said it was an ancient elf-bolt enchanted with magic. *It makes arrows fly true*, he had told her.

Her arrows had not flown true that day, she thought; but she did not know much about the charm stone. Thomas had given her the yew bow too, which her father and brother had taught her to use. She wore the necklace in remembrance of her great-grandfather, deciding that its true magic was as a reminder of Thomas, inspiring her to be the best archer she could be, and to reach for courage and boldness.

Pulling in a shaky breath, she looked out through the branches. No one was about in the forest. She would be safe here for a while. But she must find a way to help the others somehow. Returning to Kincraig for help would take days, even if she could find a way to do that. Perhaps a nearby sheriff might provide help more quickly. There would be a village nearby where she could inquire.

Another thought struck her. Had the attackers intended to take her too? She was fairly sure they had snatched Lilias deliberately. Though Margaret Keith was an earl's daughter and a Marischal's niece, she had no value otherwise. She did not even have a husband to pay her ransom, having refused four betrothals.

But she possessed something that might be valuable to some—an elf-bolt that had belonged to Thomas the Rhymer, given to him by the Queen of Faery, said to be imbued with magic. And one of the attackers had the Rhymer's brooch. If she could get the brooch back, could she barter those precious items in exchange for a king's daughter and a hero's son? Yet she did not know who had Lilias and Andrew, though the attackers were likely enemies of Robert Bruce.

But she had no answers to such questions yet. She needed to retrace her steps, leave the forest, find the attack site, try to find out who the attackers were and where they might have taken the hostages. But how?

For a moment, she felt utterly defeated.

Years ago, one of her suitors had refused a betrothal, insisting that Lady Margaret Keith was bad luck; he said the girl could bring bad luck to a man faster than thunder brought lightning. She had brought ill fortune to others, he claimed, who had agreed to take her for a bride.

The proof, apparently, was that Sir Duncan Campbell had been unfortunate enough to be yoked to her. Even though the betrothal was broken, he had been captured by the English and had died in captivity. Bad luck indeed, said this fellow.

Other suitors had died too, one of age and infirmity during the betrothal negotiations. Another—Sir Brian Lauder, a knight in his prime, intelligent and considerate in their one meeting, a man she almost considered—had died in a skirmish before any agreement could be made. After that, her father had negotiated with a fourth suitor—but that man had harshly rejected her on the excuse that she would bring him poor luck, even death.

Ridiculous. She knew that. What her suitors did not know was that Margaret Keith had refused those betrothals against her father's wishes. She was not bad luck for anyone. She was brokenhearted and did not want to marry. As for her first suitor, she had transformed Duncan Campbell into an ideal, the perfect knight, the lover tragically lost, the one man she would have loved forever had fate allowed.

Now, in this dilemma, she had no husband, no father, and no brother nearby to help her. No matter. She would make her own luck. The wellbeing of others—Lilias, Andrew, the captured men—depended on what she did now. She alone could help.

Drawing a fortifying breath, she pulled back a pine bough and listened again for pursuers. The forest was so quiet that she ventured out and began to walk back along the path the way she had come, her steps cautious.

Soon she heard a voice somewhere in the forest sounds. She froze.

"*Margaret!*" The whisper cut through the trees. "*Meg!*"

It was a familiar voice. And only kin and friends knew her shortened name.

"Andrew? Andrew! *Here!*" She ran forward a few steps.

Nearby, bushes rustled and swayed, and a lanky blond boy with blood trickling down one side of his face emerged. Andrew Murray. She ran to him.

"Oh, Andrew! I thought you were—oh, your head! You are hurt!" His thick golden hair was blood stained, the side of his face scraped. He cradled his left arm.

"I am fine," he said as she hugged him. Then she turned to usher him back to the shelter of the huge pine. "Are you hurt, Meg? They took Lady Lilias and the men."

"I know. Sit down. Let me see your wounds." She pushed him to sit.

"I must go after her," he insisted. "I will ride after those rogues!"

"Then you would not return in one piece. Tilt your head, let me see," she instructed. His forehead was bruised and his cheek scraped, and he was holding his forearm. She crawled away briefly to grab some of the nettle leaves and wild garlic that she had seen growing nearby. Dipping them in the stream that ran beneath the slope, she returned to wipe damp leaves over his wounds. Then she pulled at the hem of the linen shift under her woolen gown and tore the fabric to create a few strips. She tucked nettle and garlic in the bandage and wrapped his head. He winced.

"There," she said. "Let me see your arm."

"I twisted my wrist when I fell—oww," he muttered.

She wrapped linen around his wrist and made a simple sling with the longest piece. "Try not to use it for now. It does not seem broken, but I am no healer. If my sister Rowena were here, she would know what was wrong."

"And she would be gentle. Ow," he said as she positioned his wrist.

"Luckily she is away, or she might have been abducted too. How did you get away?"

"The rope knots were loose enough that I slipped free. I saw you roll down a bank and run, so I watched for a chance and did the same. Then I went in the same direction hoping to find you. But what should we do now?"

She sighed. "We can do little before morning. It will be dark soon. Best we rest here. There is a clear stream nearby, and I can find berries and such for us to eat. And we will think of a way to help Lilias."

"How?" He shook his head. "I am sorry that I could not stop them."

"You did your best. And I am sorry I did not pull my bow fast enough to take them down."

"You hit one. He complained about it. And your bow fell, I saw it. I wish I had a weapon. My father would have killed those men," he added, scowling. Margaret knew Andrew idolized his heroic father, although he barely remembered him.

"Your father was a great man, and he would be proud of you for being strong and clever with a righteous heart. We both tried. Remember that. And we have each other. We can solve this. I just wish I knew where we are now."

"This part of the forest runs east away from Loch Lomond," Andrew said. "Sir Hugh told me they were taking us northeast. We went about four miles north, then east, he figured."

"Sir Hugh—was he hurt?"

"He took a blow to the head, otherwise they would never have taken him. Four others were with us. And Sir Quentin

Douglas, a young knight sent by Bruce."

"I remember him. Did Sir Hugh say if this forest is in the Lennox?"

"Aye, he said we were not far from Dunbarton Castle when we were attacked just south of the loch. Sir John Menteith holds Dunbarton. He is sheriff of Dunbartonshire. I think he is not well liked, though."

"Could we go to him for help? We need a sheriff."

"Not him! He may be part of this. I saw the badges some of the attackers wore. The design was a yellow shield with a band of black and white checks. That is Menteith's crest."

"Are you sure?"

"Sir Hugh saw it too and mentioned it to me and Quentin. One of the attackers struck him for saying so. He fell, and Quentin helped him up."

Margaret frowned. "If Menteith has Lilias and the men, we should try to find a Scottish sheriff, not an English one, to confront him."

"Sir John Menteith is Scots, but he supports Edward. I have heard that. But why would he send men after us?"

"Lilias," she said. "I think that would be the reason. Was she hurt?"

"Not hurt, but angry. She fought like a wildcat, did you see?"

"I saw some of it. I took a knock to the head and was foggy for a bit." She touched her temple. "It feels somewhat better now."

"Good. Best be careful, though. Lilias put up a fuss for sure. She called them names until someone gagged her and bound her wrists and feet so she would stop punching and yelling. Sir Quentin demanded they let her go, but they struck him with a pole and gave him a broken nose and black eye. Oh, Meg, this is awful! Perhaps we should go to Kincraig right away for help."

"We would need horses or a cart. It would take too long. When our escort does not arrive to meet the boat, men will come looking for us, but we cannot wait for that. We must do something quickly." Margaret shook her head, thinking. "Whoever took Lilias and the others will act swiftly to hide them. Perhaps even ransom them."

"We passed an inn along the way just before we were attacked. I will go there to see if I can hear any news. We might be able to hire a messenger to ride to Kincraig."

"Possibly. We will go in the morning." She glanced through the pine boughs, seeing the gathering darkness. She hoped they had not been followed.

"If we can find the place where we were attacked, we might find your bow and some other things there."

"And we should find a priest to bless the dead. But we do need a sheriff," she said. "There is one in Stirlingshire. I wonder where we could find him."

"I will ask at the inn."

She began to feel a tiny ray of hope. As darkness fell, she and Andrew made beds of pine needles and oak leaves. The stream provided cold, clear water that they drank from cupped hands, and Margaret found wild strawberries along the banks, as well as dandelion greens. They ate in silence and slept exhausted under the eaves of the pine.

"THAT BRIGHT HAIR will give you away," Andrew said next morning as they neared the inn. "The thugs will be searching for a red-haired girl. Stay under those trees while I go to the inn to ask around."

She paced—the long walk had tried her sore knee—and worried for a while until he returned. He carried a bulky cloth bag on one shoulder and her quiver and bow on the other. His grin was wide.

"My things!" she cried. "Where did you find them?"

"I ran past the inn a bit and found the place where we were

taken down. I found this too." He opened the cloth sack and brought out an unsheathed dagger. "It was lost by one of the men. There are three dead there."

"A priest must bless them and arrange burial. And a sheriff can help find whoever attacked and stole the king's daughter. What else do you have there?"

He rummaged to produce a cloth-wrapped packet. "Meat pie! Mutton and barley. The woman at the inn gave it to me, with ale." He drew out a small pottery jug, and another packet wrapped in parchment. "And cheese. She only asked a half-penny, but the coins you gave me were not clipped, so I gave her a whole penny. She gave me clothing too, seeing blood on my shirt."

"What did you tell her?"

"That I witnessed an ambush along the road and escaped without being seen. She promised to send word to the Stirling-shire sheriff and said he might come this way in a few days for a woodland court and a village fair. She gave me extra food too," he added. "I did not say there were two of us in case someone overheard."

"How kind of her." Margaret drew out the folded things—a tunic shirt, woolen trews, a knitted hat, patched hose. Though old and worn, they were clean.

"She said her son wore them, but he was killed in a battle. There will be a court for public complaints and hearings near the village soon. It is not far from here. We could stay in the forest until then. The sheriff might be there. I learned something else too."

"What is that? Are you hungry?" She opened the wrapped pie and broke it, steam rising, in half, then handed Andrew a wedge.

"This is good," he mumbled, then swallowed. "The dame in the inn said men were in there last night, saying that Sir John Menteith's men saved a young lady whose escort was attacked by brigands, that they brought her to safety."

"Saved her!" She blinked. "His men were the brigands.

Where did they take her?"

"To the protection of her family, so the dame heard."

"Impossible!"

"The woodland court will be an ayre court, the innkeeper's wife said."

"An ayre? I know of those. They are outdoor courts overseen by regional justiciars instead of just sheriffs. A judge in an ayre court can hear grievances and decide cases. If only we had proof, we could bring a complaint against Menteith."

"I saw the badges. I can witness that they were Menteith's men. A justiciar of northern Scotland will be there to hear complaints, the good dame said. She said he comes here once or twice a year."

"Menteith is also a sheriff, so that could be trouble," she said. "We cannot accuse a sheriff of wrongdoing without evidence."

"There are dead men lying in a field, Margaret. Someone should know of it."

"Aye. We must report the ambush. If Menteith is there, I want to talk to him."

"Why? To ask if he stole Lady Lilias away? It is too risky! Let the sheriff or the judge do that. The dame at the inn also said a market will be held in the village. We might learn something there that would help."

"With luck, we will get assistance from the judge."

"Meg," Andrew said, "will they believe us? It sounds like a wild tale."

"It does." She sighed. "And we should be careful about mentioning Lady Lilias Bruce in a public court. There are so many English about."

"What if I followed Menteith to see if he has Lady Lilias at Dunbarton Castle? You could wait in the forest and I would come back with Bruce's daughter and all our men."

He was so young, so earnest. Margaret smiled, shook her head. "You dear lad! Now who would take a risk?"

"What then, Meg?" He sounded desperate. Her heart went

out to him.

The cloak and its contents—the dagger, the bow, the clothing—tugged at her thoughts. How could they make use of those? She felt responsible for Andrew and Lilias and there was little time. This sat on her shoulders.

"There might be something else we can do. Listen…"

CHAPTER THREE

"I HOPE WE are near done hearing cases," said Sir Constantine Murray of Pitcairn, sheriff-deputy of Stirlingshire, as he resumed his seat on a bench in a woodland grove beside the justiciar.

"It has been a long day," agreed Sir Duncan Campbell, laird of Brechlinn and justiciar of the north of Scotland. He was glad his old friend Con Murray had been assigned to the ayre court with him. They sat at a trestle table in a sunny clearing bordered by birches edging a forest lush with spring growth. Beyond an expanse of flowery meadow lay a village and a bustling market fair. Savory cooking and sweet baking smells wafted toward the grove.

"I am hungry, Brechlinn," Constantine said as he rifled through another stack of parchments handed to him by Duncan's clerk.

"Aye, but we have work to do. Just a few left."

"Have you read Menteith's complaint? Robbed of sheep and cattle, he claims."

"I glanced through. I suspect Sir John and his sheep could cause a parcel of trouble. He was complaining loudly about it not long ago."

"Ah, and here he comes, looking determined to defend himself."

Duncan glanced up. Spring sunshine filtered over the crowd

of people gathered in the clearing as Sir John Menteith, sheriff of Dunbartonshire, shoved his way through. A burly man in his thirties, near Duncan's age but looking much older, he wore a long yellow surcoat and chainmail with his usual surly scowl.

Menteith was unlikely to wait his turn, Duncan knew. Ayre courts meted out justice for those needing to present complaints beyond the sheriff court—and also provided a diversion as entertaining as games at a market fair. He had presided over many such courts in the past few years, and felt it was work well done. But the cacophony of voices, music, the lowing of cows being sold, the *thunk* of stones being tossed, and *thwack* of arrows at the archery butts was a tempting distraction after a long day. And the smells of smoky meats and savory foods made his stomach growl.

He just wanted to grab a meat pie and a fresh ale and watch a race or an archery competition. He wanted to look for a length of woven cloth to send to his sister Isabel, expecting a child in her husband's Hebridean stronghold.

First, he had to hear more cases, and knew Sir John Menteith could be tiresome. Years ago, he and Constantine had shared a dungeon cell with Menteith, who had been a decent sort, though more interested in his welfare over others'. After their release, he had heard the fellow had pandered to King Edward and prospered for it, while Duncan and others lessened their service to Edward in favor of justice for Scots.

Following his father's death, Duncan had to appeal for his inherited position as a Scots justiciar. Even so, he managed to cross Edward's tyranny in secret and worthwhile ways, and continued to take that risk.

"Patrick Fraser." Duncan turned to the young clerk seated with them shuffling parchments. "I need the account of the incident involving Menteith."

"Here, sir." Patrick handed him a rolled parchment.

"Sheep, cattle—and a man gravely injured in a dispute over livestock. Con, shall I review this as justiciar, or will you keep it in the sheriff court?"

"We could manage it in the Stirlingshire court, but since Menteith is sheriff of Dunbartonshire, better it goes to the justiciary. I thought you might like the, ah, privilege."

"Did you now," Duncan drawled.

Constantine chuckled. "Sir John says he expects the decision to go his way."

"He deserves a chance to be heard, but he can wait. Patrick," Duncan said, "ask Sir John to stand aside until we call him." As the clerk got to his feet, Duncan looked through other parchments. "What more do we have?"

"A few cases reviewed by the sheriff court need final decisions. A land dispute. A breach of promise—that girl is angry," he muttered. "A tussle over well rights, another over grazing rights." Constantine gave him a page and its copy. "An annulment."

Duncan set those aside. "The Church decides that, not the justiciary."

"But this is a hotheaded dispute over the girl's tocher," Constantine said. "Her family wants it determined by a higher civil authority than the sheriff."

Duncan scowled. The mention of a breach of promise and dowry dispute unsettled him for a moment. Just old guilt rising again.

"An abbot must recommend it to a bishop to approve or send on to Rome. Patrick, take these pages," he said as the clerk returned. Dipping ink, Duncan scribbled a note and his name. "Inform this party their complaint must go to the nearest abbey. Give the copy to Father Ambrose. He is over there and can take it to his abbot."

As Patrick hastened off again, Duncan sighed. "They will not have an annulment before autumn, if the Church moves even that fast."

"Aye. Dissolving such an agreement can be a sticky matter. Ah, sorry, Duncan."

He had no reply for that. "Next?"

"A new claim. Incident along the road past Druimin." Constantine unfolded another parchment. "A witness told an innkeeper, who conveyed it to the Stirlingshire sheriff a few days ago. It came to me. My men are investigating. They found three bodies to be blessed and buried, left in a field after some encounter. Not good. Here."

Duncan took the page. "Who is the claimant?"

"Menteith is arguing against it."

"I cannot wait," he drawled. "Who was the witness?"

"A young Andrew Murray, the innkeeper said. That name gave me a pause, but several Murrays bear that name. Not just my older brother."

"Your brother was the finest Andrew Murray of the lot. He was a good man when he was captured with us, and a brilliant general beside William Wallace. A tragedy for Scotland when he died after the battle at Stirling Bridge. Any who share that name should be proud. He had a little son called Andrew too. How old now?"

"My nephew would be twelve or thirteen. But he fosters with the Keiths and is safe there. He would hardly be wandering the Druimin Road witnessing attacks. But this witness might be a distant kinsman. He is not expected to be here, though."

"Ah," Duncan said. "Apparently Sir John has waited long enough." He watched as the sheriff pushed through the crowd to cross the sunlit clearing toward the table. Then Duncan's attention was caught by someone in the crowd.

Sunshine glowed on the head of a young woman in the crowd whose uncovered hair shone bright as copper, her face pure and beautiful. Tall and slim, she stood in a green cloak, her bronze-and-copper hair spilling over her shoulder in one fat plait. Her gaze was keen, her eyes like jewels under arched brows. Golden sunlight and the white flowers of a hawthorn tree formed nearly a halo behind her.

He stared. She stood still, a beautiful statue amid the bustling crowd. A blond lad stood beside her, a quiver strap across his chest, bow upright in his hand like a walking stick. He spoke. She nodded.

He noticed that her gaze seemed fixed on Menteith. Even at a distance, Duncan saw a spark of temper and pride in the lifted chin, slim shoulders, high pink blush. Then she glanced around the clearing at the people, the table and the men seated there.

Her eyes went wide as she looked straight at Duncan.

By God, he thought, she looked familiar. He had been holding ayre courts for three years in the region and might have seen her before. Yet something tapped at his memory.

Margaret Keith. That was who she resembled. He sucked in a breath, stunned. Yet Margaret Keith could not be here in this place, in the middle of a local crowd. The strong, fire-haired Celtic beauty he was looking at now was not the fragile, whimsical young girl he remembered, but the resemblance was startling. He had hurt that girl so deeply that she had gone into a convent, so his father had heard.

Guilt had conjured her. This girl was just a beauty who reminded him of the one he had never forgotten. He still wondered what could have been if he not made a terrible error.

Fate had not only stepped in the way, it had taken over and thrown his life into turmoil. Once captured and imprisoned, several years had passed before he returned to Scotland a free man. Even then, he moved around, never establishing a home, never finding time for peace, never taking a wife.

Poor little Margaret Keith. He had loved her in his way, remembering and cherishing her bright, wild spirit. Had she not become a nun, she would have married someone else. She did not need Sir Duncan Campbell, knight, laird, justiciar, prisoner, rebel, working openly and reluctantly for one king and secretly, loyally, for another.

The young woman glared at him, then at Menteith again. Certainly she seemed displeased; perhaps she had a legal complaint to air. The lad beside her, holding the bow, whispered to her. Something was going on there.

"Who is that lass, the redhead?" he asked quietly. "Did she submit a complaint?"

"Not that I know. Bonny thing." Constantine leaned toward him. "I do not trust Menteith. Be wary."

"Aye, but he gets his say." He tapped his fingers on the table as Menteith approached.

Tough and wiry, Menteith was not a tall man but the crowd parted for him as he moved with force and fury. His round, beefy face above a brown beard, his red cheeks and dark eyes, his tense shoulders, all spoke of a man who carried anger in every step.

"Campbell. Murray," he snapped. "I am here for recompense."

"Sir John," Duncan greeted. "Taking your turn ahead of others, I see."

"I am sheriff of Dunbartonshire and lord of Dunbarton Castle. I do not have time to wait. I presume you read the papers."

"I have. State your complaint," Duncan replied.

"Those thieving MacRuaris took eight of my sheep and two of my cows a month ago. I want compensation for the animals."

Duncan studied the parchment. "This occurred on your property at Loch Roskie?" He looked up. "You can prove the theft? Do you have witnesses?"

"I know they did it. My men reported it to me. That is enough proof."

"You lost livestock, but a MacRuari was badly hurt and may die. Which has more value, sir?"

"I would get no money for that fellow at market," Menteith growled.

But some say you got a good price for betraying Wallace, Duncan thought. Beside him, Constantine Murray, who knew that rumor too, said nothing.

"I trust you will take care of this matter, Campbell. Because I am a sheriff, it must be decided by another court, but that deputy"—he looked at Constantine—"has no authority in Stirlingshire except when that sheriff is away."

"I do have authority. I decided you need a justiciar," Murray said.

Menteith ignored him. "Campbell, your father would have seen to this for me."

"Would he?" Duncan asked mildly. "But he is no longer with us."

"And you hold his title of justiciar in the north. You have the look of him too. I am sure I can expect the same courtesy from you that he would have given."

"We shall see."

Menteith curled his lip. "You even have the same damned castle ruin on the edge of my lands, which your father refused to sign over to me as I petitioned. Perhaps you stole my sheep and cows to fill the byre at Brechlinn."

"I am not inclined to ride out in the middle of the night to steal livestock." Duncan glared at him. "You are accusing the MacRuaris, sir, but if the fellow dies, that puts a darker turn on these charges."

"No one is innocent in Scotland these days with so many changes in loyalty and secret alliances. Are you accusing me because I support Edward?" Menteith seemed full of himself.

"Why would I bother? Are you admitting guilt here?"

"Of course not."

"Some do make secret bargains," Constantine agreed. "For their own benefit."

Menteith caught his meaning, his cheeks ruddy. Duncan sat silent. He would not poke the beast of William Wallace's fate here and hoped Murray would refrain too.

"Sir John, we have other cases today," Constantine went on. "Perhaps your livestock went over the stile in the night, as some do."

"They are too stupid to do that. Someone led them."

"Then explain the attack on a MacRuari on your land," Duncan said bluntly.

"I came here to report the theft and swear that neither I nor my men harmed him. All I know is he and his brothers stole my sheep and cows, and I am owed for the beasts. That is my only declaration. I expect you will be neighborly in your decision, Sir Duncan."

"I am sworn to be neutral, not neighborly."

"Your inherited responsibility should include courtesy," Menteith said.

"I inherited this position to provide impartial and educated opinions of matters with regard to Scots law and Brehon law, where the latter applies in the Highlands." Duncan said the words almost by rote, having explained himself in several woodland courts for the past four years.

"Brehon law?" Menteith's eyebrows shot up. "I want *cro* if Gaelic law applies."

"It does apply in this region, but under that law, the injured man has the right to demand payment. You would not get the fee."

Menteith waved a hand. "Then make your decision. I do not have time for this." He turned away.

"You are not excused," Duncan snapped as Constantine handed him a new page.

"Look at this," his friend murmured.

"As sheriff of Dunbartonshire, I am excusing myself," Menteith said.

"One more question." Duncan regarded the page in his hands.

"What is that?" Menteith fisted his hands. "I have duties to tend to."

"As do we all," Duncan murmured. "But it seems there was a recent incident along the Druimin Road east of Loch Lomond. Sir Constantine?"

"Aye. A few days ago, an escort party was attacked there. Three men were found dead in a nearby field. There were signs of a skirmish, with hoofprints, discarded weaponry, and other signs. A torn badge showed the Menteith insigne."

"I know nothing about that."

Constantine leaned forward. "Sir. According to the account of an innkeeper along that road, men wearing your badge and insignia were overheard at the inn saying they had taken a lady in a skirmish with others. A young lady."

"What my men say in their cups is not my concern."

"A witness reported similar details."

"Sir John, you are attached to this issue because your badge was seen," Duncan said. "Your men were overheard mentioning your name and an altercation that occurred on that road. And there are signs of an incident."

"Since it happened on the east side of the loch, it is a Stirlingshire concern," Constantine said. "Do you know of a skirmish, sir, or of a lady taken in that area?"

"Think carefully," Duncan warned.

"Oh, that one!" Menteith waved a hand. "Not a lady. A child. You confused me."

"What do you know of it?" Constantine asked.

"My men witnessed a theft along the road. Brigands. They interfered to rescue a young girl and her escort. They took the ruffians down and escorted the girl and the others to her kinsmen. It is done. It has naught to do with me."

"Who are her kin?"

"MacDougalls. She was fortunate my men intercepted those brigands."

Duncan masked his reaction. His father had died at the hands of MacDougalls years ago. The name would always rankle, but just now, it puzzled him.

"A minor incident," Menteith said with a shrug.

"Not if men were killed," Duncan snapped.

"Brigands died. I am not responsible for those deaths."

"Nor responsible in any matter today, it seems. Who was the girl?" Duncan asked.

Menteith shrugged. "Daughter of a Highland laird. She needed assistance. A good deed done is no matter for a justiciary. We are finished here."

"I will decide that. Sir Constantine will need to take accounts from your men. You may be questioned too."

"But I am leaving today," Menteith said.

"Going where?" Constantine asked. "If you will be at Loch Roskie instead of Dunbarton, we will find you there."

"I have properties in the north. Other responsibilities. You understand."

"Of course." Duncan studied the page in his hand. "Well. The other party in the dispute of missing livestock and an injury has not shown up today."

"Nor will they, coward MacRuaris," Menteith said.

Duncan ignored that. "Then you are done for now. But stay nearby and remain on your lands until Sir Constantine can determine more about the matter along the Druimin road."

"I told you I cannot stay."

Constantine tapped another parchment. "Sir John, I have a statement from one of the men who removed the dead from that place. He says the deceased were knights, not brigands. Two wore laurels on their badges. The Keith insignia."

Duncan froze, his hands stilled. Keith! He had not seen the page Murray held. His thoughts went to the Keiths of Kincraig, but there were other Keiths, fine men all, though none resided in this region. Why would they travel through Stirlingshire to escort a young girl to meet MacDougalls? Now Menteith's claim made little sense.

"Likely the thugs stole gear belonging to others," Menteith insisted.

"Best pray so," Constantine said. "Trouble will surely stir if Keith men were killed on a Stirlingshire road and a girl taken."

Reminded of the girl who resembled Margaret Keith, Duncan glanced toward the crowd. She was gone.

"That girl was delivered to her kin, I tell you." Menteith was turning redder.

"The highest-ranking Keith is Marischal of Scotland," Duncan said. "He will want to know if Keiths were involved—and slain."

"All a misunderstanding. I am expected in the market square now to judge pigs and pies. And you, neighbor?" Menteith turned to Duncan. "You should join the archery contest. Years back, you were a fine shot. There is a handsome prize."

"I will consider it," Duncan said, frowning at the man's sudden casualness.

"Indeed. Best watch your back at Brechlinn, sir. Watch your sheep."

"I would, if I had any."

"Did he just imply a threat?" Constantine murmured.

"Could be. But he had best stay away from Brechlinn."

"Your property is remote enough to protect what you are doing for Bruce there," his friend said low. "But you may need more guards on the walls. Send word if so."

"I should increase the watch at Brechlinn, but Scots soldiers are thin on the ground these days. Bring a few men if you can spare them."

"I may do that soon. Bruce relies on you. I am pleased to quietly help."

"Very quietly. Here is Patrick. What else must we do here? I am starving."

"MEG, YOU HEARD what Menteith told them," Andrew said. "He rides north today, and he seems in a hurry. If he moves Lilias, we may never find her."

"I thought the same. And if they send a ransom request to her father, it may be too late." Margaret paced the forest floor beyond the village. In the shelter of beeches and oaks, sunlight tinting the new leaves green, she and Andrew had found a pocket in the forest close to the village and the woodland court, yet dense enough to hide them. "If only we could delay Menteith from leaving."

"Impossible. We have been here for near a week, and now that we have finally found him, he is leaving today." He shoved a hand through his hair.

"I have an idea. But before we return to the village fair, I need to change."

"Change? Why?"

She ducked behind the wide trunk of the beech with its low branches and grabbed the bundled cloak with the things Andrew had acquired at the inn. Pulling off her green gown and hiding it under a tree, she stepped into woolen trews, drew them up and crammed her linen shift inside, trying to thicken her curving waistline as she pulled the waist cord. Next she tugged on a tunic of drab brown, then black stockings, shoving her feet into her boots, glad she had worn those to travel from Kincraig.

Emerging from the tree cover, she spread her arms. "What do you think?"

"You look like a lad with ribbons and long braids."

"Oh!" She wrapped her braids, plaited with cream ribbons, around her head and stuffed her hair under a generous black woolen cap that came with the gifted clothing. "We will go to the village as two lads."

"You need to sheathe a dagger in your belt to look more manly. But I do not think you can manage it even then," he added.

Sending him a wry look, Margaret took up her belt of plain leather, detached the embroidered purse buttoned there, and slung the belt low over her hips. Next she took up her green cloak and flipped it; the lining had a plaid pattern of green with blue and black. She fastened it around her throat as best she could with the pewter cloak pin the innkeeper's wife had included.

"Give me the bow and the quiver, if you please, and keep the dagger for yourself."

"What is your plan?" He handed her the bow and adjusted the quiver strap over her back. Then he took up the dagger, wrapped it in cloth, and stuck it in his belt. "What shall we do in the village? Listen and spy?"

"We can find Menteith judging contests."

"But we have neither pigs nor pies."

"If there is an archery contest, I could enter. Then I could try to have a word with him."

"And ask nicely if he stole Lilias?" He scoffed.

"Well, maybe not nicely." She patted the bow.

"You are a madwoman. Do not act rashly! I am just a lad and would not dare confront him without a sheriff there."

"We shall see." She led the way out of the forest.

"I thought you might accuse him at the court."

"It was not the right time. He has some trouble, though. They are watching him. That could go well for us."

"We should look for the justiciar or the sheriff. One was a Murray. If I tell him my name, he might listen."

"Who was the other? I did not hear his name."

"A Campbell."

"Oh?" She busied herself adjusting the bow on her shoulder.

"One of the sons of Cailean Mòr of Lochawe who was killed years back. I heard the knights at Kincraig talk about it once."

Her heart quickened. "I did hear that." She recalled that the justiciar was handsome enough to stand out among other men—and he had seemed oddly familiar. When Andrew said the name, she felt stunned.

But he could not be Duncan Dhu Campbell. Yet he had black hair that shone in the sunlight, keen blue eyes, a rare smile, crooked and sincere, and a way of tilting his head to listen, really listen, to others. Oh. Her heart surged.

But Duncan Campbell was dead. Her father had told her so, years ago. He had been captured in battle and taken into England with a hundred other captive Scottish lords. He had perished in captivity.

If that justiciar was a Campbell of Lochawe, he could be one of Duncan's brothers. That would explain the resemblance. Whoever he was, if he could bring justice for Lilias and go after Menteith, she would have to approach him. Lilias and the captured men were her highest concern just now.

"There are sporting contests at the village fair today," Andrew was saying. "Foot races, horse races, tossing stones, and such. A contest at the archery butts too."

"Good. You are swift of foot. And I am good with the bow."

"Skilled with a bow, but a fire-haired female. And a mad one at that."

She shoved him hard, which she thought a lad might do. He stumbled, laughing.

CHAPTER FOUR

DUNCAN TOOK ANOTHER bite of a meat pie, wild fowl mixed with currants in a spicy sauce and thick crust, as he walked through the market square. Hearing raucous cheering, he saw people gathered at the edge of a meadow watching a foot race. Curious, licking his fingers, he stopped to watch seven runners pounding along an earthen track, feet flying, hair sweeping back. Two lads had a good lead, and one wore a sling on one arm—the blond lad with the bow and arrow he had seen earlier beside the girl who resembled Margaret Keith with her bright hair and faery grace.

The lass he could not forget, his one-time betrothed, with whom he shared a gyrfalcon. The girl he should have married. He had never lost his remorse over it.

For a moment, he wished he could see her again, if only to apologize and tell her what only a few trusted friends knew—that he still protected their gyrfalcon at remote Brechlinn. Even if she never forgave him, she would be pleased to know that.

Standing there, he searched for the red-haired lass to no avail. When the golden-haired lad lost narrowly, Duncan applauded the winner and the other for persistence. When the lad left, Duncan followed, hoping he would find the redheaded girl.

He felt distracted by the need to find her, as if seeing her would refresh the memory of a girl he cherished. Craved. Wished he could see again.

He lingered as the boy bought an oatcake, then saw him wave a greeting to another lad, a slender, leggy fellow in a brown tunic, plaid cloak, and black cap. This one had a youthful, beardless face partly obscured by the draped cloak hood.

Perhaps this was just his brother. Duncan shrugged and headed in another direction. Now he scanned the busy crowd for a glimpse of Menteith, who was judging some of the contests. The man's explanation of stolen sheep and cows, and then of a girl attacked by brigands, did not sit right. He wanted to know more.

Duncan knew from experience that Sir John was not the most trustworthy of men. He had learned that after Dunbar, when Menteith, Constantine, Andrew Murray, Duncan, and over a hundred other young Scottish lords had been taken prisoner. Staying with Menteith and others in England for a while, Duncan had been sent to Flanders with one group, Menteith remained captive in England. Later, to obtain release, Menteith had pledged to Edward again, and had given up the names of others to gain favor.

Duncan was aware of the pressure Edward inflicted on Scottish nobles. He had been a recipient of that too. But though he understood the circumstances, he had little respect for the man's actions.

Looking around, he could not find the woman who looked like Margaret Keith. Well, he told himself, it was just guilt and regret tugging at him again. He felt it too often.

Ahead, he saw an archery contest. That was one of his favorite pastimes, a skill he had honed growing up with brothers, shooting at hay bales, apples, shields, painted images on wood, even coins when they dared each other's eye and skill. He often bested the others; he had an unfailing eye for a target. But archery was not considered a skill for knights, but was left to archers trained to the bow and crossbow. Knights relied on swords, lances, combat from horseback. But he preferred the bow for hunting and sport.

And he hated war. He had no taste for it, good as he was with sword, shield, lance, and arrow, good as he was with wrestling a man to the ground. He had size and strength, agility, a keen eye and mind. But he disliked conflict and admired the law far more for resolving differences.

A few years ago, meeting with Robert Bruce in Ireland, he had earned that earl's trust—now the king's trust—for his grasp of the law and his discretion. As laird of remote Brechlinn Castle, he was able to help Bruce by channeling fugitive Scottish rebels through his castle, sending them on from there to Ireland or other safe locations. Recently he had taken in some of the priests the English called "false preachers," loyal Scottish clergymen arrested for advocating war and stirring rebellion. Duncan had been involved in releasing them on bail, and he took it further, secretly, by sheltering them.

Released and protected, then freed, the priests had stubbornly resumed their activities, so the English were often looking for them. Edward's lieutenants sent word out that the priests, including a bishop, were behaving worse than ever by praising Bruce and the Scottish cause to stir Scots against English domination.

As justiciar, Duncan was expected to help corner and punish these priests. But he was more inclined to discreetly help them. When he next returned to Brechlinn, which lay at the northern end of Loch Lomond, he would fulfill requests from Bruce over any orders from Edward's commanders in Stirling.

But now, he only wanted a hot bannock and a cup of ale. The spring air felt clear and cool, the mood around him merry. As he strolled through, he nodded here and there in greeting, though most gave a curt nod or looked away.

"People are afraid to talk to you, man," said Constantine Murray, falling into step with him. "The grim justiciar who looks so stern. Here comes a Campbell, son of a clan chief so great, he is practically a Highland myth. His son upholds the law, so best watch out, for he never smiles."

"If I had something to smile about, I would," Duncan said.

"My father was bigger than life, brave and brash and fair. Me, I am a quiet man, hey. And Scotland is a grim place these days. Years back, we were both happier, I vow, as new knights ready for adventure."

"Those were good days. And then we were brave and brash enough to leap to the Scottish side and thumb our noses at the English. But we were captured."

"A hard lesson. But I do smile sometimes." His mother often said he was too serious, but it suited him. Reserve and secrecy were comfortable, and necessary in a judge.

"That glower you favor is the look of the reckoner who sees a person's guilt. Adults avoid you. Children run from you—see," Constantine added as two small boys, chasing a leather ball, stopped, stared, and raced off.

Duncan huffed. "I am hardly evil."

"Stern but fair, I give you that."

"When a regional justiciar must decide life or death in a woodland court, it sits heavy on a man sometimes. Thankfully I did not have to do that here."

"Listen, lad, you are like a brother to me, so I will give you some advice. Someday you will need to marry and settle down. Lighten your mood and be more approachable."

"What, join in the merriment here? Enter a contest and be a champion? That will not attract the love of my life." Huh, he thought. The love of his life—realized too late, his own fault— had chosen to be a nun.

"How about a foot race?"

"That last pie I ate would slow me down. Very well. I will try my hand at archery."

"Then the others may as well go home."

"Winning a prize might make me smile," Duncan said. Constantine laughed.

He halted, noticing archery butts set up on a long field just beyond the village. Onlookers gathered there, applauding as a few archers lined up to take turns. Duncan saw Sir John Menteith standing with others, apparently acting as a contest judge.

"Now there is the very spirit of honor," Constantine muttered.

"Nock!" called a man Duncan recognized as the miller. "Mark! Draw!"

Arrows were loosed and hit the painted targets tacked into hay bales.

"Good shots," Duncan said.

"Go on, be as approachable as you can be. Join the contest. You will likely win the prize, so you can chat with Sir John and find out what more he knows about that attack. I am curious. What happened along the road, and why were his men there?"

"I agree. Ah, he is displaying the prize now. A pretty bauble." Duncan saw Menteith hold up a shiny silver thing to show the crowd.

"Win it and find someone who would like that pretty *bijou*."

"Ha. Well, I must find me a bow first."

"Put your name on the list. I will fetch you a bow and meet you back here."

Minutes later, having added his name to the list held by a lad serving as clerk for the contest, Duncan went to stand with other contestants. Constantine Murray returned, bow and quiver in hand. A tall, brawny, black-haired man walked with him.

"Good Lord," Duncan said in surprise. "Malcolm! What are you doing here? You look good!" He took the man's hand. "I have not seen you since we were last in Ireland."

"And before that, escapees in France. But I did not want to serve in Edward's army any longer." Malcolm, fugitive Earl of Lennox, spat on the ground.

"Nor did Constantine or I. Malcolm, draw up your hood. Menteith is here."

"So I see. God's bones, it is a pleasure to find you both together. I have a message." Malcolm Lennox pulled his hood down over his dark curly hair. "But here I am skulking about, having been ousted by Menteith, courtesy of Edward of England."

"Someday that will be corrected. You have business here?" Duncan asked.

"A word with both of you, aye, from—Robert."

"Aye then." Duncan glanced at Constantine, both knowing who Malcolm meant. Lennox was a big man, beyond thirty years, with deep brown eyes and nearly black hair, his black beard long and full and streaked with silver, his brown cloak and tunic tattered and plain. Not much of a disguise, Duncan thought; Lord Lennox was a striking fellow in any crowd, and his voice, deep and rich and distinctive, carried far. But the man kept his voice muted as he spoke with them.

"Can we talk here?" he murmured.

"If you whisper and keep that great head down and covered," Constantine said. "Is that gray I see in your beard?"

"Life is hard, lad. I should be judging contests and eating pies," he said. "But I am not willing to serve King Edward, so there go my lands." He shrugged.

"The king you admire will get your lands back someday," Duncan said. "Did he send you here?"

"He sent me to find you both. He awaits the arrival of a very important lady who came this way, and he needs to know her status. She has disappeared," he added.

"A fugitive from king's justice?" Duncan asked in a low tone. "Was she on her way to Brechlinn? I have three guests there, priests who will be moved soon. My men will do that before I return, but we have room for more."

"I have news about that as well. Another cleric will be sent to you to be conveyed to the Isles. But not this lady."

"And what of her?'

"Bruce arranged for her to be taken safely to the Isles. But she never arrived at the Firth to meet the ship. I am here to find out why, and to alert you both as justiciar and sheriff's deputy. He needs to know she is safe. I am to bring back any news."

"Who is she?"

"A very significant and very young lady."

Exchanging a glance with Constantine, Duncan frowned. "We heard of a young girl traveling this way with an escort party," he said. "They were ambushed by brigands. She was rescued by another party, and taken to meet her kinfolk."

"But that girl was a child," Constantine added.

"Who were the kinfolk?" Lennox asked.

"MacDougalls, we were told," Duncan said.

"Not the same lady then. I cannot say more here." Malcolm glanced around.

"Menteith's men saved the girl, so he claims," Duncan went on.

"The one we must find was accompanied by Keiths and some of Bruce's men."

A cold chill ran through him. "Keiths?"

"Henry Keith and his sisters hosted the young lady at Kincraig for a while, until Robert requested that she be sent to Ireland. It was arranged that one of the Keith sisters would help escort her out of Scotland."

"Keith's sisters are still at Kincraig?" Duncan asked.

"One is at Dalrinnie, I hear, having married a Seton. There are two others."

"The Seton who runs with the outlaws in the Ettrick Forest?" Constantine asked. "I know of him. A good and loyal fellow."

"Aye. Bruce trusts him," Duncan added. His heart was pounding unaccountably. "And the other sisters? Are there three?"

"I do not know how many sisters Henry has, but I have heard they are beauties, desirable to any man, and even more desirable for their kinsmen and their fortune. I only know Bruce wanted this young lady taken from Kincraig to Ireland. But if the child you mention went to MacDougalls, she is not the one I seek."

Mention of the Keith sisters had shaken him, but Duncan nodded. "I will find out what I can. Give me a day or so."

"Very well. I will find you again. Bruce has gone south, have you heard? Men are gathering behind him in great numbers in the southwest."

"We heard." Constantine nodded. "Word is spreading that his forces are growing. Duncan, they are calling for the next set of archers. Here." He handed the bow and quiver to Duncan. "We will cheer you on, hey."

Shouldering the weapon, Duncan went to join the several archers standing near the butts. Waiting his turn, he took a few moments to check the bow, a good ashen one with a powerful pull. The arrows were good too, neatly fletched with goose feathers. Their plain steel bodkin points would fly straight and true to pierce a target. Satisfied, he stood patiently by as names were called. He would be last.

Two shots were allowed each contestant, the targets easy enough—a pair of flower garlands varying in color and size. Each archer showed decent skill, Duncan thought, as he watched two farm lads and a grizzled crofter hit near the edges of the garlands, fluttering petals to the ground. The next archer hit the center of one garland and wildly missed the next shot.

"Marcus Murray," the clerk called.

Murray? Duncan narrowed his eyes. The lad appeared to be the one he had seen with the blond fellow in the foot race. Bundled in cloak and cap, the slender lad in the black cap brought his bow up, nocked the arrow, stretched the string, eyed the targets.

Duncan sensed an uncanny calm in one so young. The lad acted as if he heard nothing around him, seeing only the target. His first arrow struck near the garland's center. His second shot was a finger's-width to the side, measured by a lad who ran forward to pluck arrows from the targets, while the dog with him fetched arrows from the ground, bringing them back to those overseeing the competition.

"Sir Duncan Campbell of Brechlinn," the clerk called out, standing near Menteith.

Duncan stepped forward as the young archer in the black cap stepped away. The boy looked pale, even shaken, despite his previous calm. He glanced at Duncan, a flash of green eyes—young and anxious. Perhaps he did not like justiciars.

"Well done," Duncan said, to offer encouragement. The lad turned away.

He took his position next, nocked, sighted, taking a moment to get the feel of a bow he had never used. The bow was good, the arrow shaft straight, the target an easy twenty or so yards off. Then he pulled. The bodkin point sailed to pierce the hole made by the lad in the black cap. His second arrow hit very near the center of the garland.

The crowd applauded as Duncan stepped aside. The miller's lad fetched the arrows while the miller and another tacked up another garland. Each competitor shot and stepped aside. Duncan waited, hands wrapped around the upright bow.

Young Marcus Murray stepped up again, shooting with impressive calm and accuracy. Several shots later, Duncan was not surprised when the competition winnowed down to Marcus and himself.

"Which of you will win the prize?" Menteith crowed, holding up the brooch. It flashed blue and silver in the sunlight.

Beside him, Marcus Murray made a sound, a sort of gasp that became a cough.

Duncan reached out and clapped him on the shoulder. "Fine? You can win that brooch. Just go easy."

"Huh," the lad grumbled. "I want that brooch."

Odd, Duncan thought, that low, husky voice, that intense glance at Menteith. But it was just a cloak pin. He had a half dozen in a wooden box. He did not need another.

The final target was set up—three wooden hoops of graduated size, the smallest less than a palm wide, a true challenge. One shot would be allowed for each ring.

Duncan struck near the center, and so did the boy, their arrows tight together inside the first two hoops. He held back a bit with his shot. He did not want to best such a talented young archer. Marcus was so shy, he barely looked up, even when the crowd cheered him. Yet the lad gave Duncan a genuine challenge. Though thin and barely muscled, his aim was true.

Their third set of shots hit directly into the smallest hoop, the arrows so tightly together inside the circle that the miller turned to Sir John.

"Should both win?"

"Give them one more," Menteith said. "I want to see that strapling boy beat the justiciar. Bring another target. That painted sign."

Two boys carried out a banner and tacked it to the hay bales, the cloth blowing a bit in the spring breeze. As the boys stepped back and Duncan saw the banner, he clenched his bow in startled response. The image was a white falcon in mid-flight, wings spread. White feathers had been glued to the painted wings, giving it an eerie realism.

Beside him, Marcus Murray gasped and tugged at his cap. Duncan saw a reddish curl slip free, tucked back again. He frowned.

He studied the boy more closely, noticing what he had not before: the finely shaped profile and pale skin; slim, graceful fingers adjusting the cap; long, smooth, shapely legs; and despite the bulky clothing, a distinct curve at hip and breast.

No need to look for the red-haired lass. She stood just beside him. What the devil? He could not sort it out quickly.

"A falcon," Menteith announced. "A gyrfalcon—the bird only kings can fly! Have you ever seen one, Sir Duncan? The boy never has, surely, but perhaps you have."

"I have. Magnificent birds." Duncan glanced at the young archer. Under the ill-fitting cap, the girl's cheeks were stained pink.

"I have heard they fly wild in Scotland. One of my men saw a white falcon not long ago. We should trap it together, you and I, since our lands converge."

"Likely impossible to trap such a thing," Duncan said carefully.

"Well, shoot the eye of that falcon and you win the prize!" Menteith raised the silver brooch. It caught the sunlight. "One shot each will determine the winner."

Marcus—the girl—was breathing audibly fast, gripping the upright bow. Duncan watched her, his brow creased. It was her turn, but she looked shaken.

"Nock!" the miller called. "Mark!"

"Steady," Duncan murmured, as the girl fumbled with her bow. "The falcon looks real, but do not let it throw you."

"You shoot first," she answered in a husky voice, and moved back.

Duncan stepped forward. Taking a moment, he raised the bow, nocked, sighted the bird, focused on the eye. All the while he masked the fiery thread of anger that grew within. Was Menteith's unsettling choice deliberate? Had he seen the falcon recently?

The thought hit hard, cutting into his focus. Few knew about the rare gyrfalcon he kept at Brechlinn. Had someone sighted her over the glen when he or his men exercised the birds? He was always cautious and reminded others to be careful as well.

Heart pounding, he wondered why the girl seemed startled by the painted white bird too. Then it struck him. He knew of only one lass who might react like that to the sight of a white gyrfalcon. But it could not be. That girl was likely praying in a convent.

He flexed his fingers on the bow, propped the arrow shaft along his hand, tilted, tightened the string, sighted. Too distract-ed, he lowered the bow, lifted, refocused.

"Steady, sir," the girl murmured. "It is just a target." Her voice was husky, earnest, yet enticingly feminine. He glanced at her. A strand of red-gold hair slipped free of the dull black cap again. Her gaze met his. Gorgeous green irises full of recognition. She looked away.

Margaret. Safe and well, just here beside him, when he thought her locked away praying somewhere. Here, where he could touch her, talk to her. More than surprise, he felt sheer relief.

Taking a breath, he loosed the arrow into the eye of the bird.

CHAPTER FIVE

NOT ONLY WAS Duncan Dhu Campbell standing next to her, vigorous and stunning, black-haired and blue-eyed, tall and strong. Not only was he the only archer to give her a challenge today. He was, quite frankly, alive.

But how could that be? No one had ever brought news of his survival.

She glanced at him, away, back again. He had matured into a beautiful man, wearing traditional Highland dress—a woolen tunic belted over trews, with a length of plaid draped across his torso, pinned on one shoulder and caught by a leather belt. His hair, nearly black with glints of dark bronze, was tousled nearly to his shoulders. He was unshaven with a scruff of dark bristles on his lean cheeks; his nose had an elegant curve; his dark-blue eyes were long-lidded; his mouth quirked, his gaze was keen.

Her knees went weak and her hands trembled. *Duncan.*

She needed to take the next shot. She tried to focus, to calm herself. Her thoughts were racing, scattered with shock.

Years ago, she had been ill and raw with heartbreak when she had learned that Duncan had been captured in a terrible battle. Later she was told that he had perished in captivity, she had been free of the betrothal and free of dreams and infatuation. Of love.

She had remained in the convent, sick and heartsick. Two years later, she had come home, and her father had begun arranging other betrothals. She had refused each one. All the while, her inner will and her stubbornness grew stronger. She resolved never to marry, and instead, threw herself into helping at Kincraig. She never wanted to risk her heart again. She could not forget Duncan Campbell, and she worried about the gyrfalcon's fate.

Now Duncan stood next to her, handsome, robust, charismatic, and mysterious. She did not know how to feel—though a sudden urge to throw herself at him nearly overtook her. He was alive. He looked more than hearty—he was compelling.

Clutching the bow, she shook. His arrow struck the target and he stepped back in silence as a boy ran to pluck the arrow from the target.

"Leave it!" Menteith shouted. "Let the second archer split the shaft!"

Split an arrow shaft? She had skill, but few archers had the precise aim and power to do that. Yet she could not lose her great-grandfather's brooch to Duncan Campbell or anyone else. She had to win and claim the prize. Then she must find a way to accuse Menteith. Here was the justiciar she needed, in the most surprising way possible.

Fate, or saints and angels, had somehow arranged all this. Menteith. The brooch. The justiciar. And dear God—Duncan. What she did next would determine if Lilias was found soon—or too late. And it might even determine her own future.

She swallowed, then took a shaky breath and raised the bow. Once more Menteith brazenly displayed her brooch, holding it aloft, then tossing it to the table as if it was nothing. To her, that pin was a legacy and a promise, trust and magic.

And evidence, she realized. Menteith's possession of it was proof he had a role in taking Lilias de Bruce.

She sighted down the shaft, closed her eyes, saw the fletched arrow in her mind. Opening her eyes, she released the bolt.

Her arrow grazed Campbell's, tearing the feathers. But the point bounced off the target at an angle and clattered to the ground.

"Winner! Sir Duncan Campbell, Justiciary of the North, is the archery champion!" Menteith bellowed. He waved the brooch high, silver glinting.

She had lost. Margaret lowered her head. The crowd applauded. Beside her, Duncan Campbell sighed as if exasperated.

"They are waiting, sir." She could not look at him. "Claim your prize."

"You did well." His voice was gruff as he shouldered his bow and quiver and walked away. She watched his broad-shouldered back, his confident stride, saw how he ignored the praise as he passed.

Menteith handed him the brooch and a small pouch of coins and the two men spoke. Margaret walked closer, hoping to hear.

"No matter to me," Menteith was saying. "I will be away in the north."

"I prefer you stay until the Stirlingshire sheriff finishes his inquiry."

"I have more pressing matters to attend to."

If Menteith left, Margaret might never find Lilias. She had to get word to Bruce and her brother. But she had to do something now. Menteith could not leave yet.

"Sir!" she called impulsively. Her thoughts were spinning, a plan forming even as she called out. "My lord Dunbarton! I wish to challenge the winner!"

Both Menteith and Campbell turned. "Challenge?" Menteith asked.

"A—bonus shot!" That was it. She came forward. "For the brooch."

"This thing?" Menteith asked. "But you lost."

"I need a pin for my cloak," she said, keeping her naturally husky voice low. "And I need coin more than Sir Justice does."

"No chance!" someone called. "No one can beat the justiciar at the archery!"

"I could shoot that brooch off the top of his head," she said boldly.

Laughter rose, but she hardly heard it. She felt desperate to delay Menteith, ready to say anything, *do* anything. *You stole Bruce's daughter*, she wanted to yell out.

Instead she had to be bold and earn the crowd's goodwill. It was clear that Campbell and the other sheriff wanted Menteith to stay in the area too. That would help.

"Give me a chance to win that brooch and earn some silver to buy my supper!" Hearing laughter in the crowd, she sensed they supported the lad over the justiciar.

Menteith cocked a brow. "Very well. One arrow each. Winner takes all. I would not mind seeing Campbell defeated." He gave a harsh laugh. "Then we are done."

She returned to the butts, Campbell with her. When she reached into the quiver for another arrow, she glanced at him. His steady, searing blue gaze threw her off.

"You first," she said, and stepped back. Instinctively she reached for the chain at her neck, but only set her hand to her upper chest for a moment. She dared not reveal the pink stone arrowhead caged in silver. No crofter's lad would wear such a thing. But the Rhymer's elf-bolt gave her courage, and thoughts of Thomas gave her courage too.

The elf-bolt will go wherever thee sends it, she remembered him saying once. Good. She would send it to hit that target and solve at least part of her dilemma.

Duncan Campbell set the arrow, stretched the string and took aim. Waited. Then he released the arrow. The banner fluttered and tore as he hit the very eye of the falcon.

She could not let him have the brooch. He could keep the coins. And she desperately needed Menteith to be delayed somehow. But she could not think about that now.

Lifting the bow, she sighted the target. The false falcon's wings rippled as if to fly away in the breeze. Duncan Campbell stood to the side, his sheer presence disrupting her focus so much that she could hardly think. Dear saints. She hoped he did not recognize her. She wanted to talk with him—she had so many questions—but not now.

Not yet. Lilias's safety was essential to her.

Menteith crossed the green to observe them closely. She ignored the man's glower and Duncan's silence as she raised the bow, tightened the string, sighted down the shaft. So much was at stake—hitting the eye, winning the brooch, delaying Menteith until she had a chance to alert Campbell to him. It all seemed impossible.

She breathed long and deep, seeking calm.

"Easy now," Campbell murmured softly. His voice was a balm. On the exhale, she let go the string.

The arrow shaft skated past the banner and the hay bale, curved askew toward the earth—and struck Menteith as he walked over the grass. With a scream, he fell.

Dear God, what went wrong? Stunned, she stared.

"What the devil," Duncan Campbell growled, and ran toward the sheriff.

Margaret stood frozen, stunned. The justiciar dropped to a knee beside Sir John, who cradled his leg, shrieking, and pointed at her.

"He shot me! Arrest that boy!"

Grabbing quiver and bow, Margaret whirled and ran toward the forest even as she heard shouts and the trample of boots behind her.

"ARROWSHOT! I AM done for—the blood—I cannot walk—" Menteith groaned.

"Quiet! You will live," Duncan barked. "Someone fetch Father Ambrose," he called, having seen the priest earlier, aware he worked in the abbey's small infirmary. Duncan waited beside Menteith, who moaned and clutched his foot.

When Ambrose rushed toward them, Duncan stood, grateful. The priest would have the patience to deal with Sir John. Duncan did not.

"Let me see." Ambrose eased the man's boot off. "Oh dear,

back o' the ankle. Not a good place to be arrowshot."

"There is no good place to be arrowshot!" Menteith snapped. "Campbell, why are you standing there? Get that boy! My men are chasing him while you dawdle!"

"Sir," Duncan said, turning. He saw immediately that Marcus Murray—Margaret Keith, he corrected—had vanished already. The lad who had fetched arrows earlier ran toward him, holding feathered shafts.

"Sir, these are yours and the lad's."

With quick thanks, he shoved them into his quiver, took up the bow—he might need it—and strode across the meadow toward the forest. Several knights in chainmail, swords drawn, ran toward the woodland as well, entering at various points to cover as much ground as they could.

He had to find Margaret before they did.

Hearing his name, he stopped as Murray and Lennox rushed toward him.

"Menteith is squealing like a pig, though just nicked in the leg," Lennox said.

"Let the priest tend him," Duncan said. "We must find that— lad before Menteith's men do, or there will be the devil to pay."

"He entered the forest there." Lennox pointed. "We can track him."

As they ran, Duncan saw the blond lad with the sling, and realized he had to be Margaret Keith's friend—and might know where she had fled.

"We need to follow that boy," Duncan said, leading his friends at an angle into the forest, hurrying before the lad could vanish in a maze of leaf and shadow.

Duncan gestured. "One of you go east, the other west. I will head straight on. Circle after half a mile, and we will soon cross paths. Look for the boy or—both lads."

"Aye!" Constantine angled eastward and Lennox headed west, where afternoon sun sent golden beams through the leaves. Duncan plunged ahead.

Soon he saw traces of someone passing by recently—crushed leaves, a footprint on pine needles, a snag of wool on a bush. Seeing reddish-gold threads of hair sparkling along a branch, he hurried on.

From various directions came shouts and the noise of men in armor crashing through the woodland. Determined, he pushed through a thicket of scrub and headed up a hill where saplings grew thick and straight.

Something dark fluttered on a bush—a black cap with lappets. He snatched it, stuffed it in his belt, then went higher. Bushes rustled as if something went through. Duncan took the slope in long strides, stepping over fallen logs, wondering if Margaret Keith would go to earth like a rabbit or climb like a squirrel.

On the ridge above, he glimpsed armor and cloaks as two knights moved between the trees. On the hillside, yellow gorse and dark juniper swayed. Duncan saw a boot and a brown tunic vanish. He took the hill in stealthy steps now, focused on finding her before she was spotted by Menteith's men.

Then he saw a pale hand, the curve of a bow, a wild mass of reddish curls whipping through tall bushes. Duncan cut to one side, slid into thick ferns and nudged between birch saplings.

Seeing a boot, he lunged, grabbing her ankle and dragging her toward him while she wriggled and twisted. "Come here," he growled.

Pulling her under one arm, he tossed her face down as she tried to wrench free, and hauled her deeper into a wild growth of bushes and ferns, dragging fragrant remnants of juniper along. Sinking low, he yanked her hard against him, her slim body all elbows and knees and shoving hands. He rolled until he lay across her, trapping her while she twisted beneath him like a wild thing.

"Let me go!"

"Be still, you wee rascal," he hissed, and clamped a hand over her mouth. She tried to bite him. He held her tighter, but when he saw fright in her eyes, he eased up.

"I will not hurt you. Be still," he whispered. "There are

guards up there. Hush if you value your life."

She stopped. He rolled, then sat up and pulled her against his chest in the iron band of his arms. She whimpered in protest or in pain.

"Let me go," she gasped again.

"Listen to me," he said, low and fierce at her ear. "They will kill you if they find you. I will not. *Hush.*"

Voices sounded above, very close. She went still and lay against him, his cheek resting on the mass of her tangled hair, red as flames amid the green shadows that hid them. Under his arm, he could feel her heart pounding.

Several moments passed. Finally, there was silence all around. When he was sure the men were gone, he loosened his grip. "Sorry," he grumbled.

She bit his finger. He winced and swore, pulled her tightly against him again. She weighed little for all her strength, and she fought, twisting, pulling, scratching.

"Wildcat," he said. "If I let you go, you are surely dead, but not by my hand."

She went limp again. He wondered if he had squeezed the breath out of her. He released his hold a little more, but she twisted quick, so he tightened again.

"Quiet. And do not bite me." When she nodded, he relaxed his fingers cupping her jaw. He did not relax his steely embrace.

"Beast," she said, then bent her knee and kicked back, hitting him hard on the thigh—too high for comfort. He rolled to press her to earth, his weight on her back.

"Margaret Keith, you have gone feral, I swear," he breathed.

She froze. Then a sob tore free. "You! Hateful beast!"

"So you remember me. Sit up, wildcat." He lifted her upright to lean against him in a cavern of ferns and juniper, bordered by thorny bushes that he tried to avoid, but a prickly frond slapped her cheek.

"Ow," she said. "Thorns. Oww."

"Sorry. Wicked stuff, gorse." He shifted, pulling her to him, one arm braced over her chest, fingers tight on her arm. "We need to stay clear of the thorns, but we cannot move from here. I am sorry if you are hurt."

"Not the gorse. My shoulder. My knee. Let me up," she gasped. "Why do you hide with me? You would hand me over to them if they came by."

"I will not. They would kill you without hesitation. I, at least, would ask questions before I throttled you." He winced as another thorn scraped his hand.

Scuttling with her toward the softer haven of the ferns, he settled behind her, trapping her in his arms and folding a leg over her knee. "Sit still. Tilt your head. Let me see if I can get these." He scraped a thorn from her cheek, brushed the blood away with his thumb, then pulled a few prickly bits tangled in her hair.

"Thank you," she whispered.

"Now," he murmured, "tell me what the devil is going on."

"Did I kill him?" she asked softly.

"Sir John? He will be fine."

"Good. The arrow shaft must have been warped."

He grunted. "It was not. I saw it. Perfectly straight. It should have gone into the target—or into Menteith, where you sent it."

"I aimed at the target. Are you justiciar in the north?"

"Aye," he grunted.

"So you can arrest someone? Imprison them?"

"I may do so now if you do not tell me what this is about."

"You could arrest Menteith?"

"Or you. Sit still," he insisted as she twisted again. "Explain why you were dressed as a lad and then assaulted a local lord and a sheriff, none of which is in your favor. Be still, I say. Here. Put this on." He snatched the black cap and yanked it over her head. "That hair is bright as fire and will surely give us away."

She tugged it down, cramming her hair messily into the cap, but a few tendrils hung down. When she looked up at him, her eyes, in the ferny surroundings, were green glinting with amber. He stared.

God, she was beautiful, he thought, distracted. Even with blood on her cheek, tear tracks down her face, a scattering of freckles; moss-green eyes and straight dark brows lowered in a glower; and thorns and flowers in her hair, she was the fey creature he remembered.

"I did not assault him," she said.

"You damned well did, my lady. Why do you want me to arrest him?"

"He did something evil." She glanced through the bushes toward the hill. "Are they gone?"

"Wait." He paused a beat. "I think so. You stirred up quite a kerfuffle. Is your friend part of this scheme too? The lad in the foot race. I saw you with him."

"Just a friend. No scheme. Menteith did an evil deed and must be stopped."

"Some might agree with you, but we cannot punish the man without evidence of this evil deed. Have you stolen any livestock recently?"

"What? Of course not. You must listen to me."

"I can hardly wait. Go back to why you shot him."

"It was accidental."

"I saw your skill. You could have bested me and taken the prize."

"I want that prize. Do you have the brooch?"

"I left it with Menteith. It is hardly important. Tell me why you shot him. I saw you do it, so you cannot deny it."

"I did not mean to. I only wanted the brooch. Is he badly hurt?"

"He thinks so. But he is not going anywhere for a while."

"Good." She grimaced, trying to wrest herself free. "You can arrest him."

"Sit still," he whispered. Far off, he heard the crush of twigs underfoot. When the sound died, he loosened his hold a bit. "Why do you want me to arrest him?"

"He abducted a girl."

"What—" He shook his head, bewildered. "What proof do you have?"

"I know he did. There is my proof."

"Huh. Where is this girl?"

"If I knew, I would not be here."

"Ah." This was odd. He thought of the incident along the road, the young girl taken in the ambush, Menteith's men escorting her to her family. And Lennox was looking for a girl too. What connected them? "Abduction is a serious charge. Until I can determine what happened, I will keep you in custody."

She paused. "Prison?"

"Somewhere Menteith cannot reach you would be good."

"But—shh!" She tapped his arm. "Someone is coming!"

He stilled. Footsteps crushed closer. Duncan parted juniper and fern and peered out. "It is fine. He is not a Dunbarton man."

She looked, then tensed in his arms. "The sheriff of Stirling!"

"Con Murray!" Duncan called softly, shaking the bushes. "Over here!"

"What are you doing?" Margaret hissed.

Constantine turned, then climbed toward them as a second man appeared.

"Malcolm! This way," Murray said. Soon two pairs of booted feet stood near the bushes. Held in Duncan's arms, Margaret Keith tried to flee.

"Hold!" He had to let go so he could stand, and as he grabbed for her again, she took to her feet and started to bolt. He shot out a hand, caught her arm, and tugged her with him out of the bushes.

"And here is the archer lad," Lennox said.

"Come with us," Constantine beckoned as Margaret Keith ducked her head, black cap secure. Duncan stayed quiet, letting explanations wait.

"Shall we take him to Dunbarton Castle?" Constantine asked.

"Sir John will not treat the lad kindly if you go there," Lennox warned.

"True. I will take him up the loch to Brechlinn." Duncan pulled on Margaret's arm as she tried to yank free. When she winced in pain, he stopped.

Lennox went past them to retrieve the two bows and two quivers discarded beside the bushes and joined them as they turned to find their way through the forest.

"Go ahead, Con," Duncan said. "Find Menteith's men and tell them I have the archer in my custody. I will deal with him. Menteith does not need to trouble himself. Lennox," he said, "I know you have other business here, but if you have time to head north, come with us."

"Do you need a guard for your snarling pup? I can do that."

"Where are we going?" the pup asked, tugging against Duncan's grip.

"To find a boat." Duncan yanked her black cap lower. "Keep quiet."

CHAPTER SIX

TUCKED IN THE curved bow of the long birlinn, Margaret lifted her face to a chilly breeze. High above, the wind billowed the square sail. Awkwardly, her hands tied together, she pulled a plaid blanket around her. Malcolm Lennox had tossed it toward her when they had boarded the birlinn. It smelled of sheep and fish.

"To hide your bonds, lad," he had said.

Nearby, Sir Duncan Campbell stood silent, looking out over the water.

She flexed her right knee to ease the ache that plagued her. She had been injured in the attack on the escort party, and the mad race through the forest had not helped. Wincing, she was glad of the blanket that warmed her and hid her bound hands and feet.

Earlier, Duncan Campbell had tied ropes around her to keep her in place. Only he and Lennox knew she was a prisoner. Even Campbell's clerk, a lanky young man with fair hair and a fetching smile, did not know. No one else aboard the boat paid any mind to a lad in dull clothes and a black cap; she was just the sulking adolescent accompanying the justiciar on the great loch. The sail would take three or four hours from what she had overheard.

Traveling on the birlinn were a few farmers, sheep as well, several animals clustered near the upright mast, bleating and shuffling about. The helmsman and his two strapping sons sailed the craft, worked the ropes, and took up oars if the wind stilled.

The water was calm and as blue as glass as the boat skimmed along. The clinker-built birlinn sat low, equipped with twelve oars with four in use.

Margaret watched the water sluice past and looked out at the pebbled shoreline and the hills and woodland beyond as the boat passed one small island after another. Brechlinn Castle was their destination. She heard it belonged to Sir Duncan, a remote fortress at the northern head of the loch. He intended to tuck her away there for her own protection while he sorted out the matter, or so he claimed.

He had said little about her identity or his. That needed sorting too, she thought.

But most immediate was the matter of Lilias Bruce. She had not yet had a chance to explain what had happened. During the journey, Duncan Campbell kept his distance, talking to Lennox or the helmsman. He seemed to be avoiding her, though he sent Lennox over to her.

"Sir Duncan wants to know if you are comfortable."

"I am not," she said, seated on a bale of hay between barrels. "Why does he care?"

"For some reason he does, which is good for you. Do you want ale?"

"No more." Earlier she had sipped ale and had a crust of bread. But she could not piss over the boat's side as she noticed some men doing, so she was loath to drink more. "Where are my bow and arrows?"

"I brought them aboard. But you will have no chance to use them. You might decide to shoot that justiciar over there."

She scowled. "I just want my things."

"They are safe."

"Thank you," she said grudgingly. She had no quarrel with Malcolm Lennox, who had been helpful. A brawny man with glossy black hair, a big, easy smile, and dark eyes that seemed to see through her, he gave her a bemused tilt of his head now.

"Aye then. Watch that sheep," he said, as one walked past bleating. Margaret leaned away. Lennox went back to stand with Campbell.

Now and then Duncan Campbell glanced her way as he talked with Lennox. She lifted her chin and looked away.

Leaning her head against the nearest barrel, she closed her eyes and sought rest while the boat moved over the loch. The rocking motion made her slightly queasy at first, then eased her into sleep.

⸎⟫⟪⸎

"THAT LAD," MALCOLM said, "is a lass. Did you know?"

"Aye." Duncan was not surprised that Malcolm, a clever sort, saw it too.

"A puzzle, hey." Lennox gave him a careful glance. "Would you lock up a lass at Brechlinn?"

"Best she be there for now. There is a woman nearby who sometimes comes to help. Perhaps she can stay for a bit."

"What does that wee bit lass have against Menteith to shoot him?"

"I mean to find out. She says she did not do it deliberately. The arrow was off, she claims."

"That lass is no poor shot." Malcolm sat back. "Though if I could stick an arrow in Sir John, I might do it. He has been disruptive to the valiant efforts of good Scotsmen. Some want him out of the way. But she is not that sort, is my guess."

"Aye," Duncan said. "I meant to ask earlier—have you any news of, er, misbehaving clergy?"

Malcolm gave him a wicked grin. "The false preachers employed by Bruce, as the English claim? The holy men charged with advocating war, that lot?"

"And said to be behaving worse than ever," he agreed with a half laugh.

"The English are in fits over these poorly behaved priests. Did you sentence some of them?"

"Aymer de Valence, Edward's loyal lieutenant, sent them to one of my courts. I released three on bail. They later went through Brechlinn and out to the Isles."

"Ah. So long as De Valence does not know."

"I am not inclined to report it. I gave my vow to comply with certain measures of justice, but I will not volunteer what they do not need to know."

"If we had more naughty priests in need of better justice than Edward would dispense, what would you say?" Malcolm cast him a side glance.

"I can help them."

"Bruce thought so. You can expect another soon. It is a help, but also dangerous."

"Brechlinn's location is an advantage. No one will look there. A small ramshackle castle held by a justiciar who is no trouble at all. Use that as you see fit."

"A good place to hide a lass who is not a lad, as well."

"For now, until I understand the circumstances. Malcolm, you came north to look for a girl and her escort. Tell me more."

Lennox blew out a breath. "Bruce would want you to know. She is his bastard daughter. He has a few by-blow children, and to his credit, cares about each one and protects them well."

"So I have heard. How old is this lass?"

"She is the first of three or four now. I would not be surprised if he has more. He loves his queen, but—" He shrugged. "Elisabeth is thirteen."

Menteith had mentioned a girl who supposedly belonged to the MacDougalls. "Twelve is the age of consent for girls. That wee lass is a valuable marriage property."

"And if she has been taken, or God forbid, harmed, it is dire indeed, especially with the other Bruce women captured by English," Malcolm emphasized. "Duncan, I know your brother's wife is one of the captured royal women. I am sorry."

"Aye. Neill's wife is Lady Mary Bruce. She is one of the women locked in iron cages and exposed on castle battlements."

"No wonder Bruce is desperate to protect any Scotswomen close to him. He has set trusted men on the task—myself, Sir William Seton. You," Malcolm added. "He wants your help in finding his daughter's escort and ensuring she reaches the west. But I have no news of them. They have vanished."

"The wee bit lass over there," Duncan murmured, "spoke of a missing girl."

"Did she. Is there proof?"

"In the court today, an incident came to our attention." He detailed what he knew of the attack on the road, and Menteith's claim that his men had rescued a girl. "If that was a lie and she is not a MacDougall, could she be Bruce's girl?"

"If so, we have a problem," Lennox said.

"We do indeed." Duncan looked down the length of the birlinn, past ropes, crates, and woolly sheep, to the slight girl draped in an old plaid, asleep against a barrel.

"I am thinking your wee bit lass is another problem."

"More than you know," Duncan muttered.

IF SHE STILL believed in dreams, having lost that trust years ago, they would be born and flourish at Brechlinn. Margaret sat in a small boat while Lennox rowed them up the last part of the loch—the birlinn had docked to let them depart, turning south again. Now they headed for a castle that jutted up from a narrow peninsula. Fieldstone walls and a blocky keep rose from the green and rocky sward to form a powerful silhouette against a twilight sky streaked pink and gold. The castle was power and beauty and welcome, its reflection almost magical in the calm sheen of the water.

She caught back a sob of yearning that came out of nowhere.

The pull she felt to the castle was strong, as if she were coming home. But this was not her home. It was her prison. And it was another barrier in her search for Lilias.

The urge to tell Duncan what troubled her most overwhelmed her. She half rose.

"Sit," Campbell growled. "Do not think to leap into the water and swim."

"I will add Brechlinn is a very good swimmer," Malcolm Lennox said.

She sat, frustrated, on the verge of tears, unable to tell them what they most needed to know. She did not even know if it was safe to reveal what happened to Bruce's daughter—what if Campbell was for Edward? Then Lilias would be in more danger. Though she thought Lennox would be receptive; Edward had given his lands to Menteith, after all.

She rubbed her aching knee. Her feet and hands were free now, for Campbell had untied her before guiding her to the small rowboat to cross the water toward Brechlinn.

For a moment, she savored the sweet clean breezes, the wild vista of water and trees and hills at the remote northern end of the loch. The castle seemed to be the only touch of civilization.

But she could not savor anything for long. Lilias's unknown fate hung over her like a pall. And now Andrew was gone again too. Her eyes welled with tears. She dashed them away. Duncan Campbell gave her a sharp glance.

Lennox oared the small craft beside a wooden dock and secured the ropes to a post. Duncan brought her out, guiding her up to the castle that sat on a rocky thrust of land. They followed stone steps up to a doorway set inside a stone arch. Margaret heard dogs barking distantly as Campbell pounded on the door. After a bit, the door opened.

A huge man blocked the threshold, torchlight behind him. He wore a tunic and stockings without boots, a helmet crooked on his head as if hastily added. In his hand was a chunk of cheese. He tore his teeth into it, chewed, and considered them.

"Back so soon? Who is the bairn?"

"I am not a bairn," Margaret muttered.

"Good to see you too, Bran," Campbell said. "Fetch us some food up to the tower if you will." He stepped inside with Margaret as Bran stepped back, Lennox following.

"Am I a servant? Hold, you there! Hold!" he shouted as three dogs came skidding around a corner. "Stay! Dinna scare the bairn!"

As the dogs pushed closer, Bran caught two huge hounds by their collars. They stilled, both brindled gray, one dark and one light, both standing near as tall as Margaret's shoulder. The third, a small terrier, slipped between Bran's legs.

Margaret squatted to greet the little dog, glad for a happy welcome. She let it sniff at her, then ruffled its head and coat. The two larger dogs stepped forward cautiously, sniffed, and let her pet their magnificent heads. Then they both turned to Campbell.

"Hey, you. Good lad, good girl. Stay," he said, and stood with a hand on either head. Margaret straightened as the brown terrier jumped for more attention. "The wee one is Broom," Campbell said. "This is Freya. The big lad here is Mungo."

She patted heads, shoulders, the small one eager, the two larger dogs calm and regal. "Beautiful sighthounds, and the wee cairn is lovely too."

Bran grunted. "A bundle of mischief, that one."

"Bran," Duncan Campbell said, "bring something upstairs for us in a bit. We are starved. And send to the village to fetch your sister here, if you will."

"It is late to fetch her. Gone gloaming already."

"We need her help. The lad is injured."

Then Duncan Campbell took Margaret's arm gently as he led her along a dim corridor. Lennox and Bran followed, the dogs weaving in and out. They greeted Lennox and were curious about her, but craved Campbell's attention. Reaching a passage-way, Bran held cheese out to lure the dogs away with him.

Campbell led Margaret up a turning stair, Lennox behind

them. The wedge steps were worn and treacherous in the shadows, the only light the yellow gleam of a wall torch.

On the third level, a stone platform with two doors, Duncan Campbell opened the right-hand door, fitted with a latch and brackets.

"Go in," he directed, guiding her inside the dark room. "You will stay here."

She turned. "Is there a candle? Can I make a fire in the brazier? I am a bit hungry," she added, plaintive and hoping. She had expected to be led down to a grim cell rather than to what appeared to be a bedchamber.

Silhouetted in the doorway against torchlight, his face was inscrutable. "Someone will see to your needs." He shut the door before she could reply. Then she heard the decisive click of a latch and a thunk as a wooden bar slid into brackets. Footsteps sounded as Campbell and Lennox descended the stairs.

So it was a prison after all. Fear ran through her and she folded her arms against it. Turning again, she peered through the shadows.

The room was small and sparsely furnished, with a narrow bed against one wall, covered in a plaid blanket with a few folded linens. Red woolen curtains strung on ropes were draped partly around the bed. Nearby was a small wooden table and a bench.

An iron brazier stood cold and dark in a corner, but the promise of heat reassured her, if she could find flint and kindling. A wooden cupboard on spindly legs filled another corner; on top of that was a candlestick, a cup and bowl, a stack of small books. But she did not see a flint. Hearths and braziers generally were not put out entirely, and could be quickly ignited. She hoped someone would bring a light to banish the damp chill and shadows.

A tall arched window was framed by wooden shutters beneath a top section of leaded glass roundels. She crossed to the window and opened one of the unlatched shutters to find the window open with no barrier. But as she peered down, she saw the tower wall and a long drop to the bailey yard.

She breathed in the cool damp air carried off the loch and rose on her toes to lean on the stone sill. The view overlooked the curtain wall planted on the peninsula at the water's edge. Far beyond, hills and tall pines were dark against the twilight sky.

Closing the shutter against the chill, she sat on the bed and gathered a blanket around her, shivering. The mattress rustled, giving off a dusty blend of heather and pine.

The chamber seemed more suited to the occasional guest than a captive. Cold and empty now, it would be comfortable with a fire in the brazier. But the drawbar was a telling detail that said she was definitely a prisoner.

She rubbed her aching shoulder and then her knee as fatigue crept through her bones. Time seemed to pour by, and she had found no way to help Lilias yet. Her sense of frustration and desperation increased.

Though she regretted Menteith's wounding, she had not done it deliberately. Somehow the arrow's track had curved to catch him. She did not understand how that had happened. Then Campbell, doubting her innocence, had dragged her to the far end of the loch, leaving Menteith hours away. She had lost Andrew Murray again, and could only hope he would find his way back to Kincraig, or wait in the hiding place in the forest until she could get away.

And Lilias de Bruce might be more in danger with every sunset and sunrise. Margaret either had to convince Campbell to help, or had to get out of Brechlinn.

Hungry, thirsty, tired, feeling despair overtaking her, she stretched out on the bare mattress, curled in the old plaid, and fell asleep.

A rattling at the door woke her suddenly and she sat up in deep darkness, dazed, wondering where she was, just as the door burst open. A blaze of candlelight flowed inside with Bran MacArthur, a mountain of a man carrying a flaming brand in one fist, a plate in the other, and a jug tucked under his arm. Another person stood on the stone platform in shadows. Skirts. A female.

Margaret stood, clutching the plaid around her.

"Here you go, bairn." Bran set a wooden platter on the table along with the ceramic jug. "This is all I could find—cheese, oatcake, more cheese. And a bit of dried meat, though it be tough. Ale is here too. Not fancy." He cocked a brow, regarding her. "By the look of you, rags and dirt, I doubt you are used to fine things—but there is something about you. Something," he repeated thoughtfully. "Do you come from a fine household? Servant or such? Either way, a boy will be hungry."

She approached cautiously, for Bran towered, an intimidating sight. He wore no helmet now, his hair a brown riot, his eyes crinkled, irises pale and surprisingly pretty.

"Thank you." She tore off a bit of cheese. "There is a cup on the shelf."

"Huh. So there is." With a long step and a longer reach, he snatched it up. "Here. Eat. Brechlinn says you need it." He sloshed dark ale into the wooden cup. "Later you can piss in that bucket in the corner. Or in the tub. There's one coming up."

"Tub?" Margaret saw a woman enter the room through the shadows.

"Here's my sister, come to tend to you." He jabbed a thumb toward the doorway. "Campbell says you are injured. He thinks the wee bairnie needs a mother."

"I am not a bairn. And I am not injured badly, just a twisted knee and shoulder. They will heal." Her mouth was already crammed with cheese that was buttery soft and wonderfully good. She glanced toward the door. "Sister?"

"Aye." The woman came into the circle of candlclight and set a basket on the table. "I am Euphemia MacArthur." Her voice was warm.

Margaret blinked, expecting a female version of Bran, large and beefy, perhaps disagreeable. But Euphemia MacArthur was young, a large woman yet small beside her massive brother. Where he was creased and scruffy, untidy and scowling, she was lovely, golden pink, and calm in a gray gown. Her round face was pleasant, her form generous and curving, her honey-gold braids were wrapped about her head in a pretty frame. Her eyes were ice blue under arched brows, and her dimpled smile brightened the room.

"After you eat and bathe, I will tend to your wounds."

"A soak in a hot bath will do. You can both leave."

"Sir Duncan asked me to see you. He says you had a trying day and need to rest here in the guest chamber."

"Is that what he calls it," she said wryly.

"Sorry?" Euphemia looked baffled.

"Are you wanting that oatcake?" Bran asked.

Margaret shook her head and handed it to him. She smiled at Euphemia, feeling relief despite all. The past few days had been difficult. Having sisters, she found she missed the company and comfort of a female friend, and here was a kind stranger. Food, candlelight, and the prospect of a bath would help too. But the hospitality originated with Duncan Campbell.

"Thank you, Euphemia."

"It is Effie, if you will. Here is the bath," the woman said, as Margaret heard a noisy clunking and scraping outside the room. A lanky boy stepped through the doorway, dragging an empty wooden tub that he had pulled from another room. He rolled it to the middle of the chamber. An old man followed, lugging a basin of steaming water that he dumped into the tub.

"Not much, but we will fetch more," the old man said. He beckoned to the lad and both disappeared down the steps.

"Thank you, Hector, Artan. Bran, it is chilly in here," Euphemia told her brother. "The shutters should stay closed and that brazier should never go out. This room should always be ready in case Sir Duncan brings a guest."

"It is a waste to keep it fresh. No one has used it since the last priest we—"

"Give me a candle," Effie said briskly. Taking it, she knelt beside the brazier in the corner, lit a twist of cloth, and applied the flame to a small stack of peat bricks inside the brazier. "This will take a while. Do eat," she told Margaret, standing. "Bran, you may go. Please tell them to hurry with the bathwater."

While Margaret ate, Euphemia moved around the room, tucking sheets on the bed, adding blankets. The old man and the boy returned with buckets to pour streams of water into the tub, vapor rising.

Euphemia thanked them as they left, shut the door, and went to the table to open the basket. She took out a ball of gooey soap and rolled linen toweling.

"Now then, my dear," she said quietly, "let us get you into that tub."

Margaret stared. "Do you know—"

"Aye. Duncan told me, and Malcolm Lennox knows too. My brother thinks you are a lad and will not guess otherwise until he is told. Duncan asked me to help you. He says your arm is hurt, or your knee. Warm compresses will help. Do you want those clothes, or this?" She dipped into the basket to hold up a soft drape of dark blue cloth. "I thought to lend it to you."

"It is lovely," Margaret said.

"I brought a shift too. You might be tall enough to wear my gowns with a belt, but they will be large on you. Are you done eating? Sorry. Bran does not know much about serving food."

"He was kind to bring it. And I appreciate the gown."

"You should give up that awful cap too. Oh, my saints!" Euphemia said as Margaret tugged it from her head, red-gold tresses spilling out. "What glorious hair! Though not a lucky color, is it, such red, they say. But you have been a lucky girl, and you are in a good place here. I brought a comb too, if you like."

"Effie MacArthur, I rather love you," Margaret said.

CHAPTER SEVEN

D UNCAN STROLLED ACROSS the bailey yard, cheese in hand—reminding himself to ask Euphemia if she could make some decent meals while she was here—and looked around at the castle in the blue twilight. Somehow its features and flaws showed fresh in the light. Trotting beside him, one of the tall hounds gave a low woof.

"I know, Mungo," Duncan murmured. "Look at this place. Stout and strong once, aye, and we have done some work. But there is more to do."

Several years ago, while he had still been in Ireland, the English had ridden north and had attacked the small garrison his brother had assigned to Brechlinn, setting it on fire and bringing part of it to rubble. Since his return, Duncan had done what he could to repair it, but there was work to do yet.

"The outer wall is still broken just there," he told the dog, "and the ivy is higher than ever. The smithy is in disuse, even with the new anvil we put in. We do not have a smith. Still, it is a good fortress, if sparse and broken in places. We can make something of it someday. What do you think, hey?"

The leggy hound gave a soft woof, and Duncan huffed agreement. "Not much of a home, but I do not need much just now. A place to rest and somewhere for hounds and hawks. And friends. That is enough, hey." He rubbed the dog's head.

Along the curtain wall, ivy climbed the stone like dark fingers, and on the battlement just two guards strolled. The yard was nearly empty but for a cart—the brewer, Bran's good friend, must be here again, he realized—along with some barrels and stacks of hay, a broken wheel and other remnants in stone and wood of the place it had once been and could be again. Everywhere, inside and out, needed attention. Brechlinn Castle needed new life. Its laird did too.

Later for that. Always later, he told himself sourly, but for the birds. His priorities were the birds and other secrets he kept.

Mungo woofed, and Duncan saw Bran MacArthur lumbering through the shadowed yard. He hailed his seneschal and stopped to wait.

"How did things go?" he asked.

"Good. We brought food to the lad and set up a bath. Effie is up there. She is happy to mother anyone. The bairn says his injury is naught and a hot soak will do."

"When Effie leaves, ask Hector to sit outside the door until midnight, and set Artan there the rest of the night. Give them blankets but tell them to be alert to movement. And I want a man watching the tower, and two more watching the gate."

"That slip of a lad will not go out the window. It is a far drop and he has no rope."

"Still, we will watch the door and the window. Where is Lennox?"

"In the library looking at the dusty books you keep chained there. As if we would steal them." Bran rolled his eyes. "You off to see Greta and the rest?"

"I AM. HOW are they?" Duncan strolled again, Bran and the dog with him.

"Fine and good. Artan and I take them out regularly. The youngest has the devil of a temper. Watch her. Duncan, we need more men here," he added low. "Only a few of us are left, with most riding south weeks ago."

"Constantine Murray is looking into it. If word gets to the

English that this garrison is short of men, De Valence at Stirling may send soldiers in Edward's name."

"*Tcha*," Bran said and spit on the ground.

"I must tread that line, as you know. What of the priests?" he asked quietly.

"There were three here when you left for the ayre court. Gone now, off to the west and the Isles, as Bruce requested."

"Good. Menteith may be keeping an eye on us. So we must be careful."

"Will there be more priests and renegades, sir? With Lennox here, I wondered."

"Possibly. We need to be ready. Put the word out that we seek more men, quietly if you will—crofters and shepherds still in the glens, sons willing to be soldiers and someday knights. Any available for the Scottish cause are welcome here."

"We will train them if needed."

"You will make good work of it, as a fine seneschal and a good companion in arms these years." He clapped Bran on the shoulder.

They reached the mews, a two-story wooden structure with a thatched roof and tall windows covered in lattice. As Duncan opened the door, Bran set off again, whistling Mungo to him. The dog hesitated, then followed the seneschal.

Duncan stepped into the dark and quiet.

She perched on a stand made of birch, her pale beauty a soft light in a shadowy corner. He took a thick leather glove from a wall hook and slid it on, then moved with soft steps over straw and woodchips toward her.

Cocking her head, the gyrfalcon waited, expectant. A delicate silver bell chimed on the jesses around her ankle. She cheeped, shifted.

"Hey, Greta," he murmured. He lifted his hand and she stepped to the glove, golden talons gripping his wrist snugly. Her power surged, then waned as she settled there, familiar, accepting.

He wanted to bring Margaret here to show her that their bird was safe and well. He imagined her smile at the discovery. Soon he would do that. For now, he needed a little distance to think, and guessed she needed that too. Yet there were matters that needed settling between them.

"I am home, Greta," he murmured, untying her jesses with one hand, twisting them around his fingers. "Aurelia, hey you," he said then, hearing another cheep.

A peregrine falcon sat on a nearby perch, restless, her little dark head tipped against her shoulder. She regarded him as if miffed that he had come to Greta first.

"I took you out to fly the field last time I was here," he reminded Aurelia, reaching out his hand to brush the speckled breast feathers. She blinked, used to his presence.

He turned back to Greta, looking her over, studying the delicate feathery textures of her breast and back like a physician. He sensed contentment as her feathers roused. Earlier, Bran would have fed the birds; they sat replete, Greta relaxed on his fist.

Greta was an incomparable bird, a king's bird discovered and kept by a mere knight, though an earl's son. Ten years now she had been his, though once she had been Edward's bird. He could only pray the English king never learned that she still lived, and that a Scottish lord protected her in the remote northern hills.

A Norwegian gyrfalcon, nearly white but for a faint gray striping over her breast feathers, she was cloud-colored, a rare and beautiful bird. She had grown large, and so fast on the hunt that each time Duncan took her out and let her off the leash, she could turn into a swift, pale, lethal blur.

"Ah, Smoke. Good sir," he said, crossing toward another bird, a small tiercel, a male gyrfalcon, pale gray striped with dark gray. Smoke was smaller than his mate, Greta. Years back, they had bonded as a couple and had a family. Banshee was one of their brood, white like her mother, young still, asleep on a corner perch. And Tay, a pale gray tiercel, faintly marked in a pretty pattern. He loved the birds, though sometimes they reminded him of what he had lost—a wife, a family, the loving partnership that Margaret Keith had once described to him. The loss was his own doing, at least in part.

But by some miracle, Margaret was here, now, at Brechlinn. He felt a wash of disbelief. He had named Greta for Margaret so he would never forget.

Aurelia cheeped, catching his attention. She was a peregrine of modest size, brown and gold, slim and elegant. A bird from his father's mews, raised by Sir Bernard, she always wanted attention. But she was his, and King Edward could not lay claim to her.

He had not yet achieved all that Brechlinn Castle needed, but he made sure the mews was the best it could be. There was room for the birds to have freedom and some interior flight in a place where they were safe, healthy, and comfortable.

He kept his birds discreetly, for he could not easily explain owning gyrfalcons, and he dreaded word reaching Edward. In earlier days, the English king liked nothing better than the gift of a beautiful bird of prey. The king was ill and vengeful now, but he might return a favor for a gift of trained birds. Duncan could not risk anyone learning about the gyrfalcons. And although English decrees about owning gyrfalcons did not apply in Scotland, Edward would not care about that.

After spending some time with the birds, he left the mews to cross toward the tower. He glanced up. Candlelight glowed in a single window on the third level. He felt pulled there, as if some unseen strand stretched between him and the redheaded girl, a strand spun years ago in innocence and hope. It was still fixed in his heart.

The Keith girl had no place in his life now, nor did he expect her to have any love for him, though he harbored feelings for her and always had. He just needed to discover why she was in the Highlands, why she had shot Menteith, and what she knew about the missing girl. Then he would return her safely to Kincraig. He owed her that at least.

He had questions, but should wait until morning.

The candlelight was still bright in the tower window, and he felt again the deep pull of some invisible, strand—an irresistible one. Margaret Keith was here. Some things could not wait until morning. He had to see her again. He had to know this was real.

He strode for the tower.

CHAPTER EIGHT

Lilias

L ILIAS WOKE WITH a start to sunbeams slicing through a shuttered window, the light falling across her face. Sitting up, she rubbed a hand over her eyes, pushing back her dark hair, loose from its braiding, and looked around. She leaned against plump pillows, all but swallowed up in a huge postered bed draped in golden damask curtains, her knees and feet small bumps under blankets and a pale embroidered coverlet. The thick mattress smelled of lavender and rose petals with a hint of herbs and resinous bog myrtle. The damask curtains let in a wedge of sunlight. Sliding her legs to the edge of the bed, she sat up and pushed aside the curtaining damask. Where was she?

Ah. Trapped. Imprisoned. She remembered now. Days ago— a week or more?—she had been dragged from her horse in a commotion of men and swords and shouting. Tossed over a saddle, she had been carried away on horseback for hours, then dumped over someone's broad shoulder and taken up a torchlit stairway. Terrified, she fought, kicked, shrieking until a hand had clapped over her mouth to shut her up. Pushed into a darkened room, she was tossed on a bed. The man left, and a woman, silent and grim, brought her a drink and some food. Throat dry, she swallowed thirstily. Soon, all had gone blurry and she had slept.

Days had gone by, slow and silent, seeing only the woman, getting few answers to her volley of questions. Where was she, who had taken her, where were her friends? What happened to the men of her escort? The woman said little, shaking her head, asking her what she wanted to eat, if she wanted a book or needlework, if she preferred wine or ale.

"I am thirteen," she said. "Bring me water for my health. If you bring spirits, water them." She was served hot herbal infusions and watered ale. Her head always seemed foggy, so that she slept often and did little. Today she felt that way again.

She shook her head, sitting with stockinged feet dangling from the edge of the great bed. The room was not large, nearly filled by the enormous bed. The walls were whitewashed and plain, but there was a shelf with a few books that she looked through now and then. The raftered ceiling beams were painted in a flowery design that she had all but memorized. A patterned rug covered part of the planked floor. Daylight spilled through the latched shutters covering a tall window.

A fire in a stone hearth made the room feel too warm, with the sun shining bright outside. She wanted to go outside but had not been allowed. On a table, a tray held a glass goblet, a pottery jug, a pewter plate with apples and cheese. In a shadowy corner, a curtain partly concealed a chamber pot and a table with linens and a bowl of water. Near the window, a leather chair was pushed against a table holding a pot of wildflowers.

The room's arched wooden door, trimmed in black iron, was latched shut. She knew the latch was bolted. She heard it every time the woman came in and went out.

Locked in a pretty room fit for a princess. Perhaps they thought she was one. But she was only the eldest illegitimate daughter of the earl who last year had declared himself King of Scots. The title of princess now belonged to her younger half-sister, Marjorie, just eleven years old and a captive in England with her other kinswomen.

Now both Robert Bruce's daughters were prisoners, thousands of miles apart. But Lilias had a better chance of escaping than her half-sister.

Sliding to the floor from the big bed, she went to the table, sloshed the jug contents and sniffed, discovering watered ale. She poured a little into the glass cup, then sniffed the liquid again. The serving woman often gave her something at night that made her feel groggy and vaguely aware of her surroundings. She dipped a finger into the watery ale and touched it to her tongue, then tried to remember what she had learned about herbs and infusions that made one sleepy.

A sweetish, earthy funk traced through the brighter taste of ale. Wrinkling her nose, she thought about what Lady Rowena Keith, Margaret's sister, had taught her about herbs. Valerian! That had an earthy taste. It was a helpful herb unless the dose was too high. One could fall asleep quickly and feel awful upon waking.

She gave the apple an uncertain glance—it could be tainted—and walked the room, bored, trying to be more alert. Using the little chamber pot and cleaning her face and hands, she smoothed her clothing, the same blue woolen gown that Robert Bruce's sister had given her, with the same pale embroidered stockings and chemise that she had been wearing when the escort had been attacked. So her days went. So slowly.

Shuddering at the memory of the attack, she wondered what had become of Lady Margaret and Andrew Murray and the kind knights of the escort. She had learned nothing of them since coming here.

Sitting in the chair, she paged through a book mindlessly and tried to still her fears, trying to imitate the natural calm of Lady Rowena and the courage and spirit of Lady Margaret. She had boldness in her, she knew that, but the days, the fear—and perhaps the herbal infusions—had eroded that.

Hearing the door latch rattle, she folded her hands and straightened her shoulders. She wanted to seem calm and brave and look like a king's daughter. Her father would expect it.

The servant woman who had come every day entered again, wearing a plain dun-colored gown and a white head kerchief that did not obscure her sour expression. Carrying a small jug and a covered bowl, she placed them on the table and poured liquid into the cup. Picking up the other pitcher, she nodded to Lilias.

"My lady. To break your fast."

"What is in the cup? I will not be dosed again. You have been giving me valerian."

The woman raised her eyebrows high. "My lady, there was naught in the drink to harm you. Just a little to calm you."

"Too high a dose. Go to whoever is holding me here," she said, "and tell them I will neither eat nor drink until I know it is harmless."

"If you wish." The woman went to the door, then stopped. "Oh! Sir William!"

She backed away as the door opened wider and a man stepped into the room. He glanced at the servant, then Lilias, frowning. A tall man, dark haired and dark eyed, he wore a long blood-red surcoat with silver embroidery, an expensive garment, with a black tunic and boots. He was a handsome knight, not as old as her father but older than Sir Henry Keith or Sir Hugh Stewart.

"Lady Elisabeth, greetings," he said to Lilias; she had not shared her affectionate name here. Let them call use her formal name. He turned to the servant, who looked discontent. "Dame Brigit, speak. Is there a problem here?"

"Sir, my lady says she will no longer eat or drink for fear of being poisoned."

"That is not exactly what I said." Lilias stepped forward.

He glanced at her, then at the woman. "She is a child and will do as she is told. Damc Brigit brought you food. You will eat it."

"I am being given sleeping draughts against my will."

"You need it, from the ruckus that I heard. You are calmer and should thank the good dame for that."

"She should know a slight girl needs a slight dose. Where am I, and who are you?'

"Sir William de Soulis."

"De Soulis? My father mentioned the name. I thought De Soulis was dead."

"My uncle Walter was killed recently. Why does it matter to a child?"

"When I hear things, I think about them. Why am I in this place?"

"This is Roskie Castle, which belongs to Sir John Menteith, sheriff of Dunbartonshire. You are his guest."

"Guest! I hear the drawbar each time the door closes."

"We must protect you from harm."

"Better if my escort and I had been left alone. Why were we attacked? Where are my men and companions now? Who told you my name?"

"A knight in your escort. Before he died, alas."

"Did you slay him?" She sounded bolder than she felt. Her legs trembled so under her gown that she put a hand on the table to stay upright.

"Child," he said. "Be fair and grateful. Did you forget that Sir John's men tried to save you? You were attacked. You are under the sheriff's protection after a rescue from brigands."

"That is not true."

"A child may see things differently than an adult. You may eat and drink without fear. No one will harm you here."

"A real sheriff would send word to my father. He is—" She stopped, about to say the one name she should protect.

"We know who your father is." He turned to leave the room, beckoning the servant out as well. The door shut, the bar dropped, the latch fixed.

CHAPTER NINE

HECTOR SAT OUTSIDE the girl's door, dozing against the wall. He opened an eye as Duncan approached.

"Sir! Effie MacArthur is down the kitchens making a late supper. I will tell you Effie does not like that bar on the door. But I told her we follow Brechlinn's orders, not hers. But she said to leave the tub so as not to disturb the guest."

"Aye. Go have your supper, and send someone up with food for the—guest."

As the old man headed down the steps. Duncan knocked. Hearing no response, he lifted crossbar and latch and entered.

The room was dark but for candlelight. Hearing splashes as he stepped inside, he saw the wooden tub with its draped cloth liner, water puddling on the floor. Visible in the gleam of water was the girl's head, bare shoulders, and hands scooping water in sparkling streams over russet hair.

"Euphemia, did you—oh!" Margaret glanced at him, eyes widening.

Suddenly he felt like an awkward young knight again. "I—uh—"

"Sir Duncan," she said crisply. The tub was deep but not wide, so she sat knees high, head and shoulders visible. Over the elegant sweep of her collarbones, a silver chain glinted between the lush curves of her breasts.

At that glimpse, his body surged and he sucked in a breath. "I thought we could speak. I could come back."

"This is your home." She waved a hand and rested an arm along the top edge of the tub covered by the cloth liner. Rivulets ran down to pool on the floor. Her arms were lean and limber; he recalled her strength and skill in pulling a bow.

"My home." His gruff voice betrayed a churn of discomfort.

"I thought you might shut me in a dungeon, so I am thankful to be here, even if you barricade the door." She dipped her hand in the water, releasing a glitter of water droplets. She was enchanting and distracting. He needed to focus.

"The dungeon is not available at present."

"Too full already with those who have displeased the laird of Brechlinn?"

"Too flooded with spring rains." The ancient structure, seated on the edge of the loch, did not fare well in heavy rain. Last year, an English raiding party set fire to it, undoing what work he had accomplished.

She gave him a sour look and sank lower, knees high, head tipped back. She had a graceful profile, a swan-like throat. He swallowed, stood silent.

"I thought you were Effie come to help me."

"She is making supper."

"Are there no kitchen servants?"

"We are just a few here. Effie MacArthur helps when she can."

"So there is no one to deter the laird from entering a lady's quarters?"

"Most of them think you are a lad." He watched her shoulders ripple as she lifted slim arms to sluice more water over her head.

"You and Effie know about me. Anyone else?"

"Lennox guessed on the boat."

"A smart man. Lovely man." She slid a glance at him. "Considerate. He would not burst into a lady's bath. I think he did not want me kept captive."

"He has a soft heart."

"And does the laird of Brechlinn."

"Is this a dungeon? It is not." He went to the table that held a basket and folded linens beside a chair holding a gown of dark blue. He picked up some things to carry toward her. She glanced over her shoulder, covered the tops of her breasts.

"What are you doing?" She sank lower.

"Being considerate. Just leaving a towel and clothing for you." He dropped the things to the floor. She stretched an arm out and down, fingers flexing.

"I cannot reach. Hand me a linen please. Then will you leave?"

When he lifted the toweling, she snatched it so fast the cloth trailed in the bathwater. She tucked the wet, translucent fabric over the high curves of her breasts. Another quick, inadvertent glimpse made his blood run hotter.

"Here." He handed her another cloth.

"Thank you. Go, please. Send Effie here when she is done in the kitchen."

"Euphemia MacArthur is not a servant. She is a friend."

"Then I apologize. I thought her a housekeeper or suchlike." She raked fingers through her hair, water trickling over her shoulders. "I need to get out now."

"I will wait. Tell me when you are ready." He turned to face the door, taking a sidestep so she could see his back.

He heard splashing as she stood, heard a foot meet the floor softly, then another, and finally, cloth rustling.

"There," she said after a few moments.

He turned. The blue dress draped in generous folds on her tall and slender frame, dragging on the floor, its neckline slipping off one shoulder. The silver chain gleamed on her damp neck, its pendant hidden beneath the bodice. Her hair, dark and wet, trailed in ripples to her waist. Duncan breathed against another surge; the woman affected him despite all. He had never been able to distance himself from the memory of her, and now she was two strides away, grown and womanly.

"Lady Margaret." *How well I remember you*, he wanted to say. *How beautiful you have become.* He kept his gaze steady on hers.

"Sir Duncan." She lifted her chin, her neck long and graceful, her attitude clear in the tight lips, flared nostrils, hooded glance. Defiant, indignant.

Duncan pondered what to say, where to begin. Should he apologize? Tell her he had always cared for her? He stood silent. Then she touched her shoulder with a little wincing frown. "How is the shoulder? The knee?"

"Both will heal. What do you want of me, Duncan Campbell? Brechlinn, they call you now? Laird of Brechlinn and Justiciar of the North? And you been here all this time, and never let us know you were whole and well? No apologies?"

"Apologies?" He frowned; she read him too easily. "Why the disguise, Margaret Keith? I thought you a lad at the archery butts." He did not mention that his first glimpse of the red-haired lass in the crowd had left him stunned, and somehow relieved.

"I thought you were dead. Clearly not."

So that rumor had reached the Keiths. "I was a prisoner for years. I escaped with others—a long story. And I heard you entered a convent. You do not look like a nun to me. We can discuss all that later."

"To what point? It is done between us."

"At the moment, we have a more pressing matter between us. Why did you shoot Sir John Menteith?"

"An accident. I told you that. Though it could turn out to be a blessing."

"Not for him."

She huffed. He could not take his gaze from her. He wanted to drink in her vibrant presence here, let himself feel simple joy in that. He wanted to take in her wild beauty—she had matured into a desirable woman. And he wanted to understand what stirred now in his heart, the feelings he had locked up with regret and rumor. But his innate reserve, the ordeal of the last years, and the need to protect his secrets had given him the habit of wariness.

"You spoke of a missing girl. Tell me more," he said.

Thoughts flickered through her green eyes. He sensed she was torn somehow. "I shot Menteith by accident. Truly. But if it delays him, all the better. You see, I believe he has Bruce's daughter."

"Bruce's daughter." He waited.

"Aye. You cannot keep me here," she said urgently. "I must find her."

"Is it your responsibility?"

"Aye!!"

That puzzled him utterly. "I have lawful cause to keep you until I am satisfied with the answers. But this warren only gets deeper."

"Since I am innocent of malice. You can let me go. I must find Lady Lilias!"

"Lilias?"

"Lady Elisabeth. Bruce's bastard child. She is so important. You cannot know."

"I can," he said slowly. "You, a slip of a lass, saving a king's daughter? What proof do you have that Menteith had aught to do with this—missing daughter?"

"Menteith was involved. I know it, I."

The phrase startled him. His mother had said that when her sense of Sight made her certain of something. By nature, he trusted that phrase. But he could not trust Margaret Keith until he knew how this all fit together.

"Such a wild claim needs proof."

She raised her hands in frustration. "You are an authority of the law. You can help. I have no one else to turn to, no time to fetch help from my kin. If you refuse, I must see to finding her myself!"

"If there was evidence, I would help. But you must stay here for now."

"I will not. There is no time to wait." She folded her arms.

"Best we keep you here in case you try something else foolish."

"Duncan Campbell." She lowered her brows. By God, she had a fierce beauty. "Promise me you will help if I can prove this."

"I will." His heart thumped. She stood close enough now that he leaned back a bit, too aware of the tug between them, that strand pulling, unseen but keenly felt.

"I will do whatever I must," she conceded. "I should have gone to Menteith earlier and demanded to know what he did with Lady Lilias Bruce."

"If you had done that, you might be looking at a noose just now. Be glad I took you away. Tell me why I should believe you. Sir John said his men came upon brigands attacking a party along the road. They rescued a girl, a laird's daughter. They escorted her to meet her kin. He made no mention of Bruce."

"You should believe me," she said, "because I was part of her escort."

A prickle went down his spine. Constantine had said Keith men were found dead at the site of the attack. This was beginning to make uncanny sense. But he would be cautious until he knew more.

"You got away," he said.

"So did a friend. He saw the men's badges—black and white checks on yellow. Menteith of Dunbarton, though they were the ones acting like brigands!"

"Where was your escort headed?"

"West to meet a boat, then out to the Isles and Ireland. They attacked us, I tell you. Where did they take the girl? What did Menteith say?"

That matched Lennox's account. "MacDougalls." He nearly spit out the name.

She stepped closer, eyes intent, cheeks flushed. "If they did take her there, we can rescue her. You are the justiciar. I appeal to you."

"You want me to ride to stir the MacDougalls further? They do not support Bruce and the Scots cause as it is." Now he threw a hand up in exasperation. "We need abundant proof to accuse them or Menteith of any action against Bruce or his own."

"We have enough." Her eyes were bright with conviction. "I was there. The prize you won—there is your proof."

"Prize?"

"The brooch that Menteith had and gave to you. It is mine. I lost it that day."

"Interesting." He scowled, looking away, thinking. He had not even claimed the thing but left it with Menteith. "Are you sure?"

"Oh!" She blew out a breath. "Let Menteith sit by the fireside with his injured foot. There is a useful delay while we take Lilias back. And the men—the other men in the escort. They can all be rescued. Then you, sir, will thank me for that wayward shot."

"I will not. And no one will hie off to accuse anyone, especially Menteith, a sheriff and an earl, without good cause."

"What more do you need? I saw them. My friend saw them and their badges. Later he had my brooch. I know in my heart he is part of it. Do not waste time looking for more proof. Help me, please!"

"Where is she? See? Even with proof, we cannot make a move yet. Your friend, is he the lad with you in the village?"

"Andrew. He fostered at Kincraig."

"Andrew Murray? The witness who spoke to the innkeeper?" When she nodded, he went on. "The hero's son?"

She frowned a little. "Aye."

"I knew his father. I know his kin."

"All the more reason to join me in finding Lilias and Andrew too. I do not know where he went once you took me. Both are my responsibility, you see."

"How so? This is a considerable burden for a lass alone."

"If I you believe me, Duncan Campbell, then I am not alone."

He wanted to believe her. He ached to say so. But his training, his obligation, and the risk in accusing Menteith, who was in Edward's pocket, had to be considered.

She took his silence for refusal. "If you must ponder for so long, I will find someone else. Lennox is here. I can ask him." She took a step toward the door.

He reached out and took her arm, knowing the door was unlatched. "Neither Lennox nor I will accuse Menteith of taking a king's daughter without strong proof."

She pulled her arm and winced. He let go. "You are a justiciar. Please—"

"As a justiciar, I am obliged to ensure the law is followed."

"Oh! You!" She stamped her bare foot, the dress nearly slipping off her shoulder. "Then let me go and I will do this myself and you can ensure all the law you want later."

His mouth twitched in a flicker of amusement, seeing a flash of the young Margaret he had come to love. And had hurt. He scowled. "It is late. You need to rest. We will both think more clearly in the morning. These accusations have more consequence than you know."

"I do know. But I hoped you were—the man I imagined you to be."

"You thought me dead, so that is curious."

"I meant I thought you would take quick action to help a king's daughter."

"At the risk of poking a heinous enemy, I will be deliberate. But if I have reason, you will see swift justice. I promise you that."

Her gaze was intent, jewel-like. "You broke a promise once."

"Long ago. Not again." Outside the door, he heard footsteps. A knock followed, and he turned to open the door to Euphemia holding a tray. He stood back as she entered. She sent him a concerned look.

"All is well?" she asked.

"Well enough. I was just leaving."

"Thank you, Euphemia." Margaret's smile was wan. "I am

hungry. That smells good." So she could be gracious after all, this wild thing, Duncan thought.

"Just bacon with pease pudding and bannocks. Best I could do, as my brother has let the larder go empty again. I must come here more often, Brechlinn, if you will leave Bran in charge," she added. "He and the other men would wait 'til Doomsday before they would prepare a decent meal. Will you stay, sir?"

"I will eat downstairs. Lady Margaret, we will talk later." He opened the door.

"Lady?" Euphemia raised her brows.

He nodded, then shut the door, and after a moment, dropped the bar in place, resolved to return soon to let Euphemia out. His friend would expect an explanation, and he owed her that.

But he would not chance that Margaret Keith might convince good-hearted Euphemia to let her leave the room—and Brechlinn Castle.

CHAPTER TEN

Restored by a bit of bacon, a bannock, and a swallow of ale, Duncan headed up the stairs to free Euphemia. Opening the door, he heard laughter and saw Margaret seated while Effie stood combing and braiding the rich length of her hair. Seeing Duncan, Effie finished her task, took up the tray, and went to the door.

"Lady Margaret," she said as she left. The girl smiled, but when Duncan gave her a nod, she looked away with a tilted chin.

He followed Effie outside, barred the door, and took the tray as they descended the steps. Once past the central stone pillar and out of earshot, Effie paused on the downward step and turned to face him.

"So, Lady Margaret Keith. She was your betrothed, the one you—"

"That was years ago. Did she mention it?"

"Not to me. She only said she needed the protection of guising as a lad. Some women must resort to that. Men can be fools," she added. "She also said you brought her here against her will. I did not press her because she is tired and in pain. But I want the truth from you. Did you bring her here by force? Though I cannot see it of you."

"I did not, Effie. She wounded a man, so she is in my custody for now. That is all."

"Is it? The air was thick enough to slice through between you two. You lock her in like a criminal. Bran thinks you brought a lad up from the end of the loch to help here. Lennox avoided my question, so he knows something. What is it?" Hand on hip, she blocked his way.

"She entered an archery contest and shot Sir John Menteith," he said as Euphemia gasped. "She claims it was an accident. But I cannot leave her in Menteith's jurisdiction until I know what happened. I do not trust the man. So I brought her up the loch. Even so, he could come looking for her here. He thinks she is a lad."

"If it was an accident, then she is innocent, and you cannot hold her."

"It needs sorting out before I can release her."

"And the rest of it? The betrothal." Her ice-blue gaze was honest.

"All in the past." He sighed, considering her, his good friend since childhood years. She was like a sister to him, Bran like a brother. Effie had married, was a mother, was a widow. He would do anything for Euphemia and Bran and their kin.

But some matters he would keep to himself.

"The betrothal was dissolved years ago, before I rode for Edward, before I was captured and all that followed. It is done."

"Is it? She remembers. So do you. I felt it between you just now. That was more than a childhood betrothal."

"She was thirteen, I was twenty. Both young, foolish. Much has happened since. It is forgotten."

"And yet is not. You are changed even since I saw you last. Your eyes are more blue, more alight. You are keen on something. What has tapped your wicked old soul?" She poked his chest, smiled.

"I am just glad to be home, my dear, with my friends and falcons."

"Huh! Content in this pile of rubble with a handful of misfit knights, and falcons you cannot admit to owning? Oh aye. Something has changed." With a knowing smile, she took the tray and went down the steps, leaving him standing in shadows.

She was right. He knew it, though he was not sure what it meant.

LATER, HE WALKED through the shadowy great hall, past its low-burning hearth, and opened the narrow door that led into a snug, low-ceilinged room. Brechlinn's modest library held a small table, two chairs, and a hefty set of wooden shelves to which nearly fifty leather-bound volumes were chained. Part of his father's library, now his, with books added as he found time and silver.

Malcolm, Earl of Lennox, was sprawled in a leather chair, one leg extended as he studied the painted pages of the heavy volume cradled in his big hands. A brass chain draped from the book's spine to the nearby shelf. He looked up.

"I found a volume of the Anglo-Saxon chronicles. Fascinating account." He tapped a page. "Look here—it speaks of the outlawing of an earl believed to be a traitor to the king, long ago. He admitted to betrayal 'before all the men gathered there,' so it says, and he was expelled. Then he returned with ships from Norway. Interesting."

"Ah, that. 'And yet it is too tedious to tell how it all came about,'" he quoted. "Not a good precedent for your situation. You are no traitor, Malcolm."

"But cruelly expelled from my lands. I have no Norwegian ships, though. I might borrow a few from Ireland if Bruce backs my bid to reclaim The Lennox from Menteith."

"He would back you if he could spare the ships and men. Speaking of Ireland," Duncan said, taking a chair, "we may have trouble."

"The wee bit lass upstairs?"

"And more. Menteith may have Bruce's girl, though he claimed that the girl his men rescued on the road was taken up to the MacDougalls."

Malcolm set the book aside and leaned forward. "Tell me more."

Explaining what he knew and had reasoned thus far, Duncan drew a breath and then mentioned the broken betrothal. Malcolm huffed.

"I remember. You are still unhappy over it. That wee bit lass, here? God's foot! What an odd coincidence. Providence brought her to you. So perhaps it is a miracle."

"I hold no faith in miracles, nor do I trust Providence to mess about in my life."

"Says the justice man. But think, now. Lady Margaret escaped, or she would have been taken too. If Menteith arranged this deliberately—though he claims not—I wonder if Margaret was part of his scheme, considering who she is."

"Henry Keith's sister and a niece of the Marischal of Scotland?"

"And a granddaughter of Thomas the Rhymer."

Duncan looked up sharply. He had forgotten that. "Certainly Henry and the Marischal, too, would be incensed over harm done to a Keith daughter, not to mention Bruce's lass. But True Thomas is long dead. What bearing would that have on this?"

"Bruce said the Rhymer left part of his legacy to the Keiths of Kincraig. Last autumn, one sister—she married William Seton—was pursued by Edward's men. Something to do with the Rhymer's legacy."

"Why would Edward care about that?"

"A book of prophecies or some such. But he never got it. And since the sisters are co-heiresses, he may hunt them too, their brother as well. Edward wants something that belonged to Thomas the Rhymer. But they say he is mad, and growing more so."

"Mad or cunning, either is dangerous," Duncan muttered. "So Liam Seton married a Keith sister? I did not know. He carries out tasks for Bruce. I would think the fact that she is Bruce's daughter would be enough reason for Edward—perhaps through Menteith—to order her pursued and caught."

"True, with the queen and others captured by English, Bruce

has tasked Seton and others to watch over certain Scottish noblewomen. That would include the child. Henry Keith and Liam Seton would have been discreet in arranging to move the Bruce girl, and Margaret Keith with her. Apparently someone found out."

"Menteith sends spies about," Duncan said. "Sheriffs communicate with one another, so perhaps there was word of the escort. Given the rumors about Menteith's previous deeds, he would be wary. Perhaps he had someone watching Henry Keith."

"Menteith's deed—betraying Wallace, as many suspect?"

"That he sent that good man to a horrible death, aye. So he is not above threatening Scotswomen who have ties to Bruce. But a lass close to Thomas the Rhymer—that is more difficult to understand."

"Bruce trusted Thomas, who carried out missions for him."

"Ah. Then he had knowledge Edward would covet."

"He had magic Edward would covet. Predictions. Potions. Who knows? Listen, Brechlinn. If your wee lass has something Auld Thomas gave her, Edward will want it. He never got the whatnot off her sister."

"I see. This is making more sense. Margaret Keith was with Bruce's lass, and she may have something of the Rhymer's as well. So both lasses might be targets. If Menteith, Edward's sworn man despite his Scots blood, is behind it, this may be another arm of Edward's revenge against Bruce. Yet there is something else at work here."

"It seems so. But we cannot divine it sitting here."

"Lady Margaret wants us to go after Menteith. For now, we will keep a close eye."

"Thanks to your lady, he will be stuck by the fireside nursing his foot for a while."

Duncan sent him a sour glance.

MOONBEAMS SHINING THROUGH the window woke Margaret often until she finally sat up in the darkness. Yawning, she went to the window and pulled open a shutter for a breath of cool air. Beyond the wall, the rippling loch reflected the moon's gleam.

From the tower's height she could see the bailey as well as the outer curtain wall that sheared down to the water. Out there, she spotted a rowing boat beached on the pebbled shore.

If she could get to that boat, she could row down the loch and return to the forest to look for Andrew. If Duncan Campbell would not act soon, she would find her own way through this predicament. She felt so strongly that she bore responsibility for Andrew and Lilias—she could not bear to think either might come to harm.

The last few years had honed her natural independence, changing a dreamer, a naïve lass with a wild streak, into a stronger, more insistent soul. Within a year of Duncan Campbell's rejection, she was in a convent, ill and grieving—thinking him lost, thinking her chances gone. Healing slowly, she discovered her ability to be determined and capable, while her stubbornness, and that wild streak, only grew. She refused to marry her father's choices and decided she would never be a bride. So be it.

Yet meeting Duncan again, she felt relieved and aye, joyful that he was alive and well after all. Seeing that he had become a reserved, competent, certain, very handsome man reminded her of what she had lost—what they could have had. Even more, she realized what she had gained without him. She was a stronger woman because of it. If she were honest with herself, she owed him for stirring that in her.

She had to rely on her determination and her impulsiveness to solve this dilemma. Yet she was stuck waiting for the justiciar—her dear Duncan Dhu, precious in memory though she did not know the man well at all—to decide what he would do.

Gazing out at the battlement, she saw two guards looking out over the loch. Far off, a dog barked and went silent; she heard the steady shush of the water but little else. The guards moved out of sight, and she would have turned away, but looked down.

A cart sat at the base of the tower keep, filled with hay, bales piled beside it. The sight gave her a sudden, tempting, mad thought. *Escape.*

Months ago, her sister Tamsin had escaped a castle tower using a makeshift rope of bedlinens in a desperate bid to avoid a marriage imposed by King Edward. Tamsin had climbed down only to encounter a knight waiting outside the castle walls for his own purposes. He helped her make a fortuitous escape, and that adventure had led to a life Tamsin had never anticipated.

Could Tamsin's mad scheme solve Margaret's situation too? But Tamsin's tower had been on an outer wall, so that she escaped into a forest with the knight's help. Here, even if Margaret could climb out and land in the cart, she would have to get through the bailey and out the gate. With luck, she could find a small postern gate at the back and escape unseen in the darkness.

She looked around. Tamsin had tied together an abundance of linens and things. This bedchamber held only a few blankets and linens; knotted together, they might not be long enough. Still, even halfway down, she could fall safely into the hay.

She had to try. Duncan was a deliberate soul, which suited him and his work. She was his fiery opposite, and could not sit here longer without acting.

Flexing her shoulder, she decided it would support her; she could nurse it and her knee to full strength later. For now, all she wanted was to get away to search for Andrew and Lilias. Rushing around the room, she collected what she could find and began working fervently to tie the corners of blankets and linens together in fat knots, glad of her nimble strength from bow practice. Once the lengths were knotted together, she stretched the rope out. Too short.

She removed Euphemia's too-large blue dress and tied the arms to a blanket corner. That left her shivering in a thin shift, but the tunic and trews she had worn as a lad were folded on the bench. Quickly she scrambled into those and pulled on her boots.

Too impatient to search for the black cap, she tossed her single braid back.

Tying one end of the makeshift rope around a leg of the bed, the heaviest item in the room, she carried the rope's length to window. Then she dragged the bench to the window and climbed up, resting a hip on the stone sill. The wind on her face was cool and damp. She looked down. A mistake. The drop was long.

Reeling back, she leaned a shoulder against the window frame, facing darkness and the snapping chill, waiting for the dizziness to pass. Then she dragged the awkward fabric rope closer and spilled it over the sill.

The weight of it shifted the bed forward, wooden legs scraping over the floor, dreadfully loud. She stopped, heart pounding, and glanced at the battlements. No sign of the guards. She leaned out again as a swift breeze cut past.

She rose on her toes to assess how to get out the window. As children, she and her siblings had climbed on a rope over a deep stream and pool by Kincraig. That was how Tamsin learned to climb down a rope. So there was no reason she could not do this too. Taking a breath, she leaned out, drawing a breath to conquer dizziness and the fear that this was an idiotic thing to attempt. She hoisted up on her arms, hands pressed on the windowsill, and with a little leap, set one hip on the sill. Bracing her hands, she began to wriggle about, realizing she needed to turn so that she could climb down the rope while facing the outer wall.

A door slammed. "God's bones!"

Surging out of the darkness, two strong hands grabbed her under the arms to yank her back into the room. Startled, she twisted to see Duncan's scowl as he pulled her hard against him and held her fast.

"What the devil are you doing?" he growled. Then he lifted her, though she kicked and writhed, carried her, and all but tossed her on the bed.

She wriggled enough to throw him off balance so that he tumbled with her. Frame and mattress lurched under the combined force of their fall and the bed shifted, the rope's weight pulling it toward the sill. Jumping to his feet, Duncan grabbed the rope and turned. He jabbed a finger at her in the moonlight.

"Stay there. Do not dare move!"

She sat up, breathing hard, as he snaked the rope into the room so fast and in such agitation that its end whipped backward and into her lap. Then he slammed the shutters, rattling the glass in the upper arch, and turned to glare again.

"God's very bones, you gave me a hell of a fright! What were you thinking?"

"I was thinking I should leave." She returned his glare.

"You could have been killed." He pulled the cloth rope off her and threw it on the floor, then lifted a boot to push the bed back against the wall. Margaret bounced as it hit.

"I did not know you had such a temper," she said.

"I did not, until I saw this. What the devil am I to do with you?"

"Let me go or help me."

"I will not help you jump out a window."

"Then open the door," she said.

He shoved his hair back—thick, dark and glossy, it had fallen in his eyes. Why did she notice the way moonlight glinted over those black waves? Why did it look so soft and appealing? She scowled to dispel the thought.

"Are you hurt?" he asked.

"Only where you grabbed my ribs." She tucked her hands under her arms.

"I was just saving your life."

"I would have been fine. There is a wagon filled with hay down there."

"From this height, on that ridiculous rope, the cart would have broken apart, if you were lucky enough to hit that target rather than fall to the ground."

"I always hit the target."

"I have noticed. And you were a climber too, as I recall.

Climbed a tree once, and fell out."

He remembered. "For all the good it did then."

"Meaning?"

"I never saw that beautiful falcon again. I never saw you again until lately. Did you send her back to the king to earn your reward?"

"The only reward King Edward ever gave me was a long stint in prison." He sat on the bed beside her, mattress rustling, sinking. She scooted away. "Do not fret. I will not touch you, unless you try to escape again."

"Then what do you mean to do here?"

He blew out a harsh breath, as if he struggled with the question. Reaching out, he took up the fabric rope and began to untie the knots. Shaking a blanket free, he tossed it over her. He freed another blanket for himself.

"I mean to sleep here tonight."

"What! You cannot!"

He lay back, not beside her but lying opposite, his head at the other end, and pulled the blanket high, bending his arm for a pillow. Long legs and big feet in big boots created an effective barrier. Margaret would have to climb over him to get out of the bed, which now sagged in the middle.

"Lie down," he said. "You are going nowhere."

"You cannot stay here." She scooted back, pulling her blanket high as she leaned against the wall. "You need to leave."

"Someone must ensure you do not break your troublesome neck."

"Not here, not in my very bed."

"I am no threat. I still have a rusty sense of honor." He lifted on his elbow to regard her. "I want to know you will be here in the morning."

"It is discourteous to treat a lady thus, even a captive so wrongfully held. Get off the bed and out of my room." She kicked him.

"Oof. Here." He grabbed a linen sheet from the tangle on the floor and crammed the length of it between them. "There. A wall."

"What is that supposed to do?"

"It is customary in Germania, among other places, for two people who are betrothed or courting to share a bed with a bolt or board between them." He patted the wadded cloth. "Lay back and go to sleep."

"This is not Germania and we are no longer betrothed. That was your choice, as I recall. And I will not lie here with you all night."

"Near me, not with me. And not all night. I just want to be sure you will not try to go out the window again and fall on your bonny head." Lying on his side, he shifted his topmost leg to rest it firmly over hers, cloth bunched between. She felt his strength and tension sure as an iron lock. "Go to sleep, Margaret Keith."

"You go to sleep." Her gaze drifted to the door. She did not think he had set the drawbar in place.

"If you are hoping the drawbar is still up," he said, as if he read her thoughts, "I will fix it in place again. Just do not try the window again. That is all I ask."

"I was thinking about it," she admitted.

"I feared so. But that cart will not be there long. It belongs to the brewer who brings ale and supplies for our larder. Euphemia MacArthur sent for him today. He sometimes plays dice and drinks half his ale with Bran and Hector before he heads home. And your rope is shorter now by two blankets and a sheet. Remember that."

"Beast," she said, scrunching down to pull the blanket over her.

"Wildcat," he said. "Going out on a rope of blankets. Dear God. Sleep now."

"My sister escaped a tower on a rope of linens."

"Is that where you got the inspiration?"

"She needed to escape a threat. I thought I could do the same."

"You are not threatened here, my girl. Did she survive the fall?"

"She was fine. A knight came by who aided her, since she was being pursued."

"Fortunate she did not break her neck. Who was in pursuit?" He half turned in the darkness. The low rumble of his voice sent a warm thrill through her. "Is this the Keith daughter who lately married Seton of Dalrinnie?"

"You heard of that?"

"Lennox mentioned it. Apparently King Edward caused trouble for the lady over something she possessed."

"A book. Edward demanded to take what did not belong to him."

"It is sometimes his habit."

"Sometimes! He expects all Scotland to buckle under his bidding until he owns every plot of land, every castle, board, blanket, and book we own. Our very lives too."

"Go easy, wildcat. Though many would agree with you."

"I suppose you would not, since you are in Edward's employ."

"My position as justiciar is overseen by Edward and his commanders. I did give him my knight's oath, but that was to preserve life and limb. I do what I must. But I would not say I am in his employ, exactly."

"You cooperate with the English rule of law."

"I keep to Scots' law, lass."

"You still have a castle, while Edward takes any Scottish castle he can."

"Brechlinn is small and too remote to bother. They did come through and tried to burn it down, but I am rebuilding. My father left it to me and I am grateful to have it."

"I remember your father. I liked him. My father is gone now."

"I know. I was sorry to hear it."

"I remember hearing that the great Caelin Mor Campbell had been killed. My father was upset. He said he was a good man, the best of his kind."

"Aye, and taken down heinously," he growled. She felt the chill in it.

"So you have his position as justice now. That seems a good thing for you."

"I do my best. So your sister had something the king wanted?" he went on. "Would you have anything Edward might covet?"

The brooch. She caught her breath. Would Edward covet the Rhymer's brooch as he had coveted the book that Tamsin had? "An—item a king would want? I doubt it."

"Good. If you had something valuable, it might be another reason your escort was attacked. You could be a target on Edward's orders."

That surprised her. "King Robert's daughter was the target. And Menteith's knights came after us, not Edward's. So you believe me now about the attack?"

"Possibly."

"Decide, Sir Justiciar. We have no time."

"You have grown a sharp tongue since I saw you last."

"I was a child with dreams. Now I know dreams do not usually come true, and I must be bold to defend myself. That needs a sharp tongue sometimes."

"And a sharp arrow."

Instinctively her hand went to the pendant at her throat, the ancient arrowhead that brought her a sense of comfort and safety. "You said you would leave soon. I am tired and would sleep."

"In a while. Quiet now."

Lying in the darkness, she wanted him to stay, so much that she felt the pull of that desire. His solid presence eased loneliness and fear. She was tempted, in the quiet and dark, to tell him she was glad he was alive. But he began to snore, and soon enough, her eyelids grew heavy.

CHAPTER ELEVEN

SOMETIME LATER, SHE woke to a murky near-dawn, feeling so warm and cozy that she curled sleepily under the blanket. Then she startled, realizing with a gasp that Duncan Campbell still lay beside her. Not only that, he had turned while she slept, his head beside her small pillow. She stared at his shoulder haloed in the brazier's glow.

Reaching out, she tapped his back. "Campbell," she whispered. *"Donnchadh!"*

"Mmhh." He rocked a little as she pushed.

"You are still here," she whispered.

"Shh." His hand came over his shoulder to pat her fingers. Turning around to face her, the mattress sagged and rustled. His eyes were closed. "Shh. Tired. Sleep now."

"You cannot stay."

The suffused light of near dawn showed his closed eyes, his lashes thick dark crescents. His tousled dark hair drifted over his brow. His chin was bristly. He was beautiful. He had to leave. She poked his shoulder.

"Donnchadh!" Somehow his Gaelic name kept coming to her lips.

He lifted his hand to soothe it over her hair. "Hush, my dear."

"I am not your dear," she whispered. "I am your captive. Your prisoner."

He gave a sigh, his fingers sliding to her jaw, tracing there.

"That is unfortunate."

"What?" She waited. He was silent. She poked his chest. "Are you awake?"

He huffed. "I am now."

"You must go. What is unfortunate?"

He blinked, opened his eyes, dark blue, heavily lashed. Her heart seemed to flip. He had to leave. "Duncan!"

"Did I say—damn. Listen now, aye?" His quiet voice poured out like dark honey. "What happened between us long ago was unfortunate. It caused you trouble and hurt. I regret that."

She caught her breath. "It is done. Leave it be."

"If you are upset still, I understand." His hand cupped her shoulder. "But you are right. It is done."

"You could have let me know you were—not dead."

"If I had known you thought it, I might have done so."

"We all thought it. We heard you were taken and died in captivity. Your own kin were unsure when my father sent word to ask."

"There was no way to send word and we did not know what word was out there when we were prisoners. I was kept in England for a long while with other Scottish knights. Then some of us were sent to Flanders to fight for Edward in another war."

"Flanders?"

"Why let knights sit in a dungeon when they can fight in your army? It was a condition of release. But even that was withdrawn. After another year, several of us escaped to France, where the Scots have allies. We were there for a long time before we found a way to Ireland. I stayed up there working for the Scottish cause. I returned home for brief visits only. After that," he murmured, "my father was murdered. My mother and my brothers needed me. And I took on the role of justiciar."

"We heard only that you had died."

"There was no reason to send word to your father. I assumed you hated me, and that your kin despised me as well. Besides, I had heard you were gone."

"I never hated you. Gone?"

"I remember your words, lass. They stayed with me for years. Gone into a convent and took the veil."

"I went there for some time, but left again. How did you hear that?"

"I was kept in an English castle where we sometimes had news of Scotland. I heard Sir Robert Keith's daughter had gone into a nunnery from heartbreak. It hit me deep."

She propped up on an elbow. "I did go to a convent. But not because of you. I was ill. A fever, not heartbreak. I was upset with you, true. But I heard you had died, and it made me—very sad."

"Did it?"

"It did. My mother and I both had fevers, a summer ague, you see. My father took us to an infirmary where we stayed for weeks, then we went to the priory at Lincluden to recover. I got stronger," she said. "My mother grew weaker. She lingered and died."

"I am sorry," he murmured.

"I stayed after she died. I thought about becoming a nun." She shrugged. "But I was not suited to that life. I was—uh, asked to leave."

"Asked to leave a convent?" He sounded surprised.

"Wildcat," she said simply. "I do not like rules."

He chuckled. "I see that. So neither of us knew the truth about the other."

"Would it have mattered?"

"It would." He cleared his throat. "I heard the rumor of my death, but I thought it affected only my family. I am sorry it troubled you."

"And my father. He was saddened. He said you were a good knight." She had not wanted to hear it at the time. Now she lay facing him, warm and relaxed, aware that he must leave. Yet she wanted these quiet moments to linger. "Can I ask—did you ever marry? If you had a wife here, you would not be in this bed."

"I am just here keeping a certain lass in custody. I have no wife."

Tilting her head, she wondered if he had ever fallen in love. Should it matter to her now? She had never loved any suitor but him, but she kept that to herself.

"I never had time to marry," he went on. "And you? Surely your father looked for another match for such a daughter as you."

She smiled in the darkness at that. Stretched out beside him in the darkness of the half-curtained bed felt dreamlike, a cocoon of shadows and moonlight and drowsy warmth. Time vanished, hurt faded. His resonant voice, his very presence felt magical, thrilling through her. Truth felt natural here.

"My father arranged three more betrothals. Four in all. I refused—three of them."

He gave a surprised huff. "Three! What was wrong with the fellows?"

"Two died," she said. "Three, counting you. The fourth one refused me before I had the chance."

"By the saints, lass, you would be a desirable bride for any man. But bad luck for some to die before—well. I am sorry."

"Not bad luck. I decided I would have to make my own luck. Make my own way. I decided I did not want to marry."

"Was that my doing?" he asked. She heard regret soften his words.

"My own doing. Besides, I thought you were dead. But instead you were captured, imprisoned. Tortured." She shuddered.

"But I was cordially held for the most part, since my father was an important Scots lord who could pay ransom. But it was never asked of him. Instead, I was sent to Flanders to fight for the English. But no one was treated that badly."

"You were held, kept from your family. No wife, no children. No happiness."

He gave a little huff. "You imagine a good deal of woe on my behalf."

"The elderly nuns said I was woeful, cursed because of my red hair, green eyes, and freckles. Only witches and demons have such, they said. My sisters are beautiful and talented—Tamsin is blond, so gentle and smart. Rowena is dark-haired and kind and practical. I have the devil's red curls and a temper to match."

"I agree with the temper. And I would wager you are as much a beauty as your sisters," he added. "But redheads are not cursed. What nonsense. My mother was redheaded, as are others in her family. Not a one is cursed. They are all good, smart, spirited women."

"I rather like my hair. But some distrust red-haired folk." She was blushing. Had he called her beautiful just then?

"Superstition. My mother said it began with the Viking raids long ago. It was not red hair that brought bad luck and trouble, but the Vikings themselves. You are no doubt as lovely and gifted as your sisters. I am surprised that you never married."

She shrugged. "Both my sisters were married and widowed—Tamsin married again. Rowena was wed for a short time, but her husband perished. I think my father worried about my future, so he arranged these betrothals, though I told Papa I did not want to marry. The first—after you, that is," she added, "was older than my father but kind. He died a week after agreeing to marry me. The next one was young, a good knight, but he was killed in a skirmish. I never had a chance to know him. So I told Papa I would be the plain girl and take care of him in his elder years."

"I know that tradition in some families. But you are no plain girl." She heard the kind amusement in his voice. It thrummed all through her.

"That role often falls to an unmarried daughter. I told Papa I would take care of the castle household as he aged. But he did not live much longer. I did learn to direct the household, and I took up the bow and arrow."

"You were already doing that when I saw you at Innis Connell."

"I had stopped, but Grandda left me a fine bow, so I took it up again. I did not really want to count linens. I wanted to defend the castle if it was necessary, so that I could truly help at Kincraig after Papa died, and when my brother went away to Selkirk."

"He is deputy sheriff there now, I hear."

"Aye, now. Then there was a fourth promise, you see. A Scottish knight, son of a Guardian of the Realm. Prestigious. Papa thought it would be a fine match. But he rejected me too."

"Margaret, I never rejected you," he murmured. "I was young. I was not ready. Neither were you."

"Well, it was a refusal," she pointed out. "This fellow refused too, after he had signed the promise and accepted the tocher. He took coin and a land grant, and Papa set the wedding—he would not listen to me. He was that concerned about my future. The man was courteous enough, but I did not have a good feeling about him. And then he changed his mind, which proved me right. Though he returned the coin, he kept the land. He said he was misled."

"Misled!"

"He had heard that my other suitors had died and he wanted no part of that sort of luck. My brother is petitioning to regain the lands."

"Legally," Duncan said, ever the justiciar, "it could go in your brother's favor. But it sounds to me that you are better off without such a one."

"I think so too."

The darkness was lifting. Soon the household would rise. Duncan had to leave, she thought. But this wrapping of warmth and honesty was filling her like sunshine in a dim room. She had needed this, and was only just realizing it. Here, in the quiet, listening and caring, Duncan Campbell was all she had dreamed he might be—gentle, kind, patient. His closeness, simple as it was, felt magical.

She wanted to tell him she had loved him since childhood, had loved him even thinking him gone. She had made him an ideal knight, the perfect husband and lover, the man she would never have, and whom none could match.

But she blushed at the thought and kept silent. He would

think her foolish. Yet one question had always troubled her. "Duncan, did you ever want to marry me?"

He sat up, swung his legs over the side of the bed and gave a long exhale. She dreaded his answer. He looked ready to leave, not ready to answer.

"I did," he said finally. "But I would not marry a girl of thirteen. And I did not want you to wait. If I did not return, you would have been widowed without even a marriage."

"I would have waited." She sat up and scooted to the edge to sit beside him.

"I know. But it is done. Let it be forgotten. We are not the same as we were then."

"We are not," she agreed. "You did the honorable thing, then, that day."

"I believed so at the time. Later I was not so sure."

"Neither was I," she said with a half-laugh. "What now?"

"This matter of Menteith and Lady Lilias must be resolved. That is the most important, aye?"

"Thank you," she said in a whispered rush of relief. "Can we ride out?"

"I do not trust the man. And I agree that what you say may be possible. But Sir John is an officer appointed by Edward to uphold Scottish and English law, just as I am. I have to consider that until I know more."

"You say you do not trust him. Do you know him well?"

"We were captured at Dunbar and held together with others—our friend the Earl of Lennox, Sir Constantine. Sir Andrew Murray too. I know Menteith all too well."

"Then why hold back? We can accuse him now. Taking Lilias is treason."

"Which means I must be very careful how I approach this. And—" he paused, "I have some matters here at Brechlinn that must be protected at all costs. If this goes wrong, I could lose all that. Menteith—is not a forgiving sort. Which is why I brought you here."

She nodded, grateful. This time with him was a revelation. Something had shifted within her, as if she had crossed a bridge that spanned the past to this exact moment.

Drawing a breath, she leaned a little toward him, her shoulder brushing his arm, part apology, part plea. Feeling shy, a little uncertain but wanting so much to take the risk of it, she nudged him. A step toward peace, forgiveness. She was not sure what. But she wanted, desperately just then, to cross the distance between them.

In silence, he set an arm around her shoulders. Another step, a gesture they both needed. His body felt warm, solid, his strength palpable. She glanced up at his aquiline features in the shadows, the dark brows and long-lidded eyes, the fine arch of the nose, the mouth's tenderness in a lean masculine face.

"Would we solve this problem of Lilias and then go our ways?" she asked.

"I hope it is that simple."

"I see." She was not sure what he meant by that. A powerful urge to mark this moment before he left, before the distance between them opened up again. "Can I—give you something? Before you go."

His arm light on her shoulders, he moved back to look at her. "What is that?"

She leaned toward him quickly and touched his bristled jaw, the beard like fine sand over his skin, and raised her face. He leaned down and she kissed his lips. Soft yet firm, warm and supple, his mouth moved over hers. He broke away.

"Lass—"

"I used to dream about—well, it is done. I just wanted to do that. Take it as my apology."

"You have nothing to apologize for. You dreamed about us?"

"Sometimes."

A little exhale. "I was a lout then. A fool."

"I was a fool too. But later, even when I thought you dead, I still—" She stopped, feeling a hot blush rise, not sure she was ready to admit her feelings.

"Still what?" His hand rubbed her shoulder affectionately, like a friend. If it were to be over, she could be honest.

"I—I wanted to love you." It was perhaps the most difficult thing she had ever admitted to anyone. "I suppose I loved the *idea* of you. And I was sad you were gone, and I did not want to let that go."

His fingers stilled. He was silent.

She could not look at him. "You should leave. The past is the past, but I understand better now. And you have your secrets and I will not ask. I only ask your help in one matter. And I hope—I hope you will do that for me."

"Margaret." He paused. "I felt a trace—of that too. Feelings that stayed with me. Guilt. Regret that I hurt you. And more," he murmured. "But it has been ten years, and life has become quite complicated."

"I know." She smiled, anticipating the refusal again, yet she felt something powerful, sudden, billow warm through her. Compassion, forgiveness. Love.

She surged toward him, looping her arms around his neck, wanting for one moment here in this cocoon, to grab her countless dreams before he left, and the sun rose, and everything changed again. Pressing her lips to his, she drew back.

But he pulled her to him, slipping his hands along her jaw. He tilted her head back and kissed her in a way that she had not dared to kiss him. Her simple kiss took on a force, a fervor, that drove through her body, swirled, heated. With a soft moan, she curved to him, slid her hands into the thick silk of his hair. He stirred another kiss, tender at first, then lightning.

He pulled her into his arms, turning her across his body, kissing her again. A fiery sense stirred in her, like the euphoric punch of releasing a perfect arrow—or the wild delight of a dream coming true—

But he straightened away, brought her up to sit. "Sorry. That was not well done."

"I did not mind," she breathed. It had felt like something left undone between them, something that needed to happen. A resolution of sorts.

He stood, a tall dark shadow in a long tunic, a long-haired, broad-shouldered, dark archangel gazing at down at her, all beauty and banked power. He reached down and lifted her chin.

"Margaret Keith," he murmured. "Still the dreamer. I am glad. Go back to sleep. I will see you later."

He turned and walked out, closing the door behind him. Margaret heard the drop of the drawbar. Lying back on the still-warm blankets, she blinked back tears.

She had made a fool of herself. Her dreams were a fancy after all. He did not share them—his life was very different from hers, and a decade was a lot of time to leap.

Then she would be content with the good fortune of finding him again, knowing he was well. And she would go on with her life, determined, keeping her spine straight, showing strength and doing what she liked. His decision years ago had caused her to toughen her spirit, even if he did not know.

CHAPTER TWELVE

Lilias

A KNOCK AT the door made Lilias jump. She sat on the bed stitching an embroidery piece on a wooden frame, having asked Dame Brigit to bring her some needlework to occupy her during the long hours. She had been here several days, she thought. Dame Brigit came each day at morning and again late afternoon.

No one knocked at midday. She heard the bar lift, the latch creak, and Brigit poked her head inside.

"Lady Elisabeth, the sheriff wants to see you in the hall. Come with me."

Lilias stood, puzzled. In all this time, Sir John Menteith had not asked to see her. Perhaps her father had come to fetch her! She followed the woman down stone steps to a corridor, then up to a door opened by a guard dressed in the red and gold of Edward of England. Seeing that, Lilias frowned.

Finally the housekeeper led her into a large hall with a high ceiling and a bright fire in a central iron basket. A trestle table and benches were arranged in the middle of the room. At the other end, a man sat in a chair near a glowing brazier. Pillows were crammed around him, and his foot was propped on a stool with another cushion. He beckoned her forward but did not rise.

"Lady Elisabeth," he said as she approached. "I am Sir John. Take a seat."

She did. He gestured for Brigit to leave, and the woman crossed the room to sit under a window with a basket of sewing work. Beyond the tall windows, Lilias saw green hills and a small loch. She wished she was out there, running from this place toward her father and her friends.

Lilias regarded him. Sir John was perhaps her father's age, brown-haired with a plain, round face and a close-trimmed beard. He wore a fur-trimmed robe over a tunic, and his foot on the stool was wrapped in cloth bandages.

"You are Sheriff of Dunbartonshire?" she asked.

"And Earl of Lennox, aye."

She tilted her head. "I know the Earl of Lennox. He is a tall man with black hair and a big beard. You are not he."

"That man is no longer earl of these lands."

"Oh now! Is he dead?"

"Outlawed. A traitor. Dispossessed of his lands."

"Are you one of King Edward's men? I thought you were Scottish."

"I am. I was appointed by King Edward to command this region."

"Am I a prisoner of the English?"

"You are safe here. Not a prisoner."

"Then you can let me go."

"Hah! Where would you go?"

"I would send word to my kin to fetch me."

"Your father is too busy to fetch you. That is why I must keep you safe, until he can send someone for you." He moved, winced. She looked again at his bandaged foot.

"What is wrong with your foot?"

"I took an arrow. A young lad shot me."

"In battle?"

"I wish it were so noble! An archery contest. Then the coward ran. He is in the custody of a justiciar now. If he were in my custody, he would be hanged by now."

"When did it happen?"

"Well over a week ago."

"And your foot is not much better?"

"I can hardly put weight on it. The physician applied a poultice and maggots and said he would return to cauterize it if it did not heal." He waved a hand. "Not your concern, child. It still pains me, so I will send for the doctor."

"He should have cauterized it the first time he saw it. May I look at it?"

He gave her an odd glance. "Why would you want to do that?"

"I want to be a physician. I am learning the healing arts."

He laughed. "A physician! That is no work for a female, or a girl of your rank."

"I am not a princess, if that is what you mean. There is only one princess of Scotland and she is a prisoner of the English king."

"Huh. So you want to be an herb-woman? I suppose your mother was a servant on Carrick lands when your father was the young earl."

"My mother was the daughter of a great lord. She died when I was born."

"Then she would not want her girl to be an herb-wife."

"I will be a physician. I will go to university and learn medical arts."

"Impossible!" He laughed.

"Women can be physicians too. In Italy, women can attend university and earn a doctorate. That is what they call it. And that is what I will do."

"And how would you get to Italy?"

"I will find a way. My father says I am the most determined of his children."

"Dreams of a child! Your father will marry you off to someone important. Who does he want for you, has he said?"

"I do not talk about my father with strangers." She had begun to fear that Menteith meant danger for her father, so she must protect whatever she knew. "Let me see your foot, sir."

"What are you, twelve? I am not showing my foot to a child."

"I will be fourteen in October."

"Marriageable age."

She ignored that. "Your physician is not helpful. That poultice should have been changed and a new one applied days ago. I know some things. Let me see your foot. I have been studying with a healing woman, you see," she explained.

"A crofter's wife, I suppose. Superstition and kitchen herbs."

"She is a noble lady, and very knowledgeable and experienced. She is tutoring me." Something told her not to name Lady Rowena Keith.

"And that makes you an expert? Females think they know everything."

"Let me see your foot, sir."

"Insistent little wench." He beckoned. "I will not have you coming up sick over the sight of a wound."

Lilias knelt by the stool and began to unwrap the bandages. "I will not be sick. I have seen worse than this," she said as she pulled the bandages off gently. She had not, but she was not squeamish, either. "They say air is good for wounds and a dry wound may not fester."

"You cannot possibly know what a physician knows."

She said nothing as she examined his foot. He winced constantly as she unraveled the fabric strips carefully. "I must ask Dame Brigit to bring warm water and cloths, and some herbs that could help."

"Woman!" he called. "The lass wants hot water and herbs."

Lilias looked up. "Please bring willow, comfrey and yarrow, if you have them. Garlic and honey as well, and some strong drink, like *aqua vitae* or *uisge beatha*. And clean cloths." She had seen Lady Rowena Keith tend wounds this way, and they cleared up nicely. She could do the same for the sheriff, who was clearly suffering.

Most of his foot looked normal enough, but the heel was swollen and warm to the touch. The wound, a puncture, was deep and dark and curling at the edges. It had not yet begun to smell, but she feared that would develop soon. Dame Brigit came quickly enough with a pot of hot water, a bowl and cloths, and a basket of herbs.

"It needs to be cleaned and treated," Lilias told the sheriff, and set to work, trying to look calm and knowledgeable in imitation of Lady Rowena. She asked Dame Brigit to stand by to lend a hand.

Sir John winced, jumping now and then as Lilias gently bathed his foot. Setting Dame Brigit to that task, she turned to make a poultice of herbs, honey, and crushed garlic in cloth. Then she wiped the wound with strong spirits, which made him near leap out of his chair and swear under his breath. She soothed it with honey.

Applying the fresh poultice to his heel, she secured it with clean bandage strips. Then she stood, wiping her hands on a clean cloth. "It will heal better now. But you must rest it so that the wound will close itself into a scar. If you want, I can cauterize it for you."

"I am not letting a wee lass touch a hot poker to my foot!"

"Then wait for it to heal, which will take longer." She rubbed a little honey on her hands, dipped them in clean water, then dried them. Lady Rowena insisted on cleanliness, a harmless habit.

"It feels a bit more comfortable. I suppose I should thank you," he grunted. "But I will not pay you a physician's fee, though I fear you will ask for it. If you do get to Italy and earn a degree, you can ask me for payment then."

"I will ask for a different payment. Tell me what happened to the others in my escort. Where are my friends and the men of my party?"

"They are being taken care of, I promise you."

"What of Lady Margaret Keith and Andrew Murray?"

"Who?" He looked startled. "Keith and Murray? I do not know them."

She did not like the sound of any of this. Something was very wrong, and it was clear she was not a guest here. Fear began to trickle down her spine.

"My fee is that you send me back to my kin and my friends."

He smiled. "I am your only friend now. You are a remarkable lass, perhaps more valuable than I thought."

A bad feeling plunged through her. He obviously had a scheme. He was a threat to her father, not an ally as she had first hoped.

"Have some strong spirits," she said, "and rest your foot. Go nowhere for at least a fortnight."

"A scrap of a lass ordering a sheriff?" He laughed. "I would send word to your father if I knew where he was. Do you?"

"I do not." She had an idea where, but she knew by now that her father would not trust Sir John. Suddenly she wished desperately that Sir Henry Keith or Sir William Seton, the good knights who had bid her escort farewell at Kincraig, would learn of the attack and come looking for her and the others.

Menteith drained the liquid in his cup and motioned for Dame Brigit to fill it again. "Lady Elisabeth, you can leave now. I am done with children for the day."

She spun and walked away, Dame Brigit hurrying after her. Just as they reached the door, it was pushed open. She stepped back.

A man entered the room—Sir William de Soulis again. He looked brawny and huge in a red surcoat over chain mail. He had long dark hair and very dark eyes. He stopped, arching one brow.

"Lady Elisabeth," he purred, and walked past. "Sir John! You spoke with Bruce's whelp? What does she know?"

"Not much. A troublesome chit. But she bandaged my foot, if you can believe it."

Dame Brigit held the door open, and Lilias glided through, head high. She might be a whelp and a bastard, but she was a king's daughter.

And she would find a way to leave this place soon, by any means.

CHAPTER THIRTEEN

ORNING SUNBEAMS FLOWED downward, rinsing shadows from the castle walls as Duncan left the slate-roofed kitchen building for the keep. He took the steps by twos as he went up the turning stair, balancing a wooden bowl and a jug in his hands, with a gown of moss-green wool over his arm. Reaching the third level, he knocked, upended the drawbar, and shoved the door open.

Light streamed through the glassed window arch, making the red plaid drapes around the empty bed very bright. Margaret Keith sat on a bench, turning as he entered. She wore the too-large blue gown again, her unplaited hair a mass of loopy curls. With her perfect oval face and green eyes, she looked elvish and adorable. His heart leaped.

She crossed her arms. "What is this?"

"Something to break your fast." He set bowl and jug on the table. "Bran made porridge. It is not too bad. I thought you might be hungry."

"Thank you. I did not expect to see you today. You seemed so busy yesterday."

"I was." Though he had sat with his clerk, Patrick, considering legal documents much of the day, Margaret had never been far from his thoughts. He set the green gown on the bench. "Here, I found this for you."

"For me?" She looked up at him in surprise. "A pretty color."

It reminded him of her eyes. "It should fit better than Effie's clothing. This belonged to my sister, I think. Brechlinn was a family castle before it came to me, and there are chests of our old things here. You can have other garments if this one suits."

"Thank you." She gave a shy smile as she poured ale into a cup. "Will you have some?"

He shook his head. "Margaret—I owe you another apology. I did not mean to—the other morning—good God," he muttered, flustered. The heat of a blush filled his face. The girl had a damnable effect on him. Always had.

"I am the one should be sorry. That kiss was my idea, not yours."

"Oh, I was part of it."

"If you apologize, do so for keeping me here."

"Ah, the wildcat is back."

"The wildcat is impatient, desperate to act while you ponder." She scowled at him now, then sat to dip a spoon into the oats. She ate in silence for a moment.

"I will not act impulsively in this. It is too important. I discussed it with Lennox. We agree we need to act. I have been looking through some recent changes in the laws to see what rights I still have over sheriffs."

"Lilias is a hostage. And Andrew is missing."

"He is likely still in the forest wherever you were staying. We will find him. And if your feeling about Menteith is correct, we may have to negotiate to get her back. Remember that Bruce's women have been held for months. Give me a few days."

"And me? Your hostage here?"

"I am considering that too. Eat and change. I want to show you something."

"What, your gallows?"

"Margaret," he groaned.

"Wait there." She took up the gown and went to the bed, climbed up on the flat mattress, and tugged the curtain closed. He heard the bed creak and rustle, then she yanked the curtain open and stepped down.

He blinked. She was transformed. The gown skimmed over her lithe body, enhancing womanly curves and draping down over her scuffed leather boots. Her hair, spilling free in loose curls, gleamed like new bronze, and the gown's color reflected her forest-green eyes. She was a vision, even more so than the girl with wet curls in Effie's too-large gown, or the redhead he had glimpsed days ago.

Again, Margaret Keith took his breath away, stopped his thinking for a moment.

He glanced up and down her body, recalling the moments when she had felt so good in his arms. He wanted that closeness, those kisses with her; wanted all of her, but had cut it short for her sake and his. His pragmatic nature saw complications more easily than dreams; his manly urges saw no issue and needed restraint. But his heart saw only Margaret, the girl he had hurt and had missed. And he wanted her deeply.

For a few hours the other night, they had moved toward truth and acceptance. She had opened up to him in the impulsive and enchanting way he remembered in the girl, and found fascinating in the woman. But he had stopped himself, for it was not right to take her as if he had a claim. He did not.

He knew his faults and strengths, what he did well, where he went astray in most things. For years, he had known that he loved Margaret Keith, loved what he knew of her, loved the memory of her and what might have been. And he knew he had erred.

But he was not the most spontaneous fellow, changing on a quick urge. He took his time in things, serious and aloof, cautious and careful. Margaret was his near opposite—impulsive and quick, leaping before thinking, following her heart over her head. He thought before he leaped. But when he acted, it was decisive and certain.

But he wanted this spitfire lass with every part of his being and body, with a craving unlike he had ever felt.

"Well?" she said, turning in the green gown. "It does fit. Thank you."

He merely nodded. "I thought it might. Good. Now take up your cloak." He went to the door, gripping the latch a little too hard.

"We are going outside? Where?" She fetched her cloak, green with a plaid lining, a good cloak, he noticed. As she tied the cord that strung through the base of the hood, he noticed a gash in the wool.

"You tore your cloak. Is that how you lost your cloak pin?"

"They tore my cloak in the ambush. Menteith had my brooch and I want it back. And I would love some fresh air just now," she said as he held the door open for her.

The thought of her being manhandled in an ambush sent a stab of fiery anger through him. He was even more convinced that something must be done. But if he said so now, this lass would expect immediate action. When he moved, it would be deliberate and effective.

"I thought you might like to go out through a door instead of a window."

She twisted her mouth in silent reply and descended the steps ahead of him. The light scent of lavender wafted with her. He recalled that scent in her hair when they had kissed, the same scent of the soap when she had bathed. That sight came back to him unbidden, and he felt a tug of yearning.

Stop, he told himself. He was a justiciar, not a heartsick lover.

LIFTING HER FACE to the morning light, Margaret breathed in the bracing springtime air as she followed Duncan Campbell. He led her to a structure with wattle walls and a thatched roof, two stories tall with latticed windows. She looked at him in surprise.

"A mews? You keep birds here?"

"A few." He opened the door and she stepped inside.

As she entered, she heard the rustle of wings and the chime of tiny bells. Sunlight cast the shadows of the wooden lattice on tall windows. A raftered ceiling soared high overhead, giving the small building a spacious feeling.

A few birds sat on various perches, six or eight birds of various sizes, some hooded, some sleeping with heads tucked. Duncan touched her elbow. "Over here."

In a far corner, a large white bird perched on a stand made of slender tree limbs. A falcon, she saw; it stepped back and forth a little, bells chiming on jesses. Dark eyes beneath arrowed brows flashed the visitors a searing look.

Caught for a moment by that piercing avian gaze, she gasped. "A gyrfalcon?"

"Aye." Duncan had an expectant smile.

"Is she—oh, the same—"

"She is. This is Lady Greta."

"You kept her!" Margaret smiled up at him, feeling truly joyful in that moment.

"All this time."

"How old is she now?"

"Eleven, is my guess. They live thirteen or fourteen years in the wild, but in a mews with all their needs met, they easily live twenty years. She was a juvenile when we found her."

"Oh, Greta, you beauty," Margaret said, speaking softly. Greta fluttered her wings, her leather jesses looped to the perch.

Duncan reached into his belt pouch to pull out a bit of flesh meat from a wrapped packet. He offered it, and the bird scooped it quickly but casually, as if in dismissal and irritation with him.

"Greta is a little unhappy with me. I have been away."

"She missed you."

"Bran takes good care of her when I am gone. These birds are a bit lazy and like the convenience of being kept. When we take them out, they fly as long as they like, and always—well, usually—come back. They like the easy source of food, the shelter, the care in a mews."

"She looks very healthy. I do not remember her being so white."

"She was a juvenile when you saw her, with dull coloring for protection. A snowy gyrfalcon is a very valuable bird." He gave her a quick glance.

"I know." Memories flooded her. "You just fed her. Is she still upset with you?"

"Perhaps. Today I brought a friend."

Margaret blushed. "She does not like strangers?"

"They do not love them generally, but she seems calm with you. Perhaps she remembers you. She is very intelligent and might recognize your voice or your hair. The color would catch her attention."

She put a hand to her hair, wild and unplaited that day. "I thought you might have sent her to King Edward. I wondered if that happened after we—" She stopped.

"I never wanted to send her back, nor did my father. When I left to fulfill my knight service, he kept her at Innis Connell. And before I left, my brother Iain and I trapped the wild tiercel so she had a companion. Do you remember him?"

"The gray falcon. The male."

"Aye. We caught and trained him. Smoke, we call him. He is over there."

She glanced toward a smaller gray bird, asleep on his perch. "Could Edward lay claim to him as well? None but a king is permitted to keep gyrfalcons."

"So the English say. But that is not the case in Scotland. Earls and some others may keep them. My father was an earl, my brother is earl now. I am the son of an earl and so there is some right there. But no one in Scotland fusses about such things. King Robert has no court, and he has far more important matters on his mind. And no one can prove she was Edward's bird."

"I kept your promise, Duncan. I never told anyone, even when I thought you were dead."

"Thank you for that."

"But it is a risk for you to have her. Edward is so fierce about anything to do with the Scots. If he should find out—"

"It is a bit of a risk. But Brechlinn is remote. I brought her here three years ago, once I could spend more time in Scotland. Before that, she stayed at Innis Connell with Smoke and their growing brood. Some were born there, some here. My brothers have a few of their juveniles. We also keep Tay here—for Taibshe, ghost. And Banshee, his sister. She is young yet, but will be a white beauty like her mother."

"Where are they?" She turned. The mews had dark corners and niches, and places where sunbeams fell bright, transparent, full of motes.

"There and there. Tay is sleeping too. Lazy lad." He indicated a smaller bird, gray barred in darker gray, and a larger pale bird, both with the distinctive arrow-shaped brow of the other falcons.

"I am glad they are safe here."

"The risk is a bit more now that Menteith has land along the loch. Our lands meet to the east. He was granted the Lennox, confiscated from Malcolm when Edward outlawed him. So Lennox works for Bruce now. That," he added, "is confidential."

She smiled, glad of that sign of his trust. "Would Menteith see the birds if you fly them here?"

"It is possible. I am careful where I take them."

"Will you always keep her here, or take her to Innis Connell or perhaps Ireland?"

"Some travel with their hawks and falcons from place to place, but I do not find it good for the birds' wellbeing to move them often. This is their home now. It is familiar and the land suits their preferences—wide open spaces, with mountains, rocky heights, fields and forests, cool temperatures, a northern clime. They like the freedom here."

"I am glad you never sent her to Edward. He would not have cared about her. He would only see that a Scot had her."

"A Scot, a Campbell, a cousin to Bruce. That would have merited his anger. Well," he said, "I wanted you to see that she is safe."

"I always wondered. I even prayed for her safety."

He smiled, then went grim. "Margaret, can I trust you with this?"

"I gave you my promise years ago. She is our bird. Or at least, she was." She looked away.

"And can I trust you not to run again?" He tilted his head.

"Set a guard on me if you do not believe me." She watched Greta. "Now I know why you do not want to bring attention to Brechlinn. You need to protect these birds."

"I do."

"Would you take me out when you go hawking next? I have flown hawks at Kincraig for years. We had a busy mews when Papa was alive—peregrines and goshawks, merlins, kestrels. But never a gyrfalcon."

"We could go this afternoon. I have not had a good outing with the birds for a while."

"So you would trust me to leave the castle?" She smiled a little.

"With me, aye. I will talk to Bran, and Lennox may want to go with us too." He walked to the door. "So now you know one of my secrets."

"And I will keep it. Could I fly Greta?"

"Not yet. You should have one easier to handle at first."

"I like her name."

"Greta," he said, opening the door, "is a short form of Margaret."

She gave him a startled look as she stepped outside.

"Ah, Bran!" He strode out into the yard as if his words had not struck her, though she stood staring after him. He had named the bird for her?

Bran approached, an astonished look on his face, his gaze fixed on Margaret. One of the big gray hounds was with him; Mungo, she remembered. The hound, tall enough to tip his head on her shoulder, bumped against her hoping for a pat. She obliged. Bran continued to stare at her.

"Good morning, Bran," she said brightly.

"Good morning—er—"

"This is Lady Margaret Keith," Duncan said smoothly.

"Uh, greetings. She, uh—" Bran frowned, looked toward the gate, puzzled.

Duncan laughed. "You will remember her dressed as a lad, Bran."

He widened his eyes. "The archer lad?"

"The lady needed to hide from some who were looking for her."

"Sorry, my lady. I truly did not see it."

"It would be a useless disguise if everyone guessed easily." She smiled.

"I suppose! Duncan, what can I do for you and the lady this fine morning?"

"You are cheerful today."

"A lady is present, sir."

"Of course. Well. We will take some birds out later today. Have the horses ready, with one for yourself and Lennox too. We will go north a bit."

"We will need the ponies up there. The walking is tough. Can the lady ride or walk that far?"

"I will be fine," she said.

"Aye then. Sir, if you are looking for Lennox, he is in the kitchen eating the last of my oatcakes. I burned them badly this time, but he says he likes them. The dogs were needing me and I forgot they were on the griddle. The cakes, I mean. Not the dogs. My lady," Bran said with a clumsy bow, and walked away.

"He likes you. He does not like everyone," Duncan said. "You are kind to him. I appreciate it," he said briskly. "Later, then. I will find you a falconer's glove. Come up the stairs now, and back to your chamber." He walked backwards as he spoke.

"Will you draw the bar this time?"

"We shall see."

"Could I have a book or two from your library? I looked at the others there already."

"I will send some up for you." He led her into the keep and up the stairs. At her bedchamber door, she stepped inside and turned. "I believe there is a book of Arthur's tales if you like it. Though it is in French," he said.

"That will do. I will see you later." She smiled, tremulous. Hoping. Not certain that she could hope, unsure yet what he felt. His outer reserve contrasted to the inner passion he had shown her, spun her about. The other night he had responded to her vitally, passionately, and yet drew away. Perhaps she had been too impulsive, his closeness stirring her, his kindness misleading her.

Duncan Campbell kept himself to himself. Perhaps for him, this new peace between them was enough.

"I have matters to attend, cases and suchlike. I will see you later."

Ah. She smiled. "Thank you for showing me the birds. That was kind of you."

"I wanted you to know she was here, and safe." He opened the door and stood back as she entered. His smile was pensive as he shut the door.

A long moment passed. She did not hear the bar slip into place.

So, trust was offered. Perhaps she should not hope for more.

CHAPTER FOURTEEN

THEY HEADED NORTH out of Brechlinn and followed the course of a narrow river through a green glen where curving foothills stretched toward far mountains. Margaret looked about, savoring the sunlight, the wind, the freedom. The Highland air was fresh and wild, the clouds high overhead, and she felt content. What she had missed these days, she realized, was simply being outside—the air, the hills, the forest that always fed her spirit and gave her a sense that all was well, at least for the moment.

Bran had saddled four garron ponies, the short, heavy-set, shaggy Highland breed that was so surefooted on slopes and rocky ground. Secure on the garron's wide back, Margaret hooked her knee around the pommel of the sidesaddle Bran had thoughtfully provided, though she could have ridden a man's saddle if needed.

Duncan, Bran, and Lennox, all big men, looked a bit awkward on the ponies, she thought, their boots brushing grasses and bracken at times. Normally knights rode huge chargers or even larger destriers. But as Highlanders, they were perfectly at ease on the garrons. She knew they could not easily take larger horses through some parts of the Highlands, and she was grateful for her mount's gentle, intrepid character.

Duncan rode beside her while Bran and Lennox rode ahead, accompanied by the two large dogs, Mungo and Freya, that moved about freely, running off and coming back as they pleased.

"Your hounds are enormous," she said.

"Wolfhounds, aye. They need big spaces, indoors and out. They are happy here."

"And the birds, they are fine with the dogs?"

"They tolerate each other."

On her thick leather glove, she carried Aurelia, the peregrine falcon, compact and powerful, dark-feathered with a creamy breast. Her large dark eyes were striking, ringed in gold, hence her name; her fierce expression and flickering eyes seemed to see all. She was not hooded, as Duncan said she was well-behaved and would not pull at her jesses or launch away on her own. Duncan carried Greta hooded in red leather.

"How far will we go with the horses?" she asked. "You said we would walk with the birds in open spaces."

"We will. I want to take you north through Glen Falloch to the waterfall, not far ahead. Further north is the village of Crianlarich, and west of here, a quick route to the western Highlands and the Isles. East lie hills and moorland, with Stirling less than a day's ride. Either way is a good outing for hawks and falcons."

"Duncan should have told you," said Malcolm Lennox, slowing his garron, "that along the eastern side of the great loch below Brechlinn are my lands. I am lending the Lennox to Sir John for now, until it pleases me not to."

Duncan laughed. "A loan, is it?"

"I stomach it better that way until I have it back."

"Indeed, you must have it back soon forthwith," Margaret said.

"Duncan Dhu, I am a bit in love with your lady." The earl smiled at her.

"And Greta thanks you," Duncan retorted.

"Greta my love, none but you," Lennox replied, giving Margaret a wink as he urged his garron forward to join Bran again. Margaret smiled.

"Lennox makes you laugh," she observed. "He is a cheerful fellow."

"Another in his situation might be angry and resentful. Yet he can smile even so. He is a rare man and a rare friend."

He smiled too, his eyes twinkling, but soon the humor faded as he looked about, wary and alert. As serious as he could be, he was easygoing with his friends—and she had felt some of that with him the other night in her bedchamber.

She felt as if a taut and curious chain connected them, invisible but in place for years. It had always been there, even when she had believed he was gone, for he had stayed in her thoughts, her prayers, her dreams, an unforgettable soul. And as she grew from child to woman, he had grown in her imagination.

Glancing at him again, she saw the same handsome, virile man who had appeared in her dreams, with his crooked smile, a sleepy droop in his eyelids when he was thoughtful, a spark of wit in deep blue eyes. What she had imagined was true in the man. That was a marvel to her. How could that be?

He pointed ahead. "Do you hear that?"

She did—the rushing sound of water everywhere, so that she could not tell where it originated. The air was filled with texture, power, and moisture.

"A waterfall!"

"Just through those trees, but we must leave the ponies for a bit. Bran! Malcolm!" he called as they turned. "I want to show Lady Margaret the falls. Take the birds and go ahead to the moor by the river if you will. We will meet you soon."

Quickly they transferred the birds, Greta to Bran, Aurelia to Lennox, both wearing heavy falconer's gloves. They had birds too, carried on a fifth horse in a wicker cage. The birds cheeped, restless, wings fluttering.

"They are anxious to fly," Bran said.

"Let them go if you like. We will be along shortly," Duncan said as the two men left, their garrons proceeding steadily over a rocky incline.

"We can leave the garrons here and walk toward the falls," Duncan told Margaret, dismounting to help her from her seat. She walked with him along an earthen path that cut through a woodland of oak and birch that merged with a rocky gorge. The river cut through, fast and frothy, dipping and cascading. Ahead, Margaret saw a long white trail of water.

"Come look," Duncan said, offering his hand when the way grew steep. He helped her balance on the slick stones of the rugged gorge above the fast, narrow river.

The falls roared now, white and spectacular, surrounded by trees, the water thundering into a wide pool filled with eddies and whirlpools, growing calmer near its banks.

"It's beautiful!" she said, raising her voice as he leaned to hear her.

"The Falls of Falloch. Part of the river that flows south to join Loch Lomond just above Brechlin." He too raised his voice. "The birds like it here," he went on. "Sometimes we release them near the falls. They fly over the hills, all around, and come back. They know we will be here waiting for them."

He took her hand again to guide her closer to the falls. She felt the spray on her face and hair, her gown blowing back against her legs. The immense thunder and beauty of the waterfall seemed to dominate all around it.

"It feels so cleansing," she said. "In the air. In the spirit."

"It does. Come this way." He led her down the rocky slope to the edge of the pool, where the sound faded a bit and the water was calmer.

"There is a legend about this place," he said. "They say the faery ilk have always inhabited this place, and that their magic infuses the water and the stones and trees all around here."

"What a lovely thought," Margaret said.

"If you look around the pool, you might find small stones with holes in them. Faery magic formed the holes, so they say. If you look through the holes, you might see the future."

"Seeing-stones." She stared up at him in surprise. Her great-grandfather had such stones and had gifted a special one to her—the very brooch Menteith had offered as a prize and Duncan had refused. She wanted that brooch back, though its importance paled in comparison to rescuing Lilias and finding Andrew.

"Seeing-stones, aye. I find it hard to believe in such things. I have also heard that a stone with a hole in it has been beaten with water for ages longer than we can know. The relentless flow makes more sense than faery stones."

"I believe in them."

"I am not surprised. There are whole crops of them here. Look around." He washed the toe of his boot back and forth, then stooped to dip his hand into the water and brought up two or three in the palm of his hand. "Just here."

"What lovely faery stones!" She took one of them. "My great-grandfather had some of them. He said they were magical things."

"Thomas the Rhymer ought to know." He sounded amused. "We played by the falls as lads and would try to tell the future with such stones. We played at being Thomas the Rhymer, truth be told." He grinned.

She laughed. "He called them seeing-stones and truth stones and he showed us how to use them. I did not have much success with it. Though now and then I saw something unusual." She did not say more, sensing his skepticism.

He brought one of the stones to his left eye. "I just see water and rocks."

"Wait a bit. You might see the future."

He chuckled. "Seeing the future would be useful. I hear King Edward has a passion for gathering prophets and seers and astrologers and such so he can know the future."

"He only wants to hear that he will succeed."

"True. Go on, take a look. You have been taught by the master of such things."

She raised one of the small stones to her eye. "Grandda had some beautiful seeing-stones. He gave me one," she ventured.

"Did he?"

She drew a breath. "The brooch. The cloak pin that I lost."

"The one that was taken from you?" He stared at her, tilting his head.

"The one you did not take when Menteith offered it."

"You had just shot the man," he reminded her. "The brooch did not seem important at the time. I swear, lass, I would have given it to you had I known." He gave her a rueful smile. "Did the faery queen give it to your grandfather?"

"So he said. And he always told the truth. Always," she added firmly.

"True Thomas, aye. There are stories that he met the faery queen and went with her into that realm for a few years, then came back with a gift of prophecy and truth-telling."

"Seven years, they say, though he said it seemed like three or less. From the day he returned, he made predictions, and sometimes used seeing-stones to show him what was otherwise unknown." She sighed, thinking of the blue and silver brooch, Thomas's truth stone.

Impatience swamped her then. Lilias was somewhere, and Andrew, and the brooch too—and yet she was here with Duncan Campbell. The power of that had a strong pull, but she must not let it overtake what was most important.

He looked at her, tipping his head. "What is it, lady? If I could give you the cloak pin now, I would. If I could bring Lady Lilias back to you, I would."

"Would you?"

He nodded. "We will find her. And Andrew. And your pin."

It was as if he had read her thoughts, clear as the water at their feet. She nodded too, flooded with relief. He was beginning to believe her. She crouched beside the pool and waggled her fingers in water that was translucent, refreshing, and cold. She reached down to sift through sand and pebbles, tipping forward a little.

"Careful. It is slippery," Duncan said.

Scooping her hand through the water, Margaret brought her hand up and opened her palm. A stone with a hole lay in it. Standing, whirling to show him, she slipped on wet shale and one foot plunked into the water.

He was there, pulling her toward him even as she felt the tug of the current that drove the water over the falls and around the pool. His arm came about her shoulders to steady her. She shook her foot, the boot wet.

"Did you find a faery stone?"

She showed him the pale little stone, crudely pitted, its hole a perfect circle. She held it up to her eye. "I see the pool, the waterfall, the trees. I see…Bran and Lennox wondering if we are ever coming back."

"That is the truth," he said wryly.

"I see—" She stopped. Someone moved in the distance along a hill. A dark-haired girl, just a slight form in a cloak. She lowered the stone.

Just water, the falls, the trees. Frowning, she put the stone to her eye again.

"Something interesting?"

She lowered the stone. "I thought I saw—but it was just water and trees. We should find the others so we can fly the birds."

"I agree." He led her off the slick shale platform and back to the path where they had left the garrons.

"If I keep the stones we found," she said, "do you think the faery ilk would mind?"

"True Thomas's great-granddaughter? How could they object? And I am laird of Brechlinn lands, which include the falls and the pool. The stones are yours, my lady."

"Perhaps the faery ilk will bring us good luck. If they exist. Either way, we could use some luck." His smile was so tender, so quick, that she wanted to pocket it.

She looked back at the roaring, rushing falls and the mist of water in the air. "There is a veil in places like this, they say. A veil to the faery realm through the water and mist. That is why the faery stones grant visions. Grandda said a hole in a stone is like a magical doorway to another realm where the future exists, and visions show us clear what will come."

"Interesting. So you believe such things exist?"

"I truly do."

"My mother had the Sight," he said. "She knew things that sometimes proved true. We listened, though we also humored her. I wish I had known about that magical doorway when I was a lad," he went on. "I would have amazed my brothers."

Taking it for a jest—his practical, earthly nature would not be easily convinced—she laughed. The lovely moment, warm as the clasp of a hand, had passed.

When they reached the ponies, he helped her into the saddle, his hands firm at her waist, his gaze catching hers and holding it. The silence in the instant was like a lure, and she leaned toward him. But he set her on her mount and turned to his.

She was learning, in these new days with Duncan Dhu Campbell, how he had changed from the young man she remembered and dreamed about. He was a seasoned knight, a warrior, a man of the law now. He had experienced harshness that could turn a man's heart to bitterness and secrets. He did have a secretive side, but she sensed no bitterness, no anger. Just the quiet determination of a man with a sober, thoughtful nature. Yet she sensed lightness in him too, genuine amusement, affection for his friends, his dogs, his birds, his rundown castle. And affection—or at least patience—for her.

Yet something troubled him. She wanted to ask but did not feel she should probe.

Once again the idealization, the love, she had held for him since she was young came flooding back. She could not reveal those feelings, for she could not discern how he felt about her. He might think her foolish. Certainly, he thought her an impulsive and impractical soul, insisting he act to find Lilias when he insisted on caution.

Perhaps he was wise in that, she thought. While her need for quick response caused her frustration, she had to admit that he knew Menteith and understood the law and the risks far better than she did.

They rode up the slope toward the moors that swept up into hills like a vast green hammock. The river sluiced and rolled through the sloping middle ground. There, Bran and Lennox stood by their ponies, gloves empty as they watched the sky.

CHAPTER FIFTEEN

SOMETHING HAD HAPPENED at the water's edge, when Margaret had peered through the hole in the stone. Duncan had seen her go pale, as if it was no jest, as if she saw a sight through that plain wee stone that made her uneasy.

He had an uneasy feeling himself this day; perhaps it was merely that edge he felt when the birds were out flying free, that small chance they could be seen even in this remote place no matter how careful he was. But he smiled at Margaret, masking his thoughts as they joined Bran and Lennox again. He dismounted and helped Margaret to the ground.

Shading her eyes, she watched the falcon and peregrine in flight. The wind blew back her skirts and cloak and whisked her bright hair. For a moment, he could only gaze at her.

"Greta caught two larks and a ptarmigan," Bran said. "Aurelia took down a couple of larks. I gave them one and put the rest in the pouch. Effie will make a good pie of them."

"So they have hunted and fed and are just enjoying the air," Lennox said. "You two were gone a while, hey. We thought you might have fallen in."

"Is it a good pool for swimming?" Margaret asked.

"A fine place for a plunge on a warm day," Lennox said.

"The current can be rough," Duncan said. "It is easy to get pulled under."

She looked up at the clouds. "Where did the birds go?"

"Aurelia went that way like a golden arrow. The gyr found a high perch over there." Lennox pointed toward a high crop of rocks on a hillside. "She will take off again if she sees something she wants. Or if she sees you, Duncan."

Walking away, Duncan strolled toward the hill where Greta's stony perch looked like a throne. Tall pines feathered along slopes where jagged rocks clustered and water poured down in rivulets. A primeval place. As often as he came this way, he still marveled at its wild beauty.

Hearing a *kak-kak-kak*, he saw Greta lift her wings and settle, able to see for miles from her chosen seat. He turned as Margaret joined him.

"She seems content up there," she remarked.

"Aye, looking over all her kingdom like a queen. If I raise my arm and glove, she will come to me, so I will not disturb her. Let her sit."

"How far can she see, do you think?"

"Likely she could see a hare running along that mountainside over there. If she wanted, she could catch it before it goes to ground. She is very fast, our girl." The words slipped out before he knew it.

She smiled bright as a sunbeam at that. "Aurelia is very fast, too. She went sailing past and vanished."

"Peregrines are said to be the fastest of the falcons. In all the world, there is nothing faster than a peregrine but lightning." He smiled, proud of his birds, glad to be out here in the open where they could be free. "This is a good place for them. Isolated," he said, indicating the hills, the sky.

"You love your birds. And this place."

"I do."

"And you love your castle, your kin, and your friends."

"Aye." He glanced at her, arching a brow. What was she was about with this?

"And you love the work you do."

"Most of it."

"Why do you do that work? Is it that you support the English king and his laws? Is it obligation or love for the law?"

"Does it matter?"

"It must to you."

"What about to you?"

"I am thinking you are a man of integrity, and so—I am beginning to understand why you have not acted to rescue the king's daughter."

"So I need not explain caution to one so impatient?" He smiled a little.

"I am trying, Duncan Dhu. But it is not easy. Look! Is that Aurelia?"

He saw the peregrine, very high now, hover and tip its wings back, then streamline in a fast dive, a flash of gold and gray that all but disappeared. "She went into a stoop. Must have seen a temptation beyond the hill. The lads are going there now. Shall we go see? How is your stomach for such things?"

"I will be fine." As she fell into step beside him, he spared a glance for Greta, who still watched sharp and serene on her high rock.

Beyond a swell in the moor, Duncan saw the peregrine mantling over her kill, plucking quickly. He put up a hand, and Margaret, Bran, and Lennox paused.

"Once she starts to feed, she will not take kindly if we try to remove it," Duncan said. "We will wait while she feasts."

After a moment, Bran walked up a hill, shaded his eyes, then turned to come back. "Knights," he said, pointing. "Riding this way from the glen to the east."

"Curious," Duncan said. "We had best learn their business. I do not want them to spot my lass."

"Me?" Margaret said.

"Greta," he said, and saw her brow twitch. "You too, daughter of Keiths, shooter of sheriffs."

Her cheeks went crimson. Lennox burst out laughing. "Seeing this lady," the earl said, "no one would mistake her for the archer lad. What became of him, by the way?"

"Shooter of sheriffs?" Bran asked, looking bewildered.

"Lady Margaret disguised herself," Duncan told Bran, "after a kerfuffle with Menteith at the archery butts."

"She shot that bastard? Good," Bran said.

"I did not mean to," Margaret said. "If those are Menteith's men, they may ask about it," Duncan said, just as the riders appeared at the crest of the hill. "They are coming this way."

With a glance for the rocky cliff where Greta had been resting, Duncan saw with relief that the bird had left her perch. He prayed she would remain out of sight for a while.

"Odd," Bran said. "Few riders come this way. The drover's track is a rough run through the mountains. These rogues look headed toward the river. Ah, see their shields? Yellow with black and white checks."

Lennox groaned. "Menteith."

"He rarely comes to Brechlinn or sends his men this way. And he is laid up with a bad foot," Duncan said. "Well, let us see what they want." He set out for the hill, casting a glance around for the gyrfalcon as he went.

Margaret caught up with him. "What about the falcons?"

"These men would not care about a peregrine. But a white gyr will raise questions. Luckily, she has flown off for now."

"If she reappears, I shall marvel to see a white bird. And so will you."

He nodded. His mind whirled with concerns, not just the gyrfalcon, but the new task for Bruce—the arrival of another renegade priest—and now this question of the king's missing daughter. Not least of all, he was concerned about the lass beside him, her welfare. Her place in his life.

"Watch your step. The hillside is rocky." He took her elbow on the incline.

"Rocky enough that the men will not come down the hill on those horses," she said, looking toward the riders paused at the top of the hill.

"They are on chargers, which says they did not intend to come this far. Something brought them here, but what?" He hoped they had not seen the gyrfalcon on one of her long sweeps across the sky.

"Hey! Sir!" one of the knights called, and began to descend on horseback.

Duncan lifted a hand, glad that Bran and Lennox kept a little distance with Margaret, staying close enough to guard. "Sir, what is your business?"

The man, in chainmail and a red surcoat, his horse wearing a short red caparison that covered the head and the barrel of the body to the knee, rode carefully down the hillside to a jutting platform of rock and turf. The other knights stayed on the ridge of the hill. Duncan noted that two wore Menteith's badge and one wore the red and gold surcoat of an English soldier.

A mixed group, Duncan thought, sent out by Menteith with something in mind.

"Duncan Campbell of Brechlinn! Is it you, sir?"

Duncan climbed closer, standing just below the rocky plat-form. For a moment, he wished he had worn chain mail, but was grateful for the simple protection of a leather hauberk over his tunic. He and his companions had not anticipated seeing others that day, and so neither he nor Bran or Lennox carried more than daggers.

"I am Campbell of Brechlinn," he answered.

"Justiciar in the north?"

"I have that title. And you?"

"Sir William de Soulis, knight of Liddesdale."

"I know the name, though we have not met." He knew the man's kinsmen and knew Sir William was heir to the lord of Liddesdale, who held his position in Scotland under King Edward. Though Scots by birth and right, the father and sons were loyal to the English. "I see that your men belong to Menteith and Edward. These are my lands. This glen is part of Brechlinn."

"We are just passing through on our way to Crianlarich."

This De Soulis was perhaps in his twenties, long legged and broad shouldered in chainmail and a red-and-white surcoat. His short dark beard elegantly defined strong features, and his eyes were deep brown under black brows. Duncan recognized the red-striped crest from his years in King Edward's service. The De Soulis family was prosperous and influential in the Scottish Borders and sided firmly with Edward, reaping advantages. Another De Soulis, Walter was his name, had been killed recently by rebels, so Duncan had heard.

"You are far from Liddesdale and the Borders, sir," he said.

"Currently I am installed at Roskie Castle, where Sir John Menteith resides at present."

"Ah." Duncan came closer. "How is his foot?"

"Recovering. He mentioned you were present when he was shot. He is better but still making a moan of it."

"I wish him a quick recovery."

"Fortunate to find you here, Campbell. Sir John asked me to stop at Brechlinn Castle on my way back from Crianlarich, but here you are. Very convenient."

"Apparently. What is the message?"

"He wants to know your progress with the boy arrested for shooting him at the archery butts. You are holding him at Brechlinn, I am told."

"I questioned the lad and decided to let him go. It was clearly an accident," he said, having no intention to bring Margaret to account for Menteith. "But I have questions for Menteith on another matter. I can call on him at Loch Roskie."

"I will tell him. But why would a justiciar handle such a simple incident as this so-called accident? I suspect Menteith will disagree with your finding."

"The deputy sheriff of Stirling was called away at the time. Tell me, why are you up here rather than in the Borders, Sir William?"

"Edward's lieutenant in Scotland assigned me to Menteith. I am being groomed for a sheriffdom. Menteith does well keeping order in the region."

"At times," Duncan allowed. "So it is an apprenticeship?"

"I would not call it that." De Soulis bristled. "Just observing and assisting. Currently we are searching for rebels. Constant work, for they are often about, elusive as the devil. Menteith is searching for some priests who escaped. You might have heard of them. He sent me out in his stead."

"I have seen no rebels hereabouts."

"As I said, they hide, sir." The knight gave a flat smile. "We have difficulty with them south of here. The Ettrick Forest especially. Rebels are everywhere, hiding and then striking out like cowards. Edward is adamant that we find every one of them."

Smug fellow, Duncan thought. Yet his mind raced. A search for rebel Scottish priests might lead to Brechlinn, where Duncan assisted those very men, hiding and then channeling them toward safety in the west. He felt a chill down his spine.

"If you think to find them in Crianlarich, there is little rebellious activity there. If you are headed that way, you are well off the road in this glen."

"We rode this way because I saw an interesting sight. A falcon trailing jesses. Where there are trained birds, there will be falconers, I thought, so curiosity brought me here with my men."

"We came out for a diversion. The lady wished to fly the peregrine. We were just heading back. I will not hold you up."

"I thought I saw a golden falcon. A peregrine for the lady. And what do you fly, sir?" De Soulis looked toward the lady, his glance keen. Margaret stood lower on the slope with Bran and Lennox. She had drawn the hood of her cloak high and had retreated behind Bran's bulk. Lennox also pulled up his hood and turned away, not wanting to be recognized near Lennox lands.

"Another hawk," Duncan replied.

"Here at the lady's whim, are you?" De Soulis peered again toward Margaret. "She looks familiar. Could it be—am I so fortunate? Is it Lady Margaret of Kincraig? My dear lady! Do come forward where I can see you."

Duncan took a step to block De Soulis's view. "How is she your concern?"

"I know Sir William," Margaret said, coming up the hillside. Duncan turned, then lifted a brow in question.

"Do you wish to speak with him?" he asked quietly.

"I should." She paused beside him and pushed back her hood. Uncovered, her braided hair was brilliant in the sunlight.

"Sir William, greetings," she said.

"Lady Margaret! It is you. What are you doing so far north of Kincraig?"

"I am with friends." Her sidelong glance at Duncan held a flicker of hesitation and a hint of a plea.

Puzzled, Duncan felt a protective surge go through him like lightning. "Lady Margaret," he told De Soulis, "is visiting Brechlinn. We—are betrothed."

De Soulis startled visibly, his horse sidestepping on the platform rock. "Betrothed? My lady, tell me that is not so!"

She stood silent. Then she nodded. "It is true."

"I wish you the best," De Soulis said. "Though I am heartbroken to hear it."

"Heartbroken? Truly?" She looked incredulous.

"Very disappointed. My lady, does your newest intended know about us?"

"Newest?" Duncan scowled. The smug tone made him want to yank the man off his horse.

"Sir William de Soulis was once my betrothed." Margaret lifted her chin.

"Ah," Duncan breathed. "That fellow." He paused to cool the fire erupting in him as he realized De Soulis must be the one who had refused her and kept her dowry lands.

"The lady is a beauty, a true prize, with a remarkable legacy in her family," De Soulis said. "And I hope she will consent to speak with me for a moment." He dismounted, sliding down to the ground in an agile drop. "My lady?"

She exhaled sharply, then sighed. Picking up the hems of gown and cloak, she walked up the incline to meet De Soulis as he moved toward her and offered his hand.

Duncan glanced toward Bran and Lennox, seeing Bran set his hand on his dagger while Lennox crossed his arms, scowling. Setting a foot higher on the incline, Duncan prepared to stride forward if she needed him as De Soulis led her away.

"Dear Margaret," he heard the man say, "you are looking well. I did not expect to see you again. I bless my luck this day," he went on. The wind picked up his voice, carrying it down the hill, snatching words away. Duncan heard more than he liked.

"Nor I you, sir," she said.

"I always held you in affection."

"Your actions did not show that."

Where was her temper? Duncan frowned. If he had betrayed her as De Soulis did, keeping her dowry lands, she would have railed at him next she saw him. Yet she sounded reasonable. Calm. Did she prefer this man? Something in his center spun, ached at the thought.

De Soulis was a handsome young knight, a favorite in Edward's circle, so Duncan had heard. The family had a powerful influence in the south. The man had charm, but it was not trustworthy charm. He felt sure of it. Again he wanted to tear the fellow away from her, and fisted his hand against it.

"My lady, you are even more beautiful than I remember. I often think on what happened and pray you understand. The refusal was my father's decision, not my own. I want you to know that." Taking her arm, he walked with her, stepping off the broad rock to the slope.

That gave him an excuse to keep hold of the lady, Duncan thought sourly. He took another step forward, watching intently, ready to move if she gave the slightest hint she wanted help.

"Not my doing, as I said. I pray you think the best of me—"

Duncan missed her answer, and could not hear what De Soulis said next as they strolled across the curve of the hill.

Margaret nodded, then shook her head. Duncan stood wary and poised to move. As she listened, she lifted her beautiful face to a cool breeze. He saw her expression soften, become more compassionate. What was she thinking?

He realized then his explanation of his actions the other night was not enough of an apology for the unhappiness he must have caused. His pride held him back from fully admitting his poor judgment as a young man.

He wanted her to believe in him again. To trust him again. But now, all he could do was stand and watch as she succumbed to De Soulis's charm and assurances.

CHAPTER SIXTEEN

"MY LADY, CAN you ever forgive me?"

Hearing the syrupy tone, Margaret forced a smile. The reason she had deigned to listen to De Soulis at all was the brooch he wore—a large circlet of worked silver with a beautiful blue stone, a translucent slice with a hole at its center crusted with tiny crystals. Thomas the Rhymer's brooch. His *clach na firin*, his truth stone.

Her brooch, pinned to this man's cloak.

From the corner of her eye, she saw Duncan take another step forward, and was grateful that he was so watchful, in case she needed quick interference. Turning, she walked with De Soulis to the rock platform where the man's horse stood.

"I am sorry," William de Soulis said. "I want your good faith again. I thought we were a worthy match—you and I, our families. Our interests."

"Interests?" She looked up.

"You are kin to the remarkable True Thomas. No doubt you learned something from him, perhaps even inherited his talents. I am deeply interested in such powers."

"I know nothing of such things. You know little of me, sir."

"I know you are a lady of caring and good family who can run a household and supervise the daily routine and needs of a busy castle—my father's property of Hermitage Castle will come to me one day. A fine fortress, though I mean to build it into a magnificent castle. I want you to be my helpmeet in that."

She stopped and looked up at him. "William," she said, "if you felt this way, why did you do what your father wanted and cancel the agreement?"

"He forced my hand. It suited his ambition, not mine. He suspected the Keiths were not as loyal to Edward as they should be. We cannot risk association with such. But I have seen my error, and have decided I will not marry unless I can be your husband." He lifted her hand to kiss a knuckle. She wanted to pull away. "One of the proud daughters of Keith of Kincraig, kin to the Marischal, kin to Thomas the Rhymer. Her hair of flame stole my heart and owns it still."

She almost curled her lip at that. Nearby, Duncan moved forward, looking stormy and disgusted. "Sir William, this is a surprising turnabout," she said sourly. She glanced at Duncan, let her eyes show a silent plea. She wanted to be done with De Soulis.

He understood. He set a foot on the rock and bounded up to stand beside her.

"Sir William, you are misguided, I fear," Duncan said. "The lady is already promised to me. Perhaps you misunderstand her situation."

"You! But look. I do not misunderstand her interest. The rosy cheeks, the sparkling eyes—"

"And the hair of flame that gives her a heinous temper?" Duncan cocked a brow.

"Sir Duncan and I were betrothed in childhood," Margaret said. "The marriage was delayed."

"That cannot be, since your father agreed on our betrothal."

"I was away for a few years," Duncan explained. Standing close to him, Margaret slipped her hand around his arm. He bent his elbow.

"Away, aye! Imprisoned! Now I recall. They said you died in Flanders fighting for the English. But you are alive and well, and back in the king's grace as a justiciar. Cleverly done, sir."

"I inherited my father's position and was granted king's approval. Let me clarify the lady's status again. She is betrothed to me."

"We are planning our wedding," she added as Duncan pressed her hand close inside his elbow. Her fingers warmed there and felt good. She exhaled, feeling an infusion of strength and calm beside him.

"As we know too well, betrothals are easily broken." De Soulis gave her a charming smile, a tilt of his handsome head. Then he sent Duncan a steely glance. "The lady knows my heart is still hers. What say you, my lady? Will you take the better offer?"

The man did not give up easily. She felt Duncan tense beside her.

"Sir," Duncan growled.

"Sir William," Margaret interrupted. "You made it clear you would not marry me, and never explained your reasoning. Yet now this sudden passion. Why?"

"I have been a tortured soul since that day. I planned to approach your brother to make amends. Finding you here is destiny."

"If only we could know our destinies," she retorted.

"Your great-grandfather had that ability. Perhaps you do as well." He smiled. It was flat. Calculating somehow.

"I will think about your request. Good day, sir. Duncan Dhu"—she used his affectionate name deliberately—"can we go now?"

Duncan nodded, curt and silent, nostrils flaring.

Just then Margaret heard a faint *ka-ka-kaaaa* in the distance. She prayed that the gyrfalcon would not suddenly sail overhead. She avoided looking up, not keen to direct the knight's attention toward the sky.

"Farewell then," De Soulis said. "I wait upon your will, my lady. You can find me with Sir John at Roskie." As he spoke, a burst of wind billowed the red cloak away from his shoulders, a fold of cloth at his throat lifting.

She had to ask now or lose the chance. "Sir, your brooch! Where did you get it?"

"This?" He shrugged. "Sir John gave it to me."

"It belongs to—Sir Duncan. Sir John was holding it for him."

"True," Duncan said. "I won the bauble in the archery contest when Menteith was injured. But in all the fuss, I did not claim my prize."

"It is more than a bauble," Margaret said. "I would very much like to have it."

"What I have is yours, my dear," Duncan murmured.

"If Sir John confirms that the brooch is yours, sir, it will be returned to you. For now, it keeps my cloak closed against the wind." De Soulis patted his shoulder.

Margaret drew a breath. "Sir—give me the brooch now in token of goodwill."

"She wants it that much?" He grinned. "Perhaps I shall keep it until she agrees to my suit."

"Give it to me now," she clipped out, "and you and Sir Duncan can both wait upon my will."

"The bauble means something to you. What is it?" De Soulis asked sharply.

"I lost my cloak pin. I like that one. Give it to me and prove your sincerity."

"What about his sincerity?" He jabbed a thumb toward Duncan.

"I gave the lady a peregrine," Duncan drawled.

Overhead, sensing motion, she glimpsed a pale winged shape disappearing into tall pines. Luckily De Soulis was busy glaring at Duncan and did not see the white bird.

Margaret did. "Quick, your answer, sir."

"Trade me your heart, lady, and this bauble is yours." His smile went flat. "If your answer saddens me, I will keep it as a reminder of you."

She raised her chin higher. "That pretty brooch might help

my heart decide."

DUNCAN WAS PROUD of her pluck. And he wanted to bury his fist in De Soulis's gut. Watching, keeping his hand fisted by his side, he saw a flash of anger, then cunning, cross the knight's face. The man leaned down from his saddle and beckoned to Margaret. She dropped her hand from Duncan's arm to approach as De Soulis spoke to her quietly, pointing at the brooch. Duncan could not hear his words, but he saw the effect on the girl.

She went pale and stepped back. Fury rushed through him and he moved forward, but De Soulis turned his horse's rump then and headed up the hill.

Margaret grabbed Duncan's arm to detain him as he moved forward, determined to haul the man down from his horse and reckon with him. She pointed upward.

He looked up to see Greta slip past a frothy cloud like a spark of sunlight and vanish again. On the hill, De Soulis paused his horse and looked up.

"What was that?"

"Just the peregrine." Margaret slipped her hand into the crook of Duncan's arm again. That simple touch was calming enough that he drew a ragged breath.

"It looked like a gyrfalcon! Large, white—Campbell, have you seen them around?"

"Occasionally," he said, trying to maintain a veneer for the lady's sake. "They are wild in the northern regions and sometimes cross over to Scotland from Norway or farther north."

"It was the peregrine," Margaret said.

"That was bigger than a peregrine and white as an angel," De Soulis said. "White gyrfalcons are the most valuable birds. If there is one around here, it must be caught."

"That looked like the peregrine to me," Duncan said casually. Margaret nodded.

De Soulis searched the sky. "What a feather in my cap to catch such a bird!" He laughed at his pun. "Well, I will leave you.

Delightful to see you, Lady Margaret. I eagerly await your reply. Then this pretty gewgaw will be yours." He patted the brooch. "Campbell, watch for gyrfalcons. Catch one and you can earn favor with Edward."

"I have all the favor I want." He pressed Margaret's hand close to his side.

"Beware that lass, sir. She is an enchantress. A faery changeling who could change a man's luck."

Wanting to wipe the smug smile from that handsome face, Duncan merely shrugged. "We shall see whose luck she changes."

The answering laugh was false and hollow as De Soulis led his horse up the slope where his companions waited at the top of the ridge.

Helping Margaret step down from the jutting platform, Duncan guided her away swiftly, his thoughts fuming. When she stumbled, he slowed for her, feeling petty about De Soulis but determined to master his temper. And his jealousy, aye.

He had not met William De Soulis until now, but knew the young Scottish knight and his kinsmen catered to Edward. That sent an uneasy crawl along his neck. The fellow was conniving; Duncan only hoped Margaret saw past the false charm. Surely De Soulis intended more than reclaiming her as his bride, but what the man's real motive was, he could not guess. Perhaps it lay in her family connections.

Then he wondered if the girl's kinship with Thomas the Rhymer fueled the knight's apparent change of heart. He was in Edward's pocket, after all, and the king had an unsavory interest in the Keith ties to True Thomas.

Duncan saw two clear risks from De Soulis: the man was too curious about the white gyrfalcon and far too interested in Margaret Keith. Either or both could mean trouble indeed.

But the knight's offer was Margaret's matter to decide. No matter what Duncan thought, what he dreaded or wanted, he would wait on her will—at least for now.

He had dull charm, he knew, compared to a knight used to

pride of place in a royal court; his gruff reserve, close-guarded secrets, and simple life in a half-ruined castle must look poor indeed. If the lass chose to walk away from Campbell of Brechlinn, he could hardly blame her.

But she was with him now, and he would make sure she was protected, and that the trouble that had brought her to the Highlands was resolved somehow. It was the least he could do to make up for the trouble he had caused her long ago.

Seeing Bran and Lennox, he waved. "We must fetch down the birds and get back quickly," he called.

"Let me make sure those fellows are gone." Bran ran up the incline.

"Lady Margaret," Duncan said, "raise your glove. Aurelia will see you and come back." She stepped away to lift her gloved hand and waited.

Within moments, the peregrine came floating, swift and golden, to flutter to the glove. Duncan produced a small hood from his belt pouch and slipped it over the bird's head.

"All clear," Bran said as he returned. "They are heading north along the track."

Duncan nodded, raising his gloved hand. He did not see Greta, and turned, searching, praying she had not been sighted by the knights on the road. "You lot go ahead," he said. "I will wait for her and follow."

"I will stay," Margaret said. "She is our bird."

He gave her a grateful smile. She was so beautiful, earnest, so vivid. He had been a young fool to let her go. The encounter with De Soulis reminded him that he could lose her before he had even tried to win her back.

He, too, had a question for Margaret Keith. The need to ask spun in his core; uncertainty spun there too. He knew he had hurt her deeply. But even more than her forgiveness, perhaps he needed to forgive himself, though such thoughts were new, foreign to him. What did she want, what did he want? The answer seemed clearer than ever. He wanted Margaret Keith to stay; wanted her in his life, his bed, his heart, desired her more with each glance, each moment. But something held him in place. Fear she would refuse, tit for tat. Fear of losing her for trying—or never trying.

"Look!" Margaret called, pointing. "Greta! Greta, love!"

Then she was there, his other love, streaming like a ray of light through the glen. Wings spread, she angled down and settled on his raised glove like a cloud, ethereal, magical. He hooded her quickly, rewarded her with a bit of food torn from a scrap in his belt pouch.

Margaret leaned close, cooing to the bird. Then she smiled at him.

Our bird. The thought of it sent a warm thrill through him, as if they were a family, bonded long ago and reunited, with no loss, no hurt. He wished it was so.

She walked beside him with their friends, toward home. For a moment he felt the urge to stop, let the others go ahead, take the girl in his arms and kiss her, linger with her in peace.

But she hurried ahead and he strode after, the hooded falcon riding his glove, the peregrine on hers. Glancing around, alert and wary, he watched for horsemen on a hillside, travelers, shepherds, any who might see them.

The snowy gyrfalcon could be seen from afar, and the bright-haired beauty beside him was all too noticeable as well. Both were beyond value to him. Keenly, desperately, he needed to hasten them home.

CHAPTER SEVENTEEN

THE DOOR OF her bedchamber showed an edge of light; the drawbar was up, the latch loose. Duncan had ushered her into the room and left without shutting the door.

Was she free to go this time? Within limits, she thought. Surely Duncan knew she needed his help as a justiciar, as a laird, as a warrior. What he did not realize is how much she needed Duncan Dhu, just him; she knew it in her heart now.

But she was tired, she told herself, and would rather rest than wander out. Rest and think, for her mind and feelings were in a tumble. The day had been exciting, exhilarating, and frightening as well. The meeting with De Soulis troubled her; and being near Duncan whirled her about, distracted her, drew her in—yet he had that protective wall around him. She would not try to breach it. A decade later, he was who he was; she wanted to know that man. Though she could not guess his feelings, she was more and more sure of hers.

For years, she had imagined herself in love with him in the way of dreams; what could have been, the handsome knight on a white charger, the saintly warrior. She had thought that was love.

Her feelings for him were changing rapidly, deepening, re-forming, tumbling like a fast river with craving, yearning, wondering. Before he had reappeared, she cherished a pure and unrealized love for the young knight who had hurt her but had nobly perished. That love, she realized now, was pallid compared to what she had begun to feel.

The shock and confusion of seeing him alive had confused her. Now past that, she felt compelled to be by his side, keenly aware of him when he was near, thinking of him when he was not; drawn to the deep timbre of his voice, the messages in his loch-blue gaze, the tenderness in his touch, and dear God, the fervor in his kiss. Quick and certain, she had fallen headlong into a heartfelt love—deep, fiery, and more consuming than she could ever have lent to the innocent ideal she had created.

William de Soulis was nothing compared to Duncan Campbell. The Lowland knight was shallow, bitter—and threatening. Yet De Soulis had Thomas's brooch—and he might be the very avenue that would lead to Lilias. She could not ignore that.

Her choices, her needs—Lilias and Andrew, the missing men, the missing truth stone—and the tug between her honed independent nature and this fast, hard craving for Duncan overwhelmed her. She needed to rest and not think for a bit.

She curled on the bed with a blanket, but her thoughts still spun. If Duncan accepted that the Rhymer's brooch proved that Menteith had taken Lilias, he would take swift action. She knew in every part of her being that he was a man of his word. But though she needed his help, she worried about the risk to him. De Soulis had seen Greta, and he was an untrustworthy soul. Duncan was not safe.

She would have to decide now between the two men if she wanted to find out what De Soulis knew. As for marriage—De Soulis had offered. Duncan had not. She had thought never to marry, but now she must choose one or the other—or refuse both.

She had been a small girl when she had given her silly, dreamy heart to black-haired Duncan Dhu, who had been just an embarrassed lad then. Later, when she was nine and he was a lanky, beautiful young man with eyes as blue as the heart of a peat fire, she had lost her young heart to his shy beauty, his quiet manners, his cheeks that stained pink with his thoughts. She knew that one day they would share a home, a castle, children, dogs, happiness. A few years later, he was the lovely shy knight who broke her heart.

The memories unsettled her. She stood, wandered about the room, sipped watered wine from a jug, glanced again at the door slightly ajar. She could walk out and leave Brechlinn. But she would stay. Duncan knew that.

On the table lay the stones that she and Duncan had found by the waterfall pool. Picking up each one, she examined them, and held one to her left eye.

She could see the window where the late afternoon sun spilled through glass roundels; there, the open door with a band of light filling the gap.

The light expanded, blurred. Something moved—a tall dark-haired man. She lowered the stone and blinked. No one was there. Peering again, she saw Duncan Campbell at the door. She lowered the stone. Just the door.

Going to the threshold, she looked out. No one was on the stairs. She raised the stone again, turned toward the window, and looked through the hole.

Tiny in the frame of the hole, a broad green field spread out in bright sun. She lowered the stone. Just the window. Lifting the stone again to look through its mystical little doorway, she saw the field again.

Then, men and horses came into view—hundreds of them. Thousands, into the distance. Lances against the sky, blood on steel, blood on the grass. A man on a horse, a brawny man, bronzed by the sun. A man in his prime with strength and power and resilience. *A king.* Words came into her mind. *A Bruce. A king. Scotland for the Scots.*

She gasped, then stepped back, lowered the stone. What was that?

Hand trembling, she set the stone on the table, went to the bed, and sat. Wrapping herself in the blanket, she closed her eyes to try to sort out what she had seen.

The stone had shown a vision, solid, frightening, and profound. *Set the stone to your eye, lass, and thee shall see what is not there*, Thomas had told her on a day, eight years ago, when he had promised the brooch and pendant would be hers. That had not been long before he died.

But this plain river stone was not the one enchanted by Thomas's faery ilk. The blue brooch stone was more powerful. She had to recover it. No one beyond Thomas's kin should have control of it. The pendant, too, was enchanted, so he had said.

She fell back on the bed with a groan, confused, stunned. She had always believed that her sisters had true gifts and she had very little. The vision was a revelation. A thrill, to be honest, yet she did not understand what it was, what she must do with it. But she would keep it to herself.

Stretching out on the bed, she curled in the plaid blanket that still smelled of Duncan slightly, wool oils mingled with the piney, smoky scent of the man. Finding the dip in the thin mattress where she had lain beside his warmth and strength and quietude, she wrapped herself up, and sooner than she knew, drifted off.

STARTLED OUT OF a forgotten dream, she sat up, surprised to find the room in shadow, the light grayed toward evening with no candles lit within. Shoving back her hair, she rose to duck behind a curtained corner to relieve herself in a chamber pot and splash her face and hands in a bowl of water set in a wall niche. As she emerged, braiding her hair, she heard a knock on the door.

"Lady Margaret?" Euphemia peered inside, then pushed the door open, a tray in her hands. "Are you awake, then?"

"I am. Oh, thank you—supper already? Is it so late?"

"Just soup with fresh ale and bannocks. I would have brought it sooner, but Duncan Campbell said he looked in not long ago and you were asleep."

"He came here? I did not know."

"He is leaving your door open now. Good! I did not like that. So you are free to go about the castle. Though if you left altogether, he might protest."

"He said nothing to me about it."

Effie rolled her eyes. "That is just his way. Keeps too much inside."

"I would leave, but—not yet." She felt a strong urge to find Lilias and Andrew, but knew she needed Duncan's help. Even when she had the frantic, mad idea to escape the tower and castle and take a boat down the loch, she had lacked a plan.

"He came up to see you, but for much of the afternoon he has been shut up in his library chamber working on documents. He travels around the region regularly for the justice courts, but spends much time reading cases and writing letters when he is here."

"A busy man." Margaret took a seat as Effie set out a bowl of soup with bannocks, cheese, a fresh jug of ale. "Will you join me?"

"I ate with my brother earlier, but thank you, my lady."

While Margaret ate, Effie spoke of the weather and the work around the castle. "Brechlinn Castle is in need of repair, you know."

"I noticed," Margaret said.

"He wants to make something fine of this place. When he first came here, the English had made sad work of the place. He hired workers and put his own back into helping them. But he was called away to Ireland, and the English came again and ruined what was done. Then they decided Brechlinn was too remote and lost interest. Now that Duncan is back, repairs have begun once more."

"The English might want men here to control the north end of Loch Lomond."

"With Menteith at the lower end, they seem to think the Highlanders at this end are not worth the bother. So Brechlinn is safe, as much as can be."

Margaret took another spoonful of soup. "This is excellent. You made this, not your brother." She chuckled.

"Certainly! With Bran in the kitchen, I cannot imagine what they eat every day. I come here often to help with the household, and with the—with guests in and out to see the laird."

Hearing the stumble, Margaret looked up. "Guests?"'

"Some come through here at times to see the laird. Legal matters and such."

"Ah." She nibbled on a bannock slathered in butter. "You know the laird well."

"We were childhood friends. Duncan and his family would stay here for weeks at a time in the summer. He and Bran were good friends. We all played together. Distant cousins, you see."

"No wonder he is fond of you and Bran."

"Aye. And good friends with my husband, years back. He is gone now." She looked away. "And he is good to my son, Owen. The boy is eleven, and wants to be a smith like his uncle in Crianlarich. Until he apprentices, Duncan gives him chores here, working in the stables, the mews, the house. Owen enjoys it."

"He is here?"

"Sometimes. You may have seen him helping here and there. His father died in a battle when Owen was small."

"I am so sorry. It happens far too often." Margaret shook her head sadly.

"Duncan makes sure we are fine. He will never ask anything in return. He is a good man. Quiet with it, and steady."

"I am not surprised." She sat back. "Thank you for supper."

"You found a stone with a hole in it?" Effie reached across the table to pick up one of the stones there. "At the falls today? It is said we can see what cannot be seen through such holes. The future and such. When we were bairns, we would find these by the pool and look through them." Effie rolled the stone in her hand, then held it to her eyes. "We invented grand stories. But I only see this plain little room."

Margaret picked up a similar stone. Tentatively she peered through it, relieved to see only the windows, wall, a bit of Effie's hair and kerchief. "Only what is here. My Grandda had such a stone, a pretty one. He was Thomas the Rhymer," she added shyly.

Effie gasped. "Your kinsman! How lovely."

"He was a lovely man, true. Gruff, but kind to us." She turned the stone in her hand. "I wanted to stay longer at the falls and the pool, but we were out with the birds. And then Sir William de Soulis rode by."

"I heard Duncan and Bran talking about it. Duncan Campbell was not impressed with the man, I saw that. We may never quite know what he is thinking, but he has a deep integrity. Depend on that." Effie gave her a long glance. "But you know that. Even with what happened years ago, you know him."

Margaret blushed. "The betrothal ended a decade ago. I am not sure I know him."

"My dear, anyone with an eye to see knows something is there. He has always cared for you."

"He has?"

She nodded. "I still see it. That quiet air in a man, that strength in his nature, can draw a woman in like a lodestone. Once you feel it, it never leaves you. Both of you care for each other."

Margaret listened in silence, frowning, sensing more.

"When that betrothal was broken, Duncan's father told my father, his cousin, 'That lad broke his own heart when he told that wee lass farewell. Broke hers too.'"

"Broke his own heart?"

"He despaired that Duncan might never marry. But then Duncan was captured and held and had no chance to even let his family know he was alive. It was years before his kin saw him again."

Margaret nodded. "Some of this I know."

"And in my bold way—Duncan may not like it but hang the lad for not being forthcoming with you—I thought you should know that he cares for you. I have been watching you both, and I just want to help. He is a thickhead." Effie leaned forward.

"Margaret. I must tell you something. Someone must tell you, for the man himself may never, and I want to kick him for it."

Margaret laughed softly. "What is that?"

"Duncan more than cares. He has always loved you, and does love you still. I am sure of it."

She caught her next breath. "Why do you think so?"

"Is he married? Has he found another since he returned to settle? He has not."

"He was never betrothed again," Margaret said, as if coming out of a fog, seeing it.

"Not a one. That lad broke his own heart, and it has never mended." She picked up another stone, fiddled with it in graceful fingers. "Broke yours too."

She tilted her chin as if to hide the truth. "We were very young."

"You never found another either."

Margaret gave a bittersweet smile. "This is no epic tale of destined love, no Saint George and his princess, no Arthur and Guinevere…" She shrugged. "Just a lad and a lass put together by their parents and perhaps not suited."

"It could be the opposite."

"My father made other arrangements for me when he thought Duncan had died. I refused each one, though Papa did not want to hear it. I did not want to marry, ever. Three more—two died."

"It is the way of things in a land as beleaguered as Scotland."

"The third one agreed, then refused after my father continued the arrangement. He changed his mind. That was William de Soulis."

"No wonder Duncan was disgusted with the man." Effie sat thoughtful. "Margaret—what if you could mend your hearts, what then?"

"We hardly know each other now." But oh, she thought. She loved him—she knew that now—and did not know, truly, what he thought or if there was real hope. Interest, perhaps, but his life was a mystery. And she had always thought her path would be to serve her family.

"There is magic there. I see it. Others do too. Bran and Lennox mentioned it. 'What was that lad thinking, to let that lass go?' Lennox said." Effie imitated his deep voice so well that Margaret gave a surprised chuckle.

"And Bran? He did not even know I was a girl!"

"He said 'If that lad is a lass, is she the one Duncan would have married if he'd kept his wits about him?'"

They both laughed outright. But Margaret sighed, turning the stone in her fingers, thinking, wanting to believe what Effie said, yet holding back.

"I am not sure about any of this," she finally said. "And I would not know what to do about it, if anything. I could not ask, not knowing how Duncan feels. Or how I feel."

"The hurt of it lingers still?"

She shrugged her shoulders, half nodded. "A little."

"See that?" Effie pointed toward the door. "He is not confining you now, so he has made a decision. Find out what it is. If you are free to go, then stay instead."

"I will. But there are matters I must see to, very soon. The welfare of others could depend on what I do."

"This missing friend? I have heard some of it. You care about her, and so you must do what you can to get her back to safety. Your heart is there. Your heart is also here though, yes? Then remain here as long as you can. You two have much to sort out."

"We would if he cares to sort it."

"He does. You are here because he wanted you safe."

"Or for his legal obligation."

Effie shook her head. "Two stubborn people seeing what is in front of them and still not seeing it. Both of you need sorting out. Duncan built such a wall around himself long ago that it would take King Edward's infernal Warwolf to break through it, that evil war machine. You might have to find a way to take down that wall. Duncan Dhu is the stubbornest of men, and perhaps the blindest. You may need to build one to get through to Duncan Dhu, the stubbornest of men. Though you are equally stubborn."

"Effie," Margaret said, smiling then, feeling affection warm through her, "you are a dear friend to your cousin. And to me."

"I like you a good deal, from the moment I saw you pretending to be a lad. And who did that fool? Only men!" She laughed. "I did not mean to trouble you with my opinion, but since Duncan might let you go again, I thought I must say something for good and all."

"Thank you."

Effie set the dishes on the tray. "I will take these to the kitchen. You are free to do what you like. But listen to your heart, my lady."

"I will try. Sometimes it is not as loud as my stubborn nature. Effie, if I have freedom here, I want to help you in the kitchen or elsewhere."

"Oh, I could not ask that of a lady! You are a guest and should not be chopping carrots and turnips with me. But if you want to visit the falcons, I think Duncan would like that. Or you could practice some archery," she added with a twinkle in her eye.

"He might object to that," Margaret said wryly. "Still, perhaps I will do that." She touched the crystal pendant at her throat.

"It is a pretty thing, that. I noticed it before. An arrowhead, a decorative one?'

Margaret smiled. "A gift from my great-grandfather."

"Then it will bring you good luck. If you want to practice archery, Sir Malcolm was oiling your bow just yesterday and added new arrows to the quiver. He remarked what a good bow it is. There arc straw targets in the yard if you want to use them."

"I would like that. I will look for him and ask for my bow."

"If you see Duncan out in the yard, remember what I said. He cares for you. I am sure of it." With a mischievous smile, Effie left the room, leaving the door wide open.

Margaret hesitated at the threshold, then stepped out, shut the door, and headed down the steps. Finding the great hall, she wandered through. Effie stood at the far end talking with servants, acting as a chatelaine for her cousin; Duncan was fortunate to have her here.

Walking past an open door, hearing male voices, she glanced inside as she passed. Duncan sat at a table looking at pages with his clerk.

As she passed, Duncan glanced up from the parchment in his hands to meet Margaret's eyes. His were piercing blue, the afternoon sun on his face. She paused, drawn in by that steady gaze. Then the clerk spoke and Duncan replied, looking away.

That instant felt motionless, timeless. The finespun strand deep within her gave an insistent tug. She walked past.

CHAPTER EIGHTEEN

H IS MIND FILLED with thoughts of a dozen orders and letters he was reviewing or writing, Duncan crossed the bailey looking for Lennox. Of all the decisions he had made lately, he had not drawn up a parchment for the lad accused by Menteith—nor would he. Just now, though, he wanted Lennox to look at some documents to lend some insight into Bruce's plans, as the man might know more than others about that.

Hearing Malcolm's voice, he glimpsed him at the far turn in the outer wall that backed up to forestland. In that section, a high wedge of stones sealed damage in the outer wall yet to be repaired. All in due time, Duncan thought as he approached.

Straw bales were set at the back wall for archery targets. Lennox stood gripping an upright longbow waiting for Margaret, who stood poised to release an arrow. Her long braid shone like rippled copper in the late sunlight. Duncan watched her draw back the bowstring and release. The arrow struck one of the bales, and Lennox called out approval. Her answering smile faded as she noticed Duncan. He felt a swirl of disappointment. He wanted that warm smile, too.

"She is a proper archer. Has not missed a shot yet," Lennox said, seeing him.

"That went too far left," Margaret said. "But I am glad to be outside with my bow again." She smiled at Duncan then, but it seemed tremulous.

He frowned slightly, wondering at her cool demeanor. Only two days ago they had taken the falcons out, had lingered at the waterfall—he would have stayed there forever with her—and then, unfortunately, they had met De Soulis. Later Duncan had left her door unbarred, making her freedom clear. He had thought that might please her.

But since seeing De Soulis, the lass had befuddled him further, even avoided him. Perhaps she was upset with De Soulis; perhaps she was upset with Duncan for not riding off in a fury to find Lilias—had he even known where to look, or how to achieve it legally and ultimately. Still, he was glad Margaret was finding ways to occupy her time with books, archery, and helping Effie here and there, which he had noticed gratefully.

She stood back. "Sir Malcolm, it is your shot."

"Hold. I need Lennox for a bit," Duncan said. "Sir, if you would, I require your opinion on some matters. Patrick has the documents in the library for you to study if you have time. I can stay with Lady Margaret," he added.

Lennox handed the longbow to Duncan. "Your turn then, Brechlinn. She might best you though. Later, my lady." He walked away.

"Are you my erstwhile guard, then?"

"Do you need one?" When she only stared at him, he shrugged. "I have work to finish, but some air will do us good before the sun drops for the evening." He raised the longbow and tugged the string. "The range of this bow is too long for those targets. The distance is better suited to your hunting bow."

"Lennox was shooting past the bales toward that postern door. But some of his shots went over the back wall." She indicated the old door, scarred with arrow shots, set in the wall. "His bowshot would catch English from here. Mine might catch a hare."

"Or a sheriff," he drawled as he took up a long arrow. He stretched the bowstring, balanced the arrow, sighted the old door.

"You still do not believe my shot was an accident."

"I still wonder what happened."

"I am a decent archer and I needed the prize. The arrow went askew. That is all."

He pulled back the string, paused, then shot. The arrow arced high and struck the wall above the door, clattering off the stone. "Your turn, my lady."

"Not bad," she said of his shot. "The brooch. I wanted it." She took up one of her arrows and stepped forward. She touched the pendant at her throat and set the bow.

"Do you always tap your necklace for luck before you shoot? It is a curious thing, that crystal you wear. Like a carved arrowhead."

"Grandda gave it to me, so it may bring some luck." She aimed and released. The arrow plunked into the center of the linen target.

"Very nice. Was that luck, a faery charm—or skill?"

"All three." She gave a reluctant smile. She was in a peculiar mood, and he wondered about it.

"Would you swear you did not intend to harm Menteith?"

"I wanted to find him, but it was not my intention to harm him." She touched the pendant again, fingers trembling. "I desperately hoped something would delay him so he would not take Lilias away if he had her. It was just luck the arrow went astray."

He nodded without reply, tipped the longbow, and released an arrow that curved high to sail over the wall. He turned and bowed almost comically, hoping for a smile.

"Too much strength," she remarked. "Now you will have to fetch the arrow. Sir Malcolm said we could send Effie's Owen out the gate to find the ones he lost."

"Come with me." He waved her ahead, and they walked across the bailey. Near the entrance gate, Bran stood talking with two Brechlinn men. Mungo, the larger of Duncan's wolfhounds, rested on the ground beside them and leaped up as Duncan approached. He ruffled the dog's head and patted the high shoulders, then gestured to Bran, who pulled the iron-studded oaken door open.

"We will be back soon. Lady Margaret, if you will. Come, Mungo!" Duncan waved the hound out ahead of them as he ushered Margaret through. Then he held up a hand, glancing this way and that to be sure it was safe before he motioned her out with him.

Overhead, the sky was going to lavender behind soft gray clouds. "We must hurry to catch the light if we want to find the arrows," Margaret said.

"Aye. Though twilight comes later now, with the days longer in May." He walked beside her, the rippling blue loch to one side, forestland to the other. They went toward the trees, crossing turf and hillocks as they followed the curtain wall toward clusters of oak and birch surrounded by ferns and a froth of tiny wildflowers, white and purple blooms. Just past the breach in the wall where stones filled the gap, Duncan walked into the trees, Margaret following. Mungo zigzagged through the grasses, nosing about.

"I do not see the arrow. It must have sailed into the trees," Margaret said.

"The woodland here catches plenty of arrows. Longer shafts from the larger bows sometimes go far into the trees. We do not always find them."

She skipped ahead, lifting her green skirt to walk through ferns and tiny blooms between saplings and older trees. The land rose and fell in low hillocks, a green and quiet forest touched by golden beams of afternoon sun. She went deeper into the trees, peering as she went.

"There—oh, just a stick. What color was the fletching?"

"Gray, I think." He turned. "This is not so easy. Usually a stable groom forages for the lost arrows."

"You do not have many servants here, soldiers either."

"I have requested more men. Here, Mungo," he called as the hound looked up from some distraction. "If he sees something interesting, he will run and we will be out here for a while."

"That would suit me. I love being in the forest best of all places."

He glanced at her, seeing the forest in her eyes, the green sparkle there, happiness pinking her cheeks. An answering glow warmed his heart. "Do you, now?"

"I do. I feel good here. It fills me somehow. It is so alive, so beautiful, so peaceful."

"Aye," he said, looking at her.

She walked on. "Will Edward send English here to add to your garrison?"

"I hope for more Scots," he said, skirting who might send them. "When enough are housed here, we will hire more servants."

"You need a cook soon and should give Effie MacArthur rooms in the castle."

He huffed and bent to rummage his hands through a patch of green ferns. "She would not live here. She has a cottage outside, in what was once a thriving village. Many left the glen after English burned some of the village once they had finished wrecking Brechlinn."

"You are rebuilding. Brechlinn will grow."

"True, but we cannot last long on Bran's cooking. Nor would I ask Euphemia to take on more, though she is willing to help."

"She has a good heart, your cousin," she commented, bending to search.

"She does, and has her own work to do as well. She weaves tartan cloth and makes a good penny in town markets."

"I did not know. How lovely! She has a son, she says."

"He is a good lad, but he does not want to be a weaver. He wants to forge steel."

"Aha!" She rose, arrow shaft in hand. "It went past this oak."

He took it. "You have a sharp eye, lass."

"And here!" She waded through ferny undergrowth and came up with another long arrow, fletched in gray feathers. Handing it to him with a look of glee, she turned to rummage further.

"Well done. Shall we head back? Mungo!" He whistled and saw the hound loping between the trees.

"Oh, Duncan, look!" When he turned back, Margaret Keith had stepped into a grove of oaks and birches, where bluebells spread in a haze of purple-blue far into the forest. The light was golden and violet here, gentling over the girl, her face, her hair, her eyes. He caught his breath at such beauty, wanting to say what he felt, yet not ready, unsure to define it or limit it in words. He saw her shiver and cross her arms.

"It is chilly, and you came out without a cloak. Come ahead."

"Not yet. We might find more arrows. I would stay here forever." She twirled around just where two birches formed an arch.

A memory went across his mind like a shooting star—lithe young Margaret in his father's courtyard, spinning, cloak swirling, bright curls spilling down her back, her face delicate and joyful. She had been innocent and full of dreams. He had spoiled that.

"You are like a forest sprite," he said gently.

"Go in if you want. I can stay with Mungo and look for arrows."

"Soon you would be chasing him over the hills. Unless your intention is just that, to run off and disappear."

"It did cross my mind."

"You are still in the custody of the justiciar. I would come after you."

"Then I will save you the trouble and stay." Under the canopy of greening branches, she spread her arms in the blur of the bluebell wood. "It is so peaceful here. It reminds me of the forest near Kincraig, which overlooks part of the northern span of the great forest of Ettrick and Selkirk. I always thought I would—" Shaking her head, she pointed. "Is that an arrow there?"

He looked. "Just a feather. You thought you would what?"

"You do not want to know." She moved ahead between trees, surging through bracken going green with spring, the shadows dimming her hair to reddish-brown.

"I do." Some urge, a twist in the center of his being, told him so.

She looked over her shoulder. "When I was very young, I wanted to be married in the forest, under the arches of the trees, like a magnificent cathedral. Grandda had predicted a forest wedding for me once."

"You mentioned it to me once." He studied the trees. "Thomas said your first betrothal would not come about, but you would be a forest bride. Something like that."

"You remembered."

"I did." Every moment of that day. Every word. "I recall you thought it a silly notion, a wedding in the forest."

She sighed. "I have learned more since then. My sister found some of his writings on scraps of parchment. He had written a verse about us. It starts, 'Three lasses, three ladies, three brides all,' with something about each of us. Part of the verse says, 'One shall loose an arrow in the heart of greenside.' I suppose that one is me."

"That prediction certainly came true." He laughed.

"But no mention of forest bride. Not all predictions come true. Even his." She met his gaze, then looked away quickly.

His heart surged with sudden compassion, seeing her disappointment. "You do not know that. Someday you will wed."

"It is not likely now. And not in a forest!" She laughed, though it was thin.

"Tell me," he said, for the question had been burning in him, "what did De Soulis want when he spoke to you before we left?"

"He wants me back. You do not." She spun to walk ahead, reaching up to shake a sapling, then bent to poke some bracken. She kept her back turned as she peered into a tangle of birch limbs and new leaves.

He followed. "I never said I did not want you."

"You made it clear years ago."

"Margaret—"

"I could decide to take his fair offer." She lifted her chin, slanted him a look.

"It is not a fair offer."

"It is an offer. Look!" This as she pulled an arrow shaft from ferny undergrowth. "I have an eye like a hawk, sir. You would have done well to keep me around."

Enough. He stepped forward, hardly thinking, plowing through the ferns toward her as if he could break the wall between him and his feelings. She had been his lost dream for so long, and now she was here—and he had yet to crack through the barrier around his heart. But her remark had touched off his guilt like a flame.

"Margaret."

"We should go," she said, back turned.

"Margaret!" He reached for her arm and spun her toward him, her skirts spiraling through the ferns. Her eyes widened in surprise when he snatched the arrow from her hand and threw it aside. He tossed his arrow down as well, and took her wrists in his hands to tug her close. She raised her forearms between her body and his.

"Margaret Keith, for love of God," he said low, furious—not with her, but himself—"what is it you want?"

"What do *you* want?" He felt the resistance in her. "Though perhaps you do not need to tell me again."

"Jesu, you are a vixen sometimes," he growled, and pulled her toward him. The desire that had lingered in him since the other night plunged through him, renewed, stronger. He tugged her so close that her breasts pressed against his woolen surcoat and tunic, against his hard-beating heart.

"What do I want? You," he said.

As her lips opened to reply, lush and ready, he kissed her. Setting his lips over hers fast and firm, he held her by the wrists, his chest hard against her full breasts, and tasted her mouth. Her lips responded and she gave a little moan. He felt her body arch closer, meeting him, pressing, drawing back. What he sought, she gave willingly, her lips opening, the small tip of her tongue meeting his. He let her wrists go and took her waist, pulling her tight against him, then slanted his face for another kiss. Her arms looped around his neck and he tilted her back as she arched, feeling as if he could not slake the thirst that pulsed through his body. The next kiss was her doing, breathless, tender, and deep. He let go of her small, taut waist and cupped her head in his hands. Kisses poured, one into the other. His heart was slamming within.

He pulled back, breathing hard, and tipped his head against hers. "Margaret."

"What," she whispered, "was that?"

"An offer." The words slipped past him. "My offer to you."

She stared at him. "Of what?"

"God's very bones, Margaret Keith, you do not forgive a man easily, do you?"

"I forgave you years ago. You never knew. Offer of what?"

Forgiven? Relief washed through him. He would say it, and so be it. "My heart."

Silent, she watched him, eyes green as the leaves surrounding her. "Truly?"

"Lass," he whispered, then sighed. He still cupped her face in his hands. "This is not easy."

"I know," she said in barely a whisper. Captured in his hands, she stood so close, her body pressed to his. He tipped his brow to hers again.

"We were young, lass. Now we are older. Wiser."

She poked him in the chest with a finger. "I want your heart. Not your guilt."

He huffed, nearly laughed. He wanted her so utterly, fully, in that moment that it nearly swamped him. Tilting her face slightly, he kissed her again, slowly this time, gently, then a deep savor. He felt her sink a little, make a soft moan. He slid a hand to her back to support her. Then he drew back a little.

"Does that," he murmured, "feel like guilt to you?"

"Not guilt," she breathed, her eyes closed. She angled her

head back, inviting more. He delved, and she raised her arms to his shoulders, drawing him as close as could be. Dipping, he kissed her again, and as she curved against him, he stepped forward and she went back. Then she was pulling him with her, moving a few steps further under the sturdy buttress of the tall oak just behind her, her back pressed to the broad trunk. Tall enough that leafy branches brushed over his hair, he tipped his head, nudged her nose, and traced his lips over her cheek.

"Here among the trees is more private," she whispered, angling her head as her lips met his.

What took him over then, kiss upon kiss, was a passion fed by an earthy, wild power he had never felt before—the luscious girl, her lips, her body; the oakwood, the wild scent of bluebells, and the green scent of leaves; her hands running along his shoulders, fingers sinking into his hair—all of it driving him onward, breathless and lost, seeking, kissing—his hands shaping her curves, fingers finding the lush swell of her breasts—her answering gasp, her next kiss welcoming more—

Mungo barking in the distance, woofing again.

This was madness. Drawing back, breath ragged, Duncan rested his brow on hers as he caught his breath and blinked, attempting to clear his thoughts. She moved her head to press her cheek to his. He realized she was up on her toes, arms looped around his neck; he held her firm in his hands, one on her hip, the other curved around her ribs, his thumb on her breast. He sucked in a breath.

"Jesu, lass." He lowered his hands, but she kept her arms around his neck. "I did not intend to—"

"Duncan Dhu," she whispered. "It is the forest. There is a sort of magic here."

"Magic in *you*." He kissed her forehead and stepped back.

"Wait." She still held him close, reaching up. "Now tell me what you want."

"Just you," he said.

"So I have a choice to make," she whispered.

"You do."

Sighing, she released him then, and he stepped back again, giving her room to come away from the sheltering oak. She looked up at the leafy green canopy, then stepped out from under the tree. Wading through bluebells and ferns, skirts trailing, she turned, framed by the green, white, silvery arch of birch trees behind her now. Winsome, faery-like, she gave him a whimsical smile.

"Well, I want that brooch," she mused.

"Ah. Is that all?" Seeing Mungo nosing through the undergrowth, he patted his thigh lightly to attract the dog, who quickened his pace. "What else do you want?"

"The key to the door where Lilias is kept."

"Fair enough. So do I. I rather thought that brooch was mine," he teased softly.

"You promised to give it to me."

"Did I?" He was distracted, heart thumping, thoughts whirling, body throbbing. He felt caught in a spell, almost a drunken state, and had to shake it off. "So you would let De Soulis court you for a brooch and a key?"

She gave a half-laugh. "I will let him *think* he is courting me."

"And you expect he will give you what you want?" He cocked a casual brow, though the question was weighted. He reached out as the hound came near and ruffled the gray head.

"Perhaps." She rustled a tree branch. "We should find the rest of those arrows."

"Forget the arrows, Margaret," he said quietly. "And if you need a brooch for your cloak, you can have your pick of mine. I have several. Take the entire jewelry casket if you like." He waved a hand.

She turned and he saw the hurt in her expression. "Duncan, what is it? Just moments ago, you—we—" She reached out in appeal.

He closed the few steps between them and took her hand. "It is just—you need never see De Soulis again, Margaret. You can have any brooch you want. And we will find Lilias without anything from him."

"But I have to see him. I must have that very pin."

"I know your great-grandfather gave it to you. But there may be another way."

"I must have it, and soon." She let go of his hand, rummaged in the ferns, came up with nothing. "I do not want much in life, Duncan. But I desperately want Lilias and the others safe soon. Very soon."

"That will happen."

"And I want my family safe in a land cursed with strife. I want you safe," she added, glancing over her shoulder. "And I need the Rhymer's blue stone in my keeping."

"I see." Frowning, he needed a little distance to regain his calm. His anger at De Soulis on her behalf muddled his thoughts. But this girl could send him reeling off balance like no other; over the years he had encountered women, certainly, but he had allowed none to breach his heart. Now, opening to her, he caught himself thinking on impulse, with his heart rather than his head. He was not used to that.

"Lilias will be safe. I promise. Lass, if I could give you whatever you want, I would. Your kin secure. A safe home. That bothersome brooch. You have your bow already, so you can shoot whomever you want."

"You are still standing." A smile quirked.

"Thank the saints."

"And I want Scotland free. I hope we agree on that. You do work for Edward." Another glance, this one uncertain.

"I want Scotland free too," he said quietly. "I only work for Edward when I must. I want you to understand that."

"Then tell me more about it." She turned full to him, eyes green, wide, cheeks pink, reddish-bronze hair mussed and lovely, sliding out of its braiding. Her beauty was simple, pure, constant. His body yearned. His heart ached for her.

"I will." He reached out to brush away a spiraled curl that

drifted over her brow. He wanted to kiss the troubled look from her eyes.

"Finding Lilias is by far the most important, and the missing men. We have lingered too long. And with them, the cloak pin."

"Aye. Tell me this. William de Soulis said something this morning that bothered you. I could not hear, but I saw its effect. I was about to throttle the man," he added.

"I suspected as much and pulled you away. He asked me if the brooch was mine. He wanted to know if it had belonged to my great-grandfather."

Something Lennox had said tapped at his memory. "Why would he ask that?"

"He must have learned about Thomas's stone somehow. But how would he guess that I might have something the Rhymer owned?"

"Your father. Inheritances are often discussed during betrothal negotiations. The groom is told what the bride will bring to the marriage. It could be that."

"Why guess the brooch was mine?"

"You were anxious about it, which caught his attention. He might have recalled that you inherited valuables from True Thomas." He saw her swift scowl. "And Menteith might know of the inheritance, too. Sheriffs are often made aware of important wills in case of disputes. Your Rhymer was a notable man."

"Could the knights who ambushed us have known too?"

"Possibly."

"Surely they wanted Lilias. But why me? For the brooch?"

"A daughter of Keith of Kincraig, and a valuable broach belonging to Thomas? Aye." The memory emerged. "The knowledge of it could have come directly from King Edward. Lennox told me that the king knew that your sister owned a particular book."

"Ah! And Menteith had the brooch, which also means he has Lilias."

"It is coming together." He turned to walk with her, the

hound between them. Margaret reached out to pat Mungo's shoulder.

"If you need proof, my siblings know that pin. My brother would recognize it."

"I need no more proof."

She stopped, her eyes bright with relief and hope. "Good. Now we will do this!"

He held up a cautioning hand. "A little more time. Constantine Murray promised the loan of more men. We do not have enough Brechlinn men to make an impression if we must confront Menteith."

"When you do that, I would ride with you."

"Margaret." He shook his head.

"I wish my brother were here. He would help. Do you know Henry?"

"I met him years ago. He was not keen to speak to me at the time, as I recall. He was very protective of you."

"He is still protective of me and my sisters. Lilias too, especially with Papa gone."

"At least we have some evidence about the escort incident now."

"I did try to tell you that all along."

"You did. I see that now."

"Surely Menteith and De Soulis, too, know something about Lilias. And the brooch," she added. "It is mine to protect, you see. The stones must never fall into the wrong hands. Grandda insisted on it."

He frowned. "Wrong hands?"

"Because of the enchantment. Listen now," she said, touching his arm. "The Rhymer's things must be kept by those who share his legacy and will honor it."

"The pendant you wear—was that his too, and under some faery spell?"

"So Thomas said. When the queen gave him the gift of truth-telling, she gave him a few treasures too, all with an enchantment."

"Your sisters and your brother as well?"

She nodded. "Tamsin was given pages of his notes and prophecies and such to create a book. Rowena has something of Grandda's too, a healing charm. I do not know much about it. She is very private about her healing work. Henry was given something too, but he has never said much about it."

"I see. Well, we are sorting through it now, my lass." He took her elbow as they stepped over a fallen log and neared the edge of the forest. The castle walls loomed, blocking the twilight so that the forest fell into deep shadow.

"Duncan—the other day when you told De Soulis we were betrothed—were you truly making an offer? Or did you say it to annoy him?"

"I did want to irritate the man," he admitted. "And I wanted to protect you."

"Am I considering two offers, or just his?"

He cocked a brow. "Would you give thought to his?"

"Should I?" She smiled a little.

"Consider mine alone." He spoke quickly, sincerely, surprising himself a bit.

She stared up at him. "I—will do that." She blushed—he saw it even in shadow—and turned to scan the ground. "Where did we put the arrows we found?"

A long, rich blast of sound caught his attention. Glancing through the trees toward the castle wall, he saw a soldier high on the battlement lifting a horn. The same pattern sounded, two long blasts, one short.

"Danger? Soldiers approaching?" Margaret asked, arrows in hand now.

"That signal means a boat is coming up the loch toward Brechlinn." He took her arm. "Hurry. Mungo, come!"

As the horn sounded again, he ran, Margaret beside him, the dog trotting ahead toward the gate.

CHAPTER NINETEEN

"WHO ARE THEY?" Margaret asked.

Duncan Campbell watched from the parapet where they stood, his arm pressed to her shoulder, his height an advantage as he leaned to look down the loch. "I have an idea who it may be now that they are closer."

Lifting on her toes, she leaned into the crenel space between the stone merlons. Far down the loch, she could see a birlinn, sails breezing out as it moved over dark glassy water that reflected a twilight sky sparkling with stars. By the time the boat reached the head of the loch, evening would be full on.

"How do you know they are coming here?" she asked.

"We are the only castle at this end of the loch. I can see helmets, armor."

"Could it be the soldiers you are expecting?"

"Perhaps, though there are not enough on board for that. I see just a few men and soldiers."

"Not Menteith," she guessed. "And he is in too much discomfort to travel."

"Unlikely to be him. Besides, he is at Loch Roskie now, east over the moor. I have not seen banners or colors yet, but I think I know who this might be. We will wait and see."

"It just makes me more concerned about Lady Lilias."

"It is unlikely this has aught to do with her, lass." He sighed. "I should tell you. I am expecting a few, ah, guests."

She looked up at him. "That does not make them sound like friends."

"Friendly, but I do not know them. Have you heard of the reports about some mischievous priests lately?"

Surprised, she nodded, remembering something her brother and others had mentioned at Kincraig. "The ones the English call naughty and irresponsible? They were arrested and punished. I heard something of it."

"I have been assisting them here and there. As a favor for Bruce."

"Oh! Oh, I see," she replied as it became clearer. "Remote Brechlinn, and you want no attention here. So it is something you must hide?"

"Or someone, until he can be moved. I need to trust you with this, aye?"

"Of course."

He set a hand on her shoulder, just an instant, a warm, sure grip that sent a delicious shiver through her. "We will soon know who it is. Bran MacArthur!" he called over his shoulder. Bran, standing on another section of the parapet watching the water turned. "Send four men to the quayside. I will join them soon. Then see what is in the larder to feed visitors."

"Sir!" Bran hastened down the steps.

"I can help." Margaret gathered her skirts. "I will go to the larder."

"You need not do that," he said.

She set a hand on her hip and faced him. "Duncan Campbell, you do not have enough help here. Either I check to see how you will feed your visitors, or I take up my bow and quiver and go down to the quay with the men. Otherwise I am useless here, another bowl, another bed."

His tipped brow showed her he noted the last word. He had a habit, she had seen, of angling one black brow high beneath a sweep of dark glossy hair, to convey doubt, disdain, amusement, or something else, adding a twist of his lips, a glint in his eyes. But just as quickly he would become inscrutable again.

"Food and a bed will always be here for you." Something sincere and tender warmed his eyes. She stared up at him, and wondered—almost afraid to think it—if her dreams could come true after so long.

In that moment, she only wanted to throw her arms around him and kiss him again. Bunching her skirts in one hand, she turned. "I—thank you. I will find the larder."

Down the steps, through the yard, she wandered into the kitchens. A quick question to a boy scrubbing pots sent her down wooden steps to the coolness of an earth-and-stone enclosure filled with shelves, where barrels and sacks held food. Barley, oats, onions, carrots, turnips, apples, a barrel of dried, seasoned meat—a small barrel of dried fish made her step back—though she knew others might like its pungency—and small casks of ale and *uisge beatha* sat on another shelf. She found three wheels of cheese in rough cloth sacks, and small jars of a few spices. While the shelves and containers held a modest variety of foods, quantities were low.

At the convent, despite being a less-than-ideal candidate, she had learned to cook and help in the kitchens. She had already learned something about directing a large household at Kincraig under her mother's tutelage, and later, with her sisters as they kept the castle for their widowed father. When her sisters were away, she had acted as chatelaine, supervising the household. She felt at home in the small Brechlinn kitchen.

Anyone could see that the larder would not produce a feast. But she had a mean hand for oatcakes, and the nuns at the convent had taught Margaret and young novices to prepare basic and satisfying meals with the simplest ingredients. This she could do. She needed to be useful to Duncan and those at Brechlinn. She rolled up her sleeves.

As she worked, she recalled the secret task Duncan had revealed, and knew why Sir Duncan Campbell, justiciar in the north and son of an earl, chose to live in modest circumstances with few men and few supplies. He did not want to bring attention to his castle—not just to protect the secret of the falcons he kept there, but also the work he did supporting those involved in defending the cause of Scotland. She smiled to herself as she peered into baskets of dried apples and cloth sacks of grain and nuts and more. Pride deepened by affection—aye, by love—filled her, knowing he trusted her with his carefully guarded secrets.

At the sound of footsteps, she turned to see Bran's tall bulk in the doorway. "My lady. You need not help."

"I am happy to do it. I think your sister and her son went home earlier."

"I sent a rider to fetch them back. What do you need?"

"Lift that sack of oats, if you will, and that small keg of butter and carry them to the worktable. And bring some salt, please. I can make oatcakes if you can light the griddle. Do we have bacon? Aye, good! I see apples saved from fall, and if there is honey and perhaps dried berries and walnuts, we shall have something good prepared."

"Thank you," Bran said. "I can burn the bacon with the best of them, but my oatcakes are like horseshoes."

She laughed, recognizing the truth. "By the time Effie arrives, the oatcakes will be coming off the griddle."

A soldier came to the door. "Bran, sir, Lennox wants you. They see who is on the way now. Sir Constantine Murray, sir, and others. Clergy and soldiers."

"Best make as many cakes as you can, my lady," Bran said.

EFFIE ARRIVED JUST as Margaret stacked a second batch of hot oatcakes on a platter and covered it with a cloth, then turned to mix melted butter into a bowl of ground oats, adding salt, a little water.

"Let me knead it," Effie said, taking the bowl. "What smells so good?"

"Chopped apples simmering in the kettle with honey, dried berries, butter. I found a little bit of precious cinnamon, and added some uisge beatha. It will stir up to a nice thickness. Also rashers of bacon over there on those griddles. Keeping the hounds out of the kitchen has been the real chore," Margaret laughed.

"I did not know you could cook or do such work, my lady," Effie said. "You offered, but I turned you down, thinking oh, she is just being kind."

"I learned a good deal of cooking and such in the convent," Margaret said.

"Convent! Were you educated there?"

"I was educated by nuns earlier, but later I spent more than three years in a convent recuperating from a serious illness. My mother was with me some of that time, but she did not survive the illness," she added low. "I stayed on for a while after that."

"Did you think to become a religious? I cannot see it, to be honest."

"I thought about it, but it was not for me. I was there—after what happened with Duncan. I was not sure what I wanted then."

"I understand, I do. Look there, I brought fresh cream and butter. I could make a soup, but with all this, it is not needed tonight. You did well. I had roasted the ptarmigan and other birds from the hawking day, and I can make a stew of those tomorrow. Oh, Duncan asked me to send you up to the hall. He mentioned it when I arrived, but I all but forgot."

"Now?"

"Aye, go on. I can see to the rest of this. They are in the great hall."

Wiping her hands on a cloth, Margaret ran for the steps, wondering why Duncan would ask for her. Sir Constantine was a sheriff's deputy, but why would he come to Brechlinn now? A thought struck her like a blow. Had the Stirlingshire sheriff sent Sir Constantine with charges for her—for the young archer in Duncan's custody? Could he do that even if the justiciar had decided not to pursue charges?

Worried, she went up the steps, down a corridor, and along

another to near the hall. Pausing, she pushed open the door. Her breath came fast, a twist of uncertainty.

The great hall was large and dim, though flickering flames in the central fire basket added light. The warm glow reflected on walls hung with shields and swords, touched tall shuttered windows and ceiling rafters, brightened the rushes on the planked floor. A scarred trestle table held ceramic jugs, cups of Venetian glass glittering with dark wine, and a scattering of parchment pages. A tiny mouse scurried by with a bit of cheese. Skirting it, she went forward.

Duncan stood with others by the table. He glanced up and beckoned her to his side even as he spoke with others. Beside him was Sir Constantine—she remembered the tall man with honey-colored hair who had been with Duncan at the ayre court. He smiled to acknowledge her. Yet the last time he had seen her, she had been dressed as a lad. Knowing he was a good friend of Duncan and Lennox, she wondered if they had already told him who that lad truly was, and that she was still at Brechlinn.

Beside Murray stood Lennox. She did not recognize the others—four knights in chainmail who murmured together, looking at elaborate maps opened up on the table. Perhaps these were men who served Constantine and the sheriffdom. Then she noticed two clergymen standing with Malcolm Lennox. One was a monk in drab brown with a shaved tonsure, who handed papers to the other cleric.

He was an older man with a silvery tonsure, wearing a dark robe cinched with a rope belt that was studded with gleaming stones above tassels. A dark capelet draped over his shoulders and a silver cross on a long chain distinguished him from the simple monk in order and status. A bishop, she thought.

She was especially surprised to be summoned to this company. A bishop visiting Brechlinn was a true puzzle. Could he be one of the irresponsible priests? That thought astonished her.

A few others stood in the shadows away from the table. Someone slipped between the soldiers to reach toward the table and grab a goblet of wine. Duncan reached out to neatly remove the cup from that hand with an amused look. Then Margaret noticed the lanky boy whose blond curls gleamed in the amber firelight. She gasped. He looked up.

"Meg!" Andrew Murray called, and ran toward her.

DUNCAN CRADLED A goblet of wine in his hands and watched the others, glad for a chance to sit back, listen, observe. Maps and documents had been set away, and now the platters and bowls of food were nearly empty after all had enjoyed thick bacon, buttery oatcakes, cheeses, and a tasty dish of spiced apples. Learning that Lady Margaret had done much of the cooking, he smiled, proud, pleased, not surprised at all that she had such abilities. He glanced toward her again.

Across the table, she sat with Andrew Murray, heads together as they murmured. They had been glad and relieved to find one another, and Margaret had been astonished to learn that Sir Constantine Murray was Andrew's uncle.

Duncan leaned toward Con Murray now. "How did you come across your nephew after we left?"

"He had been in the forest all along, where he and the archer—your Lady Margaret—had made a small camp. We combed the forest looking for the lad. He was clever and elusive, but at last we found him in a downpour, hungry and tired. He refused to talk about his archer friend, but I had heard from Lennox by then, so I told him that I knew who she was and suspected who he was. He knew I was his uncle then, though he does not remember me. I have not seen the lad since he was small. He strongly resembles his father—he has his eyes and his mop of hair."

"He is surely glad to be among kin now." Duncan turned to the bishop seated to his other side. David Murray, Bishop of Moray, was Constantine's uncle, and so great-uncle to young Andrew.

"Fortuitous," the bishop agreed. "I rode to meet Constantine once I had a message from Bruce to seek sanctuary at Brechlinn Castle. When Constantine told me about Bruce's missing daughter, it was a blessing to find young Andrew safe. Now seeing that Lady Margaret Keith is safe with you as well, I will sleep better than I have lately."

"All is well for now," Duncan said. "But we must decide how best to bring Bruce's daughter here too."

Constantine nodded. "Andrew is determined to avenge Lilias. I shall have to hold him back. And he is very protective of Lady Margaret as well. The pair of them have been through an ordeal together." He nodded toward Margaret and Andrew, still quietly talking. "My reverend uncle agreed it was best to bring Andrew here too."

Duncan nodded. He wanted Brechlinn Castle to provide safety for all of them. Yet the problem of the missing Bruce girl bothered him more deeply each day. Like Margaret, he was anxious to act.

And there was the matter of the ill-behaved clergyman as well. The Bishop of Moray had been outspoken in addressing crowds of Scots to convince them to stand against the English and lend their loyalty, their weaponry, and their fighting strength as needed toward Bruce and Scotland.

"Reverend Father," he said to the bishop, "we will make a plan to move you to safety."

"All I need, Sir Duncan, is to stay clear of the English. They would have my head for speaking out against their king."

"Aye, we heard that a certain outspoken bishop went about addressing gatherings of Scots, at first talking about the King of Heaven and then the King of Scots, and how that earthly king needs full support to save our homeland. Bold and admirable, Reverend Father. That took courage."

"A heart full of righteous anger, sir. Perhaps a touch of madness too." The bishop smiled. "And bless Robert Bruce for giving me protection, a place to hide, and the promise of transport to the west. The English king is calling for my capture and execution."

He touched his collar.

"We will take care of you," Duncan said.

"I prayed for resolution, and here you are. Heaven sent." The bishop smiled. "But you must see to the more important matter of Bruce's missing child."

"About the escort that was attacked..." Constantine said, turning to Duncan. "Andrew is convinced the rogues were Menteith's men. He saw enough to know, I think."

"There is more proof. Lady Margaret and Andrew can help piece it together."

"We must act soon. Bruce knows of it and is greatly troubled. If Menteith does have his daughter, there will be hell to pay, unless we can get her back quickly."

"Lennox," Duncan said, motioning toward Malcolm a few seats away. "A few of us will meet in the library room. Lady Margaret, Andrew..." he added. "Come with us."

AT LAST, A plan was forming on behalf of Lilias. Margaret felt a lift of hope as she stood in the doorway of the library as the men pulled chairs around the stout table there. Certain now that Duncan and the rest had the girl's welfare, and that of the missing knights, in mind, she gave a sigh of relief. The help she needed was at last here, and gathering strength.

"Will you sit, my lady?" Duncan still stood. "Your voice is important here. Andrew, bring the lady a chair."

When the lad drew out a leather chair, she sat. "I am here to answer your questions. Though I know what I would do."

"Go after Menteith with bows and swords," Duncan said.

"Wherever he is, Lady Lilias will be there. He must be taken down."

"It may come to that, but taking down a sheriff is a predicament," Constantine said. "Best we determine where the girl is and get her back without direct attack."

"We will do whatever is necessary," Duncan said.

Margaret looked around the table at those gathered—

Duncan, Lennox, Constantine, the bishop, Bran. Two Brechlinn guards stood by as well, and Andrew sat apart by the window, where a cool breeze drifted through open shutters.

Bran went to a cupboard in the corner to pour ale from a jug into several wooden cups and hand them around. Margaret accepted a cup, as did Andrew, taking one eagerly, pleased to be included. Then Bran took the last seat at the table.

Margaret glanced around the room at shelves filled with leather-bound books secured by chains. The shelves held wooden boxes too; some open, filled with parchment rolls, flat sheets, pens, ink, wax, seals, more. Duncan conducted a good deal of his legal business here, she could see.

But as she glanced at him now, she saw his intense focus. The matter of Lilias was proven to him, and just as he had promised, he was moving swiftly to solve it.

"We can be sure that Menteith will have Bruce's daughter near him. He is likely still incapacitated from that arrowshot," Duncan said. "And I am grateful for that."

He did not look at her then, but if he had, he would have seen her little smile. He rose and went to one of the boxes, removed a rolled parchment, and spread it open on the table. It was a map, she saw, as he moved a candle nearer.

"Sir William de Soulis said Menteith was at Loch Roskie while he recuperates." He tapped the location.

"Why there? Dunbarton is a stout fortress," Bran said.

"Roskie is more remote," Constantine said. "He took that chance. But it is small and not as well guarded."

"If he were at Dunbarton," said Lennox, the former owner of that castle, "he would have quick access to the firth, the sea, and a river to move her quickly."

"So that means he is not in a hurry," Duncan said. "Let us hope it means the girl is safe for now. We can make a move."

"With more men," Constantine said. "A few came with us today, but not enough for this."

"More men are coming," Lennox said. "Bruce will send men

here as soon as he can. We do not quite know when they will arrive, though. Even before word came of the attack on the escort, he intended to send more to Brechlinn, knowing they are needed."

Duncan nodded. "So you said earlier. With luck, we can expect them soon."

"He would come himself," Lennox said, "but he is gathering forces in the south. But he will be anxious about his lass and awaiting word from us."

"Just as well," Duncan said. "If Bruce headed here, that would attract more attention from the English than we want. While we can, we should arrange to move the bishop westward to ensure his safety."

"I can wait. Rescue the child first."

"If you are certain, Reverend Father," Duncan said. "We will wait a day or two more for others to join us. In the meantime, I will send patrols out toward Loch Roskie. Additional guards or unusual activity may tell us more."

"We should be careful about hunting parties as well," Lennox said.

"True. We cannot take the birds into the glen east of here," Duncan agreed. "They could fly toward Roskie. Bran, we need to fly them west for a while."

"Birds?" the bishop asked Duncan.

"We keep a mews here with a few special falcons, sir. If Menteith or his men see them, it will complicate matters. William de Soulis may have spotted them recently."

"De Soulis!" Constantine said. "Is he up here? His lands are south."

"He is here with Menteith, preparing for a sheriffdom, he said."

Constantine groaned. "If he is granted a sheriffdom, may it be far from Stirling."

"Thanks to Lady Margaret," Duncan said, "we now know Menteith had something to do with taking Bruce's daughter. We do not know quite why he would do such a thing. But he will be at Roskie for a while nursing that foot. So the girl is most likely there."

"Then we need to get inside Roskie," Lennox said. Duncan tapped a fist on the table. "We need to decide how. The patrols will help determine that."

"Sir Duncan, may I go?" Andrew asked. "I want to help."

"You can stay here, lad. Bran MacArther will fit you with a hauberk and helmet and put you on the wall walk. I trust you have a keen eye?"

"I do! I can do that, sir."

Listening, Margaret caught Duncan's eye and sent him a small smile of gratitude for including Andrew in the rescue effort.

Then Duncan leaned toward Bran and lowered his voice, but she heard him. She knew Andrew did not, seated by the window.

"At the first hint of conflict, take the lad off the wall and put him in a safe spot," Duncan murmured.

"What are you expecting, sir?"

"A passel of trouble," Duncan muttered, and turned away.

A DAY, MOVING on to two passed as Margaret found ways to help Effie, and sentries on the parapet watched for a birlinn with more men. She saw Andrew walking proudly up there too, carrying a weapon, blowing alerts on a ram's horn, even helping to tend the braziers kept at night. The time went faster than she expected, though each moment she thought about Lilias, and was grateful for the determination in Duncan and those who rode out on patrol and otherwise spent time planning. When the bishop led prayers in the great hall, she joined the group and sent hers outward for Lilias, the missing men, and protection for Duncan and those at Brechlinn.

She watched the loch too, checking from every window she passed. Bran took the bishop and a few others out to exercise the birds, heading west. Wanting to stay at Brechlinn should anything happen there, she stayed behind. When she heard Duncan tell the bishop more about Greta and the family of gyrfalcons, she knew that trust in Bishop Murray said a great deal.

"Edward does not deserve such fine falcons," the bishop replied. "Besides, in Scotland they are the privilege of earls as well as kings. I would not be surprised if one day Bruce will grant you an earldom for your services."

"I am honored that you think so, sir," Duncan said.

Helping Effie in the kitchen and elsewhere, Margaret prepared meals and attended tasks in the newly busy household. More guests meant that the few bedchambers in the tower were in use, needing dusting and fresh linens, and pallets were found for the soldiers, while Effie and Owen took a small room near the kitchen.

Owen was a big lad of eleven, with long brown hair and his mother's light-blue eyes. He had such a knowing way with the birds that Margaret wondered why he did not train with Duncan as a falconer. She mentioned so to Effie, who shrugged.

"Bran says so too, and Duncan would teach him when they are both here. But Owen wants to forge steel. It is a good craft and he will do well in his uncle's smithy."

Despite so much activity, Margaret fought impatience and concern over Lady Lilias, hoping the girl would be safe until the moment Duncan and the others found her. She distracted herself further while practicing archery with Andrew and visiting the mews with Andrew and Owen, where she watched Owen calmly handle the birds.

She saw too little of Duncan, catching a glimpse of him working with the clerk and Sir Constantine as she passed through the hall; a farewell wave when he saw her at the window as he rode out on patrol with the men to circle the glens and ensure safety; a remark or two exchanged at supper when she caught his attention for a moment. He seemed distracted and troubled.

Even with the quiet distance between them, her heart beat faster when he was near, her breath caught at his deep, resonant voice or his keen and steady gaze. Her dreams were filled with him again, as in the days before the broken betrothal, when hope brightened the future.

Each day, as the castle seemed to wait as if caught in time, she was aware that she missed him. Needed him, craved his nearness, wanted to feel the thrill of an unexpected touch, a kiss. More.

Her decision had been easily made, but William de Soulis would expect an answer from her soon. He might even come to Brechlinn to ask, though the patrol would keep him out. Her heart belonged to Duncan fully, though he seemed to have drifted away somehow. One night, she dreamed that he rowed a boat in a mist, while she called through the fog. In the dream, she feared he no longer loved her, and she did not know how to ask, or if the question was welcome.

She woke that rainy morning to hear horses in the bailey, and ran to see Duncan ride out with several knights, his cloak hood pulled up against the wet.

CHAPTER TWENTY

ON THE THIRD day, just before dawn, Margaret woke to a soft rapping on the door of her bedchamber. She could only guess at the hour, with no monastery for miles, no bells tolling prayers for the monks and across the hills too. Sitting up, she wondered why Effie tapped on her door so early without simply entering. The knocks sounded again, light and urgent. She rose, gathering a length of plaid woolen blanket around her, wearing a crumpled linen shift, her hair in one fat, messy sleeping braid. Opening the door, she gasped, startled to see Duncan silhouetted there.

"What is it?" she whispered opening the door as he slipped inside.

"A birlinn docked here not long ago," he murmured.

"Bruce's men?" She noticed he wore a long dark blue tunic over a linen shirt, a gentleman's gown, but he had dropped a brass-studded leather hauberk over the tunic, with a low-slung belt holding a sheathed dagger. "You are dressed for conflict, not guests."

"A boat arriving in the dark demands extra precaution, but now that I have seen them, they are indeed welcome. Dress, if you will, and come downstairs."

"I will be right there. Effie will need my help in the kitchen."

"You make excellent oatcakes and such, but you do not belong in the kitchen."

She tilted her head. "You never said that you like what I make for the table."

"Have I not? I do."

"You have hardly spoken to me for days, but you came here to wake me, so this must be important. We will need to feed them and find more beds."

"Important but not urgent. And thank you for helping Effie with the extra work. But I do not expect a daughter of a noble house to cook and such."

"In the convent, we all worked by turns in the kitchens, the gardens, the laundry, and all over. I did all a servant would do, and did not mind. And I do not mind helping here. My mother taught my sisters and me to have no airs even if we had the best in life. It does not serve anyone."

"You deserve the best. I would give that to you."

His soft-spoken answer thrilled all through her. "Would you?"

"Indeed so. Dress now and come down."

"Duncan, if you would let me be useful, then let me take up my bow and ride with you when you finally go to fetch Lady Lilias. Which will be soon, aye?" She nearly pleaded that as impatience and fear and worry rushed in again.

"We will fix our plans today, as we may have enough men for the task. I hope arrows are not needed. I want you safe here."

"Please, Duncan Dhu."

He sighed, reached out a hand, and cupped her cheek. Craving that touch, she leaned toward him, but he dropped his hand away and stepped back.

"Dress and come downstairs. You may know some of these guests," he added with a smile both teasing and sad. Leaving, he closed the door behind him.

For a moment, she nearly called him back to her, feeling keenly how much she missed him. But he was needed to return to the visitors, and she needed to hurry. Why had he said she knew them? Puzzled, she gathered her clothing and found a comb.

Soon, she entered the great hall, blinking at the bright flames leaping in the fire basket while darkness still shadowed the windows. Golden firelight fell on the faces of those who stood about, men in cloaks and chainmail, one woman in black, most holding cups, talking. One by one, they turned as Margaret entered. Smiles grew.

She set a hand to her heart, and tears rose. Henry—and Liam!" she said, crossing the room as she saw her brother and brother-in-law. "Agatha too!"

Arms out, she was soon enveloped in embraces.

DUNCAN SMILED, FEELING a hint of Margaret's warmth and joy as he watched her hug her brother, embrace Liam Seton, and turn with affection to the slender nun who had traveled with the group. Dame Agatha Seton—Sir Liam's sister—came with them to provide female company for Margaret and Lady Lilias, who he felt sure would be here soon. He would not entertain any lesser thought regarding the child.

Folding his arms, waiting, he wished he had acted sooner on Margaret's repeated insistence. He had wanted to believe her, but a justiciar needed firm evidence and could not rely on impulse and intuition. Yet Margaret Keith had taught him to give more rein to feelings he had learned to temper or lock away. Rely less on caution and doubt. Take more chances. And reveal the love he held inside before it was too late.

He was pleased she was happy in this moment, and content to give her the time now to enjoy it. Another wish came to him then; what if he had never walked away from her, what if her kin had accepted him into their caring fold? He wanted to give that a chance now. He hoped she would let that happen.

The morning had brought another reunion, he thought, glancing at the tall knight standing to one side. To his surprise, his brother Iain Campbell had disembarked with the rest. Three years had passed since he had seen his sibling, older by just a year.

Iain had joined a group of Scottish rebels centered in the great forests of Ettrick and Selkirk, and had all but disappeared. Just moments ago, he had explained to Duncan that he ran with Sir James Lindsay now, an outlawed laird whose name was known to nearly every sheriff and justiciar in Scotland. Through James he had met Sir Liam Seton, and now Iain, too, had been recruited to help Bruce with certain tasks—including, this time, rescuing Lilias Bruce.

Smiling at the thought, Duncan clapped his brother on the shoulder. Iain grunted. Even taller and darker than Duncan, his natural demeanor had not changed. It had always been that of a silent, somber fellow. Only a few knew he hid a good heart and a surprisingly intuitive soul. More than his brothers, Iain had inherited their mother's gift of the Sight. As a lad, he had been the only one to see strange visions through the hole in a stone.

"Once all that is done," Iain said, gesturing toward the laughing Keiths and Setons, "what is next, brother?"

"We will gather together and discuss what to do. Con and Lennox and I have a plan to share. We must act quickly now that we know who may have the Bruce girl. Iain," he said, "what do you think?"

He grunted, looked about the hall. "I think the place looks almost as good as it did when we were lads. Well done."

"What else?" Duncan sent him a wry look.

"I believe," he said in low, rumbling tones, "we will find the child. But something is... You must be wary, Duncan. There is true danger in this. But I am at your back." He clapped Duncan's shoulder hard. Margaret turned.

"So you found the Keith lass, did you?" Iain huffed. "Took you long enough."

"ARROWSHOT! WE HAD not heard that," Henry said later, as Margaret and Duncan shared what they knew with Henry and Liam. "We saw Menteith at Dunbarton Castle. He was lame with an injury, but did not explain it."

"You saw him?" Margaret asked. She leaned forward, eager to hear more, hoping they had also heard some hint of Lilias. Seeing Duncan's frown, she felt sure he was hoping the same.

"We went there to ask if he, as sheriff, knew aught of an escort expected at the Firth of Clyde that did not arrive," Liam Seton said. "He told us his men stopped an attack on an escort and took a girl to her MacDougall kin. As for the foot, I took it for gout and did not ask."

"He was shot?" Henry asked.

"Injured in the heel like Achilles of old," Duncan said. "He cannot walk or ride easily for a while. He left Dunbarton to go to his castle at Loch Roskie, a morning's ride east of here. We can thank your sister for delaying whatever plans he may have made while we puzzle out where Bruce's daughter may be."

Henry lifted a brow. "Meg delayed him?"

"I entered an archery contest. But my shot went awry. Sir John walked near just as I released the arrow." She touched the pendant at her throat.

Henry glanced at the arrow-shaped pendant; her brother knew its origin, but said nothing. "Well," he went on, "it is lucky for us that his plans changed, if he has the girl."

"He also told us his men took a girl to her MacDougall kin," Constantine said.

"We did not mention Bruce's daughter," Henry said. "He was willing to meet with me as I am deputy sheriff of Selkirk, nor did he question that Seton Dalrinnie and his sister, the prioress, were with me. Iain Campbell," he added, "stayed outside with the rest of our escort."

"Best he did not know that I was lately with rebels in Ettrick Forest," Iain said.

"When I mentioned that my sister and a fostered Murray lad were also with the missing escort," Henry said, "he went pale. It made me suspicious, I swear."

"Though he denied knowing anything, he traveled to Loch Roskie quickly afterwards, even in pain," Liam said. "He must have gone as soon as we left."

"Something made him nervous," Duncan said.

"After that, we hired a birlinn to take us up the loch, since Menteith mentioned you, sir." Henry looked at Duncan. "He told us Campbell of Brechlinn was justiciar in the north and had custody of a criminal who needed punishing. I admit I was astonished to learn you were back in Scotland."

"I am," Duncan said quietly.

"I confess, I thought you were gone, but Iain said his brother was the justiciar at Brechlinn. He explained that there was a rumor for years that you had died."

Duncan nodded. "It seems that word spread past my family. I am sorry."

"I am glad it was a false rumor," Henry said.

With a sigh of relief, Margaret glanced from her brother to Duncan. She had been uncertain how Henry might react to seeing Duncan, but her brother was a gracious sort, quick to understand. Duncan caught her glance and pressed his lips together. She saw the relief there, saw his shoulders shift in a long exhale.

"Sir John is intent on pursuing charges for this archer and said you had him in custody," Liam said. "He wants to know more. Bruce's orders directed us to Brechlinn too, on the strength of Lennox's message about the missing escort."

"Finding my sister and Andrew safe here was a great relief. I hope you will make the rest clear soon," Henry said, glancing at Margaret. She nodded her promise. "For now, it seems we have this important task in common, on orders from Bruce."

Margaret sat forward, listening intently. Her brother's calm reassured her, but she could not read him entirely. He would harbor his own opinion and not readily share it. Blond and blue-eyed, tall and strong as an oak, Henry had learned during years of knight service to show careful courtesy and school his thoughts behind a neutral mask.

"So," Henry continued, "Menteith wants me to bring word of

what the justiciar intends for this archer assailant. What are you going to tell him?"

"That I saw no reason to detain him. It was an accident," Duncan said.

Henry shook his head.

"I had to get close to Menteith," Margaret insisted. "Andrew and I suspected he had something to do with the attack on our escort. But it all went wrong, and I was caught. Sir Duncan brought me here to avoid Menteith."

"Sir John was a bit upset," Duncan explained with a shrug.

"No doubt. Thank you for keeping her safe," Henry said.

"So now," Duncan said, "we must determine how to get Lilias away from Menteith. With luck, he has her with him at Roskie Castle. Henry, if you and Liam can go there with news about this…archer lad, you can get inside and find out more."

"We could get inside, but he will be displeased with the news the lad is no longer, uh, in the area. We would be thrown out and none the wiser about Lady Lilias."

"Wait." Margaret sat up, heart pounding. "I can get inside."

"You cannot think to reveal you were his assailant," Henry said.

"Not that. I will go there to see De Soulis. He is also at Roskie Castle."

"De Soulis!" Henry exclaimed.

"We saw him recently. I have a message for him, my reply to a question he posed to me. He will want to see me. I can get inside."

"You need not do this, my lady," Duncan said sternly. She could not look at him for fear of faltering. She had a strong urge—this was a way she could move this forward, perhaps find Lilias.

"What does De Soulis want from you? He needed to approach me first." Henry turned to the others. "My sister was betrothed to him two years ago, but he broke it off. She should have nothing to do with him now. Does he want your permission to keep the land he took from us?"

"He did not mention that. He wants to renew the betrothal," she said.

"What!" Henry scowled. "He wants something else, but what?"

"That is what I am wondering," Duncan growled, catching Henry's glance.

"He told me he made a mistake, and wants another chance." She felt her cheeks fill with heat. "I promised to give him my answer. So I would be admitted to Castle Roskie, and perhaps, I could see Lilias. De Soulis might even tell me."

"Only if your answer pleases him," Duncan said. "It is far too risky."

"I agree. You cannot consider this, Meg," her brother said.

"I will go. It could change everything if I can find her. And he has something that he promised to return. The blue stone brooch," she told Henry. "Thomas's brooch."

"How did he get that?" He looked astonished.

"Menteith had it and gave it to him. I was wearing it when the escort was taken down, and it was torn away. That is strong proof that Menteith is behind this."

Duncan leaned toward her. "Margaret, you cannot do this."

"And you cannot convince me otherwise. Make your plans. My plan is to see Sir William and uncover Lilias's whereabouts as fast as possible."

WALKING THROUGH THE bailey at a quick pace, Duncan looked left and right for Margaret. She had left the hall while he had remained with the others to discuss the situation further. Now he wanted desperately to find her, and talk her out of this folly. She was not in the tower, and he was hoping to find her in the bailey.

Hearing his name, he stopped and turned to see Dame Agatha coming toward him. "Sir Duncan! Have you seen Lady Margaret?"

"I was looking for her myself," he said.

"I was hoping for the chance to visit with her. We are old friends, you see." She smiled, and he noticed the scar on one side of her face that pulled at her smile.

"Perhaps you can find her in her bedchamber," he suggested, smiling too, though he had run up those steps already to find an empty room.

She nodded, glancing around. Liam Seton's sister was young to be a prioress, and Duncan could not help but notice her beauty; she was lovely and clearly intelligent, and he wondered why she had chosen the veil. The Setons would have found an advantageous marriage for such a daughter.

Yet the deep scar that ran along one side of her perfect face, eyebrow to chin, told a silent tale of trouble and tragedy. Perhaps that had led to her choice. Perhaps some had rejected her despite her beautiful face and character. The thought made him want to make her feel even more welcome at Brechlinn.

"Thank you, Dame Agatha," he said. "Did you know Bishop Murray is staying with us as well? I am sure he would want to meet the prioress of Lincluden. I will make sure he knows you are here."

"Bishop Murray of Moray? I am delighted to know that. I will look for Lady Margaret in the tower, as you suggest." With another smile, she hurried away.

He turned in the bailey, wondering where Margaret might have gone. Her intention to see De Soulis alarmed him—perhaps she had no idea of the danger that might bring her. He wanted to talk to her, convince her that she need never see De Soulis again.

Ahead, he saw the archery butts, but the area was deserted. Seeing a familiar quiver and bow leaning against a straw bale, he had a thought and turned for gate, hailing a guard.

"Alan MacFarlane," he called. "Have you seen Lady Margaret?"

"Aye, sir. She was at the butts, but went out a while ago. Lost arrows over the gap, sir, as often happens."

"She went out without a guard?" That, too, was alarming.

"Alone, sir, but took Mungo with her. A grand guardian. If she does not return soon, I will look for her."

"I will go now. Open the gate—thank you," he said gruffly.

Moments later he was striding over turf and hillock around the span of the wall toward the forest. The sky was turning leaden gray and looked to rain. Rounding the wall past the stone-filled breach, he entered the woodland.

Soon he heard the dog's woof and saw Mungo trotting among the trees ahead. Then he saw skirts the color of a blue jay's wing sweeping between the birches. He headed that way, wanting to bring her back inside for her own safety. There was always a chance—perhaps she did not realize it—that De Soulis or even Menteith could come to Brechlinn. Margaret should never be alone outside the castle.

It also occurred to him that he could have a private moment with her out here, away from others, and talk some sense into her.

"Margaret!" he called. The air was damp, the rain hanging in the clouds, cool shadows making greens vibrant. The blue of her skirt was bright too, and the bronze and copper hue of her hair brilliant in the soft gray light.

She stepped into a gap between trees, just under arching branches, looking like a queen of faery. His heart lurched. He caught his breath.

"Are you looking for arrows? It will rain soon. Come inside." As he spoke, Mungo trotted up to him. He patted the great head almost absently, staring at Margaret.

"I lost two arrows. I found one. Go back. I will be there soon."

"They are just arrows. I will give you a dozen more. Come." He beckoned.

"Did you come out to save me from the rain, or to ask about Sir William?"

"Both." He scratched the dog's head.

"You could be useful and help me find the other bolt." She

spun away, moving through a density of ferns that swallowed the hem of her gown.

He sighed, not interested in arrows. Truly, he wanted to know what she planned to tell De Soulis. And he wanted to prevent her from stepping into danger because of it.

As she edged through a cluster of birches, the hound loped after her, nosing here and there. Duncan whistled, but Mungo trotted to catch up with the girl.

"Ingrate," Duncan muttered as he came behind them. Searching ahead, Margaret pushed bushes and bracken aside, shook branches, looking puzzled.

"Surely your arrows did not fly this far into the forest," he said.

"They could have, because I tried the longbow. Bran gave it to me."

"You are not tall enough to pull that bow."

"Which is why my shots went so far off the mark." She surged ahead, rounding a double-trunked birch and wading onward through ferns and bluebells.

Duncan went too, searching now for long, iron-tipped bodkins. They were not arrows he wanted to lose, but his mind was preoccupied. The girl turned him about like a child's wooden top, throwing him off his usual steady course.

Before he had seen Margaret Keith again, his life consisted of legal grievances and hard decisions based on justice and laws. Yet all the while, he protected and aided Bruce's allies—currently a batch of priests who had offended Edward—which put Duncan in the position of working against the laws he upheld in order to support what he knew in his heart was right and just.

And then Margaret Keith stepped into his life, blithely shaking up all he held steadfast in the same way she rustled tree branches and ferns ahead of him. What she looked for was what they both needed, he thought.

Then he realized that the guilt he had held for so long was falling away like old leaves. Forgiveness and something else had replaced it—

Love. He had always loved her, had always known it. He had acted out of a sense of honor when he was young, an honor he did not fully understand then. Now he felt honor and more in a new way. And it was strong enough to throw him off balance if he did not grow with it.

For Margaret Keith's sake, he would grow, learn, throw open doors, and shake arrows out of trees—whatever it took, he would do it. He knew he never wanted to lose her again.

The dog woofed, and just ahead, the girl threw her arms out as she tripped over something in the undergrowth. She went down in a wave of blue skirts and copper tresses and a little soft cry. Duncan ran forward, catching her under the arms before she could hit her head on a fallen tree trunk. Helping her up, he kept an arm around her shoulders.

"Are you hurt?"

"I am fine. My foot caught on something. Aha!" She bent to root in the fronds and came up with a long arrow shaft. "This was tangled there."

He took it. "A strong shot sent it this far. Good for you. I can have a longbow made to suit your height and pull, hey?"

"I would like that." She smiled in delight.

"Come then. We will go back."

"Wait. Tell me what is on your mind, Duncan Dhu. I can feel it."

He blew out a breath. They stood in a hollow of leafy branches that muffled their voices and lent privacy. "What is on my mind—is why you would risk seeing De Soulis."

"I only mean to ask for my brooch—and find out what I can about Lilias."

"Margaret, think. This is just dangerous."

"But I can get inside there easily, so I should be the one to go."

"There are other ways to find Lady Lilias. Other ways to get your brooch."

She lifted her chin. "Tell me a way better than this."

"My men and I will go to the gates and demand the girl back."

"What if she is not there? What if they shoot from the battlements? One arrow to the heart and you are slain." She poked him in the breastbone. "That worries me."

Slain indeed, by her sweet fierceness. "We have shields, bows, and fine archers."

"Give me a horse and a good bow. If they have the king's daughter, I want to be there when you bring her out."

"I will not put you at peril. We will do all we can and bring her back to you." He moved forward.

She gazed up at him. "Duncan, I cannot sit by. I need to find her."

"That responsibility you bear is tripping you up. I will do this. Refuse De Soulis from a distance. I will deliver your note."

"I want Lilias and I want my pin. He will not give either to you."

"Then I will tear it from his cloak." He dropped the arrow and placed a hand on the tree above her head, the other on a sturdy branch. She looked up at him, her head brushing his raised arm. Her copper-gilt hair sifted over his tunic like silk.

"Well," she said, "I would not mind if you tore the pin away. He deserves it."

"Ah, now we learn how you feel about the man."

"I hope you know how I feel about him. I never want to see him again. But I promised him my answer."

He leaned closer. "You do not owe him one."

She drew a breath, those magnificent moss-green eyes softening, lifting to meet his. "But I owe you one."

"When you have it."

She lifted her chin higher. Inches away now. He felt her breath soft on his face. "I suppose you have an advantage over the other knight."

"I am here. He is not." He leaned a little closer, lured in, willing.

"True." She glanced at his lips, licked hers lightly. His body surged.

"Would you—back off, Mungo," he said as the dog nosed between them.

"He wants to protect me," she said. "Mungo. Sit."

"He wants affection. Like most of us. Down." He pushed the dog away with one hand, replacing it just over her head. "The lady must decide, true. And the knight will wait. But there is a condition."

She tilted her head. "What is that? The price of a kiss?"

That surge again, hot and sure. "If that fee is offered, I would take it." Standing so close that he felt heat bloom between them, he drew a breath as hope and love and desire poured through him all at once. Bending a little, he touched his brow to hers.

She caught her breath and kept still.

"There is another price," he whispered. "The lady must promise the knight to never put herself at risk."

"I may be in harm's way now." Her gaze met his, her lips quirked in a near smile.

He hooked a finger under her chin. "You are always safe with me."

"I know," she whispered. "But I fear I have lost my heart."

"Then we will look for it somewhere in this forest, for I lost mine too."

She caught a little sob. He kissed her then, slow and sure, felt her sigh against his mouth, felt her sink a little as if she melted inside as he surely did. He had to shore up every reserve, every fiber within him, to pull back, for he burned for more.

A light rain was tapping on the leaves overhead, misting her hair, his shoulders. He let go and stepped back. "Take that reassurance as you consider your choices."

"Dear God, Duncan," she said, and reached out, grabbed his cloak, and pulled him toward her. She threw her arms around him and kissed him, soundly, surely. He pulled her against him, hands at her waist, and returned kisses until he felt her sink in his grasp. His own knees shook, his body flamed as he drew back, resting his forehead on hers.

"What is this now," he whispered.

"I am near to deciding," she breathed, and he pressed her in a full embrace, taking her in a deep kiss, lifting her full against him as his body responded, as hers answered. Then he set her on her feet again.

"Decide soon, or I am done for, lady," he said raggedly. "We should go. Where is that damned arrow?"

"Later," she blurted, breathing hard, pulling at his sleeve.

About to take hold of her again, he heard a deep sound, a long resonant echo from the direction of the castle. "We must go."

"What was that?" Holding his arm now, she peered through the trees.

"They are sounding an alarm. Mungo! Where did he—here, lad!" he beckoned, his voice oddly hoarse. The dog came toward him and Duncan ruffled the great gray head. Mungo licked Margaret's hand for more and she petted him too, her fingers over Duncan's. Trembling.

He took her arm. "Come. Something is going on."

Walking swiftly out of the woodland and around the castle wall, he saw men on chargers just outside the gate, recognizing Constantine, Lennox, Henry Keith. Bran was on foot, coming over the turf toward Duncan. "Sir!" He beckoned urgently.

"What is it?" Duncan ran, Margaret hurrying after, while the hound with great long strides reached Bran first.

"The patrol just returned. They saw soldiers in the glen to the east, riding toward the falls."

"That route could bring them here. Margaret, take the dog's collar if you will, and lead him inside." He turned. "Bran, I need a horse saddled—"

"Waiting by the gate, sir."

CHAPTER TWENTY-ONE

T HEY RODE OUT in fair silence to follow the shallow, winding river through the glen. Cutting eastward over hills and moors, the Brechlinn group slowed as a member of their patrol, having waited for them, approached on a dappled gray charger. The garrons, Duncan and the others all knew, were unsuited if the need for a chase arose.

"Alan!" Duncan rode to meet him, the others following. "What have you seen?"

"Sir, there were several riding this way, at least toward the falls. But they are gone. They turned and rode back, and just before you arrived, left the east glen."

"Then it seems as if they are returning to Roskie. Good work, Alan. We will ride along the top of the ridge to be sure they are gone. Henry, if you will come with me, then Bran and Lennox can look elsewhere. Alan, you and the others can go back."

"Aye, sir." Bran rode off with Lennox, while Alan and two others who had ridden out with Duncan and the rest rode down a slope and out of sight on their way back along the river toward Brechlinn and the great loch.

Duncan turned his horse across the shoulder of the nearest hill and Henry followed. They reached the top of the ridge overlooking the east glen. Along the length of that valley, he saw no men, no horses. Only a few sheep.

"Not very much happening here now," Henry said.

"We will watch for a little while before heading back. For now, tell me what you know of De Soulis. I only met him recently when we were out with Lady Margaret flying hawks. Falcons," he amended. "I know something of the De Soulis family and their strong loyalty to King Edward. And I know your sister has a tie to him in the past."

"And may it stay in the past," Henry said.

"She told me something of the betrothals that followed...ours. We had some discussion about what happened with her—over these last years."

"So you know some of it. You were the first to reject her, but not the only one."

"Let me say, sir, that I have regretted that day ever since. I know I made an error. No apology can make it up to the lady or her kin."

"I heard you thought it was the honorable thing to do."

"I did. I was young—honor was a simple concept then. A great deal happened quickly after that. It was a while before I had time to reflect on it."

"We heard you were captured, that you had likely perished in captivity."

"My family heard the same, unfortunately. I had no idea." He explained as quickly as he could the years in England, then Flanders and France, with the escape to Ireland.

"Iain told us some of it," Henry said. "Remarkable. I am amazed so many of you survived."

"Aye, but we did what we had to do. When I was finally able to send word to my family, it had to be done secretly. I could not risk incurring Edward's wrath."

"Edward is a hard warden. While you were gone, Margaret was in a convent. When she came home, my father felt it was well past time to find her a husband."

"She told me about that. I understand your mother died there. I am sorry."

"Those were difficult days, to be sure. After my father died, I inherited Kincraig and the guardianship of my unmarried sisters. Our great-grandfather… You know? Aye, then. When I was young, Thomas impressed upon me the need to watch over my sisters. I took it to heart. Still do."

"I missed years with my siblings. You are fortunate in your sisters."

"I am." Henry drew a breath. "It is good to know we were wrong about you, sir."

"A chain of misunderstandings. I am glad to be able to unravel some of it now. I suppose you will want to take Margaret back to Kincraig when this is over."

"Margaret is strong-willed and will do what she wants. She intended to go to Ireland with Bruce's daughter and stay there for a while, but now I wonder what she will want to do once we have Lilias back again." Henry glanced sidelong at Duncan.

"As you say, she will do as she wants." They sat in silence watching the glen until Henry pointed toward the valley floor.

"Nothing much going on down there. Sheep and goats."

"Aye. Whoever rode through earlier has gone."

"May they stay away. Liam says you do good work for Bruce," Henry said then.

Duncan took a breath. He wanted to be honest with Margaret's brother, not only to make up for the years, but because he felt that he could trust him. He gave a half nod.

"I do. The bishop—you met him at Brechlinn? We are keeping him safe until he can be moved to the Isles and the English are not intently looking for him."

"I see. If Bruce trusts you, that says all to me. It is good to know more about you. Very good." Henry nodded half to himself. "I had my reservations, but I was wrong about you. There is much to admire." He smiled quickly, as if he felt embarrassed. "I have news for my sister that I was not sure she would want to hear. But I think you should know it too. I have not had a chance to tell her yet. However, it concerns both of you."

Curious, Duncan lifted a brow. "Aye?"

"I have been going through my father's documents and belongings whenever I have time at Kincraig, which is not often, so it has taken some time. But recently, I discovered that he made an attempt to contact you just before his death."

"Contact me?"

"He had heard a rumor that you had survived and returned to your family."

"Perhaps it had to do with the dowry. Though I believe my father repaid it while I was away those years."

"On the contrary, Duncan, it has never been paid in full."

"God's bones," he growled. "I will make immediate recompense."

"No need, sir. My father decided not to ask for it. What he intended to ask you was to renew the betrothal arrangement."

Duncan stared at him. "Renew it?"

FROM THE WINDOW of her bedchamber, Margaret watched Duncan's party ride out until she could see them no longer, past the castle and heading along the narrow river stream. Seeing her brother and Duncan riding in tandem, she wondered what they might talk about. She was not certain, not quite. Though Henry was easy-going for the most part, he could have an iron stubbornness. Yet the conversation earlier gave her hope that he no longer harbored resentment toward Duncan.

Every day, every hour, she too felt old walls dissolving as she understood more about why Duncan left, what he had endured, how much honor truly meant to him.

Turning away from the gray half-light, she lit a candlestick from the glowing peat bricks in the brazier and set it on the table. Paging through a small illuminated prayer book that she had found on a shelf, her thoughts were not there, but wandering outside, flying over moor and glen with Duncan and Henry and the patrol.

A pottery bowl on the table held the little river stones that she and Duncan had found. Picking up one of them, she held it toward the window, then candle flame, but nothing remarkable appeared. She thought of the silver brooch again, with its luminous blue stone and a central hole outlined in tiny crystals.

The only way to reclaim it from De Soulis was to go to him herself. He would never relinquish it to Duncan. She was sure of that.

As for wee Lilias, she did not know—no one did—the best way to reclaim her.

Lifting the stone to her eye again, she looked toward the window, once again seeing only a small slice of hills and gray sky. Her father had once said there were ways to see distant objects closely in glass globes that made things appear larger, or small glass lenses that some could afford to aid failing eyesight. But nothing sharpened distant views.

Something moved within the small range of the stone's hole. Narrowing her eyes, she watched the landscape and saw movement again. She waited. The slope disappeared into a field of fog and a figure moved through it—then vanished. The hill and sky returned. When she had tried the stone the other day, she had seen an extraordinary sight—a battle of some kind. A true vision. But she did not know how to invite such things. They seemed random, accidental. But something appeared now and then.

Closing her eyes, she tried to recall what Thomas had told her in the year before his death, eight years ago now. Her sisters had gifts. He had said she did too. Yet what was there came and went capriciously.

Well, she thought, setting the little stone back in the bowl, if that was all she could do, it would have to be enough. The little river stones were not quite like the stone that Thomas had given her. Perhaps, when she regained that, she could try again.

Sighing, she picked up the little prayer book once more to turn its pretty pages. The rain tapped against the glass in the window arch, that repetition coaxing a yawn as she flipped the pages. Distracted, she felt anxious about Duncan and what he might encounter, and felt her stomach spin with fear as she thought about Lilias and how frightened the girl must be by now. She needed to know both were safe.

Yet she was a bit tired, and the wait might be long. Turning pages of prayers, she whispered a little prayer asking protection for Lilias, Duncan, the missing men, the gyrfalcons too—and added a little prayer for herself, wishing she might always stay here with Duncan Campbell. Drowsy with hopes and prayers, she laid her head on her arms and dozed.

Margaret. Margaret lass.

She looked around. A man stood in the shadows by the door. Thomas the Rhymer of Learmont, her great-grandfather. She sat up, reached out, but he held up a hand. "Grandda!"

Merry Margaret, dear lass, he said. *Our wee forest bride.*

"Oh, Grandda!" Tears rose in her eyes, and she felt an overflowing sense of love and kindness from him. He was younger than she remembered, fit and handsome, no longer crooked and old, with silver-white hair. His pale blue eyes held a gentle light.

Lass, the blue stone, my truth stone.

"I lost it, Grandda." She wanted to cry.

Thee must get it back. And thee must keep the elf-bolt too.

"That one is safe, see." She pulled out the silver chain and pendant to show him. "But I do not know how to use the stones you gave me, Grandda."

Just look and wait without thought or fear. The stone will show thee what it wants thee to know.

"What is it I need to know?"

Truth, dear one. The truth in thy heart. Then thee will know what thee needs.

"You said the pendant would help me. But I do not know how it can do that."

Where thee will it, the arrow will fly. Think, and do. Wee forest bride, be patient and watch. Thee will see.

"I am trying to understand. Grandda, why do you call me a forest bride?"

It has always been thy destiny. He held up a hand, stepped back, and was gone.

Rain pattered against the glass, the candle flame flickered.

Margaret opened her eyes, blinking. Her head was still on her folded arms. Just a dream—that was all. She sat up, feeling dazed. What had he told her?

Look and see. Picking up the plain little stone again, she peered through it. This time, she saw a high rocky slope, not the view framed by the window. She saw a cave opening in the slope. A girl sat there, dark-haired, wrapped in a cloak. Above, a white falcon glided. In the distance, she saw the frothy tail of a waterfall.

She blinked wide, nearly dropping the stone. Looking again, she breathed deep, and waited, as Thomas had told her in the dream.

Another image formed. Men, bloody and exhausted, some on the ground, some kneeling. One standing. Duncan leaned on his upright sword, its point in the ground. Then he collapsed, lying still—

Margaret cried out and held the stone away from her, breathing quickly. Trembling, she dared to look again. A blur of green became a forest. Two people stood there, but she could not see their faces. Chainmail on the man; a woman in a blue gown. Mist again.

Forest bride, Thomas had said. She remembered dreaming years ago of Duncan as a grown knight, herself as a lady. Just the old hopes returning.

Yet the rest was new, clear and swift images. Something had changed. The visions seemed to be more often, even using the little faery stones from the waterfall's pool.

Looking through the stone again, she saw a rainy sky, a dreary hill. Just that. An inconstant gift—but a gift. She caught her breath, grateful, hopeful, a little alarmed.

She set her hand to the pendant at her throat, always there and sometimes forgotten, its small pinkish crystal cool to her fingers, quickly warming. She remembered Thomas's words.

Where thou will it, the arrow will fly.

Did he mean the pendant would help her direct an arrow? That seemed absurd. She simply had a good eye and a knack for hitting targets. Yet Duncan had once pointed out her habit of touching the pendant before she shot the bow. She had thought she did it for luck.

Then she took in a breath, struck by a thought. The day she shot Menteith accidentally, she had desperately wished something would delay the man from leaving the area if he had Lilias. Soon after, she had taken her shot, touching her pendant first for luck. But the arrow had not gone straight and true as she expected.

It had curved to hit Menteith, almost as if it had will of its own. *Where thou will it, the arrow will fly.*

A knock sounded at the door. She jumped.

Chapter Twenty-Two

MARGARET STOOD HASTILY, smoothing her skirts, and dropped the stone back into the bowl. Opening the door, she saw Effie and Agatha waiting there.

"My lady!" Effie was holding two folded woolen blankets. "We are short of beds and rooms just now, so I was hoping you might be willing to share your chamber with Dame Agatha."

"Of course! Come in." She stepped back.

"Thank you, Margaret," Agatha murmured. "Effie, let me take those." She reached out for the blankets.

"My lady, and Dame Prioress, thank you. I must get back to the kitchen with meals to prepare and such."

"I can come help you soon," Margaret said.

"Och, you have kin and friends here. Enjoy your time with them." She smiled and stepped away. Closing the door, Margaret turned to Agatha with a smile.

"The bed is small but comfortable enough and will hold two of us, or I can sleep on the floor if you like. I was just napping a bit when you came, and—reading a book of prayers." The dream and the visions in the stone had left her feeling still a bit dazed.

"This? What a lovely wee book." Agatha picked up the book on the table.

"Please sit. It is so nice to have you here." Margaret poured watered ale into two cups and handed one to her friend. Even in the simple nun's habit of dark gray wool and a white veil, Agatha

Seton was lovely. The white woolen veil wrapped over her head and under the chin, topped by a black veil that draped over her back. Under the veils, Margaret knew Agatha's dark, curly hair would be cropped short. The stark black and white framed her delicate face and large hazel eyes lashed in black beneath black, expressive brows. Her skin was cream and rose, touched with a dimple on one side of her mouth.

Years ago, Margaret had ceased to notice the puckered scar that carved through the left eyebrow and down to tuck in one corner of her smile and dent her chin a little. It was a mark of courage and strength that added depth to her beauty and gentle character.

"I am so relieved to find you well and safe—and with Duncan Campbell!" Agatha said. "I insisted on traveling with Liam when he visited Lincluden and told me your escort had gone missing and that he and Henry were off to find out what happened. And to be honest, I needed a reason to leave the abbey for a while and get back out into the world. Sometimes it can be helpful."

Margaret tipped her head. "Are you still troubled by the incident months ago?" She remembered her sister Tamsin describing the nun's encounter with a former suitor.

Agatha shook her head. "Not that. But something is on my mind. I am thinking of leaving the order."

"Have you made a decision?" Margaret's heart leapt at the word; she had come to a decision of her own just that day.

"Nearly. The angels have provided me a little help, for Bishop Murray is here, and I asked him if he would talk with me later. I would like his advice. Perhaps his blessing."

"The bishop is here just when you need counsel—sometimes heaven works diligently on our behalf. Not always," she laughed. "There are always trials and troubles to face."

"And face them we have, my friend, both of us. Look at you here, how many years later, with Duncan Campbell, the one who broke your heart in a thousand pieces. And you thought him dead, and made the poor man all but Saint George himself. No one could say anything against him, and no other man would compare."

"No one could. Finding him alive after all—has given me much to think about."

"Very much alive, apparently." The sparkle in Agatha's eyes did not belong to a prioress. "I have seen the way you look at him, and how he returns it."

"What do you mean?"

"He looks differently at you than at others. Softer. Warmer. Have you not noticed? And how did you meet again after all this time?"

"Oh," Margaret sighed, and recounted the circumstances. "He hid with me in the forest while others were searching. That was when I recognized him, and he knew me by then too."

"Meg!" Agatha leaned forward. "Just when you needed a justiciar, your Duncan was the one who appeared. Angels direct our lives—I am sure of it. Tell me the rest."

Margaret hurried through the story. "So here we are. Agatha, I still care for him."

"As Duncan Campbell, or some impossibly virtuous warrior saint?"

"As himself. And he seems to—I think he returns the interest."

"Of course the man is attracted to you. Even I can see that. The way he watches you—it is loving. Simply that, Meg."

"He—I wondered. I hoped. But now William de Soulis is back, and awaits an answer from me. Listen." She told Agatha some of what had happened.

"De Soulis! Tell me you would never accept him. He only thinks of his own benefit, whatever it may be."

"But this time I want something from him. He may know where Lilias is. I have to find out. And he has the Rhymer's cloak pin. I must have it back."

"Be careful. That one will only bring you trouble."

"Aye," Henry Keith said, as they waited on the ridge of the hill. "My father hoped you would marry Margaret after all."

Stunned, unsure what to say, Duncan gathered the reins and urged his horse ahead, Henry riding alongside. "Why did he consider it after all that time?" he finally asked. "He was set on Margaret marrying, but he made other choices."

"Which only brought her unhappiness with each new betrothal. After you were gone, she refused to marry anyone. But Father knew she needed a strong husband, someone who could protect her—and understand how spirited she can be without trying to rule her. He wanted her to be happy. But none of the matches came about."

"She told me some of it. I feel—responsible for her troubles," Duncan admitted.

"You could never have known that you would be captured and held for years. As for the other suitors, two died, and De Soulis rejected her in the worst way. A pity, all this, for she would bring real advantage to a marriage, and be a blessing and a delight for the right man."

Duncan cleared his throat, seeing Henry's keen glance. "De Soulis wants some advantage for himself with his apparent desire to court her again."

"Aye, but what? The fellow left her in a silk gown and flowery headgear on the church steps. For all her refusal, she wanted to please my father in the end, so she agreed. I would have gladly killed Sir William that day. Later he returned part of the dowry, but kept a land grant for his trouble, he claimed. Father would have pressed for the return, but by then he was growing ill."

"But he decided to send word to me?" Duncan still felt puzzled.

"I think so. We all believed you were dead, but it seems he heard a rumor about your return. He must have intended to find out more before revealing it to us. I knew nothing until I discovered the pages he had locked away."

"I was sure my father had repaid the dowry, so I thought it

was over and done. And I heard that Margaret had stayed in the convent."

"Sir Colin offered to repay it, but Father refused it. That I knew. He said the situation was tragic enough with your death and Margaret's desire to remain in the convent. He did not want to profit from the pain of two families."

"He was a good man. I wish I had known him better." Duncan watched the empty valley below. "My father died while I was away those years."

"I heard. Sad circumstances for both sides of your broken betrothal."

"If the dowry funds were never repaid, and if the documents were not processed through the Church—" He looked at Henry.

"Then the betrothal still stands. Exactly."

He shook his head a little, as if the truth of it would settle in his brain. "Legally it would still be in effect. But Robert Keith had negotiated other betrothals."

"Only because he believed you were deceased. When he heard otherwise, he sent a message to you at Innis Connell."

"I never received it. When was this?"

"Two years ago, a little less. He died months after."

"I see. My brother Neill is earl now, but he would have been with Bruce then. He is married to Bruce's sister, Lady Mary. One of the captured royal women," he added.

"I am sorry. Edward is capable of unspeakable cruelty."

"So it seems. We have had little news about the condition of the women and Bruce has had no success resolving it. It will take time." Duncan paused. "Henry, I am sorry I never saw the message from your father."

"What would you have done if you had the message?"

He sat thoughtful in the saddle, watching the quiet glen; whoever had ridden there earlier had not returned. He thought of missed chances over ten years—but now he had hope again. "I would have been intrigued—and would have wondered if the lady would entertain the idea."

"She might well now. If you want my permission as her guardian, you have it."

Duncan huffed a little laugh of disbelief, hope, uncertainty. "It is a lot to take in."

"It is. But my father saw the truth at the end, I think."

"The truth?"

"Why do you think she refused every suitor?"

"Perhaps she was unwilling to be hurt again."

"She loved you, no matter what. My father finally saw that. She was so besotted with the idea of you, sir," Henry said, "that she refused to marry. As devoted as she was to Father, she railed at him for wanting to marry her off. But he knew she would only thrive with a man as strong-willed and stubborn as she is. A very patient man."

"I can see the need for that," Duncan drawled.

"He wanted a rare man for a rare lass. She has a wild side."

"I know." He half laughed. "I understand she was dismissed from the convent, but she never said why."

Henry chuckled. "She tried prophesying for the nuns."

"What?"

"It was my great-grandfather's doing. He gave her some stones he said were enchanted, told her she could see the future with them. She kept trying to do that. I can tell you it did not go well with the nuns. The old prioress asked her to leave."

"Her cloak pin," Duncan said. "The blue stone. She told me about it."

"Ah, you know, then. Will that make you think twice about the lass?"

"Not at all. She may do as she likes, and think as she likes. If she has something of Thomas's gift—all the better, I say."

Henry grinned. "You will do well with all of my sisters, sir. And as Meg's guardian until she marries, I would never stand in the way of her happiness. My father was right. You are the match for her."

Duncan's heart pounded, his thoughts whirled. "It would be

my life's privilege."

"Then I leave the rest to you."

"I put forth the idea recently, to be honest. She is— considering it."

"My father would be very pleased. We all would. Look, it is getting toward twilight," Henry went on.

Duncan looked up. While they had sat watching over the glen, the sky had gone from soft gray to leaden cloud cover. "And there is more rain to come."

Henry took up the reins. "If those were Menteith's men that the patrol saw earlier, it does not look like they will return. Not in this weather. We could go back."

Duncan nodded. "I will send another patrol out to be sure."

He turned his horse and headed down the western side of the hill for Brechlinn, where the woman who now owned his heart waited. And the answer she might have for him could spin his very life around.

CHAPTER TWENTY-THREE

Lilias

THAT MORNING, THE latch rattled in its unlocking, and moments later, Dame Brigit pushed open the door to Lilias's small bedchamber. She carried a tray with a bowl of porridge and a pot containing a hot herbal infusion, which she set on the table. Lilias was pleased that her request had been heard for something warm to drink in the mornings instead of watered ale, which gave her an unsettled stomach early in the day.

What surprised her even more was the rolled piece of parchment that the woman produced. When Lilias opened it, she saw a rough charcoal drawing of lines, curves, squiggles, and a track of ripples that she realized was a river.

"A map?" she asked, astonished.

"You asked me to tell you where this castle is situated. And I know that Sir John and that fellow Sir William are not telling you the truth. So I made you a drawing. Look. This is where you are. Loch Roskie," she said, tapping the page. "These are hills and moors. This way—" she pointed to one side of the crude drawing—"is Stirling Castle, which lies to the east. Over here to the west of Loch Roskie, see, are hills and a far stretch of moors. Then you see the long glen we call Glen Fada. Beyond that, into the Highlands, is another glen with a river and a waterfall. That water runs down to the head of Loch Lomond. That should tell you what you want to know."

Lilias nodded. "I saw Loch Lomond when I was traveling with my escort. We were attacked and I was stolen away, and carried by knights on a long ride—to here." She touched a crenelated square on the map. "Castle Roskie. Where we stand now."

"I thought as much." Dame Brigit shook her head. "Them men will not tell you. But I will. You are not under the mercy of their protection. You are a captive."

"I know," Lilias said.

"I heard them say they mean to ransom you. Now I never ask their business, and I do what I am told. But that troubles me. Young lass like you with such an important father, a man they mean to break. So this is where you are. I will tell you that."

"Are there other prisoners here? The men of my escort?"

"They came here with you. But they were taken to Dunbarton Castle last week. It is just you here, now."

Lilias nodded. She sipped the herbal liquid, felt it warm her stomach. She ate a little, then drew a breath to help her find her courage.

"Good dame," she said, "will you help me leave this place?"

The woman frowned. "I will not. I am just telling you what you asked."

"Oh." Disappointment swamped her. "If I followed the map, could I find friends?"

Dame Brigit shrugged. "How do I know who your friends are? If someone were to go east to Stirling, they would only find Englishers. But west over the hills and moors to the long glen, and then down the river that meets Loch Lomond, a person might find good folk at Brechlinn Castle. It stands at the north end of the great loch."

"Brechlinn. I have heard of it. My father mentioned it. A friend of his is laird."

"Do not tell me anything about your father. I want no trouble."

"Oh. Well, I suppose I must stay here then and wait for a

ransom." She sent Dame Brigit as quick glance to see how that sat with her.

"Stay or go. I will have naught to do with it. But if you go, take the map with you."

"How would I go?"

Dame Brigit picked up the tray. "That is for you to work out. I only bring you food and see to your needs. But I will tell you this, lass," she whispered. "What you have done for Sir John is a kind thing. He will never repay that kindness. So I gave you that parchment. Good day to you. I will come back with supper." She went to the door and opened it.

"Thank you." Lilias smiled to cover the fear that churned through her.

Dame Brigit left the room, and left the door unlocked.

After a while, Lilias put on her cloak, folded and creased the map and tucked it in her little belt pouch with her rosary of onyx beads and a little silver cross, and ventured out of the room. Standing on the stone steps that curved downward, she listened for a long while, hearing very little noise. Easing down the steps, she paused at a narrow window in the turret stair and looked out.

Men rode out of the gate, several in a patrol of some kind. In the lead on a tall white charger, Sir William de Soulis wore a bright red surcoat over chainmail.

Waiting until she judged the riders to be a fair distance from the castle, she tiptoed down the steps, along a corridor, following savory smells that took her past the kitchen. Servants were busy in there; she could hear Dame Brigit complaining that Sir John would not want that bland stew again for supper later in the day.

Finding the door to the kitchen garden, she stepped outside. Beyond the garden lay the back part of the curtain wall. A postern gate, just a low, square, thick door, was within sight. At the nearest corner of the bailey, two soldiers argued with one of the servants about dumping offal too near the entrance gate where they had to sit all day.

They did not notice her as she hurried across the short stretch of the bailey yard. The postern gate had a simple enough latch. She lifted it.

Then, slipping through the doorway, she ran.

CHAPTER TWENTY-FOUR

"H EY, GRETA," MARGARET murmured, moving toward the gyrfalcon on its perch. Moments before, she had entered the mews just after Duncan and the others had returned from patrol in the rain. He had not seen her, dismounting quickly to head into the keep with Constantine and Lennox, while Henry greeted her briefly. She wondered what they had seen out there, if anything; no alarms of discovery had been sounded.

For now, she meant to stay out of her bedchamber so that Agatha could nap. She had been exhausted after the long day's journey. She took another step toward the white gyrfalcon, flexing her talons on a tree limb set on a high trestle. Nearby, the peregrine was asleep, while Smoke, Greta's mate, gave a shrill *kik-kik-kik* and went silent.

Margaret paused a few feet away. "Greta, you look so well. He takes very good care of you."

Dark liquid eyes regarded her, arrowed brows tilted almost as if the bird sought a memory. Then Greta bowed her head to preen feathers as if to dismiss the human girl.

"I missed you," Margaret said. "I prayed for your wellbeing."

Greta chirred, lifting her wings slightly, fluffing her feathers, looking past her.

"Hey my lass," a man said. Margaret spun to see Duncan coming toward her.

She smiled at his affectionate greeting, then realized he addressed the bird as he stepped past her. Yet he reached out to press her elbow gently, a gesture that said he saw her too. Her heart quickened. But he greeted the bird first.

"Greta, my lass," he murmured. He reached into a pouch and produced a bit of meat, tossing it to the bird, who caught it deftly with the talons of one foot.

"Sir, you only returned and you already have meat for her?" Margaret laughed a little. "I saw you ride in moments ago."

"Ah. I went to the keep and asked after you, and Effie said you came this way. I stopped in the kitchen, thinking to bring something to the birds if I did not find you."

"You were looking for me?" She felt unaccountably pleased.

"I was. Greetings, my lady."

"Sir Duncan," she said. "Did you see riders in the glen?"

"They had gone when we arrived, riding east again, Alan said. Possibly they came from Roskie."

Watching the bird, Margaret's next thought made her gasp. "Duncan, could it be they were searching for gyrfalcons? De Soulis seemed too interested the other day."

"He did. It is possible. Margaret Keith, we must talk." His quiet words had such a sense of urgency that her heart bounded.

"Here, now?"

"Not here. The birds like their quiet. But the castle is a busy place, with Constantine and Henry meeting with men to assemble the next patrol and the bishop conferring with Seton and Lennox, and Effie directing the servants with so much to be done. We could talk in your chamber if you like."

"Dame Agatha is resting there now. She is sharing the room with me. They will all need their rest tonight, so Effie is preparing an early supper. I should help."

"She does not expect it. She knows I was looking for you. Good of you to share with the prioress."

"She is a dear friend, who said she insisted on coming with her brother when she heard of the trouble. We met at the infirmary at Holyoak when she was injured and I was ill. Then we went to Lincluden Abbey to recover. Mama, as well. Agatha stayed, and was so dedicated and capable that she was asked to be prioress after the death of the older nun, who had the position for many years."

"She is young for it, and very intelligent woman, I can see. So she was injured—I wondered why a beautiful and youthful lass would cloister herself."

"Sore wounded, aye, and a good friend to me. Though I left Lincluden, we have remained friends."

"Forgive me for asking, but she must have had a terrible mishap."

"I do not even notice the scarring now, to be honest. She has such beauty inside and out. And such fortitude and spirit. A suitor attacked her. Her brothers near killed the man."

"Jesu. I can imagine," he muttered. "I would do the same. You two had a poor betrothal in common, I suppose."

"You know I was heartbroken there," she said, glancing away. "Agatha was—devastated, with good reason, but she accepted it and grew peaceful over the years. She has the sort of calm and wisdom and kindness that makes a good prioress. She said that only months ago, she encountered the man who hurt her, and she walked away stronger for it, she said, after—well, a bit of revenge on her part, I suppose you could say."

"Oh?" He tipped a brow.

"I hear he will recover." She gave a bitter smile.

He whistled. "Well done, Dame Agatha! You have a good friend in her."

"She means a great deal to me. And I feel that I have a new friend here in Effie too. And—in you?" She felt a lift of hope.

"We need to talk." He looked grim. Anxious. Her heart sank a little.

"We could shoot arrows over the wall and search for them in the woods."

"Rain. Come with me. I know of a place where we can find privacy."

She followed him out of the mews and across the bailey, where they ran through the rain to the keep. Up the wooden steps and inside, then along a short stem corridor to another door. He beckoned for her to proceed him up a set of steep steps that turned around a pillar, a narrow space lit only by an arrowslit high up.

They climbed three levels, passing stone platforms with closed doors. Margaret clung to a sturdy rope bolted to the pillar on the steep steps. When they reached the topmost platform, she saw a single arched door.

"What is this?" she asked.

"The quietest room in the castle." He pushed the door wide.

What was so important? Did he want to convince her further about De Soulis? There was no need for that—she bristled at the thought. True, she was resolved that she would have to see De Soulis if there was no other way to find Lilias and save Thomas's blue stone. But did Duncan not trust her to see the risks and be careful?

Perhaps he simply did not know her well enough yet to understand her stubborn nature. Perhaps he did not realize how much she loved him, and could not love another.

She stepped into a shadowy and spacious room where a brazier gave off a flickering amber and light and cozy warmth to counter the cool-gray light that diffused through glass roundels in a shuttered window lashed with rain. A large wooden bed draped in dark tartan curtains filled one side of the room. By the window was a stout oak table, two chairs, and a painted cupboard. A width of thick tartan wool was spread over the planked floor. The table was piled with parchments and leather-bound books.

She turned. "The laird's bedchamber?"

He shrugged. "The only place not overrun. May I shut the door?"

"If you mean to talk about Sir William, then leave it open. I will not stay."

"I see. What would keep you here?"

She paused, then boldly met his steady gaze, her heart drumming its hopes and dreams. "I hope you know what that would be."

He inclined his head. "Margaret, I need to explain something. You must listen."

That sounded ominous. Frowning, she went to the table and sat in one of the chairs, primly arranging her skirts, folding her hands. The brazier's warmth felt good. Fortifying. Her hands went cold with a sudden unnamed fear. He took the other chair.

"Wine?" He reached for a ceramic jug and a wooden cup.

She shook her head. "Not just now."

"I think you may need it."

Dear God, what did he plan to say? She twisted her fingers, nodded.

"I only have one cup. *Baccalarius*," he explained. "Bachelor knight."

"You are not lowborn, sir, which the term describes."

"It is used more for an unmarried knight now, or was in France when I was there. *Bacalar*, they called us, our group of Scottish knights—unmarried knights, and not one of us low-born. But free, in a sense."

"Free?" Her voice squeaked as the air go out of her. Did he mean to let her go again? Perhaps he did not mean to dissuade her from accepting De Soulis after all.

She did not want De Soulis. She wanted Duncan Campbell— she wanted him so much it hurt.

He filled the cup with dark wine, offered the cup to her. She sipped. Tart yet sweet, heating her throat. She took a long gulp. He tipped a brow as she handed it back.

"Bracing for whatever news is to come?"

"You are being very mysterious."

"Best have another sip. Let me brace myself as well." He drank, slid the cup toward her.

"Good heavens," she said, after another sip. "I cannot imagine what this news is if it needs good unwatered French wine and a secluded space."

"It might be a shock, my lady. It was to me." He sighed, set an arm on the table. "I spoke with your brother today about many things. And he told me what your father had planned to do—though he died he could tell you about it. Or me."

She frowned. "You and me?"

"Henry found some papers. He discovered—" He paused. "Your father had heard a rumor that I had returned to Scotland, very much alive. He took a chance on that and sent a message to me at Innis Connell. But I was not there to receive it. It is possible only servants were there at the time. It was not passed on to me."

"Did he want the dowry? He had decided not to take the repayment."

"I know. Margaret." He clenched his fist, spread his fingers. "Our betrothal was never dissolved."

She stared, then reached for the cup at the same moment he did. It sloshed over both their hands. Duncan let it go to her. Sipping a little, she took the moment to think, to calm her fast-beating heart. Then she set it down. He took a sip.

"But how can that be?" she asked.

"This way." He explained what Henry had told him. While he spoke, she watched his long fingers, the nimble grace and strength there. An urge to reach for his hand to feel his capable, reassuring strength overwhelmed her. She kept still.

"So," he finished, and spread his open hands.

"So because the dowry was not repaid, the contract was never canceled?"

"In part. Because your father believed I was deceased, he forgave the debt. It was never sent to the abbot or a bishop to be finalized by the Church because it was thought my death dissolved it. But when Sir Robert heard that I had returned, he knew the agreement was still in place."

"What does this mean?" Stunned and confused, she leaned her forehead in her hand, then looked up. "That we are still betrothed in fact?"

"It is still a binding agreement in this moment. But we can do what we want, Margaret. We could ignore it, with the small chance that a clerk somewhere might find a document and recognize a familiar name—and if one of us had married, it could be an issue with the Church. Or it can be dissolved, just as before—or fulfilled."

She caught her breath. "What do you want to do?"

His glance was quick and keen, his brows tucked together. He ran his fingers through his dark, disheveled, too-long hair and stood, going to the window to peer out over the half shutters. Rain rattled against the glassed panel. His frowning profile was thoughtful, edged in watery twilight.

Though her thoughts whirled, she recognized how beautiful he was standing there. A quiet warrior, tall and handsome, a wise, kind, soulful man with a sharp intellect and a restrained nature that screened his thoughts.

But she could see through that reserve now. And she saw only the man she had loved for so long. Her ideals and dreams stood there in his form, far more real and tangible, whole and compelling, than she could ever have imagined.

"Duncan." She stood. "I do not want to lose you again."

"Do you still fear that?" He shook his head. "Margaret. Whatever happened then is done. I have always loved you. Always." He did not turn. "I felt—"

She stood, silent, resting a trembling hand on the table, listening.

"I felt so remorseful for hurting you. As if I had torn out my own heart."

"I am sorry," she whispered.

"I am the one who is sorry. I thought I was doing the honorable thing, sparing you the wait and uncertainty. But I learned soon that my pledge to a king was not nearly as significant as my promise to a lass I could not forget." He glanced at her, then away, cloaked in that reserve, and she saw the effort he made to talk about his feelings. She stood silent.

"I thought of you all those years," he went on, "knowing you were a woman grown by then, wondering about you. Hearing the rumors of the convent, I thought you must be the most beautiful and spirited of nuns." He gave a hoarse laugh.

She laughed a little too. "That was Agatha, not me." Her heart pounded. She wanted to run to him, but she stayed in place, feeling he needed time, the length of the room, the sound of rain, and her patience.

"We were so young, aye?" He watched the rain on the glass. "You were three when I first met you. A wee faery creature. And later, thirteen when we found the bird."

"Nearly fourteen," she whispered. "And you were twenty."

"Nearly twenty-one. And it did not feel right to me to wed such a young girl, let alone bed her, as would have been expected."

"Girls that age marry all the time." She heard her voice as if from afar.

"They do. But I could not do that. I had this rigid sense of honor and principle then. I had to prove myself a chivalrous knight. The ideal knight."

"I always thought you were," she said softly.

He shook his head. "I followed Edward for a short time and realized I could not condone his actions against the Scots, my people. So I sided with the Scots. And for years I sat in a dungeon, then in better quarters on the hope of a good ransom. Then I was shipped off to a foreign war. And so it went. Fighting in battles, existing, scheming to get away, doing what I could to survive. Ideal knight!"

"Then against all odds, you became that."

"What I learned of true honor, I learned in those years from the men around me. Sir Andrew Murray—aye, the lad's father. We shared a cell together. Sir John Comyn, who was killed by Bruce, or some say Bruce's men, in this crush of right and ambition over the throne of Scotland. But first of all, my father, a man of integrity and a soul as big as the stars. And now Robert

Bruce. He teaches all of us what dedication is. What it means to love Scotland. Persistence. Passion. Belief," he added, fisting a hand.

"You learned well, Duncan Dhu."

He looked at her then. "But I made a grave error before those years. Had we married as our families wanted then, and had I never left, I might have been a very different man than now."

"Either way, a very good man." She moved toward him. "And now?"

"And now I could be the kind of husband you deserve."

Her knees wavered. "Is that what you want?"

His sweet and rueful smile poured into her heart. "I always wanted that, Margaret. And lately I see how much, and why."

With a little soft cry, she ran to him and he opened his arms. She melted into his embrace as if she had always belonged there, as if he was some missing piece of her and she of him, found in joy. He felt so strong, warm, enveloping, that she closed her eyes to savor it, sensing his heart thumping against her cheek.

"Duncan," she whispered, and reached up to cup her hands on his dark-bristled jaw. "I thought when you wanted to talk, sounding so serious, you meant to let me go."

"Let you go? I only just found you again after so long."

"Perhaps we both needed that time," she said, as the idea of it occurred. "We both went through a great deal. I think we are stronger for it. We know what we want. What we need," she breathed.

"I know what I want. The rest is yours to decide."

She sighed, smiled. What did she want? All her dreams to come true. And in this moment, it seemed it could happen. So many dreams.

"I just want you to kiss me," she said then.

He did, taking her, leaning her back, kissing her the way he had kissed her under the arch of birches, with passion and power and all his heart blown open. He kissed her as if all the years and regrets and grief vanished, as if she had never been a child with him, or even a woman in his arms with so much time wasted between them. Instead, he kissed her as one soul would kiss another, having searched and found and merged easily at last.

"You," she said, drawing back for breath. "All this time, it was you I dreamed of. Even when it seemed impossible, thinking you were gone. I was angry and sad at first, but still yearning, still dreaming. I believed you did not want me, and still I never wanted to marry anyone else. Only you. It was only you I loved. Only you I love now."

"Dearest. Listen now." He snugged her in the circle of his arms, looking down at her. "The day I broke it off, I loved you in a way, but both of us were too young. I suppose I loved the memory of you, the thought of the woman you would become. In those days, I desperately wanted to come home to my kin— and then find you and ask forgiveness. But when I learned you were in a convent, I lost heart somewhat."

"And all the while I thought you had died. What a tangle of knots made by rumor and fate. Yet here we are."

"Here we are," he murmured. Pressed to his chest, she rose to kiss his cheek, his lips, then pulled back. "Then all is well?"

"And all shall be well. There is still the matter of De Soulis, but we are still betrothed, and he cannot dismiss that. Though we do not know what he truly wants from you, which concerns me."

"He has no claim over your betrothed. He never did," she added.

He brushed a stray curl from her brow. "No claim, but if he is angered over it, he could have ill intent. And if Menteith should ever discover you shot him, he would come after you with vengeance and the law. Remember they tried to grab you when they took Lilias. There may be a reason. Edward will do anything to punish Robert Bruce. He did order the capture of his kins-women."

"But I am not related to Bruce."

"You accompanied his daughter. And you have value of your own through your kin and the Rhymer. King Edward sent men to pursue your sister for something she owned. It is possible they meant to take you too in that ambush."

She remembered their earlier conversation about Thomas's brooch. "Since Menteith took Lilias, he may have known something about me."

"Aye, and perhaps it was a royal order—or he just wanted to please the king, knowing the king's obsession with prophecies and the Rhymer and such. It could be."

"Duncan—the stones. I nearly forgot with all this—I wanted to tell you."

"Do not fret about your brooch. I will get that for you somehow."

"Not that. The stones we found with the holes in them, remember? I did not see anything through them. But I tried again, and I saw a vision. Truly."

"The legend about the faeries at the pool is a fine one, but those stones do look rather ordinary, lass. I doubt anyone could see much but what is in front of them."

"Listen, do. At first I saw nothing. But I fell asleep for a little while, and I dreamed my great-grandfather was there. He looked so real. He told me to look through the stones again. And he mentioned his seeing-stone, the blue stone in the brooch, and said I must have it in my keeping."

"Well, if a ghost in a dream orders it, we must obey," he drawled.

She knocked his arm lightly. "When I woke up, I knew it for a dream. But I tried the stones again, and this time I saw something. A vision that was only in the stone."

His hand cupped her elbow. "What was that?"

"I saw you through the opening in the stone." At his puzzled look, she nodded. "You were standing in a field. But I was in the room, you see. And the sky was gray. It was impossible."

"In a field? Tell me about it."

"You stood in a field, but it looked to be in the aftermath of a battle. There were men lying on the ground, not moving. You were the only one standing among those poor men. Then you leaned on your sword, which was upright. But it seemed to sink down, and you fell. It was very strange. I was so frightened for you."

"Standing? And the sword sank?" Brow puckering, he looked baffled.

"I know it seems odd to see such a thing through a hole no bigger than this." She circled her finger and thumb. "But I saw it so clearly, and I am scared for you. I cannot bear for some harm to come to you. Not now, when we have found each other again."

"Hush, lass." He took her into his embrace, held her for a moment, kissed her hair, let her go. "I think I know—"

"Do not say it was nothing. It was real." She tapped her breastbone. "I know it, I."

He smiled. "My mother would say exactly that when she saw something true. And we believed it—most of the time," he added.

"There, see!"

"I see, I do. But listen. What you saw is nothing to fret over. It already happened."

"What?"

"At Dunbar, years ago. When the fighting was done, I was one of the few still left standing among the Scots. Exhausted. Wounded. I stood looking about, and leaned on my sword, and the tip sank down into the mud and the blood. I went down with it and collapsed. Listen, lass," he said, as she gasped. "That was how I was captured. I fell when the sword sank, and I was taken prisoner. That is what you saw."

"Duncan, I am sorry—and so relieved. What I saw will not happen."

A little smile as he drew her closer. "It will never happen again. You saw the past," he whispered, "and it was not something you knew. That makes me believe in those wee stones. And in you, and what you can see in the stones one."

"You believe that I saw it, then?"

"I do. I believe all you said. And I believe you inherited more than a couple of pretty stones from True Thomas. You inherited a rare gift."

"I thought I had no real ability with the stones he gave me."

"And now you know otherwise." He kissed her then, slowly, her body curving to his, yearning quick and hot as his arms tightened around her and the kiss lingered. But then he drew back, kissing her cheek, her ear. She melted at that warm breathiness poured through to her bones.

She startled in his arms at a loud rumble followed by a deafening crack. A bright flash bathed the room in silver light. Rain began to slam against the window and the outer walls. "Oh! I did not expect the storm to hit us so hard, so quickly."

"Nor did I. Some of us were planning to ride out again on patrol."

"Stay," she said. "No one was in the glen earlier, you said. They would not come out in weather like this."

"Unlikely, true. I will stay for a bit. You should go to your room and rest."

"I would not rest. Do not go yet, Duncan. There is something else to say."

"What is that, love?"

"The question I was considering." Her breath quickened in anticipation.

"Ah, that. Now that we know we are still betrothed, it truly is a question." He paused, and she knew he waited for her answer. "Have you decided?"

"I have. The betrothal—just makes me more determined to accept your suit." She lifted her chin.

"I see," he murmured, and bent to kiss her slowly, tenderly. "Well, then, Margaret Keith. Marry me."

"I will. I want to."

"Here. Now. Marry me."

She stilled in his arms, leaning back to look up at him. "Now?"

"Tonight. The bishop could marry us this evening, or in the morning. Your brother already offered his approval—though he knows his sister will do what she will regardless of what he thinks. But he seems pleased."

"I am glad of it. But tonight?" She pushed a little on his arms so that he opened his hands and let go. "I am not sure."

"It is quick. You want to think on it."

"We have done enough thinking on the matter of betrothal and marriage. I just—it would not be the sort of wedding I imagined."

"The faster we marry, the better I can protect you from what others might try to do—De Soulis. Menteith. Edward," he finished. Thunder boomed outside, rolled into new flashes of lightning. He glanced toward the window. "The men were planning to go out. I should tell them to wait."

"No one should go out on patrol just now," she said. "Wait until the storm passes. Let me stay here with you." A feeling, insistence and need and something more, a deep, luscious pull, began to fill her.

His arms went round her, drew her close. "Here?"

"Here. Forever."

"Forever, a bit at a time," he murmured as he leaned to kiss her, and she felt herself melt again in his arms. Whatever he wanted, she wanted too. Her dreams came together, a golden net that wrapped her in desire, in relief and gratefulness too. What had come about between them had suddenly become seamless, flowing as if it was always meant to be, and some barrier had finally broken away. Curving against his body, she felt a pulse begin within her—not just the drubbing of her heart, but the beat of her very blood, surging, craving, eager. She arched in his arms and gave herself to each renewed kiss, gave herself to him, opening to the gentle tip of his tongue, hard strength of him, the throb of his body against hers.

He swept her up in his arms, carried her a step or two, paused. "What do you want," he asked low. Lightning flashed again at the window as he spoke. "What do you want here and now—"

"You," she whispered with a rush of boldness. "I want to be with you. I do not want you to leave."

"You know I must. When the storm is less, aye?"

She nodded, and he turned to carry her to the great bed in the shadows, a curtained alcove of dark plaid, and inside, layered blankets and piled pillows. When he set her down, the mattress was soft enough that she sank, and sank again when he set one knee beside her. The mattress, when pressed, gave off mingled scents of lavender and heather and something piney, so fragrant that she inhaled, closed her eyes, leaned her head back. Duncan paused in the shadows, lightning and candlelight behind him, and tugged off his tunic and linen shirt. The light slipped along the hard and smooth contours of his shoulders, his arms, his torso. Lightning brightened the room again, sparkling through the weave of the plaid as he stretched out beside her.

He touched her cheek, turning her face to his in the darkness, in the fragrant cavern. She closed her eyes as he kissed her, his lips soft, tender on hers, drawing, pulling, easing open. His fingers trailed downward, tracing over her collarbones, then lower. Her body responded, ached, craved the feeling of his hands on her. With a little moan of wanting, she pressed closer, fingers spread on his chest, his heartbeat fast and sure beneath her touch. His hands at her bodice pulled at the crisscrossed ribbons threaded there, and she helped him, fingers impatient and trembling, quicker and smarter on the ties than his. A tug, a pull and draw, and the pretty moss-green gown pooled on the floor, leaving her in a linen shift.

The cloth was soft and light, so that his hands slipped easily beneath its folds. The warmth and spread of his hands over her, up and down, over her breasts and abdomen, shaping her, coaxing her to answer his touch with soft moans, kisses, inviting arches that her body simply knew—all was sheer pleasure, unexpected and so natural that she followed, curving and flowing beneath his touch, his kisses. She tugged the shift away as his lips traced over her breasts, kissed until luscious sensations surged through her, sudden and powerful. Within, her body pulsed like the thunder and rain that pounded outside, flashed within like the lightning that glimmered beyond the curtains.

Though she had long dreamed of this man, this love she felt, she had not been able to imagine this, the merging that drove thought away and let heart and desire take over, the need so strong that only her body could express what she felt now, and felt for him. She pressed against him, rolled with him, opened as he coaxed, plummeted further as his hands, fingers, found and caressed her as she burned for more, breath and heartbeat pulsing.

When he slid over her, her body instinctively knew what to do, what he wanted, what she deeply desired, so that she arched and took him into her, a sudden rich heated plunge and thrust between them that left him gasping, his breath hot against her throat and her lips. She took his breath into hers, moving like a wave with him; she could not tell where he began and she ended, a feeling of freedom such as she had never known.

All of it wove together—desire, thrill, fear, and uncertainty; losing him, finding him, not knowing where it would lead. All blended into an immensity of love that she could not define, would not limit, just let it flow over and through her. And she knew utterly, deeply, that she would always be with him, knew in the very center of her soul, her body and her being, that she had always been his, and he was hers. Troubles and wondering vanished until she stirred out of the sweet mist that had taken her over.

She kissed him simply then and lay quiet in his arms, listening to his breathing and the steady thud of his heart. In that moment, her dreams had come to be, here beside him.

CHAPTER TWENTY-FIVE
Lilias

S HE STUMBLED INTO the narrow cave on hands and knees. Standing to find the space was a natural vault just a bit higher than her head, she felt as if she entered a sanctuary as peaceful as a church, and as safe, too. The cave, a slim cleft tucked under a rocky overhang, was obscured hidden by a curtain of flowering vines and tall scrub and grasses. If she had not climbed a steep hill to avoid running across the glen floor, she might not have noticed it. But she had tripped on some rocks, turning her ankle and falling to her knees. Wincing as she looked at her bruised ankle, she glanced up. And there was the cave opening.

All the way across hills and moors, following a westerly direction from Loch Roskie, she had done her best to keep to the hills where it would be more challenging for pursuers to spot her. Most of a day and into a night, she had walked over hills, stopping to rest now and then, growing exhausted. She had taken the food left on the tray Dame Brigit had brought to her room, and ate sparingly to make it last.

But she had found plenty of clean, cool water to drink, and found some edible mushrooms and plants too—Lady Rowena Keith had taught her well, and she had been very cautious about such matters. Finally, she found the long narrow glen that matched the crude little map drawing. And after that, she discovered the low cave just as the light lowered for the day and a rainstorm blew through the glen with frightening power. But she was dry, and warm enough in her cloak, and she would be able to sleep a little with the rain drumming outside. In the morning, she would venture onward.

Just before she had found the little cave and the safety she needed, she had seen the track of a meandering river in the distance—and she thought she heard the dim rush of a waterfall. Or was that just rain? Even so, Dame Brigit's map had proved a godsend.

The cave was dark and narrow, an arched vault like a flat bubble in the middle of an expanse of rough rock. Red sandstone, she thought, running a hand over textured pinkish stone, streaked with red in places, brown in others. Iron and ochre and copper gave it color, her father had once told her. The raw stone reminded her of the walls of one of his castles. But the castle was held by the English now and her father could not go there or anywhere these days for fear of his life and the end of the cause for Scotland. He had sent her to the safety of the Keiths of Kincraig. Later, he sent an escort to take her to Ireland.

Instead, she sat in this cave, alone and all but lost, wondering what to do.

She leaned her back against the rock wall, glad to take weight off her ankle. When she had first crawled inside, her heart was thumping hard, but she felt calmer, though hurting a bit. Wincing, she bent her knee to look at her ankle. Easing off her boot, then her pale woolen stocking, she saw a bloody gash just above her bruised, swollen ankle. Wiggling her toes, she rolled her foot a little and squealed in pain. She did not think it was broken, but she could not be sure.

Cushioning her ankle in her hands, feeling some relief from that little bit of warmth, she was afraid that standing, let alone walking, would make the injury worse. Thank heavens for the cave and the rain; one provided shelter, the other a reason to stay inside for a while.

How ironic that she had helped heal Sir John's injured foot so that he was able to walk more easily, and might even be strong enough to ride out to search for her. And here she sat, nursing a twisted ankle, unable to continue her escape.

She sat shivering in the chilly cave, wrapped in her cloak, and ate what was left of an oatcake from her breakfast, and a few mushrooms she had plucked, glad she had not devoured all of it earlier in her hunger. She drank a few sips from a small silver flask that she had taken from her room at Roskie, filling it more than once that day.

Taking Brigit's folded map out of her little belt pouch, she studied it in the fading light. From what she could tell, Brechlinn Castle lay south of the falls. If she could find the waterfall, she could follow the river down to the loch and find the castle there.

But she could not walk far—her ankle ached and her body was exhausted. She had to rest. And the storm was fierce, pounding the ground, shaking the bracken, filling the sky with flashes of lightning and thunder. She would stay here, sleep for a while, and surely everything would seem better in the light of morning.

CHAPTER TWENTY-SIX

I N THE DARKNESS, Duncan rose from his bed, moving carefully lest he wake her where she slept, comfortable and warm beside him. As he dressed, he heard steady rain, but not the rumble of thunder, and no vein of lightning showed in the grim sky; the quality of the gray darkness told him dawn was near.

Sitting on the bed to pull on his boots, he heard Margaret stir, then sit up in the shadows within the curtained bed. Her hair had a bronze sheen in the low glow of the brazier, and swept down in tousled waves over her bare and beautiful body above the rumpled blankets.

"Are you leaving?" Her voice was soft and thick with sleep.

"Aye. Rest," he murmured. He leaned to kiss the top of her head.

"I cannot rest. I should not be in here." She slid her legs over the side of the bed, stretched for her shift and gown discarded on the floor and tugged them on. Sitting beside him, she braided her hair into one thick, messy plait. He stood, taking up his belt to fasten it around his hips.

"Are you going out on patrol? Wait for me," she said.

"I will not take you with me, dearling."

She sighed. "Do not go out alone. It is not safe. I feel it."

He stilled, hands on the buckle. "Do you, now? I will take Lennox or Constantine if I can stir them from their beds."

"Good. I must go back to my bedchamber. I hope Agatha is

sleeping. I would not want to explain where I have been."

"Some may wonder where we were last night. We missed supper. Thankfully no one came looking for us." He raised her chin with a finger and kissed her lips lightly. "We are betrothed, love, with all the privileges that brings. In Scotland, it is significant."

She tilted her head. "Do you mean that betrothed couples who lay together are considered married in Scotland—if they have—done the act?"

"Aye." He smiled. "If there is intention to marry, under Scots law it becomes a marriage with the act, as you say. The law recognizes such marriages. Most couples will fix it further with a ceremony, whether a private handfasting or the blessing of a priest before witnesses."

"So we are wed now?"

"In the eyes of the law, we are married." He drew her toward him, cupped his hands on her shoulders. "It rests on the intent of the groom and bride. This groom is set on it. Does the bride agree? It needs the consent of both parties."

"She agrees," she murmured, as he kissed her. "Will we have a wedding, then?"

"A wedding, handfasting, private pledge, whatever you desire, love. Wife. My wee faery queen," he whispered, brushing tendrils of hair from her brow. Then he kissed her, lingering and deep, until she was breathless and leaned into the circle of his arms. "Say what you want, and it is done."

"I want you to come back to me quickly and safely, with Lilias. Then will I decide what sort of wedding I want, if we both agree."

"We will. And I will bring her back—if I have to ride to Loch Roskie with all my men to do it. One more patrol, then I will muster them. For now, take up your shoes and I will escort you down—the turning stair can be dark as pitch."

"Hurry back with Lilias. Oh!" she said suddenly. "I began to tell you last night—and just thought of it again. You might not think it important."

"I am listening."

"When I looked through the hole in the stone, I saw something else. I just wonder if it might help, if you believe me."

"You convinced me when you described seeing me in that stone. Tell me the rest."

"I saw Lilias. At least, I think it was Lilias. A girl was running in mist or in rain. I saw a waterfall and a cave on a hill. It came and went very fast, the images. She was watching a falcon in the sky."

"Was it a dream? It sounds symbolic."

"It was not a dream. I was awake when I saw it through the hole in the stone. Are there caves near the waterfall we visited? Could it be that place? I cannot say if it was the same one. And because I had been there with you, perhaps it was just in my mind."

"But we should consider it," he said. "If she managed to get away—well. There are caves there, but Scotland is full of caves and waterfalls, in truth." He shook his head. "I will give it some thought."

"Thank you." She sighed. "I am not very experienced with this, I suppose. My sister sometimes has visions that come to her suddenly. She has learned to understand them better. But I do not yet."

"It will come with time, love. We should go." He opened the door.

Margaret picked up her shoes. "And thank you for looking for her this morning."

"Every day until she is found. I swear it." He pulled her close and kissed her.

ENTERING THE GREAT hall, Duncan walked past a dozen or more men sleeping on pallets as he crossed the room to the library that Lennox and Constantine were using for a temporary sleeping chamber. Easing the door open, he nearly tripped over Malcolm

Lennox, stretched out on a mat partially blocking the door. Beyond him, Constantine snored, and Andrew Murray slept on a pallet in the corner. Duncan gave Lennox a kick in the shin.

The man sat up abruptly. "What the devil?"

"Pray the devil has naught to do with us this day," Duncan growled. "Get your boots on and come with me. We are riding out to find a wee lass."

"Good," Lennox grunted. "Con—wake up." Constantine sat up.

"Just Lennox and I need go out," Duncan told them. "Con, gather a patrol and meet us in Glen Falloch. We will need at least a dozen in case we must ride to Roskie."

Constantine ruffled his sandy mop of hair, then called to Andrew to wake him up.

Lennox yanked on his boots in the dark and stood. "Where are we searching?"

"We are looking for a cave," Duncan said.

"Huh. There are plenty of those."

"Lady Margaret dreamed the lass was in a cave by a waterfall."

"Did she! Well, then, best start at the Falls of Falloch. Lead the way."

YEARS AGO, HE and his brothers used to run all through here, Duncan remembered as he and Lennox entered the rocky gorge where the river cut through and the falls flowed. They had played knights and lords, sheriffs and brigands, elves and ogres among these caves and hills. Memories flooded him as he went: there, the pointed rocks they had called giant's teeth; over there, cascades of water spilling into a stream; further on, a rowan tree burst forth from a rock with unmatched persistence; all around, dense woodland enveloped the gorge and made it seem like a magical realm.

There it was, the old rowan, just blooming in spring. Near that, he knew, crevices and small caves pierced the massive jumble of rocks that formed the sides of the gorge. Ahead, he heard the roar of the falls, though he could not yet see its white tail and deep pool. Shouldering the bow and quiver he had brought with him, he moved on.

With narrowed eyes, he scanned about for any niche or shadow that might be a cave. Walking along a rocky ridge, he saw Lennox exploring in another direction. Malcolm did not know the area well, but he knew Lilias. If the girl was here somewhere, she might venture out if she saw a man she knew and trusted.

And if she was in a cave near the waterfall, Margaret and her seeing-stone had a power that could not be denied.

The morning was cloudy, damp, breezy, but the rain seemed past, the sky pale and clearing. Thinking of the falcons, he remembered that Bran had mentioned taking the bishop and others out to fly the birds this morning, and had promised to head west with them, though that was no guarantee, for the birds would do what they liked. A flock of ducks arrowed overhead; their confident, noisy flight told him no birds of prey hovered nearby yet, ready to pounce.

He looked for riders too, aware that danger could come from the east glen and Loch Roskie, should De Soulis or Menteith ride out with men. If they came through the long glen toward the falls again, they might well head for Brechlinn. Were they searching for a gyrfalcon, did they want Margaret Keith, did they have Lilias Bruce? He meant to find out. But now that he thought about where he was, and what he was doing, perhaps they too had been looking for the girl.

The waterfall and gorge, the river and surrounding glen belonged to Brechlinn and the Campbells. Now the land was largely uninhabited; most of the crofters and shepherds had been driven out by the same English troops that had tried to ruin Brechlinn Castle. Folk had gone to Crianlarich and Stirling, and even west to the Isles. Duncan hoped to see them all returning home one day.

As he climbed a steep incline, he saw an outcrop of rock that rose up like a rugged crown. He remembered conquering its height as a boy. Near it, he saw Lennox coming toward him. The man raised a hand.

"Riders coming through the east glen," Lennox said. "I saw them from a height. They are far off, but if it is Menteith with them, we could have trouble."

"Keep watch. If they come closer, we will get the horses and meet them." They had left the horses in a pinewood while they went into the gorge. If Lilias was here, he prayed he could find her before any riders approached.

Every instinct he had told him she was here somewhere. He felt it with an odd sense of certainty, and had to admit that to himself. Perhaps, though he had never entertained the notion before, he had inherited something from his mother.

Margaret's visions through the stone made him wonder about such things.

"I see no sign of a cave, let alone a lass," Lennox said.

"Wrong or right, it is worth the search."

"Aye so. I will keep watch from that peak if you want to continue looking."

While Lennox headed for the outcrop, Duncan moved toward another rugged formation that he and his brothers had called their stronghold; the jagged inclines looked like a natural fortress had erupted from the earth. He tracked through a narrow pass between slopes of solid, ancient rock, hauling himself upward by gripping points of stone as he went.

Everywhere here, rocks were coated in moss and wildflowers grew in profusion, thick mats of tiny pink and yellow flowers mingled with green leaves and vines filled the cracks between the rocks and cushioned his steps as he made his way upward.

Here and there he saw crevices and shadows, none deep enough for a cave. Above, Lennox stood silhouetted against the pale-gray sky. From up there, Duncan knew his friend could see the river's course, the waterfall and glen above, and the narrow neck of the long glen to the east.

Reaching a fork in the natural pathway between the rocks, he paused to assess his next direction. He nimbly skirted a patch of prickly yellow gorse, his boot pushing and shaking the bracken as he went past. A bird flew overhead, and he stilled, watching. Just a wild hawk, hunting as it pleased. He moved on.

Something caught the corner of his sight—the gorse still shifted after his passing. About to step forward, he stopped, seeing a slight movement, a pale shadow.

For a moment he thought two eyes watched him through curtain of tangled dark hair, but as soon as he looked, they disappeared. Just a trick of shadow and light where a cluster of white flowers and dark leaves hovered. Behind that tangle was a low arched crevice. It was worth a look. He went backward a few steps and hunched down.

Something moved back there, he was sure. Not keen on prickly gorse, he took up a bit of broken shale and pushed the thorny bush aside, revealing an overhang of rock above a deep opening. He heard scurrying inside.

He hunkered down and waited. The air tensed, as if he was not the only one stilled and frozen there, barely breathing. It was not a hare or a fox, but something sentient—every instinct told him so.

"Lady Lilias?" he murmured.

Nothing. The wild hawk swooped past, far overhead. *Kee-kee-kee. . .*

"Lilias," he said softly, "I am Duncan Campbell. Your father knows me. Malcolm Lennox is here too. We have been searching for you for days."

After a long moment, the eyes appeared again. Dark blue, ringed in thick black lashes. A tangled mat of dark hair. A turned-up nose, pale cheeks scratched and streaked with dirt and tracks of tears.

"I do not know you, sir. Send Lennox to me," she said in a hoarse whisper.

A king's daughter indeed. "Malcolm, down here!" he called.

Then he held out his hand. "Come out, lass. You are safe now."

THE MORNING BROUGHT a clearing of rain with light glowing through pale, cloudy skies as Margaret dressed, pausing to look anxiously out the window, hoping to see Duncan return. Agatha had left the room to go to morning prayers with the bishop. When Margaret had returned to the room, Agatha had been sound asleep, so she made a bed of blankets on the floor and slept a little before rising just after dawn.

But if she stayed here longer, she might not hear news of Duncan. Changing out of the blue gown she wore, she went to put on a gray woolen gown that Effie had found in a storage chest. The simple gown had snug sleeves and an embroidered hem, and she dropped a short sleeveless tunic of forest green over it. She quickly braided her hair in two thick plaits and let them drape over the front, the tails reaching the leather belt slung on her hips. Then she tied a creamy silk ribbon around her brow.

A maiden's ribbon, for she had no veil or wimple yet. But she had become a bride in a passionate sense, and soon would be wife to the only man she had ever wanted. She sighed, smiled, feeling loved, trusted, treasured, and trusting. It felt like more than enough.

And today she hoped for the best news to come when Duncan returned with Lilias. Then she could truly plan for the future.

Yet worry tapped at her as she took up her green cloak against the morning chill and headed down to the bailey. The fear grew as she crossed the yard to see her brother, Agatha, and several others gathered there, including Sir Liam, Constantine, the bishop, Andrew, Bran, and a cluster of knights. She hurried over to Henry.

"Has something happened?" she asked.

Henry smiled. "All is well. Bran is about to take the bishop and a few others out with the birds for hawking and hunting. Sir Constantine is putting together a patrol. Would you like to go hawking this morning?"

"Not today. I was worried, seeing everyone here—I thought something had happened to Duncan."

Henry lifted a brow. "Duncan? Constantine said he and Lennox went out early."

"No need for concern, my lady," Constantine said. "When the patrol is organized, we will go out and meet them.

"I will go with the hawking party, to make sure they have an extra guard," Liam Seton said. "We cannot be too cautious," he added.

"I WOULD LIKE to take a morning ride, but I will not go far," Margaret said. If she could ride toward the waterfall, she might find Duncan and Lennox on their way back.

"You will need an escort," Henry cautioned.

"I can go with her," Andrew spoke up.

"I will take them out. I know the area," Iain Campbell offered. His glance toward Margaret was calm but keen, reminding her of his brother. She sensed that he was concerned about Duncan too.

"Aye then," Bran said. "I will have the grooms saddle additional horses for the hawking party, the patrol, and those taking fresh air." He gave her a sidelong glance, curious and wondering. Feeling tension in the air, Margaret wondered if some of Duncan's friends harbored a concern they did not voice.

While the horses and hawks were being readied, Effie came toward them. "If you would like to break your fast before you leave, there is food set out in the hall."

Impatient to ride out, but knowing the delay was necessary, Margaret went with the rest to the great hall, where Effie and the servants had provided a spread of dishes on a trestle table, including porridge, bacon, cheese, and more. In time they returned to the bailey, where Bran gave Margaret a sturdy pony with a sidesaddle, the same garron she had ridden before when she'd visited the falls with Duncan.

Finally they all filed through the gate, Bran leading the hawking party west and away, while Margaret, with Andrew and Sir Iain, went north toward the river.

"There is a pretty waterfall ahead if you would like to see it," Sir Iain said.

"Your brother took me there. I would love to see it again."

"No farther, though. Duncan would be displeased if you were out too long today."

"Let him take that up with me," she said, urging her pony ahead.

Iain did not protest; silence, she noticed, was his natural preference. They rode the few miles toward the waterfall quietly, and soon she heard the rumble of the falls as they approached the deep gorge that contained the falls, the pool, and part of the river.

Her concern deepened with every mile, every slope and stretch of moor and woodland. When they stopped to watch the thundering white downpour and the wide pool from afar, she turned to Iain.

"Can we leave the horses here and walk toward the falls?"

He grimaced, clearly thinking it was not a good idea, but finally agreed. "As you wish. We can leave the horses over that way."

As they entered the strip of woodland that edged along the river, she saw two horses quietly grazing, reined to trees. "Duncan and Lennox are here!" she said.

"So it seems," Iain said, frowning. Once they dismounted and tied their horses securely, Iain directed them toward a natural path slick with moisture. Margaret remembered going that way with Duncan to see the waterfall. She hurried ahead.

Andrew and Iain were slightly behind her as she followed an angled path toward the gorge. Rocks piled like high barriers in places, and trees filled the gaps with curtains of leafy branches. Soon the waterfall was closer, larger, louder as water rushed over the cliff, white and frothy and swirling, powered by the force of the drop.

"There is a pretty glen past here, as I recall," Margaret said.

"Perhaps Duncan and Lennox went that way."

"Possibly," Iain said. "These are all Brechlinn lands, but few live here now. My brother wants to bring the glen folk back. He wants them to feel safe again."

"They do not feel safe here?"

"English," he said curtly. "I will go ahead of you here. The way can be slippery, so be careful. Andrew, see to the lady." He moved on with long, sure strides.

Margaret scanned the gorge and the moors beyond the trees. Where was Duncan? As they walked along, she held the hems of her gown and cloak out of puddles, looking all around her even as she stepped carefully.

"Look over there." Andrew pointed. "Is that Duncan?"

She gasped, seeing two men moving along the rocks beyond the falls. A smaller person was with them, skirts billowing. "Lilias!"

She hurried up the rocky incline, the river rushing to her left, the waterfall increasingly noisy ahead. Iain Campbell had seen the three figures ahead too. He half-ran along the ridge toward them.

"Meg," Andrew said then. "Look through the trees."

She did, glimpsing men on horseback moving across the moors that paralleled the river and gorge. Taking up her skirt hems, she climbed faster, accepting Andrew's help. The water rushed and burbled, the mossy stones were damp and slick, and she grabbed handholds on rocks as she went upward to attain a clearer view.

Riders were coming out of the narrow western neck of Glen Fada, the long glen to the east. Two—three, Margaret counted, seeing steely flashes in the gray light, and a knight in a red-and-white striped surcoat on a black charger.

"De Soulis," she said.

"Who?"

"He is working with Menteith. I have business with him," she added.

"He may have business with Sir Duncan first. Look, the riders are heading toward the river. I hope Sir Duncan sees them."

"Sir Iain will warn them." As she spoke, Iain Campbell glanced down and motioned for Margaret and the two of them to stay where they stood and not come forward. The air seemed filled with tension, the powerful rush and noise of the falls ahead adding to that. Margaret stood, back and shoulders straight, tense.

The leader was indeed De Soulis. She saw him stop and gesture to his men, one of whom dismounted and ran toward the gorge. The jagged barrier rose dark and formidable, and the man climbed halfway and came running back. De Soulis shouted. She could not hear his words.

Glancing toward where she had last seen Duncan and the rest, she saw no one there now. In the opposite direction, Sir William seemed agitated as he rode toward the tree-lined gorge.

She could stand it no longer. "Wait here!"

"Meg, stop!" Andrew reached but missed as she moved away.

"I must speak to him," she said. "If he sees me, he will be distracted, and the others can get away. Stay here," she insisted. "They might recognize you as one who got away from the ambush."

Skirts gathered, she took the rocks carefully along the gorge, then hurried across rumpled green turf toward the knights on the moor.

CHAPTER TWENTY-SEVEN

"GOD'S VERY BONES," Lennox said, look towards the glen. "Is that your lady?"

"Where?" Duncan turned with Lilias in his arms; the girl had hurt her ankle and needed aid. He saw Margaret crossing the moor at a fair pace, her coppery hair bright in the pale light. "What is she doing here?"

"Looking for you, most like, and our wee princess."

"I am not a princess," Lilias insisted.

"You are a princess to me, and precious too," Lennox said. "Look there, that rascal De Soulis is riding to meet her."

Duncan swore under his breath. "I have to get down there. Take Lady Lilias back to Brechlinn." He handed the girl into Lennox's arms. "Go with the earl. He will take you to safety."

"Are you going to fetch Margaret Keith?" she asked. "Was she captured too?"

"She was safe with me, lass. I will make sure she stays that way."

"That man was with Sir John," she said.

"You saw him with John Menteith?"

"Aye. Sir John has our knights too, but they took them to a castle called Dunbarton. I heard them say so. Sir Hugh, Sir Quentin, and others are there."

"Excellent lass! Get her out of here, Lennox."

"Come, love. Sir Duncan will see to Lady Margaret and I will take you to safety," Lennox said. "And I will head back with as many men as we can muster. Duncan!" he called. "Is that your brother there?"

Turning, Duncan shaded his eyes. "Iain! And Andrew Murray behind him! They must have come out to find us. Take the lass and Andrew too, and send Iain to me. We will see to Margaret—and De Soulis."

He watched them go, the slight tousled-haired girl and the giant of a man who cradled her as he walked over the rocks.

Turning, Duncan moved carefully, stealthily, then hunkered down behind a cluster of boulders and saplings. Beyond the gorge and the trees, he saw Margaret pause to wait as De Soulis rode toward her.

What did she intend by this? He knew in his deepest heart that she was his, part of him now as he was part of her. There was no going back from that, no betrayal ever possible.

And yet she waited for De Soulis. The knight stopped, spoke to her from the height of his saddle. As Margaret stepped to the side, he angled his horse to face her, his back to the falls.

Ah. Duncan understood. She realized that he, Malcolm, and Lilias were nearby, and she meant to distract De Soulis from seeing them. She was giving them a chance to escape. Brave, wild, impulsive lass. His own wild, powerful need to protect her surged within him.

Wary and watchful, he set a hand to the dagger sheathed at his belt and shifted the bow on his shoulder. Hunched, he edged over the rocks, behind trees, closer to the moor. The air was chill, moist, filled with the pounding roar of the falls behind him. He watched the bright-haired lass and judged what next to do.

Hearing a low whistle, he glanced back. His brother crouched and came toward him.

"Sir William," Margaret said, "I have a message for you." *But not the one you want,* she thought, sliding a glance behind De Soulis over the rumpled moor to the gorge. Where crooked trees thrust upward, she saw movement, a man crouched and dropping down behind the rocks.

She smiled, keeping the knight's attention on her. Dropping back her hood, she showed him her braided hair with the maiden's ribbon adorning it. She had to mislead him to help Duncan and the others get Lilias to safety.

"You bring news to treasure, I hope."

She craned her head, uncomfortably aware of the huge white charger, too aware the man could pluck her up like a rag doll and carry her off. "Treasure! You did promise to return my brooch." She saw it winking blue and silver on his cloak.

He covered it with a leather-gloved hand. "First, your promise to me. You want the pin, I want our betrothal fixed again. A mistake we can correct."

"But I am betrothed to Sir Duncan."

He waved a hand. "You will benefit more marrying a De Soulis than a Campbell. Edward punishes those who support Bruce, as I suspect he does. I mean to prove it. But now, I want to know why this gewgaw is so important to you." He tapped the pin.

"It was a gift from my grandfather."

"Thomas the Rhymer." He nodded. "I know he willed some valuable items to his Keith kin. So this is one of those things."

"Kin often leave valuables to their heirs. But how did you know?"

"Your father listed some of your inheritance in our letter of betrothal. I went to the sheriff of Selkirk to confirm it, since he retains copies of local wills. You were given a pin and a pendant. Small things. But their real worth was in belonging to True Thomas. Is it enchanted, this thing? It looks like a seeing-stone."

Her heart pounded. "It is only precious to me and my family. Nothing more."

"Was it a gift from the queen of faery? Some would think it foolish or even of the devil. But I find it intriguing."

She had a terrible sense, a twisting in her gut that told her to flee. She stood firm. "Why would that interest you?"

"My own kin dabble in such things. My uncle, Walter de Soulis, whom I greatly admired, was interested in dark and magical matters. Last year, Walter was slain by treacherous Scots. I inherited some of his property. Magical armor, for one. But he did not have this," he said, tapping the brooch again. "Now I do."

She tried to laugh. "It is just a simple reminder of my Grand-da. Give it back."

"It does look like a seeing-stone. I looked through it but it would not show me anything. I have a feeling you can do that." He leaned down. "Surely he taught you."

"Give it to me—and I will show you." She said it on impulse. That would put it in her hands. Then perhaps she could run from him, get away with the others.

"So you do know!" he crowed, unfastening the hook. "Look through it, then. But I want your promise first." He held it out, snatching it away as she reached for it. "Promise to betroth. Promise to marry." He dangled the pin.

"I promise." *I promise to marry Duncan*, she thought, to make it the truth.

"Say you are mine always," he hissed, waggling the pin. Its translucent crystal stone glittered blue as the sky. Blue as Duncan's eyes.

"Always," she said, thinking of the one she loved. "Give it here."

He relinquished it. "Go on. Show me what this gewgaw does. But do not think to run." He reached down and grabbed one of her long braids, winding it around his hand like a leash. Trapped, she winced, unable to step away.

Her head was forcible tilted. "Let go!"

"Tell me what you see there." He tugged on the braid.

"I cannot do that now. It takes calm to see through a stone."

"I am calm. Look there!"

She held the stone up to her left eye, hand trembling. She saw a shaky landscape of trees, rocks, the river. Then she realized she could invent something to please him, then keep the brooch and run.

"I see—knights." She looked at trees and rocks. "I see—a proud man in armor. You. A man of power."

"Go on."

"A man who—"

But in that instant, the trees and rocks vanished—so did the white horse and the man cruelly pulling on her braid.

She saw De Soulis through the opening in the stone. He was older, gray-haired, in black tunic and boots. Wrists in ropes, head bowed. He faced a man—Bruce? She had seen Bruce, remembered the high cheekbones he shared with his daughter; he had a bold chin, a thin mouth, keen dark eyes. Here he wore a thin gold fillet on his brow. He was king. A woman was there too, a dark-haired beauty, pale and slim in the black gown and white veil of a widow or a nun. Lilias.

Traitor, Bruce said. She heard the words in her mind. *Forgiven.*

"Do not betray your king." She spoke, surprising herself. "Support him. Be loyal. Do not betray your king."

"I support Edward," he said, but his face went white. "What is it?"

"I see you with Bruce. His daughter, grown. You will have a chance for forgiveness. Take it."

"Give me that," he said, reaching down to snatch at the brooch, but she tucked it quickly into her snug gray sleeve. "You lie!"

"I saw it." She felt stunned by how easily the images came to her. The blue truth stone was powerful. She did not doubt anything that she had seen.

"Foolish woman," he snarled. "Give me that. I will have to do this myself. I cannot trust you."

"It is the truth."

"Sir William!" a voice bellowed. Hearing pounding hooves, Margaret turned, her head restrained as De Soulis tugging on her hair.

He let go of the braid to reach toward her. "Give it here!"

"*William!*" The voice roared.

De Soulis turned. Margaret stepped away—then stopped, staring. A party of knights rode toward them out of the long glen. Three men, with the leader broad-chested and scowling in chain mail and a brash yellow surcoat. Menteith, recovered enough to ride.

She backed away, poised to run. De Soulis shifted his horse to block her.

"Stay, you! Damn it, I told him I would take care of this matter," he muttered.

"Take care of what?" she asked.

"A girl slipped away from his castle. He wants her back. It is not important."

"Who is this?" Menteith demanded, riding up. "This is not Lady Elisabeth! You have the wrong one. Who are you, girl!" He reined his horse in beside De Soulis and glared at her.

She moved again, and De Soulis angled his horse again, a hoof nearly trampling her foot.

"This is Lady Margaret Keith," De Soulis said. "My betrothed, sir."

"Keith! One of the Kincraig Keiths? What do you mean, betrothed?"

"I am Margaret Keith. But he is not my betrothed." She lifted her chin. "I will leave the two of you to your business." As she moved aside again, De Soulis swung his horse around, the broad rump nearly knocking her over. He leaned down and grabbed the front of her gown, his strong grip taking a great fistful of gown and cloak.

"You are coming with me." He hauled her up, and though she tried to writhe out of his powerful grip, he dragged her over his saddle and planted her in front of him painfully. She fell across him and was trapped by his steel-covered arm.

The brooch! But she felt its pinch inside her sleeve. She still had it.

"William, what the hell are you doing?" Menteith snarled.

"Keeping her with me. We had a lovers' quarrel."

Menteith huffed. "You are here for a far more important matter. Did you find her?"

"Not yet, sir."

"Do you mean Lady Elisabeth?" Margaret snapped. She prayed Duncan and the others were gone, but she would delay these fellows as long as she could.

"What!" Menteith and De Soulis said together.

"I was with the party escorting Lady Elisabeth when she was taken. Your men killed some of our knights and captured others. But I got away."

"I know nothing of this," Menteith said.

"You do. Your men did it all on your order. Why?"

"Accusing a sheriff unfairly will bring you dire punishment, girl. Be careful what you say. You have no proof of this."

"The brooch that was stolen from me that day is my proof," she said. "You had it at the archery contest, but when Duncan Campbell did not claim it, you gave it to William de Soulis."

"You wanted that thing so you could accuse Sir John!" De Soulis shook her so hard that she grappled for balance, nearly falling. But she might be able to slide down and get away, she thought. She had done it before.

"Those lies will land you in a kettle of trouble!"

"I was there on the archery field. How is your foot, Sir John?"

"*You!*" he roared. "I knew I had seen you before—a redhaired girl was in the village with a lad. That boy must be the one who shot me! Where is he?"

"He did not shoot you. But that wound gave others time to find Lady Elisabeth." She pushed against De Soulis.

"Who found her? Where is she?" Menteith demanded.

"Give me that brooch!" De Soulis barked.

"William, shut up! That can wait," Menteith snapped. "Look over there! Someone is near the waterfall. Go after him, you fool!"

De Soulis obeyed, spurring his horse with Margaret clinging in his lap. Menteith shouted and the knights followed, Menteith as well, barreling toward the gorge.

Jostled on the horse, Margaret feared they had seen Duncan, perhaps the others. Bounced mercilessly, she clung until De Soulis slowed his horse when he could ride no closer. They had come to a barrier wall of rugged bedrock and tangled trees edging a channel of rushing water.

Reining in, De Soulis pushed Margaret out of his way as he dismounted, so that she fell hard to earth, stunned, crawling to hands and knees. He thumped to the ground beside her and yanked her to her feet.

"Come with me," he growled, dragging her across the turf and up a jumble of slate and stone and tree trunks. Below, the narrow river hurtled in cataracts toward the falls that roared not a hundred feet to the left. The sound was immense, the air filled with moisture. As she struggled on slippery, moss-covered rocks, she looked up.

And saw Duncan and Iain step out from a screen of trees just where the river swirled to pour over the cliff as the waterfall torrent. Duncan stepped forward, but stopped as his brother grabbed his arm in warning. Even across the distance, Margaret felt Duncan's gaze meet hers and hold.

That glance fortified her. She pulled in a breath and straightened. Then she kicked De Soulis, trying to escape his grasp. He ignored her, hauling her along as he climbed. Glancing back, she saw Menteith and some of his men just reaching the gorge on foot. Sir John was clumsy and slow, hampered by his injured foot.

De Soulis dragged her toward the falls and the two men who stood near it. She stumbled again on slick stones. De Soulis yanked her up savagely, wrenching her arm and shoulder.

At that, Duncan moved forward again and set a foot on a stone. Then he took the bow from his shoulder, reached for an arrow, and nocked it.

"De Soulis! Let her go!" His shout was nearly drowned by the water's roar.

"Duncan!" she screamed. De Soulis pulled her hard against him. Above, a sudden motion caught her eye. She looked up.

A white falcon glided over the treetops lining the other side of the river.

CHAPTER TWENTY-EIGHT

DUNCAN GRIPPED THE bow, fingers itching to release the arrow, yet even an accurate shot might not free Margaret. His gyrfalcon could flee faster than the wind if she wanted. A quick glance showed Greta perched on a tall pine like a tiny angel. His other angel was held tight in De Soulis's grip, with Menteith lumbering toward them and the wild falls treacherously close.

"What shall we do here," Iain murmured. "Shoot that bow and stop this?"

"Not yet. We need to get closer so we can grab Margaret safe away."

"And toss the rest of them in the deep."

He kept his gaze sharp on Margaret, but some dark urge pressed him to kill the man in the instant. Steeling himself, he kept still. Menteith reached them then, three men behind him. He swiveled his glance to see the other knights hanging back on their horses, awaiting orders.

With luck, Con Murray would be on his way with a patrol of knights ready to reinforce Duncan and Iain. But he could not wait on that.

"De Soulis!" He powered his voice over the noisy falls. "Let her go!"

"Come get her!" came the reply. "She is mine now!"

"She is my *wife*! Let her go!"

"Wife?" Iain stared at him.

"Wife?" De Soulis shouted, then barked something at Margaret and shook her.

"Enough," Duncan snarled. Raising the bow, he aimed and let the arrow loose to sail in a broad arc. It landed at De Soulis's feet. A warning.

The man launched forward, dragging Margaret in a fierce grip. Menteith followed, shouting, the words unclear in the commotion of noise from the falls. Duncan spared a glance for Greta, who sat calmly. He wished she would fly away.

"Wife!" De Soulis yelled, advancing, Margaret stumbling beside him, Menteith limping after. His men came more slowly, looking confused.

"Tell him!" De Soulis shook her. "You gave me your promise!"

"I never did." She twisted away but he set two hands on her now. She kicked him again.

"De Soulis!" Duncan reached to grab a second arrow, nocking it in a new warning. "We will annul it—or make you a widow!" De Soulis was shouting.

"That does not matter, you fool!" Menteith bellowed. "Where is the other girl?"

"The Bruce girl is safe," Duncan called.

"At Brechlinn?" Menteith shouldered in front of Margaret to face Duncan. "We will claim her there! Go! *Now!*" he shouted, motioning to his men. They ran as if relieved to leave the falls and the threat from the bow.

"Menteith," Duncan called, "you have no claim over Lilias!"

"Who?"

"Elisabeth!" Margaret shouted, just at his shoulder.

Duncan took a step forward, bow lowered but ready. "Sir John, I could arrest you for abducting Elisabeth de Bruce and for ordering an ambush on a royal party."

"You have no evidence!"

"We have proof enough from Bruce's daughter and Lady Margaret. Andrew Murray too."

"I told you that was a rescue! You may be a justiciar, but I am a sheriff. We both know you do not have enough to charge me in Edward's Scotland."

"This is not Edward's Scotland." Duncan took another step forward, making it easier to hear over the roaring water—and improving any arrowshot he might take.

"So you side with Bruce now."

"I always did. So did you, years back. But you changed your loyalty."

"We were friends once. Shared a dungeon cell. Where is your loyalty?"

"Where it belongs. Release Lady Margaret and leave Lady Lilias alone."

"But Edward would want both of them. The Rhymer's granddaughter—and Bruce's own lass! That child is a prize. You, justiciar, could benefit too."

"Trade a child? You are mad!"

"If you want your lady, then look the other way about the child. Let Edward negotiate for her return."

Duncan raised the bow again, aiming squarely. The distance was thirty feet or so now, easy enough. "Let her go or regret it."

Perhaps it was his movement or his voice that caused Greta to leave the pine and float downward, sailing just over their heads. She curved upward and fluttered to rest in a tall birch just above Duncan and Iain, perching watchful as any guardian.

MARGARET'S HEART SANK as she watched the gyrfalcon's angelic flight. She prayed the bird would vanish into the clouds, but Greta seemed intent on watching them.

"What the devil—is that a gyrfalcon?" Menteith craned his neck to look up.

"I told you I saw one out here, with Campbell!" De Soulis said.

"A white gyrfalcon—you could hang for that!" Menteith called.

"That would make this one a widow," De Soulis said. Hearing that, Margaret leaned away, feeling his tight grip raising bruises. He jerked her back toward him.

"A serious offense in England, but not in Scotland," Duncan said. "You know English law is not entirely in effect here, much as Edward wants that."

"So the gyrfalcon is yours?" Menteith asked.

"She is mine," Duncan said.

"Mine too," Margaret called out. "We found her together, and share her." She knew Duncan would not want her implicated in this, but she would not stand by and watch him risk his life for this.

"So," Menteith said. "This lass is yours, that rare falcon is yours, the king's daughter is in your custody. We have you to rights for the falcon at least. Perhaps you were the one abducted Bruce's lass, eh?" He looked at De Soulis, who shrugged.

"Again, witnesses," Duncan reminded him. "As for the falcon, my father was an earl, and by the decree of Scottish kings over generations, he had the right to own her. As his son, I have the right."

"Spouting Scots law will not protect you. You can be removed from your position. I am aware that you never gave me the rascal who shot me. That alone is suspect."

Margaret caught her breath. "You cannot condemn him for doing his work justly!"

"I could indeed. He has committed a crime against the crown. You will have to pledge your fealty all over again to Edward, Campbell! Best pray to keep your life, not just your rank." Menteith limped toward Duncan as he spoke, and De Soulis followed, holding Margaret's arm above the elbow. She stepped on his foot, twisted away, but had no recourse but to follow.

"Hold there." Duncan trained the bow on him. "Release her."

"Keep her," Menteith growled to De Soulis. "Campbell! If you want your lady back, give me the gyrfalcon—and the Bruce girl."

"I will not make that bargain." He held the bow taut. Margaret saw his forearm straining with the extended effort, saw a muscle jump in his cheek.

"Call the bird down. We will release this girl once you bring the younger girl to me. I can wait. The day is pleasant."

"We can all wait."

"But you have no glove. Here, take mine!" Menteith tore off one of his heavy leather gauntlets and threw it toward him. "It will do. Call down the bird and give her to me, and you can have this one back." He reached out to take Margaret's free arm, giving De Soulis such a vicious glare that the man let go.

She planted her heels, but Menteith's solid bulk overpowered her weight. "Come here," he said impatiently. "Campbell, give me that falcon and get that child back to me, or I swear I will toss your lady over the brink."

"The falcon will do only what she wants. Give up Lady Margaret and I will reconsider the charges I place against you."

Menteith laughed. "If you live so long! Fine. I will call that bird down myself and send her off to Edward with a note about how I discovered her. He will be pleased." Clutching Margaret in his left hand, he raised his right in the remaining leather gauntlet, held it high, waited expectantly.

Duncan lowered the bow. Margaret saw him glance toward the bird. High above their heads, Greta sat unmoving. She had keyed in to the activity, Margaret was sure—but if there was no reward in it, the bird would not care what was going on below.

Menteith raised his hand higher, waved it. Margaret knew that if the falcon was intrigued and thought the man had food, she might go to him. Then Menteith would have the bird. She could not guess what Duncan might do, for the falcon was as dear as family to him. She had to do something to change the next moments.

"I shot you," she blurted.

Menteith looked at her. "What?"

"Margaret—"

She could not look at Duncan. Beside her, De Soulis swore in disbelief. But the only way she could help Duncan now was to delay Menteith once again.

"I was the lad in the contest. In disguise. I shot you. No one else."

He yanked her around to face him, keeping his gloved hand high to lure the bird. But he laughed. "You! A poor shot if you thought to be rid of me!" He looked at Duncan. "You should have given her to me as soon as you knew."

"Her arrow bounced off the target. You were in the way. It was that simple," Duncan said. "De Soulis! Stop!" he shouted as the man took a step. "Stay there!"

"Aye, an accident—" But Margaret stopped, remembering. With her free hand, she touched her bodice where the pendant lay hidden. The little elf-bolt had determined where the arrow would go that day. There had been a reason.

So many reasons. That shot was the pendant's work. Some faery spell had acted to bring her together with Duncan again, and had brought Lilias to safety.

"You did not delay me nearly enough. I will get the Bruce girl back, and you will pay for assaulting a sheriff. Campbell, you will not get your lady back. She must face punishment. And I will have that damned bird as well."

Without releasing Margaret, he raised his gauntleted hand higher.

"Menteith!" Duncan resumed an archer's stance, raised the bow, nocked the arrow, his gaze fearsome. "Release her and stand back, or I take you down now, sheriff or none."

Seeing the dark glint in his eyes, Margaret knew he could do it—would do it—and pay the price later. She felt his intention all through her.

Kak-kak-kak-kak. Overhead came a rapid, high-pitched sound and a flutter of wings as Greta floated downward from her high perch. Her widespread wings surged once, twice, as she flew toward the man who held his gloved hand up.

Then she rotated her torso to show her talons and knocked hard into Menteith's head with a raucous screech. She rushed past and away so swiftly that Margaret felt stunned. Yet Duncan dropped the bow and ran, Iain ran, even De Soulis reached out—

But the force of the bird's attack—surely it was that—sent Menteith stumbling, sliding on slick rocks underfoot. Still clutching Margaret's arm, he teetered on the brink of the falls, then pitched backward, plunging into the water just past the terrifying edge where the torrent poured down with tremendous force.

And he pulled Margaret into the falls with him, into the wild white spray. The cold shock of the water seized her, propelled her, hurled her down the waterfall's chute. Gasping, choking, she plunged into the whirlpool to be spun about and sucked under.

The next surge of the water threw her upward to the surface as she fought with all her strength to swim, to pull herself away from the falls with its churning, battering current. She went under again, felt the undercurrent push her sideways. Coming up again for air, she tried to control her path by pumping arms and legs, while her heavy, drenched skirts pulled her down again.

When she came up for breath again, she glimpsed the flat stones that edged the pool, saw the trees framing the sky, heard the roar of the waterfall to one side now. A strong current was sweeping her toward the edge of the pool as the water circled, and she tried to swim that way. But she was pulled down again— this time by grasping hands and a bulky weight as Menteith emerged beside her. Sputtering, he pushed on her shoulders.

"Help me!" he cried, choking. She reached out to him, his weight dragging her under—his chain mail and leather hauberk would surely drown them both. As she struggled with one arm to swim forward, holding him with the other, she could feel him pulling her under instead, the churning water engulfing her.

DUNCAN TOSSED BOW and quiver aside and ran, booted feet sure on the mossy, slippery stones, the familiar steps of boyhood guiding him as he ran around the pool toward the best place to enter the water or be pulled under too by the wicked churning near the falls. Iain was behind him—De Soulis too—and he kept going, tearing off his tunic and hopping to pull off boots as he went. Reaching the shale plates by the water, ready to leap in, he looked for Margaret.

He had seen her fall in, his heart in his throat as she was sucked under and thrown out and pulled down again. As soon as he glimpsed the russet-and-gray blur of her hair and gown, heard her gasping call, he went into the water and toward her with long, powerful strokes. Drawing near, he reached for her, pulled her toward him. But she did not come easily—and he realized Menteith was dragging on her, his weight threatening to take the three of them down.

"Let go," he ordered. "John! Let go!"

But Menteith was desperate, frightened, drowning. Clinging to the girl, bigger and heavier in armor, he was a danger to all of them as he grappled and splashed.

Margaret struggled to come up again, Duncan holding her up. She hooked her arm around his neck, Menteith clinging. With all his strength, Duncan towed both of them toward the rocky shore.

Then Iain was in the water too, coming toward them, reaching them amid the whirling currents. He caught Menteith and took his bulk, leaning back to propel him toward the shore, allowing Duncan to take Margaret.

Now that he had her, he never wanted to let her go, swimming with the flow of the undercurrent until they reached the shale platform where the water lapped more slowly. There he emerged with water sluicing off of him, to carry her, all slim shaking girl and waterlogged skirts, over the rocks. Dropping to one knee, he set her down on the sandy strip edging the wilderness of bushes and trees. He gasped for breath.

"Iain," he managed, rising to go back to help.

"Go!" Margaret sat up, coughing.

He ran to the edge of the pool to see Iain going down in the water with Menteith in a frenzy, trying climbing up on him. Duncan stepped into the water, about to leap.

But he was nearly knocked down as De Soulis shoved past him and dove into the pool, wearing only a long shirt and leggings; somehow the man had stripped out of his surcoat and chain mail so that he could help. He was already swimming with long strokes toward Iain and Menteith.

"Help! God help me!" Menteith gulped, as Iain and now Sir William took hold of him and dragged him toward the shore. Together they pulled him out of the water, falling to hands and knees, Menteith lying half in and half out of the water, retching and gasping for breath.

Duncan stood over them, breathing hard, dripping. He reached down to help Iain to his feet, hugged him. As Iain went to Margaret, sitting a few feet away, Duncan extended a hand to De Soulis. He took it and came to his feet, nodding wordless thanks.

They both watched Menteith, who lay on the flat wet rock, breathing hard, pale. Neither man spoke. Then Duncan turned to the other.

"Bring him to his feet," Duncan said. "I am done with him."

He turned and walked away as De Soulis bent to help his mentor up.

Reaching Margaret in a few strides, he knelt beside her, lifted a hand to stroke wet russet hair off her brow with soothing hands, cherishing what he had nearly lost and realized he did not want to live without.

She stretched out her hand to touch his face, tracing her fingers over his bristled jaw, brushing back the wet dark hair that clung to his brow.

Seated nearby, Iain shoved back his own hair, and gave a hoarse laugh. "Look at you two," he said. "That old betrothal is good again, is it?"

"More than good," Duncan told his brother, lending a hand as

Iain stood. "Come, love, can you stand?"

"I think so." She rose with his help, and he took her wrist in his. "Ow!" she said.

"What is it?"

Sniffling, she flexed her wrist, then pushed at her sopping sleeve to extract something snagged inside. She held it out in the flat of her palm—a silver-framed brooch, a translucent blue stone with an oval opening encrusted with tiny white crystals. The thing glittered, wet and clean and shining in her hand.

"My great-grandfather's truth stone. I tucked it in my sleeve earlier. I could have lost it in the pool, but it was caught in my sleeve."

"Now that," Duncan murmured, "is a bit of a miracle."

"It is." She leaned against his chest and he gathered her into his arms, rested his cheek on her wet hair, and held her. Just that, feeling warmth return to her body and his together, feeling her arms around his waist, feeling her recover until she straightened at last and looked up. "Duncan Dhu—can we go home now?"

"Soon. I need to see to this." He looked toward the water's edge where De Soulis was clapping Menteith on the back, helping him to his feet. Sir William looked toward them, his gaze fixed on Margaret.

She held up the brooch, which winked in the light. "Thank you," she said across the stretch of shale.

"Aye," he said. "I will try to remember."

"Remember what?"

"To be loyal, as you advised." He turned away to help Menteith stagger away, while Iain got to his feet and went toward them, ready to guard.

"What was that about?" Duncan asked.

"Oh," she said, "I looked into the blue stone and it had a warning for him. I delivered it. He seems to have had a change of heart. I wonder how long it will last."

"You are an amazement to me." He leaned and kissed her brow, then set an arm around her shoulders to lead her back toward the trees. About to return to assist Iain in guarding the other two, he noticed Menteith's discarded leather gauntlet on the ground, the one Duncan had refused to take.

He picked it up, slid it on, and lifted his arm high, bending his wrist in a welcoming perch. He whistled softly.

After a moment, she came gliding out of nowhere, an angelic and magnificent creature, to alight on his wrist, the merest weight of feathers and air and beauty.

"Hey, Greta," he murmured. "Here you are with your family at last."

"Family?" Margaret asked, snug under his arm.

"Aye, love. Our bird. Our family, together now."

"Hey, Greta," she whispered. "Hey, my love."

"I was a fool to not see it then," he said. "So much time was missed."

"No matter. We have all the time we need now. We have changed, you and I, since then. Older and wiser, and now we know what we want in life."

"Aye so," he whispered, kissing the top of her head. "I know what I want."

"What is that?" She tipped her face up to his, and he kissed her slowly, gently, tenderly drawing out the kiss, letting it merge into another.

"I want forever with you," he said, "one bit at a time." She laughed against his lips, sinking into the next kiss.

He lifted his head, hearing a thundering noise above the waterfall. Straightening, he looked past the trees. In the distance, riders were coming up from the south from the direction of Brechlinn—and he saw Constantine, Henry, Malcolm, and more than a dozen men riding behind them.

"Well, look there," Iain said, coming toward them, ushering Menteith and De Soulis, who seemed complacent and exhausted. "Just in time."

"With two sheriff's deputies—Constantine and Henry— prepared to arrest a fellow sheriff. I must be here for that. Do you mind, lass? I know you are weary."

"I will stay with you always."

"Always," he murmured, keeping her close.

"You two," Iain said, "need a wedding."

Margaret laughed, silvery and sweet. Duncan smiled.

"I know," he said. "But it is her choice."

EPILOGUE

"B RECHLINN! DUNCAN!" BRAN called, hurrying through the bailey. Duncan, standing with Lennox, turned to see three monks approaching with Bran. He frowned, wondering if they brought news for Bishop Murray, who was still with them.

A fortnight after the arrests of Menteith and De Soulis, and after Henry Keith and others had brought the men of Kincraig out of Dunbarton and up to Brechlinn, the castle was bustling and busy with riders going in and out the gates, men arriving by horse or by boat, Duncan's own men heading out on patrols. Effie had brought in neighbors from the hills to help with the greater work in the household, and Margaret was helping too in organizing beds and meals and more.

Now, Duncan noticed one of the monks carried a satchel crossed over his chest in the manner of a messenger. Bruce often used monasteries to covertly communicate. With a worried glance for Lennox, he moved toward the newcomers.

"Sir Duncan Campbell?" the monk asked.

"Aye, Brother. Welcome."

"I am Brother Gideon. I have come from Holyoak in Selkirk-shire with a message for either Sir Duncan or Malcolm Lennox."

"You have us both, Brother." Duncan looked closely at the tall man with the blond tonsure. There was something familiar in the face and about the eyes.

"From the king," Gideon said, opening the satchel to withdraw a sealed parchment, which he handed to Duncan.

Accepting it, he broke the seal, read it quickly, and handed it to Lennox, who read it and nodded understanding. "So, we have our orders to bring the lass to her father, and the bishop as well. We must move quickly if we are to get them to the Firth to meet the king's birlinn tomorrow," Duncan said. Lennox nodded.

"Thank you, Brother," Duncan went on. "Will you and the others accept our hospitality and stay here? We will take you down the loch with us when we leave."

"Thank you. May I ask if Dame Agatha is here? I heard she traveled this way."

"She is. And her brother is here as well. Do you know them?"

"Very well." Gideon broke into a smile that Duncan then recognized. He had the same wide, handsome grin, good teeth and a hint of a dimple as Liam Seton and his sister Agatha shared. Gideon looked past Duncan and waved. "There they are!"

"Gideon!" Dame Agatha picked up her skirts and ran like a young girl to embrace the monk and kiss his cheek. She stepped back, her smile puckered in a deep dimple that only brightened her eyes. "Liam! Gideon is here!"

Seton hurried through the bailey to clap the monk's shoulder, grinning. Henry Keith came just behind him, greeting them as well.

"Gideon is our brother," Liam told Duncan and Lennox.

"Excellent! I did not realize. You are more than welcome. Lennox, if you will, take the good monks to the hall and ask Effie to see they are fed and refreshed. And we need to inform Liam and Henry and the rest, now that we have the king's orders."

"Aye. I will let them know and we can all discuss it later. Come this way. Good Dame Agatha, if you will," he added politely, stepping back to let her precede him as he guided them across the bailey to the keep.

Duncan turned to look for Margaret. He had come out earlier with that mission in mind but had been waylaid. Brechlinn Castle was indeed a busy place. But now he wanted to find her and let her know that they would take Lilias to meet Bruce soon.

Then he saw her hair, a bright banner, just beyond a cart filled with ale kegs brought by the brewer. She was practicing at the archery butts. He strode that way.

Just as she was readying to draw the bow, aiming at a target, she stopped and saw him. A bright smile lit her face. He savored that smile, secret and loving, and his heart warmed as he returned it. "My lady," he said, "there is some news."

"Tell me!" She set down the bow as he came near. With carts blocking part of the bailey, the practice area had become a private little corner. No wonder she had escaped here. "Someone just came in the gate, I saw. Monks to see the bishop?"

"Brothers from Holyoak, carrying a letter from Bruce. He uses that monastery often to channel messages outward. Brother Gideon and two others."

"Gideon!" She looked delighted. "Agatha and Liam's brother. There is another brother, Gideon's twin, Gilchrist. A knight. Will the monks stay here? They have come a long way."

"They will, but some of us must leave tomorrow."

"Tomorrow?" She arranged her arrows in the quiver, and looked up. "Has Bruce decided what is to be done with Sir John and Sir William?"

"He approves what we have arranged so far. He read the charges I wrote, some serious offenses for Menteith and a tentative charge of conspiracy for De Soulis. And he approves Constantine taking them down the loch to Dunbarton to detain them in Menteith's own dungeon, guarded by Stirlingshire soldiers. It will take time, but they will face a justiciary court. Not mine, of course."

"And Menteith? What of his claim on the Lennox?"

"Bruce may forfeit him for this. Either way, it will heighten the tension over the claims on the Lennox. Malcolm has a struggle ahead of him. Menteith will keep Roskie, as that is his. And there could be a tussle of authority between Edward and Bruce over it, if Edward even has the strength. They say he is very ill again." He drew a breath. "Bruce also sent orders to be carried out immediately."

"Who will leave tomorrow?" She tipped her head, and came toward him.

"Lennox and I are ordered to accompany Lady Lilias down the loch and take her to the Firth to meet another of Bruce's ships. The bishop will go with her out to the Isles, and then Ireland. But we must leave in the morning." He reached out, drew her closer. "We must leave before first light so as not to be seen. The message took time to reach us, so we must hasten."

"Before dawn!" She set a hand to her chest. "How long will you be gone? I did not think to say farewell to Lilias so soon. Am I to go with her to Ireland, as planned before all this happened?"

He shook his head. "Bruce knows the situation here. Lennox detailed much in the letter he sent a fortnight ago. The king knows we are to be married, so he asks that Dame Agatha accompany her until the party meets two of Bruce's kinswomen who will then care for Lilias. Lennox will go with us, and Bruce's men who are here. Once the girl is off to Ireland and the bishop is seen to, I will return. Lennox will take Dame Agatha back to Lincluden. But I do not know how long we will be gone. I am sorry. I know you are planning our wedding."

She took his hands in hers. "I understand. You have a good deal of work to do for Bruce with your secret guests and covert journeys. And you have justiciary cases to tend to as well. I know that. I will wait. I have waited since I was a child, Duncan Dhu. I can wait a little longer."

With a rueful smile, he lifted her hands and kissed them. "Thank you. Everything is coming together at last for us, my love."

"Aye. I will miss Lilias though. What of Andrew?"

"He can stay here with us. Constantine and the bishop suggested it."

She brightened again. "I would like that so much! He and Owen are becoming good friends. And Bran is fond of him, says he will train him up to be a great knight. And here with us, he will have a chance to see his uncle now and then."

"Aye, love. All things in their time, coming together. One thing more." He held her hands. "With so many leaving in the morning, I thought perhaps we could marry now."

"Now," she repeated. "Here and now?"

"We may not see our friends and family for a while after this. And the bishop is here."

"True. And my brother and all." She looked away with a tiny, thoughtful frown. "Oh, aye. We will do that. It will be just a quick ceremony and a small celebration, being so sudden."

"It is up to you."

She nodded. "Then this is what I choose." Pulling him close by their joined hands, she tipped her face for a kiss, long and luscious. He was reluctant to pull away, wanting to draw her deep into his arms, hold her, love her—find some private spot. But he only smiled, waited.

"The great hall can be done in candlelight and flowers," she mused. "Effie would help, and others."

"A lot of work to be done so quickly. I suppose we could do all of this in the hall."

"Wait. I have an idea." She walked away, picked up her bow, plucked an arrow from her quiver.

"I suppose that might help you think," he said.

"You said it was my choice. Watch me decide." She gave him a mischievous smile, then nocked the arrow and pulled the string back. But she lowered the bow and touched the pendant at her throat.

"You are doing that again."

"When I dreamed of my grandfather, he said this enchanted pendant would send an arrow where I wanted it to go. I want to try that now."

"Where do you want it to go?"

She smiled, drawing back the string. "Where it needs to go, Duncan Dhu. Let us see what it will do for us now."

"What do you mean?" He laughed softly at her answering, elfin smile. She was just as whimsical and fey and beautiful in that moment as she had been years ago, when he saw her spinning happily in the bailey of his father's castle.

She drew the string, tilting slightly to rest the arrow on her gripping hand, fingers light on the fletched end. For a moment she stood, eyes closed. Then she released the shaft.

A powerful shot. Duncan watched it arc past the target and sail over the castle wall. "You missed," he said.

"Then we had best go fetch it," she said with a little laugh.

Bemused, he walked with her through the commotion in the bailey and out through the open gate. As they crossed green grass toward the woodland behind the castle, he took her hand.

"Now where did that go," Margaret said. Hearing her light tone, he stopped and caught her in his arms.

"What scheme is this? Leading your unsuspecting groom into the privacy of the forest? He is happy with that plan." He drew her to him, kissed her, felt her press against him as she looped her arms around his neck and renewed the kiss, opening her lips to him, laughing softly, sweetly, against his lips. He was lost, wanting her to feel utterly lost in the moment too.

"Come with me." She took his hand and led him between the trees, through deep ferns, into the vast spread of the wild bluebells beneath the oaks and birches. "Where did that go?"

"Over there." He pointed ahead, seeing the fletching thrusting up in a thick haze of blue-violet petals between a few birch trees.

"Ah! Just where I hoped it would go." Her green eyes, as she caught his gaze, were all sparkle and whimsy, with a touch of triumph and delight. "Look up."

He did. The arrow had landed in the center of an arch of birches in a carpet of bluebells and ferns. The sun, cutting through the forest, streamed down in translucent beams. The whole area looked like an enchanted place, a natural cathedral in the forest.

"What is this place?" he asked, setting his arm around her as he looked around.

"This is where we will be married this evening, with our friends and family surrounding us. The hounds too, and the wee terrier. And the falcons. Can we bring the falcons out here as well?"

"They are part of our family too. My forest bride," he whispered. "Your dreams start now, here." Drawing her to him, he kissed her gently, and as she returned it with sweet fervor, he felt her arch against him, his forever.

"Oh, they began when I was small, and you were my handsome, honorable knight," she whispered against his lips. "And this is our lucky place, here in the forest."

"Forever so," he whispered. He kissed her. "I never knew what luck was until the day I found you again."

Author's Note

Years ago, a friend gave me a slice of polished translucent blue agate, veined in quartz and encrusted with sugary clusters of tiny crystals. It's a beautiful stone that became an inspiration when I began putting together ideas and research for *The Forest Bride*. Scotland has many tales and legends of charm stones and talismans that are said to be enchanted by faeries, or believed to be seeing-stones that provide glimpses of the future, or perhaps bring good fortune or miraculous healing. Also in Scotland as in other countries, stones with naturally formed holes created by eons of erosion may wash up on a beach or be dredged from a river. Sometimes called hag stones or witch stones, or even Druid's glass, they are said to have magical properties too.

In Scotland, a variety of charm stones are associated with Scottish clans and specific locations. Some are preserved in museums or private collections and remain curious and lovely antique chunks of quartz, agate, or other stones, banded or framed in silver, pewter, or brass. A legend or some magical characteristic may be attached.

I love the romantic notion of these charm stones, and wanted to weave that into my Highland Secrets series as part of Thomas the Rhymer's legacy for the Keith sisters (*The Scottish Bride*, *The Forest Bride*, and *The Guardian's Bride*). And so Margaret Keith in *The Forest Bride* owns—and loses for a time, to her distress—a precious blue brooch that is her seeing-stone, along with a cluster of natural holed stones. Through these magical, mysterious stones, she learns to trust her ability as a seer, part of the gift that Thomas the Rhymer gave her. The stones also inspire Sir Duncan Campbell's growth from skeptic to believer, and help Duncan and Margaret learn to trust and love again.

On a historical note, the character of Lilias Bruce was inspired by what is known of Robert Bruce's family. He was the father of several children, including his daughter Marjorie from his first marriage, and children with his queen, Elizabeth de Burgh, born in the years after she returned from extended captivity in England. From the time he was a young man, before his first marriage and even during his second, he apparently had five or six illegitimate offspring as well. That he cared equally and dearly for all of his children is supported by evidence that he gave them titles, property, and ensured good marriages. He had a natural daughter called Elizabeth, although little is known of her; in my story, Elisabeth Bruce becomes plucky young Lilias, whose abduction—as the daughter of a king—brings Margaret and Duncan together after ten years apart to try to rescue the missing girl before it is too late.

Look for another of Thomas's charm stones with very different properties owned by Rowena Keith in *The Guardian's Bride*—and in *The Scottish Bride*, Thomas's legacy exists in a messy pile of parchments bequeathed to Tamsin Keith.

Aside from the challenges and revelations that the Keith sisters encounter related to the legacy of Thomas the Rhymer, each heroine—and her hero—discover that no matter how high the stakes, how deep the challenges, how complex the threads that keep them apart or pull them together, love ultimately can resolve whatever goes awry in life. To me, that's the real magic in fiction and the real world.

I hope you enjoyed *The Forest Bride* and I hope you'll look for my other books. As always, happy reading!

Susan

About the Author

Susan King is the bestselling, award-winning author of (so far) 28 historical novels and novellas, a hefty nonfiction history, and dozens of magazine and web articles on education and the craft of writing. Her books, including mainstream historicals Lady Macbeth: A Novel and Queen Hereafter: A Novel of Margaret of Scotland, have been published by Penguin, Random House, HarperCollins, Kensington, ePublishingWorks, and Dragonblade. Praised for historical accuracy, lyrical writing, and storytelling quality, she is a USA Today bestselling author with numerous awards, nominations, and career achievement awards as well as starred reviews from Publisher's Weekly, Booklist, and Library Journal. Most of her books are set in Scotland ranging from the 11th to the 19th centuries.

Susan is a former university lecturer in art history, a private school teacher, and a founding member of one of the longest-running author blogs, "Word Wenches" (wordwenches.com). She holds a Bachelor's in studio art and English literature, a Master's in art history, and completed most of her Ph.D./ABD in medieval art history. Raised in Upstate New York, she lives in Maryland with her husband and three sons in an ever-growing family.

Website – www.susanfraserking.com

9 781963 585865